LOVE CHARADE

ALLIE MCDERMID

ALSO BY ALLIE MCDERMID

Love Charade

Love Detour

Love Magnet

1

_____

Holly Taylor plucked the headphone from her right ear. Mum was phoning for the thousandth time. She'd planned to call when she was nearer Glasgow Central Station, but the train was a good fifty minutes away yet and her mother's constant calling was getting in the way of the audiobook she wanted to finish.

She let it go to voicemail and, with a huff, stabbed at the pause button, taking a moment to compose herself. This had felt like the right thing to do as she boarded the train at London Euston four long hours ago, but the closer she got to Glasgow the tighter the grip on her stomach became. This was it: she was officially returning home with her tail between her legs.

Holly held the ringing mobile to her ear, suddenly aware she was holding her breath. She let out a wavering sigh, her heartbeat thrumming against her ribs. _It's only Mum._

'Holly, hi! Are you nearly here?' Mum said, panic clear in her voice.

'What's wrong?' Holly asked, her heart rate rising for a completely different reason now. The sound of the family's busy shop was loud on the line, so at least she wasn't in a hospital or worse.

'It's your dad.'

'What's wrong?' she repeated, straightening herself in the train's seat, on high alert. It had better not be his blood pressure again.

'That'll be two ninety-nine. Sorry, it's my daughter. I know! Have a good day.'

'Mum,' Holly scolded, her patience already non-existent.

'Sorry – customers. It's your dad. He's put his back out.'

Holly breathed a sigh of relief. 'Is he okay?'

'Oh aye, he's lying in the basement just now. I told him not to pick up that box of juice, but you know what he's like.'

'So why the ten thousand calls?'

'Well, this place is going like a fair, and we've a heck of a lot of home deliveries to get through. I know you wanted to get straight home, but do you think you could call by the shop and help out?'

Holly slumped back in the seat, her muscles relaxing now she knew it wasn't an emergency. 'Yeah, sure, no problem.'

'You're an angel! Right, I better go. Got a queue out the door.' Mum punctuated the call with an excited squeal. It was nice to hear her so happy. She'd never been like that when she worked in banking.

Holly repositioned herself, not bothering to put her audiobook back on. Instead, she focused on the countryside whizzing past the window. They were well into Scotland now. The view hadn't changed much in the last hour, aside from England's flat fields slowly being replaced with distant tumbling mountains, but a patriotic warmth hugged her bones. It felt like an age since she'd done this journey. It *had* been an age.

Christmas. Two years ago. The shop had only just opened and her visit was so whistle-stop she'd only managed to walk past it when it was closed. It would be good to see it in all its glory. Her parents had done an amazing job of building the deli up to where it was. They'd recently won Best Customer Service in the Shawlands Business Awards. No mean feat.

She checked her messages, half expecting to see a message from Shona. Nothing. Just Dad urging her to phone, and Mum's missed calls. Even after four months, her mind was on autopilot. If she ever heard from Shona again it would be too soon.

There wasn't really anyone to warn of her imminent arrival. When she'd run off to London she'd let friendships fall by the wayside. Was there anyone she knew left in Glasgow? Would they even care she was back?

She shoved her phone in her pocket.

Fuck, Holly. How did you mess this up so badly?

2

———————

Jen Berkley took a break between customers, enjoying a lull as Shawlands shoppers migrated to the local bakeries and cafes for a quick pick-me-up before resuming their shopping in the afternoon. She'd never seen an August like it.

'What you sitting on?' Chloe asked, leaning on the end of the counter.

'Just shy of eight hundred.'

Chloe whistled through her teeth. 'Woof. Wait, is that good?'

'Very good,' Jen replied, unable to hide the smile pulling at her lips. 'That's Christmas-level sales for a Tuesday.'

Chloe nodded in appreciation. 'Nice. Still going to slag off Lovefest, when it's driven your sales like that?'

Jen rolled her eyes. 'It's the name: how can I take it seriously with a name like Lovefest?'

'Just imagine the suggestions that got scrapped.' Chloe moved to the nearest shelves, her focus fixed on the copper cocktail shaker she was tumbling between her hands, pretending to inspect it. 'Had any further thoughts on what you're doing about that text?'

Jen considered her reply, and chose to ignore the question altogether. 'I've got delivery routes to plan, replen to sort, and cleaning to do. What do you want to help with?'

Chloe shot her a look. Her best friend understood better than to push it, but Jen knew that inside she was dying to dissect options in minute detail. After all, she'd hotfooted it to the shop when Jen told her who'd been in touch. Annoyance gripped her stomach once more, but Jen bit it down. It wasn't Chloe's fault. She just didn't want to talk about it.

It wasn't the text in itself that was bad. Okay: it was enough to make her want to kick the wall, but it wasn't just that. It was an accumulation of bad things that had stacked up over time, like a terrible game of Jenga, threatening to fall at any moment. Right now her tower was teetering, but if she didn't talk about the text she could keep it together. Just.

Chloe pursed her lips, weighing up her answer. 'Replen. You shout and I'll grab.'

Jen winked, keeping her bad mood under wraps. 'That's the spirit. A box of pina colada, Sex on the Beach, screwdrivers, and porn star martinis, please.'

Chloe disappeared into the storeroom, not before saluting her bestie. 'Yes, boss.'

Jen surveyed the shop, her stomach and face dropping, safe to let the facade fall now Chloe was out of sight. The store looked good. It wasn't big by any means, but it was big enough. Large enough for an ample counter, two industrial fridges – one of which was currently broken – a glass-doored freezer, and a wall of shelves. She'd kept the decor minimal and Scandi-inspired, much like her home. Light wood, sleek lines, white walls, and a little hint of industrial ruggedness with the pipework holding up her shelving. In fact, it wasn't just like her home: it was an extension of it. She'd built it from the ground up. It was her baby.

She'd always had a love of cocktails, bars, and pubs, spanning most of her career, so when the opportunity arose to open her own shop selling pre-made cocktail pouches and every imaginable sundry for making your own perfect cocktails at home, she had leapt at the chance.

It hadn't been easy, but soon she was making all the cocktails on-site, creating her own marvellous concoctions to support the better-known recipes, and selling them all over the south of Glasgow.

And now? Well. She'd be lucky if she was still here next quarter.

The spring of agitation twisted once more. Jen tensed her jaw. *Don't think about all that today. Look at all the money you've made!* But how could she not? The shop wasn't just her livelihood: it was her entire life.

And who sends a text like that out of the blue?

Chloe dumped the boxes onto the edge of the wooden counter with a thud. 'Sorry – heavy.'

'Just in the fridge please, Clo.'

'I can't believe how fast these are selling. You all out of Peachy Keens?'

'Yep, will need to make more. Fancy helping?'

'Depends. Does that include sampling?'

'If needs be.' Jen replied with a smile.

'Well, count me in!'

The bell above the door jingled, alerting them to a customer.

'Hi, how are—' Jen said, before cutting herself off. 'Hey Annie, it's yourself. How's it going?'

'You're a lesbian, yeah? Fancy a date?' Annie said, depositing a hefty folder onto the counter.

The question took Jen by surprise. Not because she wasn't out, but because people usually said hello before propositioning her. 'I, er.' Her cheeks burned red.

'Sorry, sorry,' Annie said as if waving something away. 'I'll go back to the start. How are you? Sales good? It's hoaching outside.'

'Been busy, yeah,' Jen said, her mind still occupied with the previous enquiry.

'It looks like Lovefest is going to be a roaring success, and it's only day two. I can't believe it.' Annie was head of the Shawlands Business Initiative Group, the association that organised Lovefest, and had as much riding on the festival's success as Jen did in the month's sales. What Annie lacked in height she made up with fire and determination: if anyone could pull it off, Annie could.

'Good feedback, then? Lots of smooching and canoodling?' Chloe asked with a smirk.

'Lots of feedback, yes; not so sure about the smooching. So, listen . . .'

'Yes,' Jen said, trepidation clear in her voice. She was niney-nine per cent sure Annie had a husband. And two kids, come to think of it.

'Lesbian, yes?'

'Yep.'

'Single?'

'You betcha,' Chloe chipped in, only to get daggers from Jen.

'Just what I wanted to hear,' Annie replied, with a wry smile as she tucked a loose strand from her black bob behind her ear. 'And finally, you free tonight?'

Chloe straightened herself with a wriggle, excitement

clear. They were chalk and cheese. Chloe would happily comply with anything, without even a sniff of specifics, purely for the experience. Jen, on the other hand, needed time and space to calculate. Even then, the answer was usually no. There was little better than a glass of wine and her own company.

Before Jen could protest, Chloe answered: 'She's free. What's the plan?'

'Thank the stars,' Annie said with a sigh of relief. 'It's the event tonight, in Cal's.'

'Ohh, sounds intriguing.'

'It's going to be great. Just a few minor snags, which it looks like I'm well on my way to ironing out. Right. Eight o'clock, don't be late.'

'Wait, wait, wait,' Jen said, throwing her hands up to halt further activity. 'I'm not agreeing to anything. What's this all about?'

Annie grinned. 'Thought that was a bit easy. We're officially kicking off Lovefest with a matchmaking event in Cal's, and from ticket sales, I could see we were a little short on women seeking women. Of course, we might get a few walk-ins, but I don't want to risk it. So far there are only three other ladies signed up. Not exactly the impression we were going for.'

'Matchmaking event?' Jen repeated with a gulp.

'Yes, but really, you're just there to plump numbers. You don't need to do a thing.'

'I dunno.'

'Oh, come on, Jen! It'll be fun,' Chloe said, leaning around the counter to squeeze her arm. 'What about me? Can I help make up numbers too?'

Jen scoffed. 'You? You can't pretend to be gay!'

'How so? I can act gay.'

'It's not about acting. Whatever "acting gay" is.' Jen's cheeks blushed red again: she hated debating sexuality. 'It's because as soon as you sniff out a hot single guy you're like a dog with a bone.'

'You don't think I can pretend for one night?' Chloe feigned offence.

'Not on your nelly.'

Annie picked up her folder, hugging it to her chest. 'Look, if both of you come, fantastic. But I need at least one. Free drinks? Would that do it? Please, Jen.'

Chloe was doe-eyed. 'Jen, it'll be fun. Come on, free booze! We'll have a laugh. Just what you need after today. I'm not going without you.'

Jen considered it, the unpaid bills and estimate from the fridge repair guy catching her eye. 'I have too much to do. Too many drinks to make.'

'I can help. We've got a few hours yet. Pleeease.'

Silence hung in the air: all eyes were on Jen. Her shoulders sagged under the weight of their stares. There was no point: Chloe wouldn't let this go, not with a night of free alcohol on offer. 'One drink. I'll show face, make up the numbers. That's it.'

Annie's features exploded into a grin while Chloe jumped on the spot with an excited little clap.

'You two are angels. Just one more to find now, even numbers and all that. Don't suppose you know of any more eligible ladies in the area?' Annie said, already turning on her heel to leave.

'If she did, do you think Jen would still be single?' Chloe said with a guffaw as she ducked the pen Jen had launched her way.

3

Nerves gripped Holly's stomach the closer she got to Shawlands. She was going home; there was no need to feel like this. And yet, there it was. A heavy, worsening feeling that refused to go away. Part of it was guilt, but most of it was embarrassment.

Yet, she couldn't help but smile as the taxi drove beside Queen's Park. Glasgow was affectionately referred to as the Dear Green Place, the literal translation of its name from Gaelic, and with places like Queen's Park it was easy to see why. It was huge and marked the centre of four major Southside suburbs: Strathbungo, Govanhill, Shawlands, and Battlefield.

Holly's childhood home was a hop, skip, and jump from Shawlands, in the neighbouring area of Langside. She'd often find herself in Queen's Park with one of her parents. Whether it was checking on the ducks, grabbing an ice cream near the boating pond, or spotting the squirrels, there were lots of happy memories within its gates.

She craned her neck, certain she'd seen a giant duck

floating in the pond. Her eyes must have been deceiving her. Or the locals were adding steroids to the bread.

Plenty of time to explore tomorrow. A walk would be nice; she could reacquaint herself with the area. She could already see so much had changed as the taxi came to a standstill at the traffic lights.

The Shawlands she remembered was long gone. Not that it was a bad thing. The area had a trendy feel to it now, but not in the posh student-y way the actual West End did. More like a casual glow-up. The main shopping street that ran the length of the suburb was once lined with charity shops, bookies, and empty units; not exactly a shopping destination. Now it was home to bookshops, boutiques, and enticing brunch spots. Barely an empty shop in sight. No wonder Mum and Dad's deli was doing well. This was a haven for their ideal customer. You didn't need the West when this was right on your doorstep. It was no surprise flat prices were through the roof. Not quite London prices, but she'd got a shock when investigating her options before moving home. She gulped at the thought of sleeping in her childhood bed tonight. Nothing quite screamed failure more than accepting you'd wake surrounded by popstar posters, sheets that smelled like the airing cupboard, and the nightlight you'd had since you were wee.

She sighed, awkwardly catching the taxi driver's eye in the rearview mirror. She forced a half-smile but he didn't seem to notice. Or care.

The taxi edged forward up the queue of traffic. They were now level with Langside Hall, an impressive two-storey building famously moved from its original spot, brick by brick, to where it now stood, dominating the square at the edge of Shawlands. It looked good. When she'd left for London it had almost gone to wrack and ruin, but money had obviously been invested; it was shiny and new once more. Even the ground outside looked like it had been repaved and remodelled.

Maybe it was a sign. Shawlands had been transformed almost beyond recognition; perhaps she could, too? A bit of TLC and time and she too could go from ruin, to well, maybe acceptable was a realistic goal just now.

She ran her fingers through her long brown hair and pulled at the ponytail in her half-updo, making sure it looked okay. *It's just Mum and Dad.*

The lights changed to green and they were soon in the centre of Shawlands.

'Anywhere here is fine,' Holly said, leaning forward.

The driver pulled in and before Holly knew it she was standing on the pavement, suitcase at her side, inexplicably frozen to the spot.

She let out a wavering sigh. *It's just Mum and Dad.*

The wheels of her suitcase trundled along the pavement, her legs now working of their own accord. Mum was right: the place was going like a fair. A queue snaked its way out the door.

'Excuse me, sorry, not skipping, here to work,' Holly said with a smile. The guy moved aside, not bothering to return pleasantries.

She side-stepped in, her suitcase feeling like it weighed a tonne as she negotiated it around impatient patrons.

It smelled amazing. They'd recently added toasted sandwiches, Mum's bright idea to showcase a 'cheese of the month', and the moreish aroma tickled her nostrils. Holly's stomach growled; she'd not eaten since leaving London.

Mum and Dad had done a great job with the shop's interior. She'd seen it on Instagram plenty of times, but seeing it in the flesh was a different experience altogether. It was a delightful mix of traditional grocer with modern-day deli: a large, sage-coloured dresser that wouldn't look out of place in a farm kitchen dominated the right-hand wall, with a matching table spanning nearly the length of the shop floor. Both were piled high with beautifully packaged produce: pickles, jams, dried pasta, chocolate, and spices, to cover but a few. Some were in aged wicker baskets; others stacked like proud pyramids. It was difficult not to be distracted on the way past – Holly wanted to stop and investigate. A packet of cocoa-dusted truffles looked particularly intriguing. She stopped herself; there would be plenty of time for looking later. The shop's other wall was filled head to toe with untreated pine shelving, each shelf equally bursting with produce. The pièce de résistance, though, was the deli counter, a massive glass beast that spanned nearly half the left-hand side of the shop and was packed to the brim with cheese and meat. Mum and Dad were in the zone behind the glass, dutifully serving customers as fast as they could.

She scooted round a man looking at a jar of pickled walnuts who had zero intent of moving for her, and edged closer to the counter. Dad nearly dropped the cheese he was wrapping when they made eye contact.

'Holly,' he yelped, wiping his hands on his apron as he flew out from behind the counter. 'Catherine, she's here!'

Mum's eyes searched the room, finally settling on her.

All nerves were quashed when Dad's big arms wrapped around her. She had to swallow down tears as emotion lodged in her throat.

He kissed the top of her head. 'Hello, stranger.'

'Hello, you,' Holly answered, her voice cracking slightly. 'Back's better, I see.'

'Not quite, but you know what your mum's like. Had me back on the shop floor as soon as poss.'

'Oi, I heard that,' Mum said, joining the hug.

Holly was sure she heard an *aww* from their customers and felt a little sheepish, aware all eyes were on them. Mum broke the hug first, taking her daughter by the shoulders. 'Sorry, love – it's busy today. I need to get back to work.'

'It's fine, we can catch up later,' she replied, tears still threatening.

Maybe being back wouldn't be so bad after all.

'How come you're so busy?' Holly asked as she positioned herself behind the counter, suitcase and jacket safely stowed downstairs.

'Did Mum not say? It's Lovefest,' Dad replied, trying to say the name like Barry White. As a middle-aged white guy with thinning hair, he didn't quite pull it off.

Holly screwed up her face in confusion. 'The heck is that?'

Mum spoke over her shoulder as she put another toastie on the grill. 'It's a festival the local Business Initiative group invented. Runs for the whole of August. There's loads of events on, all aimed at sparking romance.'

'Yep, all the businesses are getting involved. So we've got special hampers available for the month. Your mum's idea. And then there's matchmaking events, games, stuff like that.' Dad explained, giving Mum a wry look.

'What was that look for?' Holly asked, keeping out of the way near the coffee machine.

'What look?' Dad asked, appearing even more guilty.

'That look,' Holly said, with a nervous laugh. Time to

shut this down. 'It's only been four months since Shona and I broke up. I'm not ready.'

Mum shook her head vigorously. 'No, no. We're not going to rush you into anything. We're just excited to have you home, that's all.'

'Likely story. So, tell me more about these hampers.'

Dad beamed. 'As usual, your mother is the mastermind behind it all. One min.' He bounced off to serve a customer a selection of deli meats.

Mum picked up the conversational baton without missing a beat. 'They're called sharing platters. So, you get everything you need for a night in with a loved one plus a set of cards designed to encourage conversation.'

The baton passed back to Dad. 'Yep, so stuff like "What was your first pet?" et cetera. Ice-breakers, really. Perfect for couples who have just met.'

'Nice. You guys really are the dream team.'

'Trying our best,' Dad replied, his eyes firmly set on a generous serving of prosciutto.

'So, is that what I'm delivering for you?'

'Mainly yes, and a few other bits and pieces,' Mum said before turning her attention back to a customer. It was hard to believe the place would close in ten minutes. The crowd showed no sign of letting up.

'I'm so sorry to have you working when you've only just got here, but I don't think my back can handle lugging stuff upstairs.'

'It's okay, really. I'm glad I can be helpful.'

Mum took her chance as the queue neglected to move forward – the guy was studying his phone with a goofy look – and leaned in for a side-hug, planting a big kiss on Holly's forehead. 'So good to have you back.'

Holly gave her a squeeze in return. 'Want me to take the bin out? It's looking pretty full.'

'Yes, please!' her parents chorused in unison.

THE BASEMENT WAS AS LONG and wide as the shop floor above and was packed to the rafters with boxes of produce. Carefully stacked on the nearest table were what Holly assumed were today's orders. She surveyed them, hands on hips. The hampers looked lovely; Mum and Dad had chosen weathered wicker with tan leather straps. Very luxurious. None were fastened closed, presumably for the refrigerated goods to be added last minute, so she carefully lifted the lid of the top hamper. *Wow.* Biscuits, pickles, booze, and nibbles stared back, all nestled safely in a mound of ivory shred. Whoever got this was lucky. Kind of cool to think that Mum and Dad could be instrumental in starting romances all over the Southside. Dozens just from today, by the looks of it. Who knew how many futures they would be changing?

She closed the lid and walked towards the fire exit, absent-mindedly running a finger along the table's edge as she did so. The sour feeling from earlier had lifted; this wasn't going to be so bad after all.

The bin bag was heavy, so she hauled it up with two hands and shoved the door open, using her back for leverage against the security bar. She hadn't expected it to open so forcefully and stumbled backwards, only just keeping her footing.

She expected the cascade of lukewarm water that hit her face even less.

Her breath caught in her lungs, the bag dropping to the floor with a crack.

'Oh my God, I'm so sorry,' an unfamiliar woman's voice cried out.

'What the fuck?' Holly panted, pawing at her eyes. Whatever had been thrown at her sat in her mouth, horrid grit finding its way in-between words.

'You okay?'

Words remained lodged in Holly's throat, plugged by her thundering heart. She fixed on the blonde coming into focus. 'What did you just throw at me?'

'Throw? I didn't— well I guess I did, sorry. I wasn't paying attention.'

The dirt coated Holly's tongue and she fought the urge to spit. The woman was the colour of a tomato and looked like she wanted the ground to swallow her up, but her embarrassment didn't help a dripping Holly regain composure. 'What the hell was that?'

'Water from my bucket,' the woman replied, pointing to the offending object by her door. 'I'd just mopped the floor. Look, I'm—'

'It doesn't matter,' Holly snapped, cutting her off. 'It was an accident – let's leave it at that. I have deliveries to do.' She grabbed the bin bag and flung it into the commercial bin, before stomping back and pulling the door closed. All the while the blonde watched her every move, her jaw tensed.

The bathroom mirror confirmed Holly's worst fears. Her cream jumper was now streaked brown and clinging to her skin. Her face could be washed and the panda eyes banished, but her top? There was no saving it. She couldn't do deliveries like this.

She splashed water on her face, using the hand towel to create a little traction and remove what remained of her make-up. She looked a state, but it was better than letting the public see her with smudged eyes and pools of milky foundation.

Washing her jumper wasn't an option. There was no way to dry it before deliveries started. Anger bubbled below the surface, threatening to manifest as tears.

Footsteps on the stairs signalled someone was coming. She couldn't hide the mess; she'd have to let Mum and Dad down.

'What's happened?' Mum asked, coming into view in the mirror.

'That cow next door soaked me.'

Mum's face scrunched at her choice of words. 'Jen? She wouldn't do that.'

'Well, obviously not on purpose.' Holly relented, hands gripping the sink. 'She threw her mop bucket water and it caught me square in the face.'

'Ah.' Mum stepped forward, placing a comforting hand on Holly's shoulder.

'I can't do deliveries like this.' Her voice was almost a squeak.

'We've got some polo shirts left from last year's Christmas temps. Your dad was too tight to get the logo embossed, but they're the deli's brand colour – they'll do for now.'

Holly nodded, her face betraying the fury that still rumbled inside her. 'I look a mess.'

'You're not too bad. Pop your hair up and no one will know any better.'

'What a start to my new career as deli delivery driver.' She forced a smile.

'The only way is up,' Mum said with a wink.

4

_____

She'd done this as retaliation. No doubt about it. Jen's knuckles whitened as she shoved her fists into her hoodie's pockets, watching her driver circle for the third time. Parking was rubbish outside the shop so she'd come to an agreement with Taylor's Deli. She got the spot closest to her shop at closing because her delivery driver, Ben, was on the clock and finding a space and loading up the van could take forever, especially if it was far away, and every minute ate into her already tight budget.

'I told you hiring a driver for the month was a mistake,' Jen growled to a lingering Chloe.

'He'll get a space. Chill.'

'I could do it on my own.'

'You've got seventy orders to fulfil. You just had me double-check the route and it says it will take him three hours.'

'So?'

'So, you still need to make the cocktails you've sold out of. You can't do everything.'

'I did until last week.'

'And you got that weird rash thing in your armpit.'

'Hey, shh,' Jen said, slicing a hand through the air to silence her best friend. 'I used cream. It's gone.'

'Still, not great if you burn yourself out.'

'She's not even loading her car.'

'Probably still cleaning herself up after you assaulted her. Come back inside.'

'Don't, I feel terrible,' Jen said, rubbing at her temple as she ventured back into the shop.

'Why did you throw it so high, anyway? Her shoes would have been bad enough.'

'I dunno. I was thinking about that text, and I got mad and I just flung it.'

'Ready to talk about it? You know it will help. You wouldn't have told me otherwise.'

Jen sighed, arching her back as leaned on the counter. 'It's ju—'

The door opened and in flew a hurried-looking Ben. 'Parking spot agreement is already out the window, I see?' He flashed a smile at Chloe, who returned it with bravado. He really wasn't Chloe's type – he was slim, with glasses and a penchant for checked shirts – but he was lovely, and an asset Jen desperately hoped she could keep on the team, especially with Christmas around the corner.

'Just a blip.'

'Jen assaulted their new driver.'

'You what?' Ben laughed nervously, his eyes darting to Jen for the explanation.

'Right, settle down, that's how rumours start. I accidentally soaked her with my mop bucket.'

'We've all been there,' Ben said, his face returning to its usual cheeky self, ready for action. He was on a mission, well aware how tight Jen's budget was and wanting to earn brownie points. 'So, what orders have you got for me today?'

Jen stepped aside, letting him see the counter. 'All loaded on the app. You parked close, or do you want us to carry some?'

Ben eyed the boxes. 'I'm just across the road, up that cul-de-sac, but it would be quicker if you helped. You know what it's like getting crossed here.'

'No problem,' Jen replied, forcing a smile. She'd have words with the new girl tomorrow.

'I REALLY WISH you hadn't roped me into this,' Jen whined as they walked down to Cal's. It was only five minutes away, but with every step she got slower.

'Oh, come on, it'll be fun.' Chloe gave Jen's bicep a squeeze, her other arm linked with her best friend's. 'Another drink and you'll be fine.'

They'd snuck a few shots while making tomorrow's cocktail pouches and, although she hated to admit Chloe was right, alcohol was helping take the edge off her sense of impending doom.

'You know I don't like playing with others.'

'Which is exactly why this will be good for you.' Chloe stabbed the button for the green man. 'Three years is too long. You need to get back out there.'

'I'm happy on my own.' Chloe's face told her she didn't believe Jen one bit. Riding solo wasn't bad. Only one person could let you down: yourself. 'It's not worth the hassle.'

'Ready to tell me what the text said yet?'

Jen rolled her eyes, setting off across the road as the lights changed. 'She just wanted to know how I was.'

'That's it? After all these years, that's it?'

'Yep.'

'What exactly did it say?'

'Just hello, yap, yap, yap, how are you?'

'It's the yaps that I'm concerned about. You're sure it was definitely her?'

'That's what the yaps were.' Jen stopped in her tracks, yanking Chloe to the side. 'Look, I really don't want to do this. Can we go get drunk somewhere else?'

'We promised Annie. Let's show face, look helpful, then we'll get a bottle of wine and go back to mine. We can craft a reply to you-know-who.'

'You think I should reply?' She'd expected this to be a chuck-it-in-the-fuck-it-bucket case.

'Erm, yeesss! No one sends a message like that after three years and doesn't have an ulterior motive.'

Jen cocked an eyebrow, unsure. 'I don't think I want to talk to her.'

'Then we'll talk about that too. Explore our options.' Chloe pulled her in the direction of Cal's.

'Urgh.'

'Come on. Free booze. Focus on the free booze.'

'That equates to a free hangover tomorrow.'

'Stop being such a stick-in-the-mud.'

'Sorry, you're right, you're right,' Jen said, physically attempting to shake off her bad mood as they reached the overspill of smokers outside Cal's. 'Worries aside, I'm going to enjoy tonight.'

'That's the spirit. Talking of spirits, shots first?'

'No more shots,' Jen replied, pulling a face. She could still feel the vodka sloshing about in her stomach. 'In fact, I might start with a spritzer.'

Chloe's face looked like a puppy sucking on a lemon. 'That had better be a joke,' she jibed with a smile.

The bar was packed. More than either of them had ever seen before.

A grin spread across Jen's face; she was unable to hide her glee at another Shawlands business doing well. Day two and Annie was already killing it.

Cal's was one of the biggest bars in Shawlands, situated right in the very centre, but it wasn't just location that had helped cement it as one of the Southside's hottest spots. It spanned the space between the two main roads in the district; an impressive feat in itself, but it was the way Cal's snaked around its neighbours that really sealed the deal. Its odd, cubic layout meant it was really three-in-one. The front space was a cosy lounge, all cocktails and candlelight; the back was a raucous bar with burgers worth dying for; the middle was a pub-come-club. You could start at one side, migrate to the other, and end the night in the centre of the action. Something for everyone and every possible kind of night. You never stayed for just one drink at Cal's, and that was a promise and not a threat.

Chloe grabbed Jen's hand and weaved them through the throng of punters in the cocktail bar. Jen had often considered opening her own place, but with competition like Cal's, there was no point. She was better staying in her lane and focusing on the stay-at-home crowd.

It wasn't long before they'd made it to the middle. There were no doors or inner walls in Cal's. Just an unspoken knowledge of where each area ended and the other began. Tonight, though, there were a few, kind of subtle, clues. The twelve-foot LOVEFEST banner hanging from the ceiling being the biggest of them all.

Jen forced a gulp. This suddenly felt way too real.

The lights were low, but Jen could see a sea of nervous faces studying them as they entered. She felt out of place, her hands forgetting what the hell they were meant to be doing and becoming instantly clammy. She dropped Chloe's grip and stuffed them in her pockets.

Annie was right to want to balance the numbers. It looked decidedly hetero. Not that she could ever judge who was gay or not, but it just wasn't the right vibe for a gay event. There was far too much awkward mingling already. Too many blokes in ill-fitting shirts.

Chloe shot her a smile. 'You ready?'

'As ever.'

Both headed for the bar without discussion. Chloe wiggled her way in and took on the task of ordering. Jen scanned the crowd. A few pretty girls who would be her type, had she been looking, which she definitely wasn't. They were already talking to guys, though, so were unlikely to be one of her three supposed teammates.

A hand on the small of her back made her jump.

Annie.

'You made it! I was so worried you would be too busy.'

Jen mustered her best no-worries smile. 'Of course; happy to help. How long do you need us to stay?'

'Not raring to leave already, I hope?' Annie replied with a laugh. 'So, I need to officially start the evening with my little speech, then we have some ice-breaker games.'

'Games? You didn't say there would be games.'

'Relax – it's okay. They're ways to get conversation flowing so no one is left standing on their own. Speaking of which, if you see anyone looking lost, can you go be their pal? Just for a bit, to get things started for them?'

Jen couldn't help but sigh. 'Okay.'

'An angel as always. Right, I better go kick things off.'

Chloe appeared by Jen's side, already sipping on her wine. 'Everything okay?'

'Just getting the low-down from Annie. We're to befriend any stragglers.'

'She's obviously heard about your flair for witty conversation and fondness for talking to strangers.'

'Har fucking har.'

'So, she still wants me to gay it up?'

'You're looking forward to it, aren't you?' Jen said, a smile masked by her wine glass. She was looking forward to seeing Chloe's attempt. Maybe it would be a little payback for getting them into this mess in the first place.

'Do you know, I am. I think I'll be brilliant at fake romance,' she said, placing a hand on Jen's hip and pulling her close.

'Do that again and you're dead,' Jen said with a laugh as she stepped free.

Chloe sputtered into her wine. 'That felt so wrong. You're like my sister.'

Feedback from the mic screeched through the venue, making everyone recoil.

'Whoa, sorry about that.' Annie's voice boomed as the dance floor fell silent. 'Welcome to Lovefest!' A few whoops and claps peppered the room, but mostly a feeling of dread filtered through like a tidal wave. Annie ignored it and lumbered on. 'I'm so excited to welcome you to our first ever Lovefest event in the wonderful Cal's.' That got a few more hurrahs. 'And don't worry, I know you're all dying to get started. I'll keep this short and sweet. You'll have all received your badges on the way in.'

Chloe and Jen shot each other an *oops* look.

'The colour denotes the type of partner you're looking for, but feel free to mix it up if the mood so takes you,' Annie said with a wee wiggle of her head. 'Yellow is seeking a woman, green is seeking a man, orange is seeking either.'

Strangely, that got the biggest shout of excitement from a particular few in the crowd.

'You'll all have also received a card with half of a well-known saying. Your challenge is to find the other half by the end of the night. And with that, time to get chatting!' Annie flung her hands up like she was starting a chariot race and the crowd let out a final attempt at excitement.

'Looks like we missed something,' Jen shout-whispered into Chloe's ear.

'Just a bit. You hang here and I'll see if I can find these magic stickers.'

'You're leaving me?' Jen hissed.

'It's our job to mingle, ya single!' Chloe said, putting on a funny accent as she shimmied into the crowd.

The guy to Jen's right turned to face her, awkwardly looking at her chest as he looked for a name sticker. 'Haven't got my sticker yet,' she offered with a half-smile.

'Ah, no worries. I'm Greg.' He held out a palm and Jen could see it glistening even in the dim light.

She gave it a limp shake as she sipped her wine. Tonight was going to be long.

5

The bar was busy. Mum and Dad had said to meet at some place called Cal's. It hadn't existed when she left Glasgow. Well, the building was here, but back then it was called O'Donnell's Bar. And it definitely wasn't as appealing as Cal's. This place did cocktails, and plenty of them.

She could almost taste the martini as she double-checked their text: *Place is busy, come in from Pollokshaws Road, back left corner.* They weren't kidding. Every outside table was taken, with many people opting to stand in the spaces between in case one of the seated few decided to leave.

Holly shuffled through the bystanders at the door and made her way to the back corner. She was feeling a little better after being soaked; her hair had finally dried and she'd made peace with the fact she looked the age of a college student without her usual make-up on. The polo shirt still felt a million miles away from what she was comfortable in, but needs must. Not like she knew anyone here, anyway.

Mum popped up like a meerkat and waved wildly. They'd bagged a nice spot on a sofa, away from the hustle and bustle of the tables near the main bar.

'Hey, how's it going?' Holly asked Mum as she gave her a tight hug.

'Good! How did the deliveries go?'

Holly went to sit but Mum cupped her shoulders, keeping her upright. 'Good. What's going on?' Fear washed over her: this wasn't some sort of surprise party, was it? Or even worse, an intervention? She'd been worried things would be strained, but so far her parents had been classic Mum and Dad, just like they'd always been every Christmas and for the last few months. Maybe she'd relaxed too soon.

Dad stood up, taking a position by Mum.

Jesus.

'Listen, Holly, don't be mad,' Dad started.

'Why would I be mad? What's going on?'

Mum swiped a glass of white wine from the table and thrust it towards her. 'We were going to tell you earlier, but you seemed so upset about getting soaked that it just didn't feel right.'

'Okay,' Holly replied, her voice wavering. Her mind was torn between downing the wine or dumping it and hightailing it out of here.

Dad slapped a sticker on her chest: a huge rectangle with a yellow stripe across the top and her name scrawled in the middle. 'There's an event on tonight and Annie really needed our help.'

'Who's Annie?'

'She's head of the board for the BIG – you know, the business group that organised Lovefest.'

'Uh-huh.' This was going in an odd direction. Terror

twisted her stomach and heat flushed the back of her neck. But at least it had nothing to do with her past indiscretions.

Dad continued, 'It's really important to look like a team player, show everyone we're a serious business.'

Holly eyed the sticker on her left boob again. 'What's that got to do with the name tag?'

'There's an event tonight,' Mum replied, her eyes sympathetic. 'We need you to go, just for a while.'

'Oh no, no, no.' Holly said, trying to place the glass back on the low table. Dad gently kept her in place.

'Please, just one drink? Then come back here?' he asked.

Holly was silent. She wanted to help; of course she did. But this? *Nope.*

'Why me?'

'It's a matchmaking event and Annie was low on lesbians. She asked if we knew any and, well, we might have got excited in the moment,' Mum said with a shrug.

'So ... gay speed dating?'

'Not quite,' Dad replied. 'It's a mix. The yellow stripe means you're looking for a woman.'

'I told you, I'm not ready yet.'

'We know, we know,' Mum said, putting her hands up in mock defence. 'But, like we said, Annie wanted help. We realise this is a massive ask, but you just need to chat to a few people.'

Dad thrust a card at her, a silly grin on his face.

. . . AND INTO THE FIRE was printed in capital letters. Nothing else. 'What does this mean?'

'It's part of a well-known phrase. The idea is you chat to other people to find the other half. It's an ice-breaker thing,' Dad replied.

'Great,' Holly said, rolling her eyes.

'Please, just one drink,' Mum pleaded. 'It might be a good way to make new friends, too, now you're back.'

Holly hesitated. One drink wouldn't hurt and it would earn her massive brownie points with Mum and Dad. She downed her wine in a move that received instant looks of both shock and admiration from her parents. 'Buy me another and I'm in.'

CHATTING to strangers wasn't too bad. Most people seemed nervous; perhaps they had more riding on tonight than her. Talking was never an issue when nothing was at stake.

She'd quickly struck up conversation with a cute butch woman. Totally not her type – Holly preferred her partners to be a little more feminine – but Natalie was easy to speak to.

'So, you from around here?' Natalie asked, supping on her craft beer.

'Originally, yeah, but I spent the last few years in London.'

'Oh, wow. So, why are you back?'

Girlfriend cheated on me, I spiralled into a depression, lost my job and my flat, and had to come crawling back. 'Missed home, wanted to come back to my roots.'

'Nothing quite like Glasgow, eh?'

'It's one of a kind, no denying it. I take it you live near Shawlands too?'

'Yeah, just up the road.' Natalie paused, her eyes scanning the room. 'Listen, I think I'm going to go look for the other half of this saying, but I'll be back later, yeah?'

'Yeah, sure, sounds good,' Holly replied with a meek

smile. Abandoned by Natalie, she was alone once more. She leaned an elbow on the nearest standing table and faced the crowd, her table pals a touchy-feely man and woman.

Annie wasn't lying: the place was thin on the ground with lesbians. There was Natalie and herself; then a mousy little woman barely in her twenties; another woman with almost zero appeal to her – she looked like she was dressed to go clubbing, and who wears four-inch stilettos to a standing event?! – and a feisty, hot redhead. Holly hadn't had the guts to approach the last one yet. Although, she was currently deep in flirty conversation with a guy who looked the spit of Chadwick Boseman, so there was a possible badge mix-up there.

Not that it mattered. After Shona she needed time to heal. The truth was, she wasn't sad about Shona. Okay, maybe a little. But things had been wrong for a long time; it had just been easier to stick at it and hope something would change. It was just the straw that tipped the camel's back. No, wait. She'd mismatched too many of these damn phrases tonight. The break-up had been the final thing to push her over the edge, spiralling into a pit of dangerous self-loathing. She'd moved to London with so many hopes and dreams, only to find herself sucked into working in bars and living paycheck to paycheck. She'd achieved exactly nothing since leaving university. Mum and Dad hadn't wanted her to leave but she'd been pig-headed and done it anyway, declaring Glasgow and home a boring cesspit in the process.

She'd been a terrible daughter, and yet her parents had been nothing but ridiculously supportive the last few months. They said it was because they loved her, but she'd abandoned them, part of her knowing if she came home for too long, left the grasp of London for more than a few days, that reality would hit and she'd be lured into staying. But to do that would be admitting failure. The truth was, her heart was always in Glasgow. It had taken this year to show that. Leaving would have been better on her own terms, though, not like now. Now she'd cemented her fate as a perpetual disappointment. At least she was consistent with that. This was a fresh start, though. She was going to make it up to them; do anything they needed of her. Beginning with this event.

She realised too late that she'd been staring, lost in her own thoughts for too long, and it wasn't dead space she was looking at. It was Miss Mop Bucket herself.

There was an awkward moment of proper eye contact before Holly made her way over. Time to build a bridge.

'Come to soak some more innocent souls?' she joked.

'And I take it you've come to steal more parking spaces?' the blonde replied, deadly serious.

'Excuse me?'

'The space outside my shop. I have an agreement with the deli owners.'

'And what would that be?' Holly sipped her wine, dying to know what the heck this woman was on about. Mum and Dad hadn't mentioned anything. Had they?

'I get that space around five, if it's free. It's just how we do things.'

The woman stared her down, her pale green eyes locking with Holly's. She clocked her name tag: yellow top. *Interesting.* 'Listen, Jen. I didn't see your name on it and my parents didn't say anything, so it's free game.'

'Your parents? As in Catherine and Harry?'

'Yeah.'

'They've never mentioned you.'

'Yeah, well, I've been away.' All that time and they never mentioned her? It's not like she was expecting them to be singing her praises, but a casual name drop would have been nice in all the years they'd owned the place.

'Listen, just don't do it again,' Jen said, closing the space between them, trying to look threatening. She had a few inches on her, but Holly wasn't fazed.

In fact, she couldn't help but snigger. 'What if I do?'

'Expect another bucket of water to come your way.' Jen hid the beginnings of a smile behind her wine glass as she took a gulp, but she was anything but joking.

'You could have blinded me.' An exaggeration, but she needed to say something.

'As if. This has been lovely, but I need to remind my friend she's gay tonight.'

'You what?'

'Doesn't matter. Stay out of my spot, okay?'

Holly pulled a face, unable to think of a smart remark. Sometimes silence was better than getting the final word.

What a dick.

Never mind build a bridge – that bad boy could stay burned for all she cared.

Stiletto woman was free. No time like the present – she needed to cleanse herself of Jen's awful conversation skills. 'Hey! Holly – nice to meet you.'

'Jasmine. So, what's on your card?' the woman asked with a wink. She towered at least a head above Holly.

She produced the card from her pocket. 'And into the fire. Yours?'

'Out of the woods ...'

'Out of the woods and into the fire. Doesn't quite sound right, does it?' Holly chuckled.

'I dunno, woods can be pretty scary if you're on your own.'

To give her her dues, Jasmine was nice, odd footwear choice aside. Unlike Jen, who was giving her some serious side-eye as she chatted to the hot redhead. Holly changed her position and put her back to her. 'They can, can't they? Do you want to get another drink?'

6

Jen's head was pounding. Shots and wine at Cal's on an empty stomach was a terrible idea. Even with the chips they'd grabbed on the way home. The bottle of wine they shared in Chloe's probably hadn't helped.

She popped another paracetamol, washing it down with a glug of water.

'Still feeling rough, eh?' Chloe asked, having dropped in after her work ended. She was a barista in town and often called by when her shift finished at three. It was nice to have someone to help close up, and the fact they lived opposite each other sweetened the deal. It was always good to walk home in a pair.

'I'm never drinking on an empty stomach again,' Jen groaned.

'You always say that.'

'You're surprisingly chipper.'

'Uh-huh.'

'He's texted you, then?'

'Yes,' Chloe said, her face breaking into a toothy grin. 'We've been texting all day.'

'Told you.'

'I know, I know. I wanted to commit to the part, but he was just too cute.'

'Remind me of his name again?'

The shop door opened and the ladies chorused a hello before Chloe turned her attention back to Jen. 'Ryan.'

'Ryan, huh?'

'What does that mean?' Chloe asked with a confused smirk.

'Nothing good ever happens with a Ryan.'

'What?! You can't dismiss him purely on a name.'

'It's true,' Jen's customer said, placing a selection of cocktail pouches on the counter. 'Ryan is a total bad boy name.'

'You would really forgo this relationship based on his name?'

Jen continued ringing the cocktails through and let the customer take this one. 'No, of course not. I'm just saying: be wary. I've dated plenty of Ryans in my time to know,' he informed them.

Chloe pulled a face, making it clear she didn't believe in their misinformed opinions. 'All this without knowing the guy.'

'Just saying, Clo, be careful,' Jen said, popping the pouches in a paper bag. She was winding Chloe up, but it was impossible to know her customer's motive.

He beeped his card on the machine. 'At least you know where to come when he breaks your heart,' he said with a wink. 'Nothing like a good mojito to drown your sorrows.'

'I'll drink to that,' Jen replied. Her stomach lurched at the thought.

After a quick goodbye, Chloe looked sullen. 'You really think all Ryans are no good?'

Jen couldn't help but smile. 'Course not, you big goof. I mean, look at Ryan Reynolds.'

'Ah, Ryan Reynolds. Now, there's a Ryan I would definitely date.'

'You would date a guy even if his name was Mr Red Flag.'

Chloe opened her mouth to retaliate but was cut off by the door opening again. Annie. This was becoming a daily ritual.

'Sore heads this morning, ladies?'

'Just a bit. Evening a success, then?' Jen asked, hopeful this was just a quick visit to say thank you, although the mischievous glint in Annie's eye hinted at otherwise.

'Beyond my wildest dreams. I'm so glad you're here too, Chloe. It saves me a trip.'

'How so?' Chloe asked, leaning forward, her attention well and truly piqued.

'We're wanting to show the South how big a success Lovefest is, so Isaac's come up with a genius idea.'

Isaac was Annie's right-hand man and he was always coming up with great marketing campaigns. His most infamous being the viral music video he made last year, tempting Southsiders to do their Christmas shopping in Shawlands. Jen had been made to dress as a snowman and lip-sync to Mariah Carey.

'Am I going to have to dress up?' Jen asked, nipping any bright ideas in the bud.

'Not this time. Unless it's like a kinky thing,' Annie replied, blushing at her own joke. She chuckled under her breath before carrying on. 'We want to pick five couples and follow them over the course of Lovefest. They'll go on a date a week, experiences and such donated by the local businesses, and at the end the community will vote for a favourite couple. They'll win a cash prize and a night in a hotel.'

'Nice,' Jen said, genuinely impressed. 'What does that have to do with me?'

'I was wondering if you'd like to provide an experience? Maybe a cocktail masterclass?'

Thank God. For a brief moment she'd thought Annie was going to ask her to compete. 'Sounds great – I'd totally be up for it.'

Annie gently fist-pumped the air. 'Result. Thank you.'

'And what about me? What do you need me for?' Chloe asked, her brow knitted.

'Well, as you know, last night we asked folks who wanted to match to leave their details on the way out, and I see you and the lovely Ryan hit it off. He's a very successful graphic designer, owns a studio in the West End. He's actually a friend of a friend. Great guy.'

Chloe shot Jen a *told you* look. 'So, you want us to compete?'

'I'd love that. I'll message Ryan, of course, get his okay too. But are you keen?'

'What's the cash prize?' Jen asked.

'Forever the romantic,' Chloe said with a laugh.

'Five thousand pounds. Donated by a local philanthropist.'

'You're kidding?' Jen said, agog.

'What. The. Heck. If Ryan says no I'll find someone else to date. Hell, yeah. Count me in,' Chloe joked.

'Amazing. That's us got three straight couples and one gay, which just leaves—' Her eyes drifted to Jen.

She didn't let Annie finish the sentence. 'No.'

'You don't even know what I'm going to say.' Annie pouted.

'Right, go on then.'

'Which just leaves—' Annie said, pausing for effect. '—one lesbian couple. It wasn't exactly a hotbed of attraction last night. Sorry about that.'

'No skin off my nose. I wasn't there to meet someone.' Jen took another slug of water. She couldn't wait to get home and watch bad TV. Nothing was shifting this headache and conversation wasn't helping.

'I know, but it's really important we show the community that we represent everyone,' Annie replied.

'Not much we can do if no one matched.'

'Unless ...' Chloe said, eyebrow arched. 'I think Annie might be about to ask for a favour?' She drew the syllables of the last word out, looking to Annie for answers.

'Just a teeny one,' she replied, finger and thumb showing just how small the favour was.

'No.'

'Oh come on, Jen! It'll be fun. Me and you competing against one another.'

'It would be wrong. What about when I win? Everyone will feel cheated.' Jen masked a smile behind the water bottle's lip.

'I think you'll find me and Ryan are going to win.' Jen turned to Annie with a motion so quick it made Jen's hungover tummy flip. 'So, who you pairing her with?'

'Natalie? She had good chat,' Jen ventured.

'See,' Chloe said, flinging her arms out towards Jen like she was showing off a fancy car. 'This will be fun.'

'Natalie? Who was she?' Annie asked.

'The cute butch. Short black hair, black shirt?' Jen replied.

Annie's brow creased, deep in thought. 'No, I don't think so. But you never know. I had someone in mind, but I can ask her instead if you like. She booked online, so I can get contact info. Was Natalie your type?'

'No, but I'd at least want someone I can get on with.'

'So you're going to do it?' Chloe chimed in, eyes wide in excitement.

'Whoa, whoa. No. Definitely not. Not my thing.'

'Jen,' Chloe said, grasping her best friend's hand. 'Think of the exposure. It would be great publicity for the shop. And if you win, you can use the money to fix the fridge.'

Very true and valid points. Not that they were big enough incentive to do it. Jen shook her head. 'Too far out of my comfort zone. Sorry.'

'Look, it's okay. I understand. It was just an idea,' Annie said, stuffing her hands in her pockets. 'Dates start in a few days, so if you change your mind just message me, yeah?'

'I won't, but thank you.'

'Right. I'd best be off. Isaac and I are off to take photos of the new installation at Langside Hall.'

'What's that?' Jen asked, confused.

'We've hired a bouncy castle for the kids. Put it up in the early hours of this morning. We're going for a fairy tale love story theme. Grasping at straws for that one, but not everything can be a winner.'

Jesus, I must have been more hungover than I thought this morning. She'd walked past the square on the way to work and not even clocked it. 'I'll need to check it out on the way home.'

Annie was already halfway out the door when she spoke, forever on a mission. 'Right, bye for now, ladies! Thanks again. And Jen? Just say the word and I'll set it up.'

Chloe didn't even wait for the door to close before starting. 'Jen,' she said, dropping her voice low and slow. 'Come on, it'll be fun.'

'It'll be embarrassing.'

'Nah, listen. You need this. Take that text from Alison as a sign. You need to get back out there. Who knows, maybe your Mrs Right will see you and get in touch. Not to mention the money.'

'The money would be handy. As if I'd actually win, though.'

'Well, you definitely won't if you aren't even competing.'

Jen was silent, mulling it over. Chloe bit her bottom lip, desperate to plead the case but knowing better than to rush Jen into a decision.

An hour later and with a dozen or so customers served, Jen finally broke. 'I guess it wouldn't be so bad.'

The pigeons scattered in the square, along with probably the rest of Glasgow, at Chloe's excited squeal.

7

Holly checked her reflection as she walked past the bookies. *Not looking bad.* Not that it mattered: this wasn't an actual date. She'd been a bit miffed when Mum and Dad had thrown her into the deep end with the Lovefest event, but when Annie had asked if she'd mind going on a few dates she'd jumped at the chance. It was great to be helping Mum and Dad do their bit, plus the publicity for the shop would do wonders. It was difficult not to get carried away with thoughts of winning the money. Although she knew the chances were slim, dreams of starting her own business came to mind. It would be enough to get some prints made, at least.

Fantasies were put on hold as she reached the restaurant. Nerves made her stomach lurch. She hadn't expected that. She repositioned her summer dress again and adjusted her faux leather jacket. Her make-up was hopefully still on point. There was barely a breeze today, so her face and hair should be as good as when she left the house. Jeez, why was she suddenly feeling butterflies in her stomach?

Her legs acted on their own again, taking her up the restaurant's steps. Today's date had been sponsored by a local Italian pizzeria. It had long been a Shawlands staple, and Holly had fond memories of coming here with Mum and Dad. She had the feeling it would still look the same inside: olive-coloured leather, wood so dark it looked black, and signed photos of visiting celebs on the walls. It was good to be somewhere familiar; it helped quell her protesting stomach.

Annie was lingering at the maître d's station, partly obscured by a large palm, attention fixed on her phone. Her head snapped up when Holly approached.

'Holly, you're here!' she beamed. 'Your date's already inside. I thought I'd take the chance to update our socials while we waited.'

'I'm not late, am I?'

'No, no. Totally on time.' Annie walked into the restaurant, past the cake fridge and down the three steps to the lower level, leading Holly to the table. 'So, we'll do a few quick photos then leave you to it.'

'Sounds good.'

'Here we are.'

Annie stepped aside to reveal Jen, the arsey woman from next door. Holly's stomach dropped like a tonne of bricks.

'Jen. Lovely to see you again,' Holly dead-panned, taking a seat opposite the blonde.

Judging by the way Jen's face had fallen, she felt the same. 'And you too. I don't think I got your name?'

'Holly. Holly Taylor.'

'Like Taylor's Deli. Gotcha.'

Holly's eyes were locked so fiercely with Jen's that she almost flinched when a hand was thrust in front of her face. It belonged to a guy wearing a monstera-patterned shirt and bright green glasses. 'Isaac, hi. Pleasure to meet you.'

Holly gave it a firm shake. 'Holly; hi. You'll be taking the pictures, I presume?'

'Camera gave it away, huh?' he replied with a laugh, cradling the massive DSLR in both hands.

Jen mumbled something under her breath.

'What was that?' Holly asked, hackles raised.

'Nothing, sorry.'

Holly narrowed her eyes, unconvinced.

'Right, ladies. A few smiley pics and then we'll be off,' Annie said, clapping her hands together.

'Maybe raise your glasses like you're cheers-ing?' Isaac suggested.

It was only then Holly clocked the already filled glass. 'Ordering for me, now?'

'I asked for a bottle and they just assumed it was for both of us,' Jen shot back through gritted teeth.

'Smile, girls.' Annie ushered them on.

Holly laid on her best grin as they clinked glasses.

'Brilliant, brilliant,' Isaac said, taking shots from all angles.

Holly spied Jen from the corner of her vision, her smile never wavering. Of all the people. Should she just leave? No, that would be rude. D'Angelo's had been nice enough to gift the meal, and Shawlands was small; if one of them stormed out they'd lose a shot at the prize before the contest had even begun. Not to mention the embarrassment for Mum and Dad if word got out. She'd have to stick it out. For tonight, at least.

'Right, and one without the glasses,' Isaac said, crouching in search of a different angle.

Holly's cheeks ached from smiling but she wasn't going

to let the facade drop. Especially not in front of Jen.

'I think we've got it,' Annie said, a hand on each of their shoulders. She added, in a near whisper, 'Thanks again, ladies. Any extra drinks are on me.'

Isaac and Annie-less, awkward silence descended over the table like a heavy blanket.

'So,' Holly began.

'So.' Jen repeated.

'You look nice,' Holly said, feeling her cheeks blush. She wanted to ease into this declaration and it felt right to start with a compliment. It wasn't a lie, though. Jen's shoulder-length blonde hair was styled into beach-wave curls and she had on a checked shirt that was tight in all the right places. Under any other circumstances, Holly might have looked twice.

'Thanks,' Jen replied, taking a long draw of wine.

'I need you to know, though,' Holly said, pausing to get the words in just the right order. 'I'm not wanting anything from this. I don't want a relationship.'

'Worried I'll fall in love with you?' Jen smirked.

'I'm not saying that. I just want to be honest.'

'Good for you. For what it's worth, I don't do dating either. It's a waste of time. And I don't do one-night stands either.'

'Charming. You thought that was on the table?'

Jen blushed redder than her shirt. 'I didn't say that. I just wanted to be honest too.'

'Well, I don't do them either. So at least we agree on something.'

Silence fell once more. Holly studied the menu like there would be a test at the end of the night.

'So how did Annie manage to rope you in?' Jen finally asked, her features softening.

'I wanted to help my mum and dad. It seemed like a good chance for publicity. You?'

'Similar. How come I've never seen you around?'

'I've been—' The waiter interrupted and took their orders, complete with another bottle of wine. 'I've been in London.'

Jen rolled her eyes. 'London.'

'Yes. What's so bad about that?'

'Everybody loves London. What's it got that Glasgow doesn't?'

'A lot, actually. Opportunity, excitement.'

'Excitement? Must have been great, for you to come back.'

'I missed my mum and dad,' Holly replied, shifting in her seat.

'I've never understood the appeal. Will you go back?'

'Maybe. Hopefully soon.' Right now, it felt like that was completely off the cards, but she didn't want to admit that. Anything to ruffle Jen's feathers.

'You have a flat there?'

'Ish.'

'You can't have an "ish" flat,' Jen laughed.

'Well, I do.'

Jen's features narrowed as she studied Holly's face. 'Let me guess. A girl's involved?'

'I told you, I don't want a relationship.'

'Doesn't mean someone isn't waiting in London.'

How was this woman reading her like a book? Was she that predictable?

'There was.'

'Hah!' Jen said with a genuine smile.

'But not any more.'

'Sorry.' The smile fell and the blushed cheeks returned.

'Nah, it's fine. It happens. What about you?'

'What do you mean?' Jen topped her wine glass up and hovered the bottle above Holly's. 'More?'

'Sure, why not? I mean, why don't you date?'

'Ah.'

'You don't have to answer, sorry.'

'No, no. It's cool. Same reason I hate London.'

'I don't follow.'

'My ex fucked me over and moved to London.'

'Ah.'

'Ah indeed. It's been three years, and to be honest, I quite like being alone.'

'No one actually likes being alone.'

'Well, I do.'

Just as things were thawing out she'd made it awkward again. *Shit, come on, Holly.* If they were going to spend four dates together she had to find something to keep conversation flowing. The new bottle of wine arrived, plus two cocktails they hadn't ordered. God bless the conversational gods above.

'From Annie,' the waiter explained, seeing their confused faces. 'Enjoy!'

'What are these?' Holly asked, examining the tall glass with a raspberry balanced on the rim. The drink was red but it wasn't a martini she'd ever seen before; the liquid was almost ombre.

Jen looked equally perplexed. She twisted the glass in her hand, inspecting it from all angles. 'A martini of sorts, but they've obviously added a twist.' She thought for a moment, her eyes never leaving the glass apart from to have a sniff. 'Pineapple juice, obviously. Chambord. Vodka, naturally. Maybe some champagne, going by the bubbles. But there's something else. Can't quite figure it out.' She broke her stare, giving up on the puzzle and fixing her eyes on Holly's. 'Booze though, eh? Down the hatch.' She held the glass high, waiting for Holly to join her.

Holly couldn't help but smile as they clinked glasses. 'To Lovefest.'

'Nope. Hate the name, can't bring myself to say it. To winning five thousand pounds.'

Holly nearly choked, laughing. 'I know, right? Can you believe it? 5k.'

'Barely. That's a lot of money.' Jen smiled, her shoulders relaxing as if the booze was loosening her. 'So, when you're not stealing parking spaces and shouting at the locals, what do you do?'

Holly shot her a look, her jaw set.

'Sorry, sorry. I promise, that was an attempt at humour.' Her cheeks glowed again. It was kind of cute, how often she got embarrassed. *Nope. Rein it in, Holly.* It was the alcohol talking, for sure.

'You need to work on your punchlines.' Holly swept a hand through her fringe, giving her brain time to realign. 'I'm not doing anything at the moment. Only got here a few days ago. I'm going to focus on helping Mum and Dad for a while.'

'And what about in London? What did you do there?'

'Bar work, mostly. But nothing fancy like you. I can pull pints – that's about it.'

'What makes you think I can do fancy stuff?'

'You own a cocktail shop; you must be able to do something.'

'I try my best. That's about it.'

Jen needed more confidence in herself. Mum and Dad said hers were some of the best drinks they'd ever tried, and they weren't cocktail types. If she could impress them, she must be good. 'I don't think Annie would ask you to host a class if you weren't up to par.'

'Ach, I think she just needs to tick things off her list.'

'I didn't have you down as the modest type.'

'What did you have me down as?'

The waiter appeared with their starter: dough balls and garlic butter.

'I don't think we need to put too fine a point on that if we want to win.'

Jen stopped, mid-bite of a dough ball. 'What do you mean?'

'We want this money, yeah? We need a game plan.'

'You're going to have to elaborate.'

Holly cocked her head. Was she really not getting this? 'The public vote, yeah?' Holly lowered her voice, leaning in. 'We need to make sure we look like the best couple. Ham it up.'

'I get you. We need to make everyone believe we're a couple. And the best one, at that.'

'Bingo.'

'You okay with that?'

'Okay with what?'

'Acting like a couple?'

'Does it matter? We're just two strangers. Nothing to lose; five grand to gain.'

'Is it five grand each, or to share?'

'You know, nobody's confirmed that. We should ask Annie.'

Jen raised a dough ball, aiming for another cheers. 'To five grand. Or a two and a half; whatever.'

Holly clinked her dough ball to Jen's. 'To our five grand, girlfriend.'

8

'Oh my God, thank God you're here,' Jen said, rushing out from behind the counter when Chloe appeared.

'Whoa, what's happening?'

'I really need to pee.'

Chloe couldn't help but laugh. 'Jeez, okay, go, go!'

The shop had been non-stop today. Usually there was no issue with finding a pee break, but today? No chance. The looming weekend and Annie's social media posts had created the perfect storm, and Jen was all for it. The till had never worked so hard outside of Christmas.

Relieved, Jen returned to a cheery Chloe. 'Thank you. I was close to disaster.'

'Any time. So, how did last night go?'

Jen shrugged, not wanting to give much away.

'Oh my God, you enjoyed yourself. You actually enjoyed yourself. Hot damn.'

'Alright, steady,' Jen replied, unable to hide a smile. 'Now move out the way. I need to do the till.'

The truth was, Holly's appearance last night had thrown

her. Yes, she was the same petulant wind-up merchant she'd met at the event, but looks-wise, she'd well and truly thrown a spanner in the works. Jen had expected someone totally different, given the polo ensemble from the matchmaking event, but had that been something to do with soaking her earlier? She couldn't remember. The whole thing had been a massive blur. All Jen had focused on was finding a way to get the ground to swallow her up from sheer embarrassment, not what the poor soaked woman had been wearing.

It wasn't often Jen got flustered, but last night was something else. Holly had looked great. It had taken all Jen had to not focus on the curves of Holly's body; the way the dress cinched in just where it was needed.

'Has that gone through?'

'Huh?'

'Has that gone through?' the customer repeated, her card poised over the reader.

'Oh, yeah. You're good. Thank you.' Jen shook her thoughts free. This wasn't the time nor the place.

'Hey, how's it going?' asked the next customer, a fortysomething guy with a handful of cocktails and a set of glasses.

'Hey, yeah. Good thanks, and you?'

'Cracking. I saw your pictures online; looked like a good date. Did you have a good time?'

'Yeah, really good, thanks.' He wasn't the first to ask. The day had been filled with people wanting the backstage goss. She was getting the hang of saying what they wanted to hear. Holly had come up with a plan – a slow-burn romance – and they'd agreed on what would be appropriate in public. So far, hand-holding was as far as they would go. 'Too early to tell, but I think we clicked.'

She could feel Chloe's stare burning into her neck, but chose to ignore it.

'I could tell from the pictures. Think you'll see each other again?'

'Try and stop us,' Jen replied with a chuckle. Chloe was going to give her a permanent scar with that look. Time to get rid. 'Can you grab me some replen, Chloe?'

'Sure,' she replied, her voice dubious.

'Brill. Just the usual suspects, please.'

Chloe slinked off without another word.

The customer beeped their card, taking the till total to four figures. That was usually reserved for December. 'Can't wait to try these. I'll be back, I'm sure of it!'

'I'm sure you'll love them. Happy Lovefest,' Jen said with a wink. *Jesus fuck. Who the hell have I become?!*

'You've changed your tune,' Chloe jibed as she placed a box of pouches on the counter.

'Just feeling good after last night.'

Chloe's face said she wasn't buying it. Pouches restocked, she headed back to the counter. 'Need me to get anything else?'

'Nah, all's good.' Jen paused as she handed a lady her change. She turned back to Chloe, who was now scrolling on her phone. 'Did you not feel on a high after your date?'

'I know you. And this is fishy. Although,' Chloe said, an eyebrow raised as something caught her attention online, 'Holly is one hundred per cent your type. She didn't look like that at the event.'

Jen bit her bottom lip, attempting to suppress a smile. 'She looked good, yes. And what exactly is my type?' She laughed. 'You've only known Alison.'

Chloe pulled an *are-you-serious* face. 'Pretty boho girls who look like they should play guitar and be able to braid their hair in ten thousand different styles. She's probably an artist or something creative. Brown eyes. Brown hair. Vegan, or something quirky. Tell me I'm wrong.'

'Okay, that's spookily accurate. I'll give you that. But I don't do guitars. Not any more.'

'So, guitar notwithstanding, was I right?'

'Ish. I don't know her well enough yet. She's definitely not vegan, though. I know that.'

'Good. Because good God, that photo of me and Ryan: it's pure cheese. Have you seen what Annie posted?'

Annie flashed the screen towards Jen. It was pretty cringey. Chloe's date had been at a local brewery and Annie had captured them leaning on a cask together. It looked like a Hallmark movie poster. Jen shrugged. 'Cheese sells.'

'You've got more likes.'

'No, we do not,' Jen exclaimed, certain Chloe was pulling her leg.

'No, for real. Look.'

She was right; their picture did have more interaction. 'It'll just be because we're two women. You know what it's like.'

'Yeah, have you read the comments?' Chloe asked, pulling a face that said it all. *Yikes.*

'No, I'm purposely avoiding that. I saw Annie had posted and left it at that.'

'Some pretty creepy dudes on there.'

'Ach, it doesn't bother me. As long as they don't come in here.'

'And you're going to hell. Sorry to break it to you like that.'

Jen snapped her fingers. 'Darn. I did not see that coming.'

'Don't worry! Apparently the gay couple will be there with you.'

'At least I'll have someone to talk to. So, who's top of the popularity polls?'

'So far, Debbie and Nick are the ones to beat.' Chloe held the phone out to Jen. They looked a nice couple. They'd got to go indoor rock climbing and the photo had them standing close, Nick's arm around Debbie's waist. Their grins said it all. They were the real deal.

'Well, the games have just begun and all is still to play for. Debbie and Nick, you're going down!'

'As are you!' Chloe said, playfully dancing towards Jen.

The next customer in line was creased with laughter.

She should text Holly and let her know to avoid the comments. Maybe pass on some of Chloe's fighting talk, make a game of it. It felt nice to be a good mood. It had been a while.

9

H olly's phone vibrated on the kitchen counter and she fought the urge to instantly check what the message said. She and Jen had been messaging all evening. It certainly helped break up the hours of deliveries, and the blonde was quite funny, truth be told.

'Can I do anything else to help?' Holly asked Mum as she got the plates from the cupboard, placing cutlery on top.

'No, no. Just set the table and then we'll be good to go.'

It wouldn't take long to get everything ready, but Holly took her time, making sure everything was just right. It was nice to eat at the table. Before coming home she couldn't remember the last time she'd done it, bar Christmas. She and Shona had had opposite schedules, and any time meals were shared it was usually from the comfort of the sofa as they watched TV.

Holly took a seat, knowing better than to get in Mum's way while she was dishing up.

It wasn't long before Dad joined them. 'I thought I smelled something nice,' he said, taking his seat.

'Quiche from the shop. Lorraine for us and cheese and onion for Holly.'

'Sales go well today?' Holly asked, her mind still on her phone, dying to see what Jen had to say. She'd look after tea: now it was time to focus on her parents. 'I've never delivered so many hampers!'

'The power of the weekend. Not to mention your amazing publicity.'

Mum shook her head, the smile on her face growing wider by the second. 'It's all people spoke about today. You're a wee star.'

'Have you heard from her?' Dad asked, stabbing at a potato with his fork.

Holly felt heat blush her cheeks. 'We've been texting.'

Mum let out a squeal. 'Sorry, I know you don't want to date, but it's fun. And nice to see you making friends.'

'It's been good, yeah.' Holly relented.

'And are you ...' Dad paused, weighing up his options. 'Are you happier to be back now?'

'I don't think I ever said I wasn't happy to be back.'

'No. But we know you didn't want to leave London.'

Holly gulped, her mouth suddenly dry. 'It wasn't that I didn't want to leave. It was more the circumstances that brought it all to an end.'

Her parents nodded. Mum nibbled at her quiche, before picking at the bacon as she spoke. 'As long as you're happy, we're happy.'

'I'm not going back, if that's what you're worried about. Plenty of bars here. I can get a job no bother.'

'Is that what you want, though?' Dad asked. They'd never had such a candid conversation face to face, and emotion welled inside her.

'No, of course not.' The lump in her throat grew, but it

was now or never to say the truth. She just hadn't expected the words to come out over a handmade tart. She focused on the potatoes as she pushed them around the plate and prayed her voice would remain steady. 'It's my birthday in two days and I can't help but feel the last decade has been nothing but a string of failures. I'm sorry.'

Her parents chorused their objections. Dad gripped her hand. 'You're not a failure.'

Holly shook her head. 'I didn't achieve one thing I set out to do.'

'That doesn't mean you failed, sweetie,' Mum reassured her, giving her thigh a squeeze. 'We didn't open the deli until your dad got signed off with high blood pressure. Things change. Sometimes plans don't work out how you thought they would. It doesn't make you a failure.'

'That's different, though. You both had successful careers. I moved away with Shona to become an illustrator and make a life for myself. Instead, I worked in bar after bar, working myself to the bone and into a heap of debt. Only to be dumped and lose my job.'

Dad nodded, dissecting what she'd said. 'Okay, so the last few years haven't worked out how you hoped. But if it means anything, we don't think you're a failure.'

Holly let out a breathy sigh. It meant a lot, but it didn't change the emptiness she felt inside. It was like watching someone else's life from the outside. She cleared her throat, proud that she'd made it this far without cracking. This wasn't how she thought the night was going to play out. 'Thank you. I'll be fine. Don't worry about me.'

'Course we're going to worry, love. We're your parents.' Mum squeezed her leg again.

'I'm good. Honestly. And I'm really enjoying doing the deliveries.'

'Well, I'm glad you've got plenty to keep you going. I've had to turn the sound off on my phone – the website keeps getting orders. It's crazy!'

'Do you really think it's because I did the Lovefest date?'

'Absolutely,' mum replied with gusto. 'Everyone is dying to know what's going on. It's got Taylor's Deli on the map.'

Holly nodded, a smile forcing its way out. 'I'll have to try and give them more to talk about, then.'

10

Two days later, the initial rush of sales was dying down, but the high Jen was on showed no sign of letting up. She was off tomorrow, but a part of her wanted to open the shop, see what it would bring. She knew better, though. Working seven days in a row was a sure-fire way to burn out. *Been there, done that.*

She stood, hands on hips, and surveyed the working fridge. It could be fuller. She'd promised herself a day on the sofa tomorrow, and although a voice in her head was reasoning that coming in to make cocktail pouches wasn't really working if the shop wasn't actually open, she urged it to be quiet. She had to look after herself if she was going to make it through the quarter.

If only the second fridge was working, she could be making double. Get a few more flavour combinations on the go.

She rubbed at her temples. No point living in a dream world. There was no way she could afford it: the fridge guy said it would be at least three grand for parts and labour. If she knew the slightest thing about fridges she would have given it a go herself, but the threat of electrocution was real, not to mention coming in one morning to find it had burned the place down. No. She would have to wait until she had the funds.

Which presented its own conundrum.

The bank was sapping all her earnings, wanting huge sums on top of her loan because of missed past payments. If she could just leverage their demands she could at least buy in more supplies, stock the working fridge to capacity, earn more. Instead, she was chasing her tail. In one hand and out the other.

All this work and she didn't even have the bank balance to show for it.

The phone rang, making her jump a mile. It could go to voicemail; she'd been closed for over thirty minutes. Anyone that needed a cocktail would have to wait.

After the beep a familiar voice filled the shop, making her blood run cold as her heart hammered against her ribs.

Alison.

'I'm guessing you've changed your mobile number in three years.' She sounded almost nervous. Jen stared at the machine, anger mounting. 'Thought I'd call now and we'd have a chat when there's no customers? Must have just missed you. I'll try again tomorrow. Unless you call me back, of course.'

The line went dead and Jen found herself frozen to the spot.

How dare she? How fucking dare she?

Three years and she thinks it's okay to just text and call out of the blue? And be so blasé about it?

Jen fought the urge to rip the phone from its socket and smash it against the wall, as if it might be connected to Alison and she would feel it.

She still couldn't move, completely dumbstruck by the situation. Her chest heaved, her breath a near-pant.

'The fuck?' she growled.

Part of her wanted to call straight back and give it to Alison, no holding back, just like she'd often played out in her head. She'd got her revenge a million times over, in a million different ways, but was it now happening for real? What was the playbook on this?

Her legs remembered how to move and she began to pace, sweat blooming on the back of her neck and brow.

Chloe was with Ryan tonight; she didn't want to bother her. But what to do?

She stopped in her tracks and ran a hand through her hair.

The ball was in her court; this was her chance to decide the outcome. With no hesitation, she stormed to the phone and pressed delete.

She felt like she'd run a marathon. Her heart battered against her breastbone, unable to find its normal rhythm.

'You can't just do that,' she said to the empty room, surprised to find her voice a mere squeak.

They'd started the business together. Alison was the one to encourage it; Jen, as per, had been reluctant. Owning a business had never crossed her mind. It was a huge risk and a lot of work. That was Alison, though: she liked risks. It was fun. An adventure.

Then her music career grew bigger and suddenly Jen and the business weren't enough to keep her happy.

Jen had always known Alison wanted to make it in the industry. It was how they had met, after all – Alison had done a gig in the bar Jen worked at and the rest was history. She just hadn't realised that Alison making it meant leaving her behind.

She hadn't even been given the option to go. Alison wanted her share of the shop's capital; she had invested in starting it, and then London was calling. She didn't want their relationship complicating things. She needed to focus on her music, take risks, live life selfishly. Her words were etched on Jen's heart like a bad tattoo.

Well, she'd achieved that. And then some.

Maybe that was it. Everything had gone south and it was time to crawl back. It had been an age since Jen had tortured herself by looking at Alison's social media. With a shaking hand, she stabbed Alison's name into Google.

Jesus. Her Instagram following had risen to nearly half a million, and she had posted a link to new music three days ago. So it was unlikely things weren't going well.

What the hell did she want? She couldn't just swan back and expect them to be best pals.

A text message notification appeared at the top of the screen.

Her stomach did a flip of relief when it wasn't from Alison. *Thank God.*

Holly.

What are you up to? Finished work? Want to do something later? Xx

She fired back a reply:

I'm busy.

She didn't have time for meaningless conversation. Holly wasn't real. Yes, they'd been texting, but it was all part of the show. Or at least she assumed it was. She'd enjoyed their chats. But Holly only wanted to win the cash prize, get publicity. She'd made that clear.

Whatever her motive was for meeting up, Jen didn't need it. She didn't need anyone: letting other people in just complicated matters.

Right now, the only thing that mattered was making the business as profitable as possible.

Her phone vibrated. Holly again.

Okay. Anything I can help with? Xx

Why was she being so nice?

Three dots appeared under the last message, signalling Holly was typing again. Jen watched the screen, unable to take her eyes off the rippling ellipsis.

I can make cocktails, if that's what you're up to? I take direction well. Xx

She wasn't making Jen's mission to be alone easy. She slammed her phone onto the counter and stomped to the basement.

11

Holly ran a hand over the bubbles in her bath and let out a long, breathy sigh.

So this was thirty.

All attempts at finding someone to do something with had been fruitless. Friends from the past had moved or had babies. She hadn't even bothered to message many of them. Mum and Dad had done their best, bless them, but it wasn't what she'd envisaged for the big three-oh. Okay, she wasn't exactly in the party mood, but tea followed by blowing out a single candle on a carrot cake didn't feel like enough. Everyone was tired, herself included, but the lack of theatrics only added to her melancholy mood.

She held a mound of bubbles on her palm and blew, sending tufts of bubbly foam into the air.

She'd had plenty of well-wishes on social media, but nothing spectacular.

Had she been in London it was doubtful she would have done much. Post-Shona, there was a one hundred per cent chance she'd have done nothing. With-Shona ... who knew? It didn't matter.

When she'd been younger, thirty felt old, a million miles away. She thought she'd be married by now, maybe not quite at starting a family, but close. And work? That would be in the bag.

If she could only win this five grand, she could maybe turn some of that around. Living at home had its advantages. She could help Mum and Dad at the deli, continue paying off her credit cards, and use the prize money to start her business. It wasn't anything groundbreaking, but she wanted to start her own stationery brand. Cards, prints, coasters. She'd sell online and in local shops to start with, and then who knew? She just needed the capital to get going.

It felt wrong to be dreaming about winning, like she was teasing herself. It hadn't felt achievable before, though, and now, suddenly in the least expected way possible, it could become a reality.

Although she might have scared Jen off now. Come on too strong.

Holly scrunched up her eyes, as if closing them might change things, allowing her to rewind. She shouldn't have asked Jen to do something tonight. It was overstepping a mark. This was her forte: find something good and self-sabotage.

If she was alone in her flat she would get drunk. Living at home didn't allow for it, though. It was one of the reasons Mum and Dad had urged her to come back. Drink wasn't a problem, but she had found it the perfect solution to numbing the voice in her head. Too many nights in London had been spent doing exactly that, in the last few months. Not healthy.

Instead, she'd have her bath, put on a fresh pair of pyjamas and watch Netflix. She didn't even have the energy to draw.

Nailed it as usual, Holly.

Her phone chimed, making her jump.

Holding it as far as humanly possible from the bath's edge, she checked the message and couldn't help but smile. Jen.

A hand might be nice, actually. You still free? Xx

She'd messaged ages ago. Surely Jen wasn't still in her shop?

You're working late. Will I come to the shop? Xx

The reply was almost instant:

Got a lot to do. Pop round whenever xx

Holly's heart fluttered into action.

She placed the phone on the sink, out of harm's way, and pulled the plug. She couldn't risk lounging about; Jen didn't strike her as the patient type. It was now or never if she didn't want to spend the last few hours of her birthday in pyjamas.

She'd need to do redo her make-up, but that was an easy fix. Not like this was a mission to impress, anyway. She flung on a towel and padded to her bedroom, today's outfit in her arms, phone tucked under her chin.

She dumped the clothes on the bed. It didn't feel like the right ensemble. The jeans, yeah, they felt okay. But her floral top? Nope.

She opened her wardrobe. None of it felt right. Too formal or floaty. There was no happy in-between.

She pulled on her underwear and skinny jeans before inspecting the drawer containing her T-shirts.

Simple. Classic. Can't go wrong.

But was it right?

Why was this suddenly a big deal? Butterflies swirled in her stomach.

She was just going to help Jen; this wasn't a Lovefest thing. There would be no public eyes on them. Alone, they could just be themselves. Oh God, why was that making her feel worse?

Holly grabbed the first T-shirt her hand made contact with and held it over her torso. Light blue. *Nah.* She flung it onto the bed.

She scanned the drawer's contents and let out a huffy sigh. This shouldn't be so complicated.

Her phone chimed and she wasted no time in swiping it from the bed, happy for the circuit breaker from her thoughts.

Jen.

Can you bring some limes? Xx

Mum had limes; she'd spied them in the fruit bowl. Would that be sufficient?

I have two. Is that enough?

No kisses. She'd been too quick. Would Jen think she was mad? Should she send them now? Was that too much?

'Holly Charlotte Taylor, what the hell is wrong with you?' she scolded herself as she flopped onto the bed, allowing herself a moment to stare at the ceiling.

Chime.

Chime.

Chime.

She couldn't help but smile as she held the phone aloft, careful not to drop it on her face.

One will do. Xx

No, better make it two.

Xx

WITH TWO LIMES in her coat pocket, Holly chapped on Jen's shop door. When no answer came, she fired off a text, and sure enough, two minutes later, the stockroom door opened and Jen appeared.

Holly's breath caught.

Jen had on a sleeveless T-shirt, giving a full display of her perfectly sculpted arms. Her honey-blonde hair was tied back in a scrappy ponytail, the effects of hard work obvious; her cheeks were flushed red and sweat glistened on her skin.

Holly gulped down any bad thoughts as Jen opened the door.

'Holly, hey. In you come. Sorry, I was in the basement.'

'No worries; I've not been here long. Lead the way.' Holly played with the gold chain she'd chosen to pair with a simple black T-shirt. It was collarbone-length, but she suddenly wished she hadn't worn anything so close to her neck. Her temperature had shot up a few degrees, her heart now working overtime to push blood to more places than necessary.

Jen led her through the storage space at the rear of the shop before heading downstairs.

'It's a bit of a mess.' Jen apologised before opening the basement door. She wasn't lying. Boxes and equipment covered every available space. It was the same size as her parents' basement, but Jen had rows of racking on one side, industrial fridges on the other, and a large stainless steel prep table in the middle. A door at the back led to a little kitchenette and toilet. Unlike her mum and dad's place, here was spotless – well, minus the detritus on the floor. This was a working prep-space, and a well-run one at that. 'And you need to wear a hairnet.'

'That's cool. Just give me a second.' Holly slid the

hairband from her half-updo and scooped up the rest of her hair, twirling it into a messy bun. Her eyes fixed on the way Jen's lip twitched, like she was hiding a smile, as a hairnet was handed to her. She snapped it on. 'What do you want me to do?'

Jen grabbed the hairnet from the table and covered her own head as she sidled round to the workstation. 'Come over here – you can help pour.'

'This?' Holly asked, holding up a bottle of vodka.

'That's the one. I always start with the hard mixes, so I'm onto the easy ones now. This is the last batch, actually.'

'I thought you needed my help?'

'I did, but you took your time,' Jen replied with a smirk.

'Sorry.'

'Don't be. I'm just winding you up. Give your hands a good wash, then pour the whole bottle in there,' she said, pointing to the large mixing bowl on the table. 'Then grab the next one.'

Holly gave her hands a scrub before returning to the table, where Jen was lining up empty pouches. There was silence as the vodka glugged into the bowl. The smell was strong. This wasn't a job you could ever do hungover.

Jen cleared her throat quietly, like she might be working up to saying something.

'Did I do it wrong?'

Jen chuckled. 'No, no. Your pouring skills are top-notch.'

Holly's brow knitted. Something was off. 'What's up?'

Jen bit her top lip. 'Next bottle now.' She watched as Holly poured, before finally talking. Her voice was low, like she was embarrassed. 'I'm sorry for being grumpy earlier.'

'You were? I thought that was just your default mood,' Holly said with a smile. She had thought Jen's original *I'm busy* text was a bit off, but it was Jen. She barely knew the woman; that could be normal for her.

Jen pulled a face, amused. 'Oi. No, I was short with you and you didn't deserve it.'

'Anything you want to talk about?'

Jen unscrewed a bottle of dry vermouth and poured it into a measuring jug, studying the volume carefully. Enough poured, she spoke, her head still level with the jug. She avoided eye contact with Holly. 'I have a lot of debt and I'm kind of chasing my tail with stuff right now. Other things.' She shook her head, clearing her thoughts. 'It just got a bit much. Sorry.'

She placed a hand on Jen's back, her body heat radiating through Holly's hand and up to her cheeks. 'You don't need to apologise. I know what it feels like.'

Jen stood to face her and Holly removed her hand, the warmth on her cheeks remaining. 'It's like, I'm doing so much and I'm not getting any reward. Do you get that? I'm starting to wonder what the point is.'

Holly's features shifted to a sympathetic smile. 'The point is, you're killing it. Look how successful your business is.'

Jen laughed under her breath. 'That's kind of the issue though, isn't it? It's a business; it should be making money. Right now it's just paying off loans.'

Holly paused, turning the idea over in her head like a coin between her fingers. 'We're like ducks. Everything seems fine on the surface, but underneath, out of sight, we're working like the clappers, burning ourselves out. Everything's cool if we keep a straight face though, eh?'

'Bingo.' Jen's face softened. 'It's nice to have someone who gets it.'

'Quack quack,' Holly said, a grin taking over.

Jen let out a throaty laugh that didn't stop; tears formed in her eyes. Holly couldn't help but join in. Finally, they composed themselves, Jen shaking her head as the last wisps of laughter floated in the air between them. 'Thanks. I needed that. Now, did you bring me limes?'

'I did, but only two. You sure that's enough?' Holly asked, eying the litres of liquid in front of them.

'They're not for this. They're for us.'

12

J en was glad she'd doubled back on messaging Holly. An hour or so in the basement and she'd calmed down enough to realise that if she didn't find a distraction tonight she'd spend it going over and over how much she hated Alison, the temptation to dial 1471 and get her number growing by the minute.

Holly was doing a grand job of keeping her attention, even if she had no idea she was saving Jen the embarrassment of calling her ex. No good would come of it, no matter how many times she'd rehearsed it in her head.

The duck thing hadn't been that funny, but she'd been so cute that the giggles had got the better of Jen. And the hair? It had been tough to hide a smile. Chloe's stupidly specific observations were spot on. She never should have admitted her dream girl was Zooey Deschanel.

Jen caught herself, cottoning on to what she was confessing. *Uh-oh.*

'You okay?' Holly asked, still cutting the limes. 'You were in your own wee world there.'

Jen smiled, her cheeks reddening. 'Yeah, I'm good. Just

wondering how many times I could read *War and Peace* before you're done with those limes.'

'Hey,' Holly chuckled, laying on the fake offence.

'I need to finish sealing these pouches, then we can do the shots. That okay?'

'Sounds good to me.'

Jen watched as Holly explored the room, limes finally done. Her expressions varied from intrigued to disgusted. Cocktails were such a personal thing, and Jen didn't aim for crowd-pleasers. Try and please everyone and you'll please none. Better to go niche and get die-hard fans.

'My take on an old-fashioned,' Jen said, seeing Holly inspect a miniature bottle of elderflower tonic. 'You pair that with the pouch it's beside. Whisky and Sauternes.'

'Ah yes, Sauternes. A favourite.'

Jen shook her head, dispelling a laugh as she worked down the line of open pouches, sealing each one. 'You have no idea what that is, do you?'

'Not a scooby.'

'Do you want to guess?'

Holly thought, holding the pouch in her hand as she studied the liquid inside. Jen fought the urge to do her own studying. With her back to her, the only thing Jen really wanted to look at was the way Holly's skinny jeans hugged her hips.

Two hours ago you were content with being alone forever. It would seem the memo hadn't quite made it south yet.

'Old-fashioned is whisky, yeah?' Holly asked, putting the pouch down and wandering over to the workbench.

'Yep. One of the ingredients.'

'Sauternes. Sounds French.'

'Uh-huh.'

'Clue?'

'It's alcohol.'

Holly snorted. 'Thanks.' She paced, deep in thought. 'An alcohol that begins with. . .?'

'W.'

The brunette narrowed her eyes before shooting them wide, as if the answer had just hit square between them. 'Whisky. It's another type of whisky.'

'Close.'

'Really?'

'Not at all.'

Holly sniggered, biting on her bottom lip to hide a mischievous grin. 'Put me out of my misery.'

'Okay. It's. . .' Jen paused, building the suspense. She closed a few more pouches, enjoying making Holly wait.

'Oh, come on,' Holly urged, bouncing on the spot.

'W,' Jen lengthened the letter, making it last a few syllables. 'Wine!'

'Wine? Hmm. You learn something new every day. I didn't think that went in an old-fashioned.'

'And that's why I'm the cocktail expert. Speaking of which, these are done. Shots?'

'I thought you'd never ask.'

'Right, I'll tidy these up, you get everything ready.'

'Glasses?'

'Through that door, cupboard above the sink.'

Jen grabbed a bag of salt from the supply cupboard and lined up the limes before taking her hairnet off, pulling it taut between her two index fingers. When Holly walked back through the door she released the one closest to her, pinging the net straight into Holly's chest.

'Hey,' Holly said, laughing. 'Did you not learn your lesson last time? Forever taking me by surprise.'

'Sorry,' Jen replied, clearly not sorry at all. She did still feel bad about the whole mop bucket incident, though. 'Wasn't the best first impression, was it?'

'The less said the better.' Holly's eyes swept the length of the table before settling on Jen. 'I think you've forgotten the most important part.'

Jen stood, her eyes locked with Holly's, and failed to grasp what was missing.

'Tequila?' Holly encouraged, raising her eyebrows to exaggerate the urgency.

Jen feigned ignorance. 'Was just getting it, hold your horses.' A quick trot to the nearest shelves and she returned, booze in hand. 'I had a little left after making sunrises, so I thought it would be a good chance for some shots.'

'Woman after my own heart.' Holly pushed the empty glasses towards Jen.

'Right, get licking.'

'Huh?'

'Your hand, for the salt.' She poured two extremely generous measures. Holly didn't protest.

Holly held out a freshly licked hand and Jen spooned a dusting of salt onto it before copying the move herself, lime slice now ready between finger and thumb.

'What are we toasting?' Holly asked, holding her glass up.

'To the ducks of the world,' Jen replied, bringing hers level.

'Quack quack.'

'Quack quack.'

Their faces contorted as the sharpness of the tequila wreaked havoc with their tastebuds before being sated with lime. Jen's lips curled inward as she dumped the fruit back on the chopping board. 'Nothing like a shot on an empty stomach.'

'You've not eaten?'

'Been busy, haven't I? Speaking of which, I'll do the front stickers, you do the back, then the night is ours.'

Holly lifted the sticker sheets Jen had slid her way. 'Just right in the middle, yeah?' she asked hovering a peeled sticker over the nearest pouch.

Jen nodded. 'What's your plans tonight?'

'They had been to lay about in my pyjamas.'

'And yet you texted me.' Jen couldn't hide her wry smile.

It was Holly's turn to look sheepish. 'Correct. Dunno, just changed my mind.'

She was holding something back, Jen could feel it, but it wasn't her place to pry. She didn't know Holly well enough to push it. 'Well, if your PJs aren't still calling, do you fancy going somewhere after this? Seems a shame to do shots and not carry the night on.'

'What do you have in mind?'

'I'm thinking we avoid Shawlands. I don't think we're ready to look couple-y yet.'

'Agreed.' Holly replied, looking relieved.

It was good to know she felt the same. Jen wasn't much of an actress and it had played on her mind that the next time she and Holly were out they'd have to start on their plan. A chat was needed. Bringing it up felt awkward, though. Anything to do with relationships, real or not, made Jen's skin feel itchy.

'There's a place over in Mount Florida that's good, if you can bear to walk for ten minutes.'

'I think I can handle it.'

≈

IT WAS perfect weather for walking. The evenings were still long and the light showed no sign of turning to night any time soon.

'I keep meaning to go for a walk in the park,' Holly said as they passed one of the entrances to Queen's Park. 'But I've not found the time. Is the greenhouse still open?'

'I don't think so,' Jen replied, stuffing her hands into her denim jacket. 'But I've not been in ages.'

'Be a shame if it was closed.'

'It would. See that flat up there?' Jen asked, pointing towards the block of flats on their right.

Holly chuckled as she came to standstill. 'There's a lot of flats. Which one?'

Jen moved closer and leaned her arm over Holly's shoulder. She was a good few inches shorter and Jen liked the difference; she'd always liked being the tall one in a relationship. Not that this would be going anywhere near that territory. 'Block behind this one. Third floor up. The one with the curtains drawn.'

Jen watched as Holly counted the floors. 'Yeah, what about it?'

'That's Chloe's. I live across the landing.'

'Nice. I've always wondered what they're like inside. Odd little buildings.'

Jen stopped herself before inviting Holly to her flat there and then. Her first time out in a long time with a pretty gay girl and her body had a mind of her own. *That's all it is. These aren't actual feelings.*

'They are weird aren't they?' Jen walked on before she could change her mind about the invite. 'Not as boxy as they look, though.'

'I thought you'd be a tenement girl.'

'Nearly everyone in Glasgow lives in a tenement. It wouldn't have been a stretch,' Jen replied with a snigger.

'True. My detective skills might need some work. They're nice inside, then?'

Was she angling for an invite? *No, you're reading too much into this.* To be fair, it was a strange little development. Glasgow was a city of sandstone tenements. Jen's block of flats looked like it could be made of Duplo: little squat stacks of blocks, dozens crammed into a manicured space. She quite liked how quirky they looked, but Holly was right; her flat was kind of boxy. Especially compared to the high ceilings of the neighbouring flats. Still, Holly had lived in London. She was probably used to compact and bijou.

'I like them,' Jen said, her eyes still on Chloe's window. 'I have spent the last few years doing it up, though.'

'That's how you know Chloe, then? She's your neighbour?'

'Detective skills are sharpening, well done.'

Holly elbowed her in the ribs and Jen felt her core do a flip.

'Just making conversation, Jennifer.'

Jen pulled a face, waggling a finger at Holly as she attempted to make a noise like a wrong-answer buzzer on a quiz show. 'Wrong.'

Holly looked confused. 'Wrong to make to conversation?'

'Wrong to assume my name is Jennifer.'

'What? No. You're pulling my leg?'

'Why's it so hard to believe?'

'I just can't think of many names it would be short for.'

They walked in silence for a few metres, Holly deep in thought. 'I've got it,' she said, looking smug. 'Jenny.'

Another buzzer noise.

'Jenna?'

'Nope.'

Further silence.

'Jenessa?'

Jen snorted with laughter. 'Jenessa? That's not a name.'

'Alternative spelling of Vanessa.'

Jen shook her head, her cheeks starting to ache from smiling. 'Surprisingly, no. That's not right either.'

'Please put me out of my misery.'

'No, can do, sorry.'

'Please,' Holly pleaded.

'Nope. If I did I'd have to kill you.'

'What? No. You can't tease me like that.'

'Play your cards right and I might spill. Only my family and Chloe know the truth.'

'As your girlfriend, I think I have a right to know,' Holly retaliated, hardly able to keep a straight face.

'It's only been a week. You'll need to stick around to become part of the inner circle.'

'Challenge accepted.' Holly coughed quietly, her eyes firmly on the MOT station they were passing. 'So, this place we're going to. Do you go there often?'

'Erm, used to. Haven't been in a while. It was just the first place that sprung to mind. With so many options in Shawlands, I don't often need to travel.'

'True. Shawlands has more bars and peri-peri chicken shops than I've had hot dinners.'

'Feels like it, eh? But yeah, I used to work in Bar Orama. Doubt I'll know anyone, though. It's been about three years since I visited.'

'Bar Orama? That's a cracking name.'

'It is, isn't it? The guy that owns it, Kev, he's a right card. I think you'll like him. Sunday night it should be quiet. Unless you want to try your hand at karaoke.'

Holly's face dropped. 'Nope, never. I can't sing to save myself. Can you?'

'I've been known to sing a tune or two. Usually after a few shots.'

'Should I be worried that we just did two shots of tequila at yours?'

'You never know. What happens in Bar Orama stays in Bar Orama.'

THE REST of the walk went by in a flash. Holly was so easy to talk to. Jen's bad mood was a distant memory now, Alison's voicemail firmly cemented in the past. It felt like weeks had passed, not hours.

She learned that Holly preferred savoury to sweet. She'd studied illustration at university in Dundee. She loved bath bombs. And, she wanted to use her portion of the winnings to start a business. She's been quite reserved in sharing exactly what that business might be, but Jen got it. Sometimes an idea needed to flesh itself out before you fully shared it.

'Here we are: Bar Orama. After you,' Jen said, holding the door open.

Dolly Parton's dulcet tones spilt over them as they entered, and a few patrons sussed them out before returning to their conversations. Jen was right, it was quiet. Only a handful of the bar's two dozen tables were occupied.

She wasn't surprised to find it unchanged from when she'd last set foot in its door. The same tatty booths lined the left-hand wall, the mismatched chairs and tables hadn't even changed position, and the stage was still haloed by a shimmering silver backdrop. The only subtle difference was that the naked cowboy pictures were now slightly more faded.

A girl in a baseball cap made no effort to hide the fact she was checking Holly out as they passed, and Jen was surprised by the protective swell in her chest. She squashed it down, choosing to ignore it.

Jen was at the bar before she recognised who was serving. 'Travis, as I live and breathe. You look amazing! Your beard, oh my God,' she gushed. When she'd left, Travis had only just started taking testosterone. He was a baby-faced boy then; now he was a hairy heart-throb.

'Jen Berkley. Shut up. Is it really you?' He whipped around the bar faster than Usain Bolt on roller skates and enveloped Jen in a tight hug. 'What brings you here?'

'Fancied a few drinks. Heard it was half-decent here.'

'Only half? Don't let Kev hear you say that,' he joked.

'He about?'

'Yeah, through the back, I'll get him in a min. And who's this?' he asked with a smile, retaking his position behind the bar as he nodded towards Holly.

'This is Holly.'

Holly gave a little wave. 'Pleasure to meet you.'

'And you too.' He gave Jen a look as if he was figuring out the dynamics between the two women. 'And what can I get you to drink?'

'I'm going to have a wine – what about you?' she asked Holly.

'White? We could share a bottle?'

'Of course. Sauvignon Blanc okay?'

'Sounds good to me, and this is my treat.'

'No – you sure?'

Holly nodded, nudging Jen out the way with her hip. 'Sure. You saved me from a night in my pyjamas.'

Travis's lips curled into a sly smirk. 'Right, bottle of Savvy B coming up. You grab a seat, I'll bring it over.'

They plumped for a booth up the back and got comfy.

'It's nice in here,' Holly said, sliding her jacket off. 'I can't believe I've never been in.'

'A hidden gem of the Southside.' A thought hit Jen like a thunderbolt. 'Shit, I should have ordered food. You want anything?' Holly shook her head. 'One min, I'll be right back.'

'What have you forgotten?' Travis asked with a grin.

'Still serving food?'

Travis bobbed his head side to side, his mouth scrunched up. 'Chef's off. Kev is in the kitchen tonight.'

'Oh.'

'Oh indeed. Remember when he burned the rice and we had to close to air the place out?'

'How could I forget? What about chips? Surely he's mastered chips in three years?'

'He'll give it a bash. But hey, if I get to end my shift early, we all win. So, what's the deal with hot Holly?'

Jen looked over her shoulder as if Holly might have supernatural hearing, able to listen in over the blaring Natalie Imbruglia track. She was occupied on her phone; no chance of eavesdropping. 'Nothing.'

'But you want it to?'

It was Jen's turn to pull a face. 'Nah. I'm still not up for dating.'

Travis' eyebrows shifted into a sympathetic arch. 'Ever hear from Fuck Face?'

Jen couldn't help but laugh. 'You've always had a way

with words. No. You?' she lied. She didn't want to talk about Alison; she'd occupied enough brain space today.

'Not a peep. Thank God. Although, I'm sure if she wanted to play here Kev would say yes. She's fairly come on.' He looked guilty for praising her.

'I'm glad she's doing well. So, they our glasses?' she asked, going on tiptoe to reach over the bar.

'Patience, young grasshopper,' he chuckled, placing them comfortably in reach. 'You take them and I'll bring the wine on the way to the kitchen.'

Jen gave him a wink. 'Cheers, Travie!'

'Manage to get some food?' Holly asked as a glass was placed in front of her.

'Just chips, but they'll fill a hole.'

'Your wine, ladies. Chips, or what might resemble chips, will be out soon.'

Holly gave Jen a look. 'Long story,' she replied, pouring them each a wine. She raised her glass. 'Quack quack.'

'Is that our thing now?'

'Doesn't every couple need inside jokes?'

THE CHIPS HAD BEEN EDIBLE, so Kev had obviously come a long way since Jen had worked in Bar Orama. It was a good thing too, because they were onto their second bottle of wine.

'So, then I said to the guy,' Holly managed through choked laughter, "you'll want that to go, then?"'

Jen howled with laughter. Holly had some funny stories. 'Don't, don't, I'll wee myself.'

Her pleading only made Holly laugh harder. She placed

a hand on Jen's. Her heart rate rocketed as her tummy did a somersault.

Kev appeared at the table and Holly pulled her hand away. Jen was sad to see it go.

He placed two shots on the table. 'Fireballs. Courtesy of me.'

'You're out to cause trouble, Mr Carmichael.'

'I would never,' he replied, putting on a faux accent, full of sweetness and light. 'Just good to see you having fun.'

She was having a good night. Jen couldn't remember the last time she'd laughed like this.

She picked up the shot, raising it near eye level. 'Here's to good nights. Thanks, Kev!'

'Wait, wait,' Holly said, gently grabbing Jen's wrist before she could down the shot. 'Kev, will you take a photo of us?'

'My pleasure,' he replied, extending a hand as he waited to be passed a phone.

'Better use yours,' Holly said to Jen. 'Then you can post it on your socials.'

Jen obliged and passed her phone to Kev, although she was still a bit confused about why they needed photographic evidence of the fireballs.

'Say quack,' Holly said, holding her glass up and beaming a smile at the camera.

Jen copied her pose before pulling a few faces while Kev snapped away.

He passed the phone back to Jen. 'Have fun, ladies. And don't forget, Jen, you promised me a proper catch-up. You're not to leave it so long next time,' he said with a rueful smile.

'I won't forget. Scout's honour.' It had been good catching up with him when he'd brought the chips out earlier. She would definitely be back soon. It was time to make new memories in Bar Orama; replace the bad with good.

With Kev gone, they clinked glasses for a final time, downing the spicy cinnamon booze.

'Ooft, that'll put hairs on your chest,' Jen said, suppressing a cough. 'Right, let's look at these pics.' She positioned the phone between them, scrolling through the photos.

'They're good but they're not very. . .' Holly said, trailing off.

Jen knew exactly what she meant. 'Couple-y.'

'Nope.'

'This is never going to work, is it?'

'Hey, now. Don't give up too easily. We just need to work on this.' Holly stood, with the slightest stagger, quickly joining Jen on her side of the booth and sitting so close their legs were touching. Jen's heart picked up pace.

'Why do we need photos, anyway?'

'Because, have you not seen? Annie is reposting other couples' photos on the business thingy's stories. Debbie and Nick were yesterday. They were at home, watching a film or something.'

'You'refuckingkiddingme,' Jen said, the words coming out as one. 'Debbie and Nick are in it to win it, aren't they?'

'If we want to have a chance, we've got to be out there too. Can't have them hogging the limelight. People need to fall in love with us.'

'So, what do you suggest?'

'We need folk to believe we're the real deal, which means giving them a little peek behind the scenes.'

'Huh?'

Holly put her arm around Jen, her hand casually draped across her shoulder. 'Now our photos will look legit.'

'You really think putting your arms around me is going to seal the deal?'

'No, this isn't right,' she admitted, taking her arm back. 'But if you do this, and I hold the camera. . .' she said, taking Jen's closest arm and wrapping it around herself. 'Right, you move, so I can lean into you.'

Jen did as she was told, only just managing to keep the giggles at bay. Soon Holly was nestled into her shoulder, one hand holding onto Jen's forearm. She could feel Travis' eyes on them from the bar. She ignored him and fought to focus on the task in hand. Which was proving even more difficult than avoiding the barman's steely gaze. Holly pressed harder into her, Jen's breasts a cushion for her back. Not to mention the fact they'd contorted themselves into such an intimate position that Holly was nearly sitting on Jen's lap.

She inhaled a lungful of Holly's shampoo. She smelled fresh, like bubble bath.

'Earth to Jen, did you hear me?'

'Huh?'

'I said, you ready to look smitten?'

'Yep, good to go.'

Holly held the camera up, searching for the right angle. 'Okay, just move your head closer to mine – yep, that's it. Now smile and try to look like you fancy me.'

It wasn't hard.

13

'Ready for date two?' Holly asked Jen as they met at one of Queen's Park's side entrances.

It was hard to believe only a week had passed since D'Angelo's. It felt like a lifetime ago. Mum and Dad's deli was prospering from their little plan, in more ways than one. Annie had reposted their picture, as Holly had hoped, and had even gone so far as to do a weekly round-up of pictures from the competing couples. Only one was missing, Rachel and Mike, and Annie would surely instruct them to get snapping this week if they wanted to stay in the running. Sales had rocketed after the little round-up and they'd gained nearly 200 new followers online. Her parents were beaming.

However, they'd still not had to be a couple in public, and the thought of it made Holly nervous. Could they really pull it off?

Even meeting Jen now felt loaded, the air heavy with static between them. Should she kiss her cheek, give her a hug? What was normal? Holly tried to think back to meeting Shona in public but her mind was blank, the memories vanishing like water through a sieve.

They stood awkwardly for a heartbeat or two.

'Should we go find the guy?' Jen asked with a shrug, her hands stuffed firmly into her hoodie's front pocket.

'I guess.'

God, why did this suddenly feel so stiff?

'He said he'd be in the car park,' Jen said, wandering off.

Holly followed. Jen had on loose shorts and it wasn't long before Holly's eyes settled on her legs. They were the kind of legs that made you want to get on your knees and explore every inch until you couldn't take it any more, and—

'I'm guessing that's him with the massive van and bikes,' Jen said with a mischievous grin.

She was skating a fine line, she knew that, but ever since their impromptu night out, Holly had struggled to shake the knowledge that feelings for Jen were bubbling under the surface. Okay, maybe not so much bubbling, any more; more like an angry pot threatening to boil over should she let it. She needed to put a lid on it, though. She was still healing from Shona, and Jen had made it clear enough she didn't want a relationship. This was about money, nothing else, no matter how often she messaged Holly – which was fast becoming part of their daily routine.

Jen had been the one to suggest becoming Facebook friends, which had been a surprise. Holly didn't have her down as the sociable type. In hindsight, that was probably when things tipped past the point of no return. Not only had the messages become more frequent, but Holly now had a bank of photos to browse and by God, Jen was cute.

Holly stole a look at Jen as they walked to the van. Jen

caught her and sent a wink her way. Holly's insides melted. Maybe this wasn't going to be so awkward after all.

'Hey,' the bike guy said, standing up from where he was sitting on the rear of his open van. Two bikes leaned against its side, with a dozen more crammed in behind him. 'Connor.' He held his hand out and gave both theirs a shake as introductions were made. 'You've both ridden before, yeah? You know what Annie's like.'

Jen gave him a knowing look. Holly was clueless, but spoke first. 'I used to have a bike when I lived in London, cycled every day.'

'And you?' Connor directed to Jen.

'Not for a while, but I'm sure I'll remember.'

He nodded. Connor seemed a man of few words, and those he did part with were carefully chosen. 'Right, well. I own Cycle Nation, down on Regwood Street. Idea is, we give you a loan of these bikes and you have a cycle round the park. Sound okay?'

Not particularly taxing, but it would do. 'Sounds good,' Holly replied, wishing it wasn't quite so hot today. Or that they'd got a spa visit instead.

'Cool. Let's see what bikes fit.'

HELMETS on and bike seats adjusted to just the right heights, it was just a case of waiting for Annie and Isaac. She'd messaged Jen to say they were running late but that she hoped the fitting would fill the gap. Still no sign, though.

'How long you been doing this?' Holly asked, scrambling to fill the silence.

'Coming on five years now.'

'Still enjoy it?' Jen chipped in while fiddling with the rubber on her handlebar.

'Aye, yeah, it's good.'

He wasn't giving them much to work with. Holly searched her brain for another opener but came up short. She looked to Jen and could see a smile twitching on her lips.

'I've been thinking about getting another bike now I'm back in Glasgow. If I popped in, could you fit me with one?' A lie, but anything to avoid a triangle of awkward glances.

'Yeah, that's no problem.'

Oh my God, was every sentence a dead-end with this guy?

Jen breathed an audible sigh of relief and Holly was pleased to see Annie and Isaac round the corner to the car park.

'Sorry, guys!' Annie chimed, her usual cheery self. 'Wee bit delayed at the last date. We'll know to allow more time in the future. You good to go?'

Holly and Jen chorused their approval, maybe a little too enthusiastically.

'Right, if you guys want to wheel the bikes into the park, we can get some shots.' Isaac suggested.

'Sure, just tell us where you want us,' Jen said, pushing off.

They weren't far into the park when Isaac declared it safe to stop. 'We'll go for some shots of you standing here with the gate in the background, then I'll take an action shot of you riding off. That good?'

'Sure, no problem.' Holly didn't quite know where to stand, though. And by the look of it, Jen didn't either.

'Bit closer together, ladies,' Isaac said, gesturing with the hand not holding his camera. He squinted through the viewfinder. 'Yep, right, now turn your bikes to me.'

With their bikes on the outside, nothing but dead space

separated Jen and Holly. Where was she meant to put her hands? Holly awkwardly stepped closer to Jen as all memory of how to stand like a normal human left her head. Jen brought a hand up and let it hover, locking eyes as if asking for permission. Holly gave what she hoped was a subtle nod and Jen placed it on her hip. Even through her zippy top, she could feel how rigid Jen's muscles were. At least Holly wasn't the only one having a temporary malfunction.

In a bid to make it look like they hadn't met two seconds ago, Holly weaved an arm behind Jen and attempted to casually lean on the bike's seat. It was further than she thought, though, and she staggered a little. Jen pulled Holly closer to steady her. At least it got rid of the gap.

'Much better,' Isaac cheered, starting to snap photos.

Jen gave Holly a reassuring squeeze.

'Okay, and one looking at each other,' Isaac called.

As Holly's eyes snagged Jen's she couldn't help but feel like a bungling idiot. It was painfully obvious how fake this set-up was. Her nerves about today were justified – they should have rehearsed something beforehand.

Jen's eyes narrowed, another wry smile pulling at her lips. She clearly felt as much of a wally as Holly; her cheeks wobbled with the threat of giggles. Holly couldn't help but return the look and before she knew it Jen had barked with laughter.

'Sorry, sorry,' Jen said, trying to compose herself. She put her hand back on Holly's waist, the other still gripping the bike.

'No, no, that was good,' Isaac reassured. 'Natural.'

They hadn't been this close since Bar Orama. Holly couldn't help but notice how Jen's eyes darted to her lips before fixing back on her own stare. She was just nervous, though. They both were; cameras weren't their thing.

'You finding my face funny?' Holly joked, attempting to keep the smile on her face so Isaac could continue clicking away.

'That and other things.'

Isaac went for another angle as Annie watched on. This was taking an eternity.

'Come here often?' Holly asked.

Jen was off again. Which set Holly off. Before long their laughter was uncontrollable. Isaac seemed happy with the development. He was running about like an excited spaniel, grabbing photos from all angles.

'We're good,' he shouted.

Jen wiped a tear from the corner of her eye. 'Thank God.'

Holly creased up in another bout of hilarity.

FINALLY, they were alone and allowed to cycle. Jen was a little wobbly at first, but she soon settled into it, keeping pace with Holly no bother.

It was easy at first. This part of the park was almost flat, with the only changes being downhill.

Holly was filled with memories of the duck pond and leisurely walks with her parents. It was only ever one parent, Mum or Dad, never both at once. She'd never questioned it at the time but looking back it must have been tough being so busy. Holidays were the only time they were truly a family. Nothing made her happier than knowing Mum and Dad were living their best life now. The deli was their saving grace.

She did a double take as they passed the duck pond. 'There is a giant duck,' she shouted.

'Huh?' Jen shouted over her shoulder, making her wobble again.

Maybe best to avoid conversation for now.

Floating square in the middle of the pond was a duck, at least three feet long and half as tall. It wasn't real, of course plexiglass or something, and painted on the side were the words 'don't feed me bread'. It was good to know she hadn't been seeing things last week.

They curved left, as their only other option would take them down past the pond and out of the park, and neared a wooded area. It wasn't long before Jen hit the brakes and stopped at a fork in the road. Holly pulled to a standstill beside her.

'What way?' Jen asked, beads of sweat already clear on her face.

Holly pondered. Straight on would take them downhill, past the tennis courts, then up a sharp incline to the greenhouses. Left was an exit. Right was a hill; steep, but not as bad as the other one.

'We're going to have to do a hill at some point.'

Jen pursed her lips, weighing up her own options. 'True.'

'And the flagpole is up there – good views.'

'Also true.'

'We can go downhill to the greenhouses after, see if they're open?'

'Closed. I checked earlier. I know you wanted to visit them.'

'Aw, that's a shame.'

'Up here then?' Jen asked, motioning her head to the hill on their right.

'Aye, let's give it a go.'

It only took a few metres for Holly's thighs to burn, and judging by the work Jen's legs were doing she was feeling the same.

She didn't want to break first, but Jesus suffering fuck, this was hard work. Her legs were on fire; every rotation of the pedals was like torture. How could they only be halfway up the hill?

Jen's pace slowed and Holly focused on the shape of her thighs, the way the muscle was defined, a clear shadow running down to her knee. If she was going to let this pot spill she was going to do it for the greater good, and right now she needed a distraction from the fact her own legs were now made of lava. No harm in a little daydreaming. Needs must, and all that.

Maybe Jen would need some heat balm rubbed into her aching limbs later?

Three-quarters up the hill now. This was working. She let her mind wander further.

Toned arms, toned legs: did Jen work out? It didn't seem like her schedule would allow for it but Holly's eyes didn't lie, and that wasn't a body you got by sitting on the sofa. *I bet her stomach is just as toned.*

Holly's core awakened at the thought. She swallowed hard; visions of Jen laid bare danced in her head. Kissing up those thighs, all the way up to her navel, then back south.

The sudden screech of brakes pulled her back to reality.

'I'm going to need a breather,' Jen said, pausing at the summit. Her face was as red as a tomato.

Holly didn't need to be told twice; she pulled up beside Jen and brought her feet to the ground. The sweat was dripping off her and pooling in places she'd never known could hold liquid.

'I don't think I'm made for cycling in Scotland,' Holly said with a smile.

'You and I both. Want to find somewhere to sit for a bit?'

Holly nodded. 'I think I need it.'

Jen hopped off her bike, her attention fixed on the flagpole. It was surrounded by people, most of whom looked like boozy teenagers. 'Busy up there. Will we find somewhere else?'

'I'll go wherever you take me,' Holly said and wondered if that sounded like an odd thing to say.

Jen scanned their surroundings. 'The back of the allotments? Always quiet there.'

'Sounds like a plan. Flat too,' Holly replied, running a hand down her face to help the sweat on its way.

They pushed off in tandem, cutting through the wooded area behind the park's many eclectic sheds and greenhouses. 'Ever feel like we've been given the short straw?' Jen laughed. 'Do you know what Chloe and Ryan are doing?'

Holly shook her head. 'Please don't say a spa.'

'Close enough, well not really, but a pottery class.'

'Aw, I would have loved that. I've always wanted to try.'

'We could go ourselves some time, if you'd like?'

Holly paused, suddenly all too aware of what she'd just been dreaming about, the need to distance herself now more important than ever. Jen didn't want anything more, plus Holly wasn't in the right headspace for a relationship. But there was no denying she was attracted to her. A friendship could get messy, fast. But now wasn't the time for stepping back.

Jen grappled with the silence, attempting to fill it with as many words as possible. 'Like, as friends, obviously. Just a thought. I had fun the other night, when we went to Bar

Orama; I just thought it might be nice to do something else, as friends.'

Holly couldn't help but snigger at Jen's never-ending torrent of words.

'What?' Jen asked, somehow managing to blush an even darker shade of red than she already was.

'Nothing, you're just c—' *Jesus.* She only just caught herself before the word *cute* tumbled from her lips. *FUCK.* Holly's cheeks matched Jen's. She coughed, clearing her throat quietly and pretending that was why she'd stopped. 'I would like to go some time. With you. As friends.'

Jen's features relaxed, her shoulders visibly dropping like a weight had been lifted. Message received: friendship was on the table, nothing else.

At the rear of the allotments, not another soul was in sight as the trees opened up, revealing a spectacular view of the Southside. Not quite the postcard-perfect horizon they would have seen from the flagpole, but beautiful nonetheless. They carried on along the dirt path in search of a place to sit. Why no one had ever thought to put a bench here had always perplexed Holly.

'What about over there?' Jen said, pointing to what looked like a dry patch of grass.

'Six of one,' Holly said, twisting her bike in the new direction.

'Hey, that reminds me,' Jen said, her face lighting up. 'What was on your card at the first Lovefest event?'

'And into the fire.'

'Not a match, sorry. This date's over,' she said with a cheeky grin.

'You didn't find your match either, then? What was yours?'

'Two in the bush.'

Holly snorted with laughter. 'You're having me on.'

'No, really. I'm guessing as in "A bird in the hand is worth two in the bush".'

'Ah,' Holly replied, sense dawning. 'Two in the bush and into the fire.'

The duo erupted into giggles once more. 'I don't think it will catch on.'

'You never know.' Holly placed her bike on the grass and got comfy alongside it. 'This isn't too bad, now my legs have stopped dying.'

'I can't do that again,' Jen huffed, rubbing at her thighs as she joined Holly on the ground. 'Can we just chill here and tell Connor we went cycling?'

'Your secret's safe with me.'

Comfortable silence descended as they took in the view. A Saltire-blue sky stretched over Glasgow: tenements gave way to distant rooftops, which in turn became picturesque hills.

'It's not a bad place to call home,' Jen said, her voice quiet, like she was saying it to herself more than Holly.

'I'll say.' Holly pulled her phone from her pocket, taking a few snaps of the view to show Mum and Dad later. She couldn't resist Instagram while she was at it. 'Oh my God, have you seen this?' Annie had shared a very candid photo of Chloe and Ryan, his arms around her as they threw a pot. It was like something from a film.

'Lucky bastards,' Jen laughed. 'I'll be lucky if I can use my legs tomorrow.'

Holly sighed, bracing herself before tackling a difficult subject. 'You think we could pull that off?'

Jen snapped off a blade of grass, playing with it as she spoke. 'Dunno. I felt a bit weird when we met, like I didn't know what I should do.'

'Me too,' Holly said, her eyes growing wide with the comfort of knowing Jen felt the same. 'And that photoshoot was awkward as hell.'

'You're telling me. What are we going to do about it?'

'I've been thinking about this.' It was true. She had been thinking about it. A lot. Which was part of the reason for her wandering mind. Was it safe to go down this route or was she just acting out a misguided fantasy? No, something needed to be done before their third date, or they'd never have a chance of winning the money. 'And the public are never going to believe us if there isn't a smidgen of truth. There's an intimacy you just can't fake. Like, correct me if I'm wrong, but have Chloe and Ryan slept together? I mean, they'll at least have kissed, yeah?'

Jen shrugged as she dropped the blade of grass to the ground. 'Not sure, but yeah, they'll have kissed at least.'

'See, you can tell. There's a comfortableness about them. The awkwardness has gone. They're relaxed. Even if they're not snogging each other hello when they meet, you can tell they're not analysing a damn thing. They're just doing what feels natural. And I don't know about you, but I'm no actress; I can't pull that off with an audience. Especially if we go in cold like today.' It was one thing to be camera shy, another to be as intimate with your supposed girlfriend as you would be with a stranger in the supermarket.

'Okay,' Jen replied, drawing the word out. 'I agree with you, but what can we do about it? You want to have sex?' She laughed nervously.

'Not quite. I think that might be a bit too much. I mean, I'm committed to the part and all, but. . . ' she trailed off with a quiet laugh.

'What then? We need a set play-by-play of what we're to do?'

'Nah, too stiff. Our photos worked well the other night because we were drunk; the inhibition was gone. But we can hardly be steaming every time we meet. I think we need to break the ice, give ourselves something to work with.'

'Meaning?'

Holly's heart went into overdrive, refusing to believe she was actually going to say what she's spent hours thinking about last night. Five grand was riding on this. If she wanted to start her own business they needed to get serious about winning the money, which meant pulling out the big guns, going in strong. Holly psyched herself up, looking for the courage to push the words from her lips. 'I think we should kiss.'

14

'Now?' Jen blurted, her voice ten octaves higher than usual.

Holly sniggered. 'I'm just kidding. Plus, you never know who's hanging about – I don't think in the public eye is the best place for that experiment. I do think we need to spend some time together though, practice being in each other's spaces. Hand-holding, little touches, stuff like that. That's what makes a relationship: the little things you don't think twice about.'

'I don't know. Seems a little extreme, don'tcha think? Going to all that trouble.'

'Do you want a new fridge or not? I just think we need to clear the air, break the tension. Or nothing we do will ever look genuine. If we do it now, in our own time, then being a couple in public is going to be no big deal. Like, look at how we're sitting. We're friends at best – there's no way we're dating.'

Jen's heart was thundering, slamming against her ribs like a percussionist was using her as an xylophone, still recovering from Holly's kissing joke.

Holly continued, 'Let's start small, practice being in each other's personal space while we watch a movie or something. If we get used to each other behind closed doors it will be a cinch when we're in front of the camera. I really want to win this money, Jen. We need to try harder if we're going to beat the other couples.'

She couldn't. Lines were already blurred. The truth was, ever since their night out in Bar Orama, Jen had struggled to get Holly out of her mind. Holly only wanted to be friends, though. Would acting things out not just send confusing signals to her already muddled mind?

'I need time to think about this,' Jen said, her heart still refusing to slow down.

'Of course. I wouldn't rush you into anything.'

Could she really get close to Holly and not deepen the feelings that were now undeniable? Once that gate was open, Jen could never go back. Even allowing herself to fantasise about it had felt wrong, like she was crossing a line. It hadn't stopped her, though. She'd touched herself last night, the first time in a long time, visions of Holly between her legs playing out as she orgasmed.

Making those dreams a reality, even if it was just an act, was far too dangerous.

'Do you think we should head back soon?' Holly asked, cutting through Jen's thoughts like a knife through butter. 'Connor said we only have the bikes for an hour.'

'Yeah, probably best. No more hills though,' she replied with a chuckle. Was Holly just going to leave this conversation at that?

'If we go down here we can take the flat path back to the car park?'

'Let's do it.' It would seem she was leaving things there. Probably for the best. Or Jen would be having a heart attack.

Holly retrieved her bike, surveying the land below them. 'Of course, we could always go down here, take a shortcut to the path.'

'Fancy a race?' Jen challenged.

'You're on.' Quick as a whippet Holly was on her bike, speeding down the hill.

'Hey, that's cheating!' Jen shouted, clambering on her own bike and pushing off. She turned the pedals, to no avail: they were freewheeling now and Holly wasn't giving up her lead.

She negotiated a hummock, losing even more ground.

Jen lowered herself towards the handlebars, hoping to become a little more aerodynamic. The plan worked and she was soon closing the gap.

Not far to go now.

Holly quickly checked her rival's position, a huge grin plastered on her face.

C'mon, Jen.

A squirrel appeared from nowhere, its face a question mark as it stopped directly in Jen's intended tracks.

There was no time to think. No time for brakes.

Either she changed course or it was squirrel pancakes.

Her brakes squealed as she fought to swerve, the noise ripping through the air like a howling banshee.

The world was a blur and the next thing she knew she was flat on her back, Holly's concerned face blotting out the sky.

'Oh my God, are you okay?' she asked, crouching by Jen.

'Squirrel.'

'Huh?'

'Is the squirrel okay?' She sat up, looking for her furry buddy. Everything felt okay; a few scrapes, but that was it.

'I can't see a squirrel,' Holly replied, helping Jen sit up.

'Bastard never even stuck around to say thank you,' she said with a faint laugh. She felt like an absolute wally. Didn't look like they had an audience though, thank fuck.

Holly stood, extending a hand to Jen. 'Let me help you up.'

The agony was instant, the pain zipping through her bones like an electric shock. 'Ayuh,' she yelped, hopping around on her good leg.

Holly held her steady. 'What's up?'

'My ankle.'

'Broken?' Holly asked, tilting her head to look at the offending limb.

'I don't think so, but I can't put much weight on it.'

Holly scanned the area, her eyes settling on a bench. 'Let's get you over there and I'll take the bikes back.' She swooped under Jen's bicep, wrapping a supporting arm around her waist.

'You sure?'

'Of course, can't have you hobbling all the way to the car park. Plus, your flat's not far from here, is it?'

Jen winced as they made their first tentative steps towards the bench. 'Yeah, just across the road.'

'That settles it. I'll have you sorted in no time.'

BIKES SAFELY RETURNED, they took a slow walk back to her flat. Her ankle refused to stop throbbing. She'd had to stop a few times purely to balance on her left foot, the only thing that brought relief.

'You sure you don't want to go to the hospital?' Holly asked, hovering behind as Jen made the final steps to her landing. The banister was a godsend – limping was much easier when you could haul yourself in the right direction.

'Honestly, it's just a sprain. I'll be fine once I can get a seat.'

Holly looked sceptical. 'Only if you're sure.'

Finally on the landing, Jen allowed herself a moment to catch her breath. The reality of the situation hit like a slap in the face: Holly was at her flat. 'Do you want to come in?' she asked, scrunching one eye closed, like the question hurt more than her ankle.

'Just to get you settled.'

'I've not cleaned.'

'Then I get to see the real you,' Holly replied with a smile.

Jen sucked air in through her teeth. She wasn't messy, but is anyone ever ready for unexpected guests? She had dishes in the sink and underwear on the radiators. She was in no fit state to be running about getting things in order, though: it was how it was.

'Honestly, however bad it is, I've seen worse,' Holly said, lingering by the door.

'Just promise not to judge.'

Holly held a hand over her heart. 'You have my word.'

'Right.' Jen gave herself a moment before putting the key in the lock. 'After you.'

Holly scooped a supporting arm around her again, helping Jen into the flat. It wasn't too bad. But why had she just done a wash? Pants were everywhere. *Why am I worried about pants?* Holly didn't care about her underwear. This was just like having Chloe round, and she certainly wouldn't clean for her.

With Holly's assistance, Jen hopped down the hall and into the open plan living room-come-kitchen.

'There you go,' Holly said, holding Jen's elbow as she slowly lowered herself onto the sofa. 'Now, let me get you something for that leg.'

'Like what?'

'I dunno. Peas, or something.'

'Good luck with that,' Jen said with a smile.

Holly eyed her with suspicion, her changing features saying she understood once she opened the freezer. She checked the fridge for good measure.

'Okay, so everything we need to make cocktails, not so much on the food front. What the heck do you eat?'

'I'm rubbish at eating when I'm busy and when I remember I usually just grab a ready meal or get a delivery.' Jen took the trainer off her good foot, wincing when she loosened the laces on the bad one. Thankfully, Holly hadn't seen. She gritted her teeth as she eased the shoe off.

Holly stood, hands on hips, staring into the fridge. 'I literally don't think I've ever seen a fridge more empty.'

'Told ya.'

'Right, so nothing cold,' Holly said, wandering back to the living room and perching on the sofa by Jen. Holly patted her own thigh. 'Put it up here if you can. Let me have a look.'

'You got healing fingers now?' Jen said with a snigger. She did as she was told, though, carefully manoeuvring her leg onto Holly's. She shuddered at the sudden skin on skin contact, playing it off as pain.

'Is that sore?' Holly asked, concern clear. She gently gripped Jen's ankle in her hand and this time pain did play a part in making her grimace. 'Sorry.'

'It's fine. It'll be better tomorrow.'

Holly didn't look convinced. 'I've seen plenty rolled ankles – usually drag queens in my pub. Some cracking injuries, let me tell you, and this looks bad. You can already see the bruise coming up.'

Jen leaned forward, inspecting the limb. Holly was right: a blue tinge bloomed around her ankle bone. 'Ach, that'll fade.'

Holly skirted her fingers over the mark. Jen shivered as her nipples instantly hardened. Thank God she'd chosen to wear a loose hoodie; she wasn't used to such close proximity and even the slightest touch from Holly was driving her senses haywire. 'Did you pay that squirrel? Was this all part of the plan to touch me?'

'A girl never tells. But looks like it worked,' Holly replied with a wink, although, as if embarrassed, she dropped her hands away from Jen's leg. *Oops.*

'Well, we've started, may as well finish. What's next?'

'Huh?'

'You want to hold hands or something?'

Holly snorted. 'I mean, if you want.'

Jen bit down on her bottom lip, fighting the urge to laugh. 'This is weird, eh?'

'Maybe I was wrong. Maybe we can just be drunk every time we meet.'

'Would certainly make life easier.'

Holly paused for a second before twisting to a new position under Jen's leg, their other knees now touching. Had she done that on purpose? Where was this going? Jen's body hummed with anticipation.

'Let's style this out,' Holly said, finding the hand Jen had draped over a cushion. She laced their fingers together. A thrill of anticipation ran over Jen. 'Let's pretend we hit it off at Cal's. First date went well. We go for drinks after D'Angelo's? That sound right?'

Jen looked at Holly's hand in hers. She'd never been so

acutely aware of every millimetre of her fingers, her palm, the back of her hand. It was like she'd suddenly developed a thousand new nerves. 'Sounds about right.'

'So, maybe a little hand-holding at the table. Some flirty touching.' Holly flitted her free hand over Jen's thigh, her fingers dancing over her skin like butterfly wings. *Jesus fucking Christ.* It took all Jen had not to inhale sharply. Her core was well and truly awake, vying for the driving seat in her brain.

If Holly could play this game, so could she. Jen reached over, gliding her hand up Holly's thigh, settling not far from the hem of her shorts. She gave a gentle squeeze.

Their eyes locked. Holly's eyes darted to Jen's lips before returning to her gaze. 'Do you kiss on a first date?'

'Me personally?'

'Uh-huh.'

Jen held Holly's stare for a beat, certain she saw the same smoking embers as she was surely supplying. The fire hadn't quite started, but there was something hanging between them, like they were both fighting to keep it under wraps. Jen certainly was. If she let go, there would be no stopping the blaze.

She couldn't risk overstepping the mark, though. Not yet.

'I don't believe in sex before marriage,' Jen said, trying really hard to keep a straight face. But the wobble of her cheeks betrayed her.

Holly considered if it was a joke for a half-second too long.

'I'm kidding,' Jen offered. 'Perhaps.'

'No skin off my nose,' Holly quipped. She circled her thumb over Jen's palm, and it was a miracle Jen didn't melt into a puddle and slide right off the sofa. Holly sat back, breaking the contact, and Jen instantly missed her touch. Thankfully, she didn't have to wait long before it was rekindled. Holly tapped the knee of her good leg. 'Straighten this out.'

Jen had no clue where this was going, but she couldn't wait to find out. Holly popped her shoes off, and after a quick twist, she was nestled between Jen's legs, back to chest. They couldn't have fitted together better if they were puzzle pieces.

'Date two,' Holly instructed. Was it Jen's imagination, or was she sounding a little breathless? 'You've invited me around to watch a film.'

'Very forward of me. Obviously hoping I get lucky.'

'I should think so, especially after all that flirting I did when we went out for drinks.'

Holly's just in character. Holly's just in character.

Jen's heart threatened to pick up pace. It had been a long time, that's all it was. Yes, Holly was attractive. And yes, Holly was great company. Okay, Jen now had a habit of reaching for her phone every morning and texting Holly as soon as she woke up, but hey, where was the harm in having a new friend? Didn't mean she'd fallen head over heels for her.

Holly took Jen by the wrist and positioned her arm across her chest, settling in, pressing against Jen's boobs. She gave Jen's wrist a squeeze. Okay. This was Jen's kryptonite. She was made to be a big spoon.

Fuck.

It had been a lifetime since she held someone like this and she was surprised to discover how much she'd missed it, whether this moment was real or not. Yes, she and Chloe were often in each other's personal space, but not like this. This was the kind of intimacy only afforded to partners. Memories of being cuddled up on the couch watching films with Alison rushed back. Was she conscious of being lonely, now she was devoted to being single? Not so much. But did she miss these special moments when it was just you and the person you loved, sharing space, feeling their heartbeat, relishing the gentle rise and fall of their chest? Abso-fucking-lutely.

She'd completely blocked out how good it felt, and now her body and brain had been served such a stark reminder it was hard not to want more.

'I think we're nailing this,' Jen said, her voice almost a purr.

'Definitely better than earlier.'

Holly smelled amazing. You could tell she'd put in some effort with the bikes, but she was still fresh, outdoorsy, and the scent of her citrusy perfume lingered.

'Maybe we should have actually put a movie on,' Jen said, leaning her head on Holly's shoulder.

'I thought we were missing something.'

And yet Holly didn't move.

An hour or so like this wouldn't be the worst thing in the world. Jen edged forward, a hand on Holly's hip, keeping her in place as she worked her other arm free. Not that it felt like she was going anywhere; if anything, she was pressing harder into Jen.

She clicked the TV on, not really caring what the channel was, and repositioned her arm. A swell of desire swirled in her belly when Holly brought her hands up and regripped her forearm.

There couldn't possibly be a universe in which Holly wasn't revelling in this as much as Jen was. If she wasn't, someone get this woman an Oscar, quick.

How far to push things? The aim of the game was to get used to acting like a couple, after all.

Jen ignored the TV show, some programme about wealthy couples buying extravagant houses in the country, and focused on Holly's slender limbs. Jen's eyes traced the lines of Holly's bent knee, the one leaning against her cushion. If she'd known how Holly's toned calf was going to pop against the teal she would have bought them with a little more ceremony. Never in a million years did she see this happening when she'd picked them up in Tesco.

Next, she gave Holly's straightened leg attention, the one leaning into her own, touching at every point possible. There wasn't much Jen wouldn't give to run a tongue up that expanse of skin.

Holly shifted, sinking harder into Jen. If this was real, she would kiss Holly's neck about now. Nibble her ear a little. But that felt too far. Instead, she relieved Holly's hip of her hand, moving it to brush the back of her fingers on Holly's arm.

Holly shivered. In a good way. Jen's body tingled, alive with the sensation, every atom of her being on high alert.

'I didn't have you down as liking these types of shows,' Holly said, low and breathy.

'I'm not really watching it, to be honest,' Jen replied, purposely keeping her head low, speaking into Holly's neck.

A little brazen, perhaps. But Jen's mind was acting of its own accord now.

Holly turned, her face now millimetres from Jen's.

The move nudged Jen's leg and in the haze of the moment, she forgot her injury, letting it drop to the floor.

'Suffering fuck,' Jen yelped, her hand clutching her thigh.

'Oh my God, was that my fault?' Holly asked, her face falling.

'No, no, all me.' Jen scrunched her eyes tight, worried about the threat of tears.

Holly untangled herself, arching onto all fours then off the sofa. 'I need to find you something to put on that.'

The loss of Holly between her legs hurt more. Jen resisted the urge to grab her on the way past, pull her back in.

'You've got to have something,' Holly insisted, opening the fridge again like they might have missed a magic delivery in the last ten minutes.

Using the sofa arm for leverage, Jen stood, ignoring Holly's protests as she hopped to the kitchen. 'There might be something in the bottom drawer of the freezer. Chips, I think.' She wedged herself in the corner of the kitchen, leaning on the countertop.

Holly popped to a squat and inspected the bottom freezer drawer. 'Chips, bingo. Let's get you back to the sofa.' She held her hands out, like a parent waiting for an unsteady toddler, but Jen didn't budge.

'I know you were joking in the park, but I think we should do it,' Jen said, eager to get the words out before she lost the nerve. She had to know. She had to know what it would feel like. She couldn't come this far and let the moment pass. This was once in a lifetime stuff.

'Do what?'

'Kiss.'

'Really?' Holly's voice was nearly a squeak: surprised didn't cover it.

Had she gone too far? *Fuck.* Holly was going to know this was more than acting.

Yes, she wanted to break the tension and give their fake

relationship its best possible chance. But really, she wanted to see if these lingering feelings actually were something or if it was all in her head. She'd been perfectly happy for three years – why did this woman get to come in like a wrecking ball and flatten her carefully built walls? Chances were, there would be no spark and her confused head would finally get the message. She was horny, that was all. Mid-cycle. She wanted sex, and Holly was the closest lesbian. Nothing else.

'Anything is worth a shot, right? Five grand is on the line.' Did that sound nonchalant enough? *Please say yes.*

Holly placed the bag of chips on the counter as if it were as fragile as a bomb. 'You're one hundred per cent sure? You didn't get a concussion, or something?'

'Promise. Now can we hurry up and do this, before I chicken out?' Jen was already short of breath.

'Okay, yeah,' Holly said, looking flustered. 'Right; wow. Where do you want me?'

FUCK. Holly wasn't challenging her. This was a quick turn of events. Jen's mind felt like it was playing catch-up, watching from the outside: this couldn't be real life.

'Closer to me, please. I don't want to move.' Jen's palms were soaked, the small of her back following hot on their heels. Any closer and Holly would surely feel how hard her heart was beating. *I've said it now; no going back.*

Kissing. Did she remember how to do that? Static flooded her brain.

Holly positioned herself in front of Jen, awkwardly hovering. 'I don't really know how to start this.'

'It was your plan,' Jen replied with a grin, hiding the fact she felt close to passing out.

Holly stepped closer, straddling Jen's feet.

Jen gripped the counter, hoping her good leg wouldn't

buckle or shake. Holly placed her hands on Jen's hips, making her jump.

Holly's gaze didn't falter, her brown eyes held steady with Jen's. 'There's nothing to be nervous about.'

'I know, it's just. . . first time, and all that.'

'First time kissing ever?' Holly replied with a cheeky smile.

The joke made it better. Every muscle in Jen's body relaxed. 'Feels like it.'

Holly inched closer. 'Okay,' she said quietly. 'Let's do this.'

She closed her eyes, tilted her head, and edged closer, raising her head to Jen's level, her hands gripping tighter as she found height. Their lips were millimetres apart when Jen burst out laughing, the sound cutting through the tension of the room like a foghorn.

She couldn't help it. This was absurd. She tried to remember the last time she'd kissed in this kitchen, fogging the otherwise crystal clear image of Alison for fear of turning her stomach, but trying to latch onto a little normalcy. She'd kissed in this spot a thousand times. This was no different. Jen giggled again. *Nope.* It was ludicrous. Maybe she did have a concussion. Was this a dream?

Holly tried and failed to look serious. 'Come on, now.'

'I know, I know,' Jen said, finally getting a handle on herself. 'I'm just nervous. This doesn't feel real.'

Holly straightened herself, thinking. She removed her hands from Jen's hips and, for a brief moment, Jen thought Holly had backed out.

'We need to ease into this, set it up,' Holly said, her fingers skirting over Jen's. The tiny gesture sent a ripple of want through her, not boding well for proving her just-horny theory right.

'So, back to date two,' Holly began, her eyes finding Jen's again. Heat flushed through her body like someone had lit a fire. Hover a hand over Jen's skin and you'd feel the warmth; heck, you could toast a marshmallow if you fancied it. 'You've asked me round to watch a film or something.'

'Uh-huh.'

'We're comfy on the sofa, maybe we've had a few drinks. . . halfway through the film, you get brave and you put an arm around me, like you just did a minute ago.' She lifted Jen's hands, placing them on her own hips.

If her heart was fast before, it was supersonic now. Jen gulped, eager to know where the story was headed. She'd played out a similar scenario in her head last night. Would kissing Holly feel like she'd imagined?

'I follow your lead, and snuggle in,' Holly continued, returning her hands to Jen's hips. Never mind roasting marshmallows: Jen's insides were goo themselves. She was more than surprised her good leg was still able to hold her up. 'Then it's that tantalising moment, that bit of a date when you don't know what's going to happen. You both desperately want to kiss, but who's going to make the first move?' She dropped her voice low; it was as smooth as melted chocolate. Jen could just dive right in. 'Eventually, I get brave and close the gap.'

Jen was wet before Holly's lips had even found hers. Her brain short-circuited, all feeling flooding to her mouth and core. Her lips moved with Holly's, slowly at first, then deeper, the brunette's hand gripping tighter on her waist, drawing her closer. Her hips pressed into Jen's, pushing her back against the counter. She couldn't help but moan as Holly's tongue slipped between her parted lips, finding her own and dancing as the kiss continued.

She was hoping to stamp out any possible sparks, but

she'd started an inferno instead. This kiss could never end; she wanted to feel like this forever. It was better than anything she'd imagined, and how could it be anything but? It was beyond any kiss she'd ever experienced. If this was how Holly kissed friends, her lovers were bloody lucky.

Three years without doing this. Was she mad? This was the best feeling in the world.

Holly's soft lips moved in rhythm with her own; there was no knowing where she ended and Holly began. Her hand found its way under Holly's T-shirt, her fingers grazing hot skin, and she felt Holly smile before taking her turn to groan. Jen wallowed in the feeling, letting the moan settle on her skin, enveloping her in delicious heat. Neither was breaking the connection. Was it meant to go on for this long? Jen didn't care – she wasn't going to be the one to finish first. Desire flushed from the base of her neck to her core, a delicious path of straight-up hunger, pinging its way south like a pinball.

She could do this all day. With Holly, at least. This was the kind of kiss that ended in the bedroom with a trail of clothes marking the way.

Or it would, if this were real.

But this was a one time performance. Just two friends, snogging the life out of each other to break the ice and win some money.

Fuck, this was a stupid idea. Jen was in trouble. Serious, serious, trouble. The throbbing between her thighs and the ache in her chest confirmed her worst fears: she liked Holly. A lot.

Holly called time, but not before gently biting Jen's bottom lip. She let her speak first – right now Jen was incapable of words, never mind sentences.

'That ought to do it,' Holly said, running a finger and thumb around her lips to dry them.

'Ice well and truly shattered.' Jen's voice betrayed her, breathless and low. Her core pulsed, every beat of her heart sending a shockwave through her body.

Holly lingered, their feet still intertwined.

Was there something she could say to get a repeat performance? Jen's mind worked overtime, searching for an excuse. Nothing came fast enough.

'I didn't have you down as such a good actress,' Holly said, still not moving.

Was it in Jen's imagination or was there something going on here? The air felt heavy between them, like a balloon pregnant with possibly, just waiting to be popped.

'I'm a woman of many talents,' Jen replied, fighting the urge to grip Holly's hips again.

Holly's eyes traced Jen's face, settling on her lips, before travelling back to hold her gaze. The room felt tiny and the space between them even smaller. But it could be less. Jen lifted her hand, on a mission to find Holly's waist, but three hard raps on the door made her freeze.

Holly jumped.

'Fuck, that will be Chloe,' Jen said with a frustrated groan. 'I texted her when you were returning the bikes. Can you get it?'

'Yeah, sure.' Holly paused as if to say something, but had second thoughts and walked to the hall.

Jen ran a hand through her hair, mouthing a silent 'Fuck.'

The door clicked open and Chloe's voice filled the flat. 'Where's Jen? She okay?'

'She's fine, she's in the kitchen.'

Chloe was in the living room before Jen had a chance to

think. Everything felt wrong, like she'd forgotten how to stand normally. Suspicion oozed from every pore.

'Jen, what the hell? You okay?' Chloe asked, striding to her bestie while dumping her bag on the sofa in a seamless motion.

'I'm good – my dignity took most of the damage.'

'I'm going to go,' Holly chipped in, remaining at the door to the living room. 'Text me if you need anything, yeah?'

'Yeah, sure,' Jen replied, with a smile. But inside it was like a light going out.

Holly grabbed her shoes from the floor and there was that moment again, like her eyes were trying to say something her mouth couldn't quite muster. 'Bye, Chloe.' With the tiniest half-smile she left the room.

'Bye,' Chloe said, her eyes unmoving from Jen.

Chloe held her tongue until the front door was definitely closed.

'Why do I feel like I'm interrupting something?' Her face was one of intrigue with equal distrust.

Jen shook her head, her cheeks burning hot. 'What? No. Nothing's going on. Just ankle stuff.'

Chloe cocked her head, one hand on her hip. 'Jenevieve Berkley, you're the worst liar on the planet. Spill.'

15

When Jen had texted asking for a hand in the shop, Holly's stomach hadn't just flipped: it had done a somersault routine an Olympic gymnast would be jealous of.

She'd fucked up yesterday, and not just a little bit. This was a colossal, irreversible mistake. Her body had only just recovered from what Jen did to her. She wanted to skip down the road, high-fiving people, smiling and chatting to strangers, wishing them a good day. Then her mind would warn her heart of reality, and it was like the storm clouds gathered, soaking her to the bone, extinguishing her good mood. The cycle had been on repeat since she woke up.

Her first intention had been to break the ice. But Holly would be lying if she said there wasn't another motive. Yes, she was still navigating a break-up, but the attraction was undeniable. Busted heart or not, she was single – why not have some fun? Not that she ever thought Jen would agree to her plan.

But it was like thinking a thimbleful of wine would be enough. She'd had a taste, and now she wanted the whole bottle. It was all she could think about, from the moment she'd left Jen's flat to now, only a few hundred yards from her shop.

Of course, now there was a new problem. She'd spent the entire twenty-minute walk reasoning with herself. Jen didn't want a relationship, that much was clear. And Shona still felt so fresh. Was she ready, even if Jen did want one? After that kiss, her body was screaming *yes*. There was no harm in handing the reins of control over to the universe. She would act her part of the smitten girlfriend for the next two weeks and then deal with the consequences.

She wasn't normally one for PDAs but, like she'd explained to Jen yesterday, that's what being a couple was all about, especially if they wanted the public to believe they were the real deal. She would act on instinct; nothing was off-limits now.

She paused a few shops short of Jen's and checked her hair in the window of a boutique. Everything was as it should be.

With a final deep breath, she made the short journey to Jen's door. It wasn't too busy, only two customers inside, but she could see that Jen was sitting on a stool at the till. She was in no state to be running to the stock room for replen.

'Hey,' Holly said, trying to sound nonchalant but failing to hide the smile taking over her face. It was a relief to see Jen grinning back. She gave the blonde's shoulder a squeeze, resisting the urge to kiss her cheek. That was too far, too soon, especially with an audience. 'You okay? Need me to get anything?'

'I've made you a list,' Jen replied, tapping a piece of scrappy paper. 'Thanks again for coming in. It's not too bad, but I don't think standing on it all morning has done it any good, never mind hobbling back and forth to the stockroom.'

'Don't worry about it. I need to be next door for five, but I'm at your command until then.'

Jen held up the list. 'It's all in the back – should be straightforward, but if you can't find anything, just shout.'

'What about deliveries; do you need me to prep them?'

'You're on the ball, aren't you? I'll print them out and you can start on them after.'

Holly took the list and flashed Jen a smile. She desperately wanted another excuse to touch her. *Rein it in, Hols. This is day one.*

In the stockroom, she dumped her bag between shelving racks and set to work finding pouches. It wasn't hard: Jen's shelving was meticulous. The stockroom was tiny, just a sectioned-off area from the main shop floor, but Jen had utilised every free space: racking towered up nearly every wall, the only object being the large stainless steel fridge in the corner, and a sturdy table complete with its own shelving sat in the middle. Every box was labelled and neatly stacked. Jen obviously liked order.

She'd been worried about the state of her flat yesterday, but Holly couldn't see much out of place: a few dishes in the sink and clothes on radiators. Nothing crazy.

She gulped at the memory of Jen's underwear. High leg with a thick elasticated band around the top. Seeing that hadn't helped her overactive imagination last night. Was she wearing them today? Holly sucked on her bottom lip at the thought, heat rushing to her core.

Jen's outfit today didn't help. Skinny jeans and a patterned short-sleeved shirt, unbuttoned to show the top of a vest and just the hint of cleavage.

The heat between Holly's legs grew and she paused for

thought, her hand hovering over a pouch of Sex on the Beach.

You're here to help. Keep it in your pants, Taylor.

She couldn't actually remember the last time she'd had sex. Things were bad with Shona way before the final bell sounded. Holly had long suspected that was one of the main reasons Shona cheated, not the other way around. That's what hurt: why not just dump her? Why add insult to injury? She'd chosen to leave the question unasked, scared the answer would forever haunt her.

Why would Jen be any different? She popped a pouch of margarita onto her little stash, surprised by this new voice in her head. Shona had been nice at the start – why else would she move to London to be with her? But people change and relationships falter. Did she want to go through that again?

She shook her head, dislodging any doubts. Jen had been single three years; she wasn't some player, trying to win Holly over. The complete opposite. Jen was the one that was closed off and Holly was the one considering more.

That kiss, though. She couldn't stop replaying it in her head. She had all the time in the world to figure this out. There was no rush – Jen wasn't about to hop on Tinder and forget about her.

She double-checked the list and was surprised to find they were alone on the shop floor when she headed back. 'Where'd everybody go?'

'Just a wee lull. It happens,' Jen said with a smile. 'Get everything okay?'

'Yep, all present and correct. I need to grab the glasses, but I'll get them in a mo – didn't want to carry too much at once. These go in the fridge, yeah?'

Jen bit her bottom lip, fighting a smile. 'Yeah.'

Holly's brow knitted, her lips mirroring Jen's. 'What was that face for?'

'I was going to say something snarky but I remembered you're doing me a massive favour, so I decided to stay quiet.'

'Oh, really? So unlike you. You absolutely certain you didn't hit your head yesterday?' Holly jibed.

'I'm beginning to wonder.'

The bell above the door chimed and a couple entered as hellos were exchanged.

Pouches freshly stocked, Holly hovered behind Jen, one hand on the counter. 'I want you to show me how to use the till. Please.' She added the final word like a full stop, aware she sounded bossy otherwise.

'How come?'

'So I can take over for fifteen minutes, let you get some food later.'

'You think?' Jen asked with a smile.

'Erm, yes. And the words you're looking for are thank you.' She poked Jen in the side.

'I'm fine, but thank you.'

'Nuh-uh. I've seen your fridge, I know what you're like.'

'Circumstantial. I eat plenty.'

'Well, obviously. You're in good shape.' Holly's cheeks darkened at the unintended compliment. 'But I want to make sure you eat today.' She punctuated the sentence with another poke to the ribs.

'And what happens if I say no?' Jen replied, her lips curling at the edges.

Holly leaned close to Jen's ear, the smell of perfume filling her nostrils – spicy, woody, fruity – and kept her voice to a purr: 'You don't want to find out.' She straightened herself, Jen's eyes locked with her own.

'I guess I'd better behave then.' Her eyes lingered before

her attention turned to the couple on the shop floor. 'You guys okay? Or are you needing a hand?'

'I dunno,' the guy responded, confusion clear in his voice. 'We want to make cocktails, and we'll definitely be getting your pouches, but do we really need glasses?'

'He wants to use mugs.' His partner chipped in, her tone and face saying everything Holly needed to know.

'You can't serve a cocktail in a mug,' Holly said, trying to sound professional but wanting to laugh.

'I know, right,' he said, placing the set of glasses back on the shelf. 'But we don't have any glasses. I'm super clumsy and broke them all. So why would I pay for more?'

The woman rolled her eyes. 'I'm not drinking a pornstar martini from your bloody Benidorm mug.'

'Of course not, that's my favourite mug. I'd be using that. You'd get the one with a cat on.'

'You see what I'm dealing with?' She was trying to joke, but the frustration was obvious.

Holly rounded the counter, joining them on the shop floor. 'Jen's the cocktail expert but I've done my time around alcohol, and I can assure you if you're planning on drinking these lovely cocktails from a mug you're denying yourself a first-class experience.' She picked up the nearest set of martini glasses, tilting the box towards the guy. 'They're different shapes for a reason: they affect taste, smell, and temperature. It's like, you wouldn't play tennis with a rugby ball and expect it to be the same, would you?'

The guy turned the information over in his head, taking the glasses from Holly as he thought. 'Makes sense. It just feels like a waste of money when I'll probably have smashed the set by Christmas.'

Jen chipped in. 'See them as an investment. Otherwise, why get cocktails at all?'

'It's our anniversary, I wanted to do something special,' he said, to the glasses more than the women in the room.

'And what cocktails were you thinking?' Holly asked, guiding his partner to the fridge.

'What do you suggest?'

'Personally, I don't think you can go wrong with martinis, margaritas, or a Singapore Sling. But Jen here does a mean take on an old classic: you really have to try it to believe it.'

'We could get a few?' the lady said, her voice hopeful.

'See it as an experiment – if you get a few, you can try one in a mug and one in a glass. You come tell me if I'm wrong.'

'Deal,' the guy said, looking happy that he could still be proved right.

Holly retrieved the glasses from him and put them back on the shelf. She was thinking on her feet, reading the prices and info as she spoke, but so far it sounded like she knew the place like the back of her hand. 'If you're getting a few, you'll need a selection of glasses – gives you more reason to be careful with them, too, if you only have two of each. The good news is, Jen has an offer on: six glasses for four with her mix-and-match sets. So you're getting two free. Can't get better than that.'

'Sounds good,' the man agreed, nodding enthusiastically. His partner mouthed a silent *thank you*.

'You pick your cocktails – take your time, find your favourites – and I'll put a selection of glasses together. Don't forget, if you buy ten cocktails you'll get a stamp for each, so the next one's free.' She leaned in, like she was telling a secret. 'And I'm sure if you're nice to Jen she'll let you claim it now. She's in a good mood today.'

Holly grabbed an empty cardboard box from the shelf

and filled it with pairs of highball, martini, and margarita glasses. Happy she'd covered all bases, she placed them on the counter and returned to stand behind Jen.

'Right, show me the till, boss.'

Jen let out a quiet sigh, telling Holly she knew better than to argue. She shifted her seat and made room for Holly.

'So: search bar, type 'mix and match'. Click the photo of the glasses, select which ones are going. Bish, bash, bosh, it takes the multi-buy discount off.'

Holly nodded, taking it all in. 'Seems easy.' She squeezed in closer, shifting Jen's leg out of the way. 'My turn to do the cocktails.'

They waited patiently while the couple decided; it was a tough choice with such a great selection. Holly's eyes averted to Jen's lap and her hands, the memory of yesterday looming to the front of her mind. She wanted to skirt her fingers over Jen's, experience that frisson of excitement once again, but that would be totally inappropriate given that these people thought Jen was till-training a staff member. She settled for feeling the heat of Jen's leg against her bum instead. In a bid to keep her hands busy, she fiddled with the bow on her dress, as if pulling it tighter.

'I think this is what we need,' the man said, placing his pouches on the counter.

Jen dipped a hand to the shelf below and fetched a bag, reading each pouch name aloud as she placed them inside. 'Awesome – you're picking this up quick,' she said, putting the final cocktail away. 'Now, click on this big green button, and it will bring up the free pouches, since you so graciously offered to honour that today.'

'Appreciate that,' the guy said, clearly happy that he'd walked away with a good deal.

'Just don't drink all eleven tonight. Unless you want a sore head tomorrow. Been there, done that,' Holly joked. There were murmurs of agreement before Holly read out the total.

Transaction done, the couple left, the woman's smile showing just how much they'd saved the day.

Jen watched the door close before she spoke. 'Cocktails in a mug? Now I've heard it all.'

Holly stepped out from behind the till, although part of her had wanted to see how long Jen would have let her stay pressed against her leg.

'I've had wine in a mug when I was at uni, but a cocktail? That's a line even I wouldn't cross.'

'Good sale too, nearly a hundred pounds.'

'Is that decent?'

'I'll say. I might just need to keep you.' Jen's trademark blush flushed her cheeks. 'Listen,' she began. Oh God, was this going to be about yesterday? Holly had considered staying, feeling like something further needed to be said, but with Chloe being there, it just hadn't felt right. 'I don't want you to think this is weird, but I've got you a little present. Just a small thing.'

Oh. That didn't go in the direction she'd expected. Holly's face twisted with confusion, a smile dragging across her lips. 'Really?'

Jen's chest flushed red, the heat rising up her neck as she retrieved something from under the counter. She placed a stack of books by the till, her eyes searching Holly's, as if she was terrified this was a terrible mistake. 'They're, um, business books. I know how much it helped me to write stuff down, so...' she trailed off with a shrug.

Holly's chest filled with warmth, the hairs on the back of her neck standing to attention. This was quite possibly the most thoughtful thing anyone had ever done for her. 'You didn't need to do that,' she said, picking up the books and inspecting the covers. *Handmade Success*, *My Business Bible*, *The Handmade Business of Your Dreams*. Fuck. Holly swallowed, willing the tears away that were pawing at her surface. She hadn't even told Jen what she wanted to do; had she listened that carefully, that she was able to piece it all together? No one paid that much attention to Holly. Must be a fluke.

'Are they okay? Sorry if I got it wrong. It's just when you said about your degree, and then you pointed out those cards the other day, and then there was that printer you mentioned, and—'

'They're perfect,' Holly said, holding her voice steady. She looked at Jen, then back to the books. All she wanted to do was wrap her arms around Jen's neck and kiss her senseless. 'This means a lot. Thank you.'

Jen beamed. 'And if you need help with other stuff, boring business stuff like with HMRC, I can help there. Buy me a beer and I'll spill all my secrets.'

'I'll remember that.' Holly couldn't stop looking at the books, turning them over in her hands. How could anyone be so thoughtful? And to her, no less? Emotion swelled in her chest, threatening to creep up her throat and tumble out.

The door opened and a woman in her twenties entered, making a beeline for the fridge. Given their new rules, the company made PDAs preferable, and this customer had no expectations about what Holly's role was in the shop. She planted a quick kiss on Jen's cheek. 'Thank you, again.'

Jen looked like the cat who'd got the cream, her eyes shining like diamonds, her smile equally dazzling. 'My pleasure.'

'I'll just pop them in my bag, then I'll be back.' Holly nipped to the stockroom and let out a ragged breath. She was vibrating with the effort of keeping it together. A few more breaths and her muscles had finally calmed, as her emotions fell level.

Jen was ringing the woman's purchase up as Holly returned. They weren't destined to be alone, though, and another couple appeared. They didn't seem to have any mug drama, thank God, and were quite happy to browse themselves.

Jen looked at Holly, a glint still in her eye. 'Are you free tomorrow evening?'

'Yeah. Well, after deliveries. How come?'

Jen focused on her finger as she tapped it against the counter. 'One of my customers – turns out he fancies himself a stand-up comedian – gave me two tickets to his show. He's worried it's going to be empty or something. Would you go with me?'

'Yeah, course—'

'I'd ask Chloe but it's not really her thing.'

'Yeah, totally—'

'Like, if you don't want to—'

It was Holly's turn to cut Jen off. She took a thumb and gently brought her jaw to a standstill, closing her yapping mouth. 'I said yes.'

16

J en jumped up and down on the spot a few times, trying to rid herself of nervous energy. The pub hosting the comedy night was only up the road, so she'd asked Holly to just meet her in the shop.

Any more pacing and she'd wear a hole in her stockroom floor.

Why am I so nervous?

True to her word, yesterday Holly had nipped across the road and got Jen coffee and food before giving her fifteen minutes in the back to scoff it. She was being so nice; it was further confusing the signals coursing through her brain. *That's what friends do, you fool.*

Three years keeping her heart protected and suddenly seeing Holly made her want to open up again. It didn't make any sense. But did it need to?

A knock at the door made her jump, her heart a jackhammer rumbling against her ribs. A deep breath, quick smooth of her T-shirt, and it was go time – their first public outing as a 'couple'.

She had to wrestle the smile from her lips. Holly looked

amazing. She had on a sleeveless black T-shirt paired with a floral, high-waisted maxi skirt and black boots. A slit at the side of the skirt revealed just enough leg to make Jen gulp. There would be no pretend attraction this evening. At least not on Jen's side.

Holly propped her sunglasses on her head as she entered the shop, saying a quiet hello before she planted a quick kiss on Jen's lips.

'Hello to you too.'

'Just getting into character, although,' she said, pulling a face, 'I've got lipstick on you. Sorry.'

Jen ran a thumb over her lips, hoping Holly wouldn't see her hands were shaking from the sudden rush of adrenaline. 'Did I get it?'

'Not quite,' Holly admitted, closing the gap between them. She smelled like summer –freshly cut grass and citrus.

Jen ran a thumb over her bottom lip again. 'A little direction?' she asked with a chuckle.

'Easier if I do it,' Holly said, using her tongue to gently wet the tip of her thumb before rubbing at the edge of Jen's lower lip. 'There, got it.'

Jen's clit hardened. 'You good to go then?' she asked, surprised her voice kept steady.

'Ready when you are.'

Jen grabbed her keys off the counter and ushered Holly outside as she quickly set the shop alarm. Anything to get out of the shop and into the bustle. If she stayed alone with Holly any longer she might not be responsible for her actions.

'Ankle's better then?' Holly asked, replacing her sunglasses as they wandered out the shade.

'Still a little tender, but I'll live.'

They walked in silence for a few steps, basking in the heat of the evening sun. The air was hot and stuffy and Jen wondered if the temperature wasn't just down to the summer heat but also the throbbing between her legs.

'I'm walking, but I've just realised I have no idea where we're going,' Holly joked, her smile dazzling Jen.

'The Reading Lounge; you've never been?'

Holly shook her head. 'Doubt it ever existed back in my day.'

'You really are a stranger in your hometown, aren't you?' Jen quipped.

'Good job I have such a willing and able tour guide then, eh?'

Was this flirting? It felt like it. If it was, was it genuine or all part of the act? Chloe was in Jen's head now. She'd told her best friend everything – how could she not? She was a pressure cooker of emotion after she and Holly had kissed. 'People don't kiss friends like that!' But they did if they were in a fake relationship and on the road to winning five grand.

Holly had been clear with her expectations, but if she was going to push it, Jen would too.

'Anywhere else you want to see, just say. Nowhere's off limits.'

Holly smiled, but it was impossible to know what she was thinking behind her sunglasses.

'Late one tonight, Hols?' a familiar voice boomed.

Jen had been so busy looking at Holly she'd completely missed Harry leaning on the open door of his van.

'Hi Dad,' Holly said, 'Yeah, just off out. Shouldn't be too late, should we?'

'Nah, I'll get her home at a decent time, promise,' Jen reassured, shielding her eyes from the sun as she squinted in Harry's direction. The sun was right behind him and it was impossible to read his face. Through the glare, she could just about make out a knowing smile.

'Get her home in one piece and we'll be happy. Right, better crack on. Just been to the wholesaler.'

'Bye, Dad,' Holly said, not sounding overly impressed.

'Bye, love. Have a good night, Jen. Stay safe.'

'Will do, Mr Taylor.' Jen clocked herself, her face flashing with perplexion. She'd never called Harry that in his life. It was like she was a teenager again, meeting the parents for the first time. He didn't seem to notice. 'Do they know?' Jen asked, a question springing to life.

'Know what?'

'That we're,' she lowered her voice as they passed a crowd at the fruit and veg shop, 'fake dating?'

'Ah, kind of. I dunno. Maybe, not really. I mentioned it, but not in detail. I don't think they get it.'

Jen nodded; she'd had a similar conversation when she'd phoned her mum last week, Annie's photos raising lots of questions from her bewildered parents. They weren't the type of family that spoke about such personal things, so thankfully she could gloss over it and move on with the luxury of putting the phone down at the end of it all. Holly had to live with her parents. 'They'll have seen Annie's posts though, yeah?'

'Oh God, yeah. Dad loves social media.' Holly clicked the button for the traffic lights as they came to a standstill. 'What about your parents?'

'Mine?'

'Oh God, they're not dead are they? Shit, sorry.'

Jen couldn't help but laugh. 'Why did you suddenly jump to that conclusion?'

'Please tell me I've not just put my foot right in it?' Red travelled up Holly's neck as she bit her top lip.

'Both alive and well.'

'Thank fuck,' Holly said letting out a breathy sigh. 'You just never talk about them.'

'There's not much to say.' The green man appeared, a shrill beeping keeping pace as they crossed diagonally to the other street. 'They live in France, so I don't see them much.'

'France? Wow, so is that where you grew up?'

Jen shook her head. 'Nah, I'm a Glasgow girl through and through. I've only been to France for holidays.'

'I didn't think the accent was right. So why did they choose France?'

'*Ma mère est française. Ils ont déménagé lorsqu'ils ont pris leur retraite,*' Jen replied, speaking like she'd lived in Paris her whole life.

Holly stopped, even though she'd not quite reached the pavement. Jen pulled her forward by the elbow, unable to deny a stupid grin.

'What. The. Heck?' Holly managed, her mouth agape.

'My mum's French, but I don't shout about it. Made higher French a breeze.'

Holly was still walking at half-pace, her brain stealing her attention from the task in hand –getting to the pub, which was only a hundred yards away – while it tried to make sense of what the heck was going on. 'Right, wait, slow down. Say that again. I want to know what you said.' A smile filled her face, awe etched in her expression.

Jen chuckled. She liked throwing this curveball; it didn't happen often but it always got a good reaction from the people she let in. 'Come, walk and talk, Miss Taylor.'

'Yeah, yeah, but come on, parlez-vous Français, if you please.'

'For a start, that makes no sense, but okay. *Ma mère est*

française,' she said very slowly before talking in double time: '*Ils ont déménagé lorsqu'ils ont pris leur retraite.*'

'I've got no clue, but I like it.'

Jen chortled. 'First bit: my mother is French. Second: they moved when they retired.'

'Gotcha,' Holly said with a nod. 'Any other phrases to wow me with?'

Voulez-vous coucher avec moi instantly sprang to mind, but it was too risky. Every man and his dog knew what that meant thanks to the song. 'Plenty of time for a French lesson later; right now we need to get to Gabriel's show.' Jen held the door open, letting Holly go first. '*Après vous, mon cher ami.*'

Holly stopped in the entrance, extending a palm to Jen. 'I still don't know where I'm going. You lead the way.'

Jen scooped Holly's hand in her own, their fingers intertwining in a heartbeat, and lead her through to The Reading Lounge's bar. Holly was right, this whole being a couple thing was easier now they'd kissed.

It was busy, but nothing crazy. This part of the venue was mainly for dining and the occasional pub quiz during the summer months. She'd never quite twigged why it was called The Reading Lounge. Apart from the wallpaper masquerading as bookcases it had no obvious links to reading. Not even in the past. In fact, before it was a pub it was a pizzeria. It had a trendy vibe, nonetheless, and often hosted gigs in the small venue at the rear.

She weaved them through the diners and to the back room. Gabriel was seated at a table, a money box open in front of him.

'You made it,' he beamed. 'And this is?'

Holly gave a little wave, her other hand still firmly holding Jen's. 'Holly – thanks for inviting us.'

'My pleasure. We've had a few walk-ins but the more bums on seats the better,' he laughed.

Gabriel was one of Jen's favourite regulars. Until yesterday Jen had only known he was a librarian. Apparently, he was a budding improv artist too – it would seem everyone had their secrets.

Jen passed their tickets over and Gabriel tucked them into the money box. 'Really looking forward to this. I've never been to an improv show before.'

'You're in for a treat,' he replied, his face lighting up. 'I just hope we're not shite.'

'YOUR BEER,' Jen said, placing the pint in front of Holly. She moved her seat closer, wanting to be in touching distance of her pseudo date. If she could do kissing and hand-holding Jen wasn't going to let the side down. Gabriel wasn't the only one on stage tonight.

The room was set up like a classic comedy club – rows of staggered circular tables filled the space below the tiny stage, each one set with two seats and a candle. This was a Lovefest event, and they were obviously catering exclusively to couples.

Jen took a gulp of her beer, her other arm now resting on the back of Holly's chair.

'Jenette,' Holly said, matter-of-factly.

'Excuse me?'

'That's your name.'

Jen sniggered. 'You still on this? You know, even if you got it right I wouldn't say. You might have said it ages ago.'

Holly looked pleased with herself. 'Oh my God, is it Jenette? Really? Did I get it right?'

'If that makes you happy.' Jen's fingers found Holly's shoulder and lightly danced over her bare skin as she spoke. Sparks flew up Jen's arm, settling in her chest.

'This feels too easy.'

'What makes you set on Jenette?'

'I just googled French girl's names starting with Jen.'

'Smart.'

'The rest I'd already guessed.'

'You sure?'

Holly's eyes narrowed as she turned to face Jen head-on. Jen's fingers felt empty, the connection lost. 'Hand on heart,' she said, placing two fingers on Jen's chest. 'Have I said it already?'

Jen weighed up her options. She could let this go on, and it was fun to wind Holly up, but she also really did hate her full name, so it was probably better to put a stop to it ASAP. It was a lovely name, just not on her. The shoe had never truly fitted. If she told her now it would get it over with. She placed a hand over Holly's, pressing it harder into her chest. 'You've not said it. If I tell you, what's it worth?'

Holly paused, deep in thought as she removed her hand and traced the condensation on her beer glass. Finally, she spoke: 'You should set the price: it's your name.'

A thousand ideas sprang to mind. None of them PG. 'Why do I suddenly feel like Rumpelstiltskin?' Jen said with a chuckle.

Holly retrieved her shoulder bag from the back of her chair and fished around. 'I have gum, lip balm, my phone, and purse. Anything else will need to be an IOU.'

'How about another round of drinks in Bar Orama?'

'Consider it a deal. Although not tonight: I have a lot of deliveries to do tomorrow.'

'Deli's busy?'

'Yes. Now, don't change the subject.'

'Worth a shot.' Jen pulled her bank card from her trouser pocket and handed it to Holly. 'You tell anyone, and I mean anyone, and I will never trust you again,' she said, deadly serious.

Holly's face was a picture. 'Jenevieve. That's a lovely name. Why do you hate it so much?'

'Do I look like a Jenevieve?'

'I think it's a really pretty name.'

Jen shot Holly a look, unsure if that was a compliment or not. 'My point exactly.'

Holly handed the card back and Jen stuffed it away like it was too hot to handle. 'I think it suits you.'

The lights lowered and anticipation surged through the audience. Gabriel bounded onto the stage, along with another guy and two women, to the tune of upbeat punk music.

'Hello, hello,' Gabriel boomed, bouncing around like he was still psyching himself up.

'We're On The Spot,' one of the women chimed in, also hopping like a hyper spaniel.

The other women bounded forward, ready to do her bit. 'And welcome to our comedy night. What makes this part of Lovefest, I hear you ask?'

'Well, we set the tables for couples, that's about it,' the final guy remarked, a goofy look on his face. Their actions were exaggerated, their expressions comical. Perhaps that was the point.

It was Gabriel's turn to talk again. 'We won't waste any more time – for this scene we need one of you to shout a setting, somewhere you might go on a date.'

A few suggestions erupted from the crowd. 'I heard

club,' not-Gabriel said, a hand cupped to his ear as he pointed in the direction of the helpful audience member.

Something told Jen this wasn't going to be her cup of tea. But Gabriel was a good customer – she owed him her support. Plus, it was a good excuse to see Holly. She snuck a look at the brunette, who returned a content but dubious smile. Jen gave a wink as she found the hand Holly had resting in her lap. Their fingers laced together again like it was the most natural thing in the world.

Tonight wasn't going to be bad at all.

17

Holly laughed tentatively. This wasn't really her bag, but they were landing a few good jokes. Now and again, at least.

Besides, their performance was well and truly upstaged by Jen's hand in her lap.

It was good to see Jen leaning into the whole fake-girlfriend charade with gusto. She'd felt almost guilty when she'd greeted her with a kiss earlier. Jen was reciprocating now, though; the deception wasn't one-sided. Somehow, that made it feel okay.

And what was the whole French thing about? Holly's muscles tensed at the memory. She had no clue what Jen was saying but she didn't need to. The accent alone was enough. Jen's voice curled around her like the arms of a lover, each word caressing her skin, making every hair stand to attention. She could listen to her all day. Heck, she could read her grocery list for twenty-four hours if she did it in French.

Holly's breath caught in her throat, her heart missing a beat. She'd been so lost in her thoughts she'd absentmindedly been stroking Jen's thumb with her own. She side-eyed her. No reaction. Well, she couldn't stop now – that would be more obvious.

She traced a circle over Jen's knuckle. Holly's eyes were fixed on the stage but it might as well have just been the two of them in the room. Sound faded out; their surroundings dimmed. All that mattered in the world was Jen's hand in hers and the way it felt to run her thumb the length of Jen's finger. Every pass on Jen's soft skin sent a pang to Holly's core, as if desire was on a zip line to her very centre.

Jen had to feel this too. There was no way she could be the only one experiencing these feelings.

A conversation wasn't worth the risk, though.

The lights went up and applause sucked her back to reality and a room full of people.

'It's over already?' Holly shout-whispered in Jen's ear, joining the ovation regardless of its cause.

'Yeah, it was only on for an hour.'

An hour? How the heck had an hour passed already?

A few reserved cheers and the clapping was soon replaced by the scraping of seats and fervent chatter.

'Do you want to go somewhere for a quick drink?' Holly asked, letting the crowd disperse before she stood. 'Just somewhere local. I can't be out too long.'

'A drink would be nice.'

'How do you think it went?' Gabriel asked, leaning on the table, his energy still dialled to eleven. 'You enjoy it?'

'Yeah. It was really good,' Jen replied and looked like she meant it.

'I'm impressed,' Holly added, wanting them both to know she had totally listened to the whole show and didn't spend it fantasising about the woman beside her.

'Good, good. I thought it went well, but you can

never really tell. So listen, a few of us are going to Bazza's for drinks,' he said, throwing a thumb towards the guy who he'd shared a stage with. It looked like Bazza was doing his own recon for attendees as he joked with two pretty blonde girls on their way out. 'Do you want to join us?'

Jen looked to Holly. Was she looking for an excuse, or for Holly's approval?

'Is it far?' Holly asked, genuinely wanting to know.

'Nah, he just lives upstairs.'

Jen shrugged. 'I guess we could go for one – do you fancy it?'

'Sure, why not?'

THERE WERE MORE people at Bazza's than she'd expected. The flat was absolutely buzzing. It had been a long time since she'd been to a party in a random's flat. The whole vibe reminded her of art school – more trendy glasses than an optician's window, hair colours that would put the rainbow to shame, and not to mention the sheer eclectic mix of party patrons. Some looked like they'd come straight from their jobs as accountants: others, well, not so much. One woman was wearing a sequined waistcoat and little else.

He'd nailed the student aesthetic, too. Even down to the 80s-esque chipped counter tops in the kitchen and dubious burn on the living room carpet. Holly guessed the wasn't Bazza's first time hosting an after-party.

Gabriel had stolen Jen away, wanting to introduce her to a local jazz musician, and that had somehow become her talking to a gorgeous, dark-haired woman, who was covered in tattoos. Jen was wrapped up in the conversation, sitting on the sofa across the room, but it might as well have been in the next postcode.

This was not how Holly foresaw the evening going.

'And what about you?' the guy next to her asked. He'd been chatting away to her for ages, clearly on a mission. He was nice – slim, bit of stubble, decent teeth, shirt had seen an iron at least once in its life.

She didn't have the heart to tell him this was the wrong tree to bark up.

'Mmh?' she asked, taking a sip of the vodka and coke Gabriel had got them on arrival. It was cheap booze and tasted like absolute arse. She didn't really want any more alcohol, but it was nice to have the plastic cup as a prop, something to keep her hands busy.

'I said, where do you work?' he repeated, pushing his rimless glasses back into position.

'Oh, right, sorry. I'm a delivery driver, for a local shop.'

'What one?'

Are you meant to give real information to strangers? Her mind was too focused on the scene in front of her to concoct a lie. 'Taylor's Deli. Opposite the Co-op.'

'Ah, nice. I know the one. So—'

Holly tuned him out again. Jen and the tattooed woman shared a laugh. Jen leaned back, a hand on her face like she was exaggerating embarrassment, before composing herself. Was that Jen's type? Tattooed women who wouldn't be out of place on the cover of *Diva* magazine? Tattoos weren't really Holly's thing, but she did have a small one, at the bottom of her ribs. It was meant to be a heart, but over time it had started to resemble more of a shrivelled raisin. That's what happens when a group of art students get hold of a tattoo gun at a degree show after-party. Thankfully, she'd got off lightly, and it was easily hidden. Unlike Kerry, who would forever have a childlike cat on her calf.

'How do you know Gabriel?' Holly's would-be-suitor asked. Maybe for the second time. Holly shook her thoughts free, aware she was coming across as rude.

'My friend knows him.'

'The blonde woman from the cocktail shop?'

'That's the one. What about you?' Holly took another sip and scrunched her face in disgust. Prop or not, she didn't want it. She leaned over the sofa's edge and tucked it away from unwitting feet.

'We work together in Langside Library.'

'That must be fun.' Her tone was flat but friendly; it was the best she could muster.

'It can be. People think libraries are stuffy places, but it's like any work: it is what you make of it.'

'True that.' Holly shifted her skirt, moving the slit to the side so her knee was no longer showing. She wanted to be at home, in her pyjamas, far away from here and this droll conversation. And hot tattoo woman.

Jen was still wrapped in animated conversation. If Holly called an Uber now she could be home in ten minutes.

Holly cut the guy off, no clue what he was saying. 'Listen, I don't feel all that great. I'm going to go.'

She stood before he had a chance to change her mind, ignoring his quiet protests before he said goodbye. Jen didn't even clock her before she was nearly standing on the happy couple's toes. Her face fell as she saw Holly, the atmosphere between them as heavy as lead.

'I don't feel that great – I'm going to get an Uber,' Holly said, hands gripped around the strap of her bag.

Jen's eyes widened as her face dropped further. She

stood, reaching for one of Holly's hands. Holly held her grip, unwavering. 'What? No. Can I get you something?'

'No, really, it's fine. I just need some air and my bed. I'll see you tomorrow.'

She turned on her heel, her departure not up for discussion. Jen jogged after her, like a wounded puppy, cutting her off in the hall.

'Have I done something?'

'What? No?' Holly replied, shaking her head as she tried to sound believable. 'It's just there's too many people in there and I needed space.'

Jen nodded, her eyes unblinking. 'Can we just have a moment, before you go?'

'Sure.' Holly replied, rooted to the spot.

'Not here. Somewhere quieter.' Jen reached for Holly's hand again and this time she relented.

'Where are you taking me?' she asked as Jen led them up the close stairs.

'Your tour guide strikes again.' Jen beamed a grin at Holly as they continued upwards. Their footsteps echoed on the concrete floor, the sound of the party becoming a distant memory.

Round and round they followed the stairs, all the way to the top floor, four storeys up. Holly's face was a picture of confusion.

'Close your eyes,' Jen said, standing in Holly's way as they reached what looked like someone's front door.

'Really?'

'Yes. Trust me?'

'Of course.'

Jen's smile was infectious. Holly closed her eyes, her hand gripping Jen's tighter than ever, and allowed herself to be guided.

The sound of the street hit her first, then the cool evening air. 'Just round here,' Jen said, her voice low and her face inches from Holly's. 'Keep those eyes shut.'

There were other people here, but not many; a few voices at most. They rounded a corner before coming to a stop, Holly aware Jen was now behind her, hands covering her eyes.

'You ready?' Jen asked, her breath hot on Holly's neck.

Holly nodded, unable to speak for the smile breaking across her face. She bit her bottom lip, fighting to keep it under control.

'Okay, open your eyes.' Jen lifted her hands, stepping to Holly's side and leaning on the metal railing in front of them. She looked bloody pleased with herself.

And rightly so. Holly gasped, her breath stolen. Glasgow spanned the horizon before them, the setting sun streaking the sky pink and purple, as the city lay black below, its lights like yellow pinpricks and the occasional spire a jagged splinter against the kaleidoscope of colour above.

'Wow,' Holly said, taking in her surroundings: a rooftop garden with fairy lights strung between the dozen chimney stacks. The voices she'd heard must have been on the other side of the brickwork: here it was just Jen and Holly, in their own little world. It was pure magic. Every hair on Holly's body stood to attention, her skin turning to gooseflesh at the beauty before her.

'Not bad, huh?' Jen asked, pushing against the railing, her tricep muscles flexing.

'How did you know this was here?' Holly asked, taking her turn to lean, checking out the view below. They were bloody high. The rooftops of the neighbouring flats spanned beneath, as well as the flat top of The Reading Lounge.

'I've always known there was a rooftop garden. I've never been cause it's residents only, but I figure we're at a party, so that makes us temporary residents.' She smiled as her eyes softened, concern clear. 'You feel okay now?'

Holly nodded, still blown away by the turn of events. 'Golden, thanks.'

Jen sucked on her bottom lip like she was wrestling with the words in her head. 'Sorry I left you alone downstairs. I got roped into conversation and I couldn't wriggle out of it without looking rude.'

'It's okay. You can talk to who you want. It's not like we're really dating.'

Jen straightened herself, a devilish grin playing on her lips. 'Is that what it was? Were you jealous?'

'No? Of course not. Don't be stupid.' Holly bumped her hip into Jen's. She could never commit a crime; she was terrible under pressure, unable to lie to save herself.

'It's okay if you were.'

'You're on thin ice, Miss Berkley,' Holly jibed, raising her eyebrows as she tried to keep her face serious, but failing to hide a smirk.

'And I would hate to anger you, Miss Taylor. But, for future reference, as lovely as Tilly was, she really wasn't my type.'

'No?' Holly replied, a firework of relief exploding in her chest. She wasn't usually the jealous type but Jen was a dab hand at bringing out the unexpected in her.

'Nope. Not at all.'

'So, what is?' she asked, turning round to lean her back and elbows against the railing.

Jen sighed. 'Hard to say. I mean that's like picking your favourite book – there will always be curveballs and anomalies. It could change every day of the week depending on my mood.'

'Blonde? Brunette? Tall? Short? What did Alison look like?'

Jen winced at the name and Holly wished she could stuff it back in her mouth. Why bring her ex up?

'I can show you, if you like?' Jen said, producing her phone. A few taps and she held the device in her hand for a heartbeat, her jaw tensed as she turned it to face Holly.

'Alison Rae? Get lost. Your ex is Alison Rae?'

'You know her?' Jen asked, taken aback.

'She played a gig at my work once. Lovely girl.' Minus Holly's fringe, they weren't dissimilar. Looking like your love interest's horrible ex isn't exactly ideal, though.

Jen stuffed her phone back in her pocket, her eyes fixed on the horizon. 'She could be lovely, yes. But she treated me like shit. Let's not talk about her.'

She'd never get another chance at this topic. It was now or never. 'You don't keep in touch then?'

Jen rolled her eyes with a loud huff. 'As if.'

'Sorry. I just figured after three years, maybe you still hoped she would come back.' Why else would Jen be so adamantly single?

Jen was silent, her chest rising and falling gently as she thought. The electric sky silhouetted her perfectly, and Holly wished she could frame the image and keep it in her heart forever.

Why, oh why, had she gone down the ex route? Holly: master of saying the wrong thing.

Eventually, Jen spoke. 'Maybe at first. That's natural, I guess. But then I was just really mad. And as time went on, I realised I didn't need a relationship. Being alone was so much easier. It's not how I ever thought my life would turn out, but it is what it is, unless someone really special comes along and sweeps me off my feet.'

Jen's final sentence was a sucker punch to Holly's heart. Any future notions quashed. She'd not found that special someone in her. Duly noted. 'Fair enough,' she managed, her voice quiet.

The blonde turned, her gaze finding Holly's, her green eyes brighter than ever against the pink sky. 'You must feel the same, though. You're not looking for anything either?'

'Not indefinitely. You make it sound like you're resigned to a life of spinsterdom.'

'A few cats, I could make it work,' she replied, a smile threatening. 'Jokes aside, I've spent so long building my walls, the thought of putting myself out there and getting it wrong terrifies me.'

'What do you mean?'

'Well, what if they don't like me back? Or what if I'm not good enough? I can't take getting my heart broken again.'

'How could you not be good enough?' Holly asked, chuckling at the absurdity.

'Doesn't matter.' Jen fell silent, her eyes back on the twinkling lights of the city.

Holly thought for a moment, searching for the right way to begin. 'I understand.' She paused again, about to chicken out before deciding it was important to share. Not just for Jen: for her, too. 'I get the whole "being good enough" thing. Putting the blame on yourself. Do you know how I caught Shona cheating?'

Jen shook her head.

'There'd been a load of break-ins, so I got one of those fancy doorbell things with the camera, you know what I mean. Shona knew about it, but I think she thought it only recorded if you rang the bell. Well, I was at work one day and got a notification about movement. It was Shona and a girl I worked with, kissing at our front door.'

'Shit. What did you do?'

'You'd think I would storm home and catch them in the act, yeah?'

'You didn't?'

Holly shook her head, running her tongue over her upper back teeth as she thought. It was a painful memory, one she'd never told anyone, but Jen made her want to be an open book. 'I did my shift, went home, acted like nothing happened. I lay in bed, awake the whole night trying to figure out what I'd done wrong. How I could fix things.' She stabbed a finger to her chest, embarrassment creeping up her spine like a cold chill. 'I let it go on for months. They knew my shifts, so I guess it was easy to sneak around. I just. . .' She paused, her voice faltering. 'Looking back, Shona put doubt in my head for years before anything ever happened. Made me feel I wasn't good enough, like the cracks in the relationship were my fault. That I had to carry that burden for the both of us and she was a good person for staying with me. I know that's wrong now. It wasn't my fault. She was just a dick.' A little yelp of a laugh escaped.

Jen placed a hand on Holly's elbow and emotion rippled through her. Before leaving London she couldn't even imagine thinking that, never mind hearing the words come out of her mouth. Jen made her feel worthy: like she might actually be able to achieve something. Instead of waking up to the black pit of despair that usually occupied her chest, Holly was starting to get used to days full of possibility and hope. Regardless of Jen's intentions, she would forever be grateful for that.

Two guys rounded the corner, one sparking a cigarette before handing the lighter to his pal.

'Of course none of that was your fault,' Jen reassured, her hand sliding to rest on the small of Holly's back. 'And I thought Alison was bad.'

'For every arsehole there must be someone decent, yeah?'

'You'd hope. You cold? You've got goosebumps,' Jen said, stepping behind Holly and enveloping her in a hug, her head resting on her shoulder. 'Never let anyone tell you you're not good enough, Holly. Because I happen to think you're pretty special.'

Jen's words were like stepping out of the cold into a steamy shower. They tumbled over her, their warmth seeping into Holly's skin and settling in her bones.

Jen nuzzled further into Holly's neck. 'Don't ever forget how strong you are. Or how funny. I don't think I've ever laughed so much.' Holly could feel her smiling against her skin. Everything tingled. 'You're wonderful, Holly. You deserve to be happy. Don't let anyone tell you otherwise.'

'I bet you say that to all the girls you bring up here,' Holly said, only half-joking. Jen didn't seem like a smooth talker, but no one had ever spoken to her like that. It was tough to let the words sink in without questioning.

There was no way Jen couldn't feel how hard Holly's heart was beating. Her breath wavered, trying to calm the pounding against her ribs.

'Only the really, really, pretty ones.' Jen's chest shuddered against Holly's back as she laughed. 'Even as a joke that was too cheesy. Sorry.'

'You've had better lines.' Holly leaned back, savouring the feeling of having Jen behind her. She put her hands up, holding onto Jen's wrists.

'I blame Lovefest. It's got me saying and doing loads of things I wouldn't usually.'

'Oh yeah? What else?' Holly's voice was nearly a purr, her body and mind lost in the moment.

But, just as quickly as it started it was over. Jen stepped away, reclining once more on the railings, her body swivelled in Holly's direction. Despite the twilight, Holly could see she was blushing before she'd even spoken. 'Well, if you'd have told me a month ago I would be on a secret rooftop, kissing a smoking hot brunette, I would have laughed in your face.'

'See, you must be talking about your last conquest up here. We've not kissed,' Holly replied, her eyes sparkling with mischief.

Jen smiled at her shoes. 'That was my roundabout way of asking for permission.' She moved closer, her lips almost touching Holly's ear. 'We're meant to be couple-y in public, no? Well, we've got company.' She darted her eyes to the two blokes smoking. In the fading light, it was impossible to know if the men had even seen them.

'True,' Holly agreed. 'Those were the rules.'

Jen took her hand, leading her behind a chimney stack, the orange glow from the fairy lights the only thing illuminating them. 'Still, don't want them getting too excited.' In one swift move, Holly's back was against the chimney, Jen's thigh between her legs. The gap between their lips closed. Jen stopped short, the smile on her face saying she was enjoying teasing Holly.

How could she go from saying she didn't want a relationship to this? Holly's body couldn't take all this flip-flopping. It didn't know where it was to pump blood from one minute to the next.

Jen held her position, her hands around Holly's waist, her face enticingly close.

Two could play at this game. Holly nipped at Jen's

bottom lip before pulling back. 'Does it not defeat the purpose, being hidden away?'

'Perhaps. Just tell me if I'm to stop.' With that she dipped her head, planting hungry kisses down Holly's neck until she reached her collarbone. Her grip on Holly's waist tightened, her thigh now as deep between her legs as the skirt would allow. Holly's core pulsed, desperately wanting her to create more room, let Jen in.

As Jen's lips found hers she shifted her hands from the loops in the blonde's trousers, quickly hitching her skirt an inch or two higher. It was all they needed. Holly's breath stuttered as Jen's thigh rubbed against her centre, making her clit throb.

Surely this was too far? Friends didn't do this. Was Jen drunk? Holly frowned as Jen's lips worked in rhythm with hers, frustrated she was having such intrusive thoughts and not fully in the moment. *Does the voice in my head ever bloody shut up?*

'What is it?' Jen asked with a nervous laugh, taking a second to check their surroundings.

Holly ran her thumb over Jen's jawline. Her desire was a wildfire, burning with reckless abandon, and if she didn't call time now she was going to do something irreversibly stupid. She cupped a hand to Jen's face, settling her fingers in the woman's blonde waves.

Jen's gaze melted into hers. She knew what was coming.

Words unspoken but sadly understood, Jen stepped back, flicking at the tip of her nose with her thumb, as if the motion would dispel the last five minutes from existence.

She cleared her throat as she pulled her phone from her pocket, her voice as composed and cheery as possible. 'Photo with the fairy lights for Instagram?'

18

J en pushed open the door to Taylor's Deli, surprised but happy to find it busy. They closed half an hour after she did; there was a good chance Holly was still here.

'Hey, Harry,' Jen said, peering into the glass display counter and admiring a particularly tasty looking wheel of cheese. 'Holly still about?'

Right on cue, the brunette appeared from the basement door, a panettone in her hands. On seeing Jen she fumbled, dropping the box, only to recatch it with impressive dexterity. 'You should see me carry eggs,' she said to the customer, passing the sweet bread over. She straightened her shirt and made her way to Jen. 'Wandered into the wrong shop?' she asked with a smirk.

No one had any business looking that good in an oversized shirt and skinny jeans. Never mind the way her hair looked, up in a messy bun. Memories of kissing Holly's neck flooded back, and for a brief moment, Jen forgot why she was there.

'Jen?' Holly said, waving a hand in front of the blonde's face as if to wake her from a trance.

'Hey, Holly, hi,' she replied, her brain finally kicking into gear.

'Thank God, I thought you were actually having a moment there.' Her face contorted between humour and confusion. 'You okay?'

'Yeah, listen: Ben's van has a flat, and before I nip home for my car, I was wondering: do you fancy buddying up? Better for the environment and all that.'

Holly swallowed a smile, trying to look like she was having to consider the idea. 'Depends. What's in it for me?

'Think of it as Rumpelstiltskin's payment.' She could feel Harry's eyes on her, but ignored him.

Holly crossed her arms and her legs, putting her weight on one foot. 'I thought we agreed on a drink for that?'

'Always read the Ts & Cs. The first rule of business. I can change my mind at any time.'

'So, if I help with this I don't take you out for a drink?'

'Think of it as a swap.'

'Hmm. I don't think that sounds very fair.'

'I figure the time and conversational effort is the same, plus it will work out a heck of a lot cheaper for you.'

'I meant it wouldn't be fair if I don't also get to go for a drink.'

Jen didn't quite know what to say to that. 'We can discuss the new terms while we deliver. I want to make sure you're not swindling me,' she replied, unable to hide a sly smile.

'Me?' Holly said, feigning offence.

'I know what you're like,' Jen countered with a wink. 'So, deal?'

'I guess. Dad needs his van for the wholesaler, so I have his car. Do you have a lot?'

'It should fit. You got the back seats down?'

'Naturally.'

'Park it out front and I'll have a look, size it up. I don't know what it looks like.'

'Sorry, park it where?'

'Out front.'

Holly took a few short strides to the front of the shop and peered out the window, her arms still crossed. 'This front?'

Jen joined her at the window. 'That would make the most sense, yes.'

'And that spot?' she asked, pointing to the only one that was available – the one right outside Jen's.

'Yep.' Jen replied, refusing to rise to the bait.

Holly crossed her arms again. 'I dunno. Next door's a right moody cow. I got shouted at the last time I parked there.'

'Perhaps she was having a particularly bad day and took it out on an innocent bystander.'

'Likely story.'

Jen tickle-grabbed Holly's side and the split-second attack made her double over, play-protecting herself as she giggled. 'Alright, alright. I'll go get the car.'

JEN DIDN'T KNOW MUCH about vehicles, but Harry's roomy Volvo had ample space for both loads of deliveries. The hampers took up a lot of the boot, but with a little imaginative stacking getting the rest in was a doddle.

'You sorted the route?' Holly asked, clicking her seatbelt in.

'Yep, all done. Need me to read out the directions?' Merging routes had been surprisingly easy given that Jen had gotten Harry and Catherine using the same system last year. One click and it was fixed. If only everything in life was that simple.

'No need – there's a reason why I like to use Dad's car rather the van.' Holly retrieved her phone from the cup holder and, after a few taps, the map was displayed on the centre console's screen. '*Et voilà!*'

'Impressive. *Elle a plus qu'un joli minois.*'

'Stop showing off,' Holly teased. 'Now, buckle up.'

'Yes, boss.'

Holly started the car and the route sprang to life, the car's robotic voice telling her where to go. Jen hardly needed to be here at all. There was nowhere else she'd rather spend the evening, though.

'What do you want to listen to?' Holly said, watching the oncoming traffic for a gap.

'What do you usually play? Is this where I find out you exclusively listen to Steps?'

'Eh, do not knock one of the UK's best groups, thank you very much,' Holly replied, waving a thank you to the kind soul who had eventually let them merge onto Pollokshaws Road. 'It depends: I like Sigrid, MUNA, Betty Who, Fickle Friends, Allie X, Shura, that kind of stuff. Know any of them?'

Jen huffed out her cheeks. 'Not a single one. They real bands, or you just saying words?'

'Jenevieve Berkley, you're such an uncultured swine.'

Usually, Jen hated the sound of her full name; only her mother had the power to say it and not cause an involuntary grimace. But from Holly's mouth it sounded like a melody, an earworm she could happily listen to on repeat.

'Well, now is your time to shine. Educate me.'

'Oh, crikey. Where to begin?' Holly replied with a snicker.

'Well, let's just see what you played last,' Jen said, her finger hovering over the Spotify icon. 'You look nervous. It is Steps, isn't it?'

'You'll just have to play it and see.' Holly didn't sound convinced. This was going to be enlightening.

With a few quick taps, the car blasted MUNA's 'I Know A Place'. *Not bad.*

The song came to an end and Holly looked to Jen for approval. 'Well?'

'Good. Not my usual taste but I could tolerate that, yeah. Good beat.'

Holly's brow furrowed, her eyes fixed on the road ahead. 'Intriguing. So, what is your usual taste?'

That was a toughy. Like most people, Jen's musical taste was broad, but a few artists stood out above the rest.

'Ever heard of Wallis Bird?'

'Never – one of your favourites?'

'Absolutely.' She'd loved the *Spoons* album since it came out in 2007, but one of her favourite tracks had taken on new meaning this month and was her new go-to song. She'd found herself dancing to it in the kitchen on more than one occasion this week. It just so happened to be track one on the album, but was perhaps a little too risky given that it was about falling head over heels for someone. It was like the lyrics had been written for her and Holly.

Or should she be brave and shove it on anyway? It was the first track – she could swing it either way, should Holly mention it. Sleep hadn't come easy last night, her evening with Holly playing on a loop in her head. Holly had been jealous, no denying it, but she'd stopped the kiss Jen initiated. Her intentions were as clear as mud. Not that Jen was any better, but with so much at stake, she could hardly just tell Holly how she felt.

They were nearly at the first stop. It was the perfect opportunity to put the track on and make herself scarce.

Feeling bold, Jen ignored her racing heart and clammy hands, telling the car to play the album. The first bars played as Holly brought the car to stop.

'Right, you're doing the legwork today. Flat 4/2.'

Jen hopped out of the car and popped the boot up, taking her time to locate the hamper as she spied on Holly in the rearview mirror. Her reaction was little more than a quiet nod of appreciation. So far.

'SNACK?' Holly asked when Jen returned to the car. She gave the packet a jiggle, its contents rattling.

Not the response she was expecting. Jen had hoped for something a little more topical, perhaps not a full admission of 'I feel the same' but something at least about the lyrics. Funny how no one ever sticks to the script you write in your head.

'What the hell are they?' Jen asked, eyeing the packet emblazoned with a huge chickpea.

'Coffee-coated chickpeas – surprisingly good.'

'Yuck. I'll pass, thanks,' Jen replied, buckling her seatbelt back up.

'Honestly,' Holly said, giving the packet another shake. 'I would have knocked them too, but they're amazing. Dad had samples out the other today and now I'm hooked. Go out of your comfort zone; you might be surprised.'

What harm would it do? Jen shoved a hand in the packet, picking up a single coated chickpea. She studied it between finger and thumb. It looked like a little brown speckled egg except it was nearly perfectly round.

'Go on, it's not going to bite you,' Holly said, her face streaked with anticipation.

After a further second of inspection, Jen popped the snack in her mouth. It wasn't anywhere close to what she'd expected. She'd imagined a wet chickpea like you get in a tin, and how that would taste if you plopped it in a cup of coffee. This was crunchy, sweet but bitter, and definitely moreish.

'Bloody good, eh?' Holly looked as smug as if she'd made them herself. 'Here, have a few more. Keep your strength up for all those steps.' She tipped a handful into Jen's open palm.

'Why does that work?'

'I know, right? Who thinks up these things?' Holly hit pause on the Wallis Bird album. 'As much as I enjoyed that, I think I know what this car is lacking.'

'Uh-huh?' Jen mumbled, her mouth full of chickpeas.

'It's the deli car, so there's only one thing for it.' She clicked a few icons and brought up her playlists. There were a lot. She was quick to tap on 'Holly Taylor's Cheesy Chunes', but Jen couldn't help but notice what was at the top of Most Recently Played: an album titled *Lovefest*. She's made an album for the month? That was dedication. Maybe it was for the deli. Holly's face beamed with excitement. 'This car lacks cheese! Road trips are so much more fun when you can both sing along.'

The opening bars of Britney Spears's 'Hit Me Baby One More Time' filled the car. Jen tilted her head back, closed her eyes, and groaned, making a show of her disapproval. Holly wasted no time in belting the words out, complete with shoulder shuffles and finger-pointing.

'Let's get this show on the road,' Holly hollered.

'More like eyes on the road, Miss Taylor. I don't want to die listening to Britney.'

Holly continued her dancing, giving the chorus full welly, watching the road ahead as she grabbed for Jen's belly and tickled her. 'C'mon, you know you want to join in.'

Holly's hands safely back on the wheel, Jen held back for the remaining verse, pretending she wasn't interested until the chorus hit and she gave it her all. No point fighting it; Holly's energy was contagious.

'Yes, Jen! C'mon!' Holly cheered, her grin a mile wide.

That smile. Jen would do anything to keep seeing it.

'Any word?' Jen asked, leaning on the car door so she was positioned sideways. Sitting in the car was getting tedious – she just wanted to get home.

'Nothing yet,' Holly replied, rolling her neck.

The cheesy tunes were still on but at a considerably lower volume, their energy having waned around halfway through the deliveries before fizzling out to zero as they waited to hear back from a customer.

He'd not answered his door the first time around, so they'd come back at the end of the route, hoping he'd now be in. Unfortunately for them, he was nowhere in sight, and they were forced to park up outside his house in Giffnock and wait for Harry to give the all-clear to leave it.

Thirty minutes had passed and Jen's patience was wearing thin. Not that she wasn't enjoying Holly's company, but there were much better places to hang out than a stuffy Volvo.

'Dad will be busy with the crackers. He's maybe not

managed to get in touch yet.' Holly said, defending her father.

'More likely the guy's not bothered. You know what customers are like. Doesn't matter if our time is wasted.'

'Not wasted though, is it? You get to spend it with me.'

Jen couldn't tell if she was joking or not. Did Holly have a window into her mind? Sometimes it felt like she did: a crystal clear vision of what was going on in the darkest parts of her brain. *God, I hope not.* As if to wreak havoc, her mind threw up images of Jen's latest fantasy: fucking Holly on the rooftop last night. The way Holly had pushed down on her thigh, so hard Jen felt the heat of her core announcing how wet she was. . . it gave her shivers just to think about. She'd had been seconds away from taking things further. It wasn't a difficult task to imagine how things could have gone if Holly hadn't stopped her.

'Yo,' Holly said, clicking her fingers by Jen's nose. 'You spaced out again. You sure you're okay? I'm still worrying about concussion.'

Jen composed herself with a quiet cough. 'That was ages ago. Just tired, that's all.'

'Want some water to wake you up?' Holly reached for her water bottle, offering it to Jen.

'Only if you're happy to share. I know some people don't like sharing bottles.'

'You had your tongue in my mouth yesterday. I think I'll cope,' Holly joked, biting her bottom lip to hide a wicked grin.

Jen's cheeks beamed brighter than a fire engine. Holly was using her crystal ball again. *Quick – time to change the subject.* 'Talking of last night, we need to discuss the new terms of your swap.'

'Ah, yes, well remembered.' Holly straightened herself,

mirroring Jen's seating position and facing her as much as the steering wheel would allow. 'What do you propose?'

Jen took a slug of water and handed the bottle back. She could taste Holly's peppermint lip balm and fought to ignore the tingle in her stomach at the thought of kissing her right now, in the car. It would certainly be a good way to pass the time. 'If you still want to go to Bar Orama, I'm in.'

'Well, that was easy. I've seen they do a pub quiz on the last Thursday of the month. Fancy that?'

'Ah, yes, I know all about the quiz. I used to be the Quiz Master. Legend has it they still use my jacket.'

'What? No,' Holly replied, her eyebrows rocketing. 'Lies.'

'I swear on my mother's life. It had sequins and everything.'

Holly shook her head, a look of disbelief still plastered on her face despite the growing smile pulling at her lips. 'Photos or I don't believe you.'

Jen produced her phone from the car door. 'Actually, I do believe there are photos on Facebook,' she said with a singsong-y wiggle of her head.

'Can't wait to see this,' Holly mumbled, leaning in closer.

A lot of scrolling, through nearly nine years of photos to be exact, and lo and behold: twenty-five-year-old Jen was hosting the first Quiz Night, sequin jacket and all.

Holly's face was a picture. 'The more I find out about you, the less I feel I know. You're full of surprises.'

'I was a different woman back then. Full of hopes and dreams,' she joked.

'What happened?'

'Life.' She was only half-joking that time. 'We can't go next week – they have the Lovefest closing thing. Next month?'

Holly's eyes lit up. 'Good to know you're not getting shot of me as soon as this is over.'

'It was difficult at first, a real struggle, but I've gotten used to your company.' The song changed and Jen's attention snapped to the centre console: 'I Touch Myself' by The Divinyls. 'Nope. Nooo. Literally the worst song ever made.' Jen stabbed the skip button and breathed a sigh of relief when Christina Aguilera came on.

'It's not that bad.'

'Nuh-uh, non-negotiable. Hate it.'

'Because of the topic? Not shy, are you?' Holly jibed, giving Jen's thigh a squeeze.

Jen's cheeks burned hotter than the sun. 'It's just not something I like talking about.'

'You are shy,' Holly said, her face suddenly sympathetic but her eyes saying she was weighing up whether to wind Jen up or not. 'Consider the topic closed. I don't want to make you uncomfortable. But just to put my two cents into the ring: I think it's totally normal. I did it this morning.'

If Jen's cheeks were burning before, they were molten lava now. Thankfully some of the blood had been diverted south, or her cheeks might have actually caught fire.

She shot Holly a look that said 'shut up' in the nicest way possible. She might have said it to get a reaction. Or even worse, it might have been true. The thought of Holly touching herself mere hours ago sent Jen into a tizzy.

Holly held Jen's gaze, her smouldering stare stoking the air between them.

Jen edged forward, Holly holding steady.

What was this? Jen's heart picked up pace as her brain tried to decipher what the heck was happening. There was no air in the car, only silence as a thousand words went unsaid.

Holly's phone vibrating in the cup holder made them both flinch.

Connection broken, the temperature in the car returned to normal. Life shifted back from slow motion to its usual pace, carrying on as if nothing ever happened. That was, apart from Jen's heart. It pounded like she'd just jogged to the top of a skyscraper. Holly was a high she struggled to come down from.

'Yeah? Uh-huh,' Holly said, carrying on the one-sided conversation with her dad. 'Right, okay. Sounds good. See you later.' She hung up, replaced the phone in the holder, and turned to Jen. 'He still can't find any of these bloody cheese crackers.'

'Shite. And what about this guy? Yay or nay?' Jen replied, her voice surprisingly stable. She wanted to rewind and chuck the phone out the window before it had a chance to ring.

'He's told Dad it's no longer needed, but he'll still pay. I guess he didn't need the hamper to kick off date night,' she said with a smirk.

'Home time then?'

'Deffo. But, Dad says we can eat the hamper, like, if you fancy it? The fresh stuff would just need binned otherwise. Don't want it to go to waste.'

Jen's heart flipped with excitement. 'Sounds good. Your place or mine?'

19

Holly's eyes trailed over the contents of the open hamper on Jen's coffee table as her host grabbed plates from the kitchen.

She'd not had time to fully appreciate Jen's flat the last time she was here, her mind distracted by other matters. It was boxy, no denying it, but Jen's taste in decor made it light and airy. The living room-kitchen combo was decorated in light greys with tasteful pops of colour and wood. It had a Scandi-lilt to it. Holly very much approved.

She poked at the cheese in the hamper, interested to see what was on offer tonight. Brie. Cheddar. Havarti. Nice.

Her mind wasn't on the food, though. She'd not been lying about touching herself, and her brazenness was exciting. Flirting without flirting; it was a new concept for Holly. The thrill was intoxicating and the pay-off huge. She was sure there'd been a flicker in Jen's eyes – a hint of equal desire, a moment where they became one, both lusting after the same thing. And who wouldn't want a repeat performance of last night's epic kiss? She'd officially passed the point of no return. Whether she wanted to or not, Holly had feelings for

Jen. Plain and simple. Last night had confirmed it. Sure, she hadn't planned to fall for anyone so quickly after London, but the sooner she was honest with herself, the sooner she could concentrate on figuring Jen's intentions out.

So now she was on Jen's sofa, praying the opportunity for an encore arose. *No more phone calls, please.*

'So, where do you want to begin?' Jen asked, setting the plates on the coffee table.

Holly stifled a laugh. 'I think you're meant to do the cards first; eat as you go.'

'These bad boys?'

'That's the ones.' Holly held her hand out, waiting to take the deck of cards. 'You get us some glasses for this bubbly.'

'You're driving – I figured we'd be skipping that.'

Not if I stay over. Even thinking it made Holly's stomach lurch. Saying it out loud was never going to happen. 'One won't hurt.'

'Okay, glasses it is.'

Holly shuffled the cards before realising her parents might have placed them in a special order. Too late now.

Jen set the champagne flutes on the table before inspecting the prosecco bottle from the hamper. 'I can already tell this is going to be tasty.'

Holly watched in wonder as Jen twisted the cork free with a satisfying pop. She'd never seen it done without a towel. Her eyes raked over Jen's biceps and triceps as she fought the urge to bite her lip. Those arms were dangerous: any more moves like that and Holly wouldn't be able to control herself.

Glasses filled, Jen took her position on the sofa. It felt like there were worlds between them. As if reading Holly's mind, she shuffled closer to the middle, getting comfy with a knee against the cushions.

'So, the question every lesbian wants answered: who's going first?'

Holly snorted. 'I usually just see how the mood takes me, but you can go first today.'

'Why?' Jen's eyes creased with suspicion.

Because that's how it always plays out in my fantasies. 'Your flat. Only fair.' Holly passed Jen a stack of cards and balanced the other half on her knee. 'First, we need to toast.' She raised her glass. 'Quack, quack.'

'Quack, quack.'

Jen shifted, getting ready to tackle the first question. On looking at the card, her eyes grew wide as she blew out her cheeks. 'I take it there's no specific order to these? We're firing straight in with the big guns.'

'I shuffled and I don't think I was meant to.'

'That explains it. Holly—wait, what's your middle name?'

'Charlotte.'

'Holly Charlotte Taylor, do you want children?' Jen placed the used card on the table with a little smirk.

'Oh, Jesus. Mum and Dad haven't held back on the questions.' It was Holly's turn to puff out her cheeks as she thought. 'Yeah, someday. Not this week. Probably.'

Jen nodded in agreement. 'Nice, okay. So, what's the deal? Do I answer too, or do we just move on?'

'I think you should answer.' Holly took another sip of prosecco. She was going to need more alcohol in her bloodstream if the questions were going to be so personal. She'd Uber if she needed to. She'd expected more 'do you have any siblings?' than 'do you want to make babies?'.

Although, she was looking forward to discovering another layer of Jen. Every day was a school day with her.

'Okay, right. So, Sabine, and yes, I would love to have kids someday.'

'Sabine?'

'I asked your middle name, so you also get to know mine. You've got the full set now.'

'An honour and a privilege. Jenevieve Sabine Berkley. Suits you.'

'If you say so,' Jen replied with a wiggle of her head. 'What's your opener?'

'I'm almost too nervous to look.' Holly slowly turned over the card and breathed a sigh of relief. 'How old were you when you first kissed someone?'

'Fourteen. Boy called Lee. You?'

'Fifteen – his name was also Lee. Same boy?' she jested.

'Depends; how old are you?'

'Thirty.' She'd still not told Jen it had been her birthday. She didn't want her to think she was weird for not mentioning it at the time, but that night had been about letting loose, getting to know the woman she was fake-dating. Not outing herself as a massive Billy Nae Mates.

'Well, not unless your first kiss was with a—' Jen paused as she did the math, counting on her fingers. '—twenty-one year old.'

Holly wrinkled her nose. 'Definitely not. And what about the one that counts? How old were you when you first kissed a girl?'

Jen's eyes turned wistful, like she was replaying the memory. Did she look like that when she thought about the kisses they'd shared? 'Sixteen. Her name was Caroline. Spoiler: we didn't last long and broke up before we even really got started.'

'Aw, I was hoping for a happy ending. Marriage, few kids, maybe a dog.'

'Sorry to disappoint. What about you? And it better not have been Caroline. Although, I always wondered who she left me for,' Jen replied, chuckling as she sipped her prosecco.

'You're safe – her name was Ella. I was nineteen. Guess I was a late bloomer, so to speak.'

'For any particular reason?'

Her answer came as a shrug. 'I'm just very picky about who I kiss.'

'I'll consider myself part of an elite crew, then.' There was that wicked glint again, the one that got Holly's insides all tied up so she didn't know up from down. Time for a distraction. 'Aren't we supposed to be eating while we do this?'

'Aw, yeah, shit. Sorry, Taylor's Deli, forgot about the food. What about some tunes, too? Set the mood.'

'Sure – what do you fancy?' Holly made light work of getting to the right screen on her phone, her fingers hovering over the search bar, forever at Jen's beck and call.

'I spied a Lovefest playlist earlier. How about that? Seems topical.'

Oh no. That playlist was never intended to see the light of day. It might as well be titled *Songs That Make Me Think About Shagging Jen Berkley.* Her blood had run cold when Jen had pressed play on her last listen earlier. The universe had thrown a lifeline though, leaving only the bridge and one chorus to MUNA's classic anthem. If Jen listened to the entire two hours and twenty minutes of Holly's lovelorn mix there would be no such luck. The first song was about falling for a friend and it was the most subtle of the lot. She was going to think Holly was a complete psycho. *Shit. Holly.*

You've not said anything. Speak! Her jaw was frozen, her eyes a screensaver as her brain rebooted. Wires finally reconnected, she managed to blurt out: 'You won't like it.'

'How do you know?'

'You didn't know any of the bands I listed earlier. Wouldn't you rather listen to stuff you know?'

'If tonight is all about getting to know you, I'd like to give it a bash.'

FUCK. There was no way out of this. 'Okay, cool.' Holly hit play, turning the volume as unsuspiciously low as possible.

'Okay, my turn,' Jen said, her plate now peppered with pickings from the hamper. Holly gulped as Jen leaned over, clicking the volume up. 'Sorry, couldn't hear it over here. Right, when was the last time you felt most yourself?'

Holly thought, tuning out the music, lest she wanted to rival Jen's usually blushing cheeks. 'Do you want an honest answer?'

'Only if you're comfortable saying it.'

Holly turned the repercussions over. How could she be anything but honest with the beautiful woman sitting opposite her? 'Yesterday. On the rooftop. First time in a long time. I've never told anyone else the whole story about Shona.'

Jen's eyes bored into Holly's, her features full of so much empathy and warmth that Holly swore she felt the heat. 'I'm glad I could do that for you.' Her voice was low and slow: this was serious Jen. No snark to be seen.

'And what about you?' Holly asked, almost sounding timid.

Jen straightened herself, looking a little awkward. 'Well, you were honest, so I will be too. Not for years, but I've been damn close these last few weeks.'

There was that moment again. Eyes trained on each other; breath but a whisper. But Jen wasn't going to let it sizzle this time and shifted gears quicker than a rally driver. 'You want some of this pancetta? It's great.'

'No thanks,' Holly replied, her voice dripping with disappointment that their earlier almost-tryst wasn't rekindled. 'Vegetarian. I don't eat meat or fish.'

Jen froze, mid-chew, before swallowing with an audible gulp. 'I won't eat it if you'd rather I didn't.'

'No, no. You go for it, don't let it go to waste, but I won't touch it.'

'Okay, but just say. I don't mind being vegetarian around you.'

'And scoffing bacon sandwiches when I'm not looking?'

'As if I'd be that organised with food. You've seen my fridge.'

'True that. Okay,' Holly said, looking at her card and taking an extra-long lungful of air. 'What do you think is your best quality?'

'Easy, hands down, my boobs. Best part of my body, love them. Next question,' Jen said, no hint of sarcasm.

Holly tilted her head, half her brain having a mini-malfunction, the rest gearing up for her next sentence. 'I think it meant like, "I'm a hard worker" or something, but boobs. Okay, got it.'

'What can I say? I know my limits.' Jen's rosy cheeks said she was regretting her quick-fire response. 'What about you? Body part, please. Let's keep this playing field level.'

Tough. There wasn't much to choose from, in Holly's opinion. Jen took her silence as a chance to shine.

'Need a hand? You've got a great bum.'

Holly snorted for the second time today. 'Excuse me, you're not meant to have been looking at my bum.'

Jen threw her hands up in mock defence. 'Listen, it's a danger of the job. I might have accidentally had a wee squeeze yesterday.'

'Oh, really? I didn't notice.'

Defence turned to faux-hurt. 'You're kidding? I used some of my best moves on you.'

'You must try harder next time.'

'Noted.'

Holly danced the line again. Tiptoeing nearer the edge, hoping Jen would be the first to jump. Holly's heart upped the ante, aware she was playing a dangerous game. Jen had been more than clear that this wasn't romantic. Flirting was fine, but actually doing something? That was a different ball game.

It was Holly's turn to use the hamper. Never mind being a tool for getting to know someone, her parents had created the perfect sexual barrier. Her mind grabbed onto the thought of her parents, like catching paper blowing in the wind, and held it tight. That helped cool her down, the hunger in her chest dropping back to a gentle simmer.

'Look what else is in here,' Holly exclaimed, scooping up the chickpea packet. 'And it's the mixed sharer.' She gave the packet a wee shake in time with a shoulder shimmy.

'And, pray tell, what's so exciting about that?'

Holly studied the front of the packet, reading as she explained. 'They do seven flavours in total. This packet has them all, it's pot luck what you pick out.'

'So risqué.'

'We know how to be wild at Taylor's Deli.'

'What's the options? Any minging ones?'

'I've had most of them and liked them all. I'm not going to tell you what they are, though,' she said, playfully hiding the packet under her arm. 'I'm going to give you one, and you can guess what it is.'

'Sounds like a challenge. Count me in.' Jen straightened herself, as if readying her body and mind for what lay ahead. She pulled at her T-shirt, getting everything just so, and shut her eyes. 'Right, hit me.'

Holly tore open the packet and picked one at random. 'You keeping your eyes shut?'

'Of course. I don't want the colour to give it away. I'm no cheat.'

'You think you'll be able to guess it just on taste? It's pretty broad.'

Jen waved a hand in Holly's direction, her lips pursed as she battled a smile. Holly took the opportunity to drink her in. With no eyes on her, she could leer all she wanted. Jen did have good boobs. Holly bit her lip as her core pinged with desire. This was meant to be about hitting the reset. She shook her head as if her brain were an Etch-A-Sketch. Clear once more.

'I have a very sophisticated palate,' Jen said, unable to keep her face straight. 'Now, come on, life's boring with my eyes closed.'

'Gimme your hand then.'

'Just pop it in.'

'Where?'

'In my mouth. That's usually how people taste things.'

Okay then. It was a good thing Jen's eyes were shut. Holly couldn't hide the tremor in her hand as she brought the sweet to Jen's parted lips. She took it between her teeth, sucking the chickpea in as Holly's fingers hovered, just touching Jen's soft lips.

She snapped her eyes open and Holly pulled her hand

back like she'd just been caught stealing money from the till.

'Well?' she asked, her voice hoarse, lust clogging her throat.

Jen chewed as she thought. 'Tough one. I might need a clue. Is there fruit involved?'

'You're giving in quicker than I thought you would,' Holly teased.

'The prosecco has numbed my taste buds. Obviously.'

'Go on, have a bash and I'll let you know if you're in the right ballpark.'

Jen tilted her head up as if looking to the sky for answers. 'Strawberry. But there's something else.' She smacked her lips together, searching for the missing ingredient. 'Strawberries and cream?'

'Ooft. So close. I'm actually impressed.'

'You doubted me?' she replied, putting on the horror.

'Only for a split second. So, do you want to know what it was?'

'Yep, put me out of my misery.'

Holly paused, building the suspense. 'Raspberry—' Jen slapped her knee, gutted she was so close. '—cheesecake.'

'Never would have got that. But raspberry, how did I fudge that?' She shook her head, devastation clear, like she'd just lost the million-dollar prize on a quiz show.

'Right. My turn,' Holly said, passing the packet to Jen. She got comfy and closed her eyes. She could feel Jen gaze at her, although probably not in the same way as she'd done to her, and suddenly felt exposed. The hairs on her arms stood to attention. She smiled, but only to hide how awkward she felt.

'Open up,' Jen said, her voice deeper than usual. This little game was doing nothing to quell the fire stoking in

Holly's belly. She took her time in accepting the sweet, making a show of licking it with the tip of her tongue as she opened her eyes.

Holly put a hand up to cover her mouth, still chewing as she spoke. 'Easy. Tiramisu.'

'Right, well, that's cheating.'

'How?' Holly asked through a snigger.

'Because apparently these things are your *Mastermind* subject. Of course it's easy if you know the flavours.' Jen pulled a face, clearly not pleased with Holly's tactical advantage.

'It's all in the technique,' Holly playfully fired back as she pointed to her mouth. 'You need to do the tongue thing. The flavour's in the coating, not the chickpea.'

'Nope. I get the points, you're disqualified.'

'Sore loser, are we?'

'Nuh-uh. Just keeping things fair.' She picked up the remaining question cards, changing position so she was now sitting shoulder to shoulder with Holly. 'Ready for round two?'

Holly downed the rest of her drink. 'Bring it on.'

'I THINK we've exhausted all the decent ones,' Jen said, placing what was left of the cards back on the table.

'Feel you've learned more about me? Seen another side?'

'I'm still getting my head around what your last meal would be.'

'Omelettes are underrated.'

'And boring.'

'You really want to start this again?' Holly jibed, poking Jen in the ribs.

'Okay, okay. You win.' Jen's eyes shifted, the atmosphere between them changing in an instant, the air around them charged. 'So, before we wrap this up, fancy going off script? One question each, nothing is off-limits.'

Holly gulped. 'Nothing?'

'Nope.'

Holly considered it. Only one topic struck her as hazardous. And what were the chances of Jen asking about her feelings towards her? The notion probably wasn't even on her radar. 'Yeah, sure. I have nothing to hide.'

Jen's smile turned devious.

'I assume you already have a question in mind?' Holly asked, switching position so she was now leaning on a cushion. The only time they'd been closer was when they were kissing. Static hummed between Holly's chest and Jen's arm.

'I do, actually.'

'Why does that worry me?' The urge to reach out and stroke Jen's arm surged through Holly. She was so near; it would be so easy to do, but her muscles were frozen in place, her mind refusing to send the right signals.

'You've already agreed. No take-backs.'

'Let's get this over with, then. Come on, lay it on me,' Holly said, puffing her chest out like she was readying for battle.

Jen looked sheepish, her eyes everywhere but on Holly. 'Right.' She cleared her throat before taking a deep breath. Her voice was nearly a whisper. 'Did you really touch yourself this morning or were you just winding me up earlier?'

Holly couldn't help but laugh. 'Really? You can ask anything, anything at all, and you settle for that?'

'I just want to know, that's all.'

'Right, okay,' Holly said with a little laugh, a hand to her face as relief flooded through her. She composed herself, her attention now on the sock of the foot tucked under her bum. She pulled at it, stalling for time. She'd said it to be daring earlier, not expecting the topic to ever come back up. She clicked her tongue to the roof of her mouth, Jen's gaze an inferno across her skin. She nodded, deciding to part with the truth. 'Yeah, I did. Why do you want to know?'

Jen swivelled, her position now mirroring Holly's. For a brief moment, Holly thought she was going to take her hand and run her thumb over her open palm. It wasn't to be, so Holly stuffed her hand down the side of the cushion, not wanting to risk the temptation of completing the gesture herself. 'I've just never known anyone to be so open about it.'

'You make it sound like it's some dirty secret. We're humans. It's part of what we do.'

Jen's eyes said she agreed. She chewed on her bottom lip, thinking. 'Still, it's super taboo.'

Holly shrugged. 'I don't think it should be.'

'What did you think of?' The words came out like a freight train, fast and unyielding. They hit Holly with such force she almost flinched.

'Hey, you said one question,' she scolded, keeping it light with a laugh.

Jen's brow drooped, her eyes like a wounded puppy. 'I did.'

'And that's super personal. You can't ask a lady that,' she replied with a knowing smile.

'Ah, weird sex kink, eh?' Jen joked, lightening the atmosphere.

'Eh, no kink-shaming, please. But no. It's just there has to be a line and you're standing right on it.'

'Fair enough. To be honest, though, nothing can be worse than the whole omelette thing.'

Holly's features twisted in mock anger as she booped Jen on the nose with her finger. 'Enough.'

Holly's phone vibrated on the table, and this time she was happy to be saved by it. She skim-read the message. 'Dad's got crackers.'

'Jesus, that's a late one. Remind me again what the drama was?'

'Miss Berkley, do you mean to say you're not hanging on my every word, committing each conversation to memory?' she scoffed.

'In my defence, there's been a lot to take in tonight.'

'True,' Holly said, her face softening to a smile. 'Those crackers that you scoffed earlier, the cheese ones – they go in every hamper. Well, we ran out and so did the wholesaler.'

'Uh-huh.'

'So, we had to decide what to replace them with.'

Jen looked at the clock hanging over her breakfast table. 'Which has taken until nearly nine p.m.?'

'It's a very important decision,' Holly replied, making sure her tone matched the sincerity it deserved.

'So, what did you settle on?'

'Chilli.'

'Good. Classic. Nice choice.'

'But that's just until Wednesday. We'll be able to get more cheese for later in the week.'

'Thank the stars. I was wondering how I would sleep tonight.' Jen's voice was perfectly flat, her sarcasm impeccable after a lifetime of practice.

'You're on thin ice.' Holly was joking, of course, but it was fun to give back what Jen dished out.

'What you going to do about it?'

'I would like to ask my question now,' Holly replied, each word said with quiet purpose.

Jen wriggled on the spot. 'Shit, I'd forgotten about that.' Three glasses of prosecco had created a permanent blush to her cheeks, but Holly could tell she was already burning hotter.

'Right. Jen. Jenevieve. I would like to know. . .' She held her breath, counting to five in her head, mounting the tension. She was also delaying for her own sake. Her heart fluttered, her internal monologue screaming, *say it, say it!* Time to take a leap of faith. 'Do you enjoy kissing me?'

Jen's brow knitted, a mix of surprise and contemplation. 'Like, if you're asking if you're a good kisser, then, yeah. You're brilliant.' She shrugged.

'No. I'm asking: do you enjoy kissing *me*?' Holly laid emphasis on what she hoped were the right words, pointing between her and Jen's chests to add further clarification.

Jen scratched her cheek, thinking. 'Like, sexually?'

YES, screamed Holly's mind. She wasn't brave enough to say it, not by half. 'Whatever you feel comfortable with, but I was just meaning on a basic level. Like, do you enjoy it or is it a chore? Just part of the act?'

Jen shook her head with gusto, her blonde waves bouncing. 'Oh, no, no. Not a chore.'

It wasn't the most romantic thing she'd ever heard. but it still sent a frisson of hope over Holly. Jen didn't hate it: that was a good start. 'So, bearable then?'

'Yeah, like, as nice as kissing a friend can be. Are you really doubting your skills this much? You struck me as confident.'

Hope was dashed as quickly as it had emerged.

Holly guffawed, ignoring the sinking of her stomach. 'Me? Pull the other one.'

'I never would have known.'

The opening bars of S Club 7's 'Reach' blasted from Holly's phone, the jazzy piano making them both recoil.

'Whoa, that's not on my playlist,' Holly said, her eyes wide.

'Good tunes. I enjoyed them.' Jen reached over and picked up Holly's phone, using her knee for stability. A pop of excitement sparked in her core with the sudden contact, despite her being so blatantly friend-zoned moments before. 'But if it's finished, does that mean you need me to add to it?'

'Add? To my playlist?' Holly asked, her tone making it clear how atrocious the action would be.

Jen held the phone close to her chest, furiously typing. 'Just a few. Go on.'

Holly swiped for the mobile, narrowly missing as Jen pulled it above her head, leaning back out of reach. Her T-shirt rode up, exposing Jen's flat stomach. Holly gulped. Jen was too busy typing to notice what had stalled her. *Thank God.*

'Just one, then.'

'No,' she said with a grin, trying to reach the phone again.

With cat-like grace, Jen rolled off the sofa and onto her feet, quickly followed by Holly.

'Right, that's the first one,' Jen baited.

'No, no, no,' Holly giggled. The blonde was too quick and dodged every attack like a champion boxer. Holly changed tack and approached from a different angle, this time managing to take possession.

'Hey, hey, I wasn't done!'

'Oh, you're done,' Holly replied, unable to stop laughing. She ducked Jen's attempt at retrieval and spun around, keeping the phone close to her body.

Jen grabbed her from behind, her arms playfully locked around Holly's waist, her head on her shoulder, breath hot against Holly's skin.

Holly's core pulsed with desire, caught in the heat of the moment.

They froze, chests heaving in unison.

S Club 7 filled the room, their laughter still hanging in the air. If someone lit a match the place would surely explode – the atmosphere was so loaded that it should have come with a ticking countdown.

Jen had made it perfectly clear how she thought of her. Moment or not, she couldn't pursue anything. Not tonight. Not ever. She had to call time before she made a fool of herself.

Jen's breath still whistled in her ear as she broke the embrace, stepping away with her best attempt at a smile. 'Thank you,' she said, playfully irreverent as she wiggled the phone in Jen's direction.

It was impossible to read Jen's face.

Holly tapped the pause button, silence filling the room like a tidal wave. It made everything a thousand times worse. But she was committed now. It was a good chance to leave, especially since Jen had failed to utter a word.

Had she felt it? The way Holly's body ached for her to touch her, find an excuse to have her near, do anything to create a physical connection?

There had to be a reason for the look on Jen's face, like she'd just been winded.

'Listen,' Holly said, trying to sound aloof, 'I think my dad needs a hand unloading these crackers. Can't have him putting his back out.' She managed a half-smile. It was all she could muster, her insides now a garbled mess.

'Yeah, yeah. Of course,' Jen replied, almost dazed.

'See you tomorrow, maybe.'

'See you.'

20

She'd fucked it. Well and truly fucked it.

Jen took a breather from making cocktail pouches, pushing against the metal table's edge and arching her back.

It was her day off but she'd decided to come in and make extra, ready for a busy week ahead. Her cocktail masterclass was this week and the publicity would propel sales, so she needed to be ready.

Plus, it was a distraction from the fact Holly was ignoring her messages.

Taylor's was also closed today, and Jen wished she knew where Holly lived. *As if that's not stalkery.*

She'd been super weird last night, but Jen had convinced herself she was being paranoid. She had cracker drama to sort out. Today, though? Messages left on read. That was undeniable.

Jen picked up the measuring jug with a sigh and decanted it into the pouches.

She hadn't actually done anything. Yes, the prosecco might have gone to her head and she'd picked a play fight, but where was the harm in that? Friends could do that, right?

But God, why, why, *whyyyy* did she have to ask about the whole touching thing?

Jen winced, her whole face scrunching in disgust.

What a fucking weirdo.

If Holly hadn't cottoned onto her massive crush before last night, Jen was scuppered now. She may as well have hired a plane to tow a banner declaring it.

If the shoe was on the other foot, she would be creating distance, too.

Their moment in the car was lodged front and centre in Jen's mind, a life raft in an otherwise stormy sea. It refused to give it up, clinging on for dear life, looking for clues she could have missed and reading into the minutest details, creating connections. But what if that's all it was? A figment of her imagination? She'd seen flickers at home, but nothing as intense. She'd been afraid to let it sit and see how it played out, but she'd do anything to go back now. With no phones to interrupt, who knows what would have happened?

Courage was always easy after the fact.

She knew she was in trouble when she almost took Holly's hand. It had felt like the most natural thing in the world, to reach out, lace their fingers together, and trace Holly's palm with her thumb. She'd caught herself just in time and it felt like she'd pulled herself back from stepping in front of a speeding car. She was getting careless, and there were no second chances.

Now it felt like her insides were in the wrong place; everything just slightly out of position. To look at, she was normal, but nothing felt right. Something was always just off. Maybe she'd go for a run later, expel some energy.

Jen checked her phone again, just in case she'd missed it vibrating. Nothing.

Maybe it wasn't working.

That would make sense.

She fired off a message to Chloe, keeping it casual. She didn't need to know Jen was slowly losing her mind.

She and Alison hadn't been this complicated, but then they hadn't agreed to win a competition together or pretend to fake-date. There was no hiding their attraction; no story to weave. Just good old-fashioned physicality. Girl meets girl and *boom*.

Trust me to go this long being single and then pick the most convoluted and confusing relationship possible.

Her phone vibrated against the metal table, making her jump. Anticipation gripped Jen's stomach: it had to be Holly.

Her face fell and her shoulders sagged.

Chloe.

You did just text her.

Okay, so Jen's phone was working. Maybe Holly just didn't have a good signal. Whatever she was up to, perhaps she had enough bars to read messages, just not enough to reply? Was that a thing? It sounded like it could be a thing.

They had their third date this week. Was it going to be super awkward? *It's been one day.* She was getting ahead of herself.

She'd barely noticed her new routine until today.

It was a few texts after D'Angelos.

Which turned into adding each other on Facebook.

Then it was messages, dotted through the day.

Before Jen knew it, Holly was part of her morning routine. She was always up first, so would start the day's conversation. Like clockwork, Holly replied around eight.

Why anyone would voluntarily get up so early was beyond Jen, but she liked the company as she got ready for work.

It was nothing groundbreaking. *What are you doing today?* Pictures of ducks spotted in the wild, real or not. Constant jokes and banter. Jen found herself staying up later and later just to keep the conversation going, often falling asleep before they'd shared a proper goodnight. Which was fine, because it gave a good opener the next day.

Just had to ruin a good thing, eh?

Holly had snuck in under her radar, drip by drip, until she was well and truly embedded.

And now Jen had been thinking with her heart, not her head, and pushed away the one human that made her feel like a complete person.

There has to be a way to fix this.

Vodka poured, she set to work on sealing the pouches. This was good manual labour, something to keep her body and mind occupied. But there were only so many pouches she could make.

I'll go for a run. Then watch a film or something.

Tomorrow would be rinse and repeat. Just like always. A month ago she would have loved days off like this.

Impatience was a serpent wrapped around her insides, getting tighter by the minute, and concentrating on the task at hand was impossible.

This is ridiculous.

Jen checked her phone again. *Right. Nope, let's hide it. Let's hide the phone and you can only look at it between cocktails.*

She marched the offending mobile to the back of the basement, putting it out of sight and out of mind behind a box of brown sugar.

Were relationships meant to feel like this? Like all of you ached, your stomach was a mess, and your brain felt squidgy? She'd never felt like this before. How can six hours of radio silence do this to a person?

Holly was under her skin. Regardless of what was going on, this was a serious wake-up call. She couldn't carry on like this. She was a struck match, caught in the moment before ignition, forever on the edge.

Should she message again? *I don't want to look desperate.*

She'd already done two in a row.

A double message. That looked forlorn.

A third? Holly was going to know Jen was in over her head.

Jen grabbed the sticker sheet and got to work, finishing the pouches. She shook her head as she worked, chuckling to herself. 'You've finally lost it.'

You're overreacting, idiot.

How would Holly know? This was obviously to do with something totally unrelated. Maybe she was visiting a sick relative, or at the cinema. . . seeing a six-hour film that started at the crack of dawn. Jen had been super guarded: there was no way Holly could have figured out her true intentions.

If she could just hear and know Holly was okay, that they were okay, she could stop feeling like life was on pause.

The brown sugar rumbled.

Or did it?

Was she hearing phantom vibrations now?

I'll finish these stickers, then I'll check. There's no rush.

The stickers were finished in record time. Her hands shook with adrenaline as she finally held the phone.

It was Holly!

Her muscles tensed with excitement.

Everything was going to be fine.

'What the fuck?' Jen blurted, her words ringing in the prep room.

One tiny message: *Sorry, busy today.*

That was it.

No kisses.

They're closed today: how can she be busy?

There was no more paranoia. This was full-blown confirmed.

Jen hung her head, defeat ringing in her ears in the form of her booming heart. What to do now?

21

Holly skimmed the sole of her shoe over the masonry sticking out from the grass.

Mum and Dad were off wandering around the castle grounds again, so she'd taken the chance to steal some alone time.

Bothwell Castle had sounded great over breakfast, but there was only so much that crumbling turrets and unfinished guardhouses could distract you.

She sighed, a little louder than intended, and got a funny look from a passing dog-walker. She forced a half-smile and was gifted a sympathetic one in return.

Her phone vibrated against her hand in her jacket pocket.

It would be Jen.

She turned over the message in her head again. Going from one extreme to another wasn't ideal, but needs must.

Jen probably wouldn't even care. Or notice.

Her exit from Jen's wasn't the most inconspicuous, but she really had helped Dad with the crackers, and again this morning before the castle, so it wasn't a lie. She was busy: no harm, no foul.

So why did it feel like she was being shady as hell?

Reality had hit like a tonne of bricks last night. Whatever was between her and Jen was firmly on the friendship side of the tracks. At least for Jen. She had to respect that. The only way to get a handle on her heart was to distance herself.

She'd been living in a fantasy world, imagining moments between them that never happened. And yesterday evening, with Jen's arms around her waist, she'd been seconds away from ruining everything.

Jen was her friend, nothing more.

Her phone was a hot coal in her pocket, threatening to burn through if she didn't read the message.

Holly traipsed around to the other side of the remaining circular guardhouse, kidding herself it was super interesting. Why bother to start to build it, then give up? The information plaque didn't give anything away. Change of heart, perhaps: they no longer wanted to keep the riff-raff out.

She felt bad for not being with Mum and Dad, but her mind was a constant buzz of thoughts: she'd found herself distracted and irritable all day. It wasn't fair to take her mood out on them. She was much better keeping to herself and letting them enjoy the day.

A group of teenagers hung out by the park's entrance and Holly felt like they were watching her. Can't a lone woman wander about the grounds and lose her mind in peace?

She pulled out her phone, distracting herself from their gaze. Her lock screen gave enough away without showing Jen she'd read it.

Just wanted to know you were okay. Wha. . .

The urge to know what the rest said was like a vice around her stomach.

This is ridiculous.

Three weeks ago she didn't even know this woman existed. Now she felt like she wanted to cry at the thought of Jen not liking her back.

Still feeling the teens' eyes on her, Holly went in search of a quiet spot. There were no benches near the castle but she wouldn't have wanted to chance one anyway; she needed space.

Nowhere was perfect, so she settled for a patch of grass by the biggest, most intact turret. She took a seat and rested her arms and head on her knees, probably looking like the biggest sad sack on Planet Earth.

She'd brought this on herself, playing dangerous games with her heart.

With another sigh Holly looked to the sky, basking in the heat of the afternoon sun. Under any other circumstances, today would have been glorious. There was barely a cloud in the sky: it was a perfect summer's day.

But it felt like storm clouds were overhead, heavy and black, blotting out any chance she had of enjoying it.

Might as well bite the bullet.

Holly whipped her phone out and read the remainder of Jen's text. She just wanted to know what she was up to. Nothing groundbreaking. She'd reply later. If she texted back straight away they'd be right back into old habits. Creating physical distance wouldn't be enough – she had to get Jen out her head as well.

She settled her chin on her arms again, watching a dog run with an impressively large stick: the thing was three times as big as him. Holly chuckled quietly as it negotiated a walker coming his way, unaware of how much room he was taking up and forcing the woman to jump from the path.

Everything ached from how much Jen and she had laughed yesterday, her stomach muscles constantly dull. She couldn't remember the last time she'd felt like this, if ever. If laughter was the best medicine, Jen was the cure for all.

Maybe I should just text her back now.

'You okay, love?' Dad's voice made her jump. She'd not even seen them approaching.

'We're going to go for a walk down by the river if you want to join us?' Mum asked, her features a picture of concern.

'That would be nice,' Holly replied, trying hard to sound chipper.

They walked in silence for a while, Holly keeping her attention on the surrounding trees and meandering river. But she could tell that loaded conversation hung in the air, right on the tip of her parents' tongues. She bit down on her anger; it wasn't their fault she was so irritable.

'Look, Hols,' Dad said, stopping as he pointed to the riverbank across the water. 'A crane.'

The bird waded through the water, tall and imposing, looking for food.

The tension grew heavier as the three of them stood, watching the bird but not really watching. A question hung in the air, like thought bubbles above her parents' heads.

Holly stuffed her hands in her jacket pockets, bracing herself for whatever was coming.

'Are you—' Mum began, taking the time to choose her words carefully. 'Are you sad again, Holly?'

Holly spun to face her mother, her brow creased. 'Sad?'

'It's okay, love,' Dad reassured.

'Do you think, maybe, you might reconsider the doctors? They can help with these things. There's no shame in tablets.' Mum had the best intentions. Holly wrestled the comeback that threatened to spill out.

She watched the riverbank again, scanning the tree line for the bird. All she could spot was a lone duck.

'Not that kind of sad,' she eventually managed.

'What kind, then?' Dad asked. 'Can we help?'

Holly chewed on her lip, unable to face her parents. Their stares held more weight than the stupid crumbling turrets that towered in the distance.

'It's a Holly problem. Don't worry about it,' she said, her voice unsteady. *Don't cry in public, Holly.*

Dad placed a hand on her back. 'We're your parents. A Holly problem is our problem. Whether you want it to be or not.'

Mum padded round to her side, Holly now the filling in a sad sandwich.

'There's no pressure, but sharing can be good. And you never know – us old codgers might even have a solution.'

Holly's mouth twitched with the threat of a smile. 'I don't know what I ever did to deserve you.'

'I hope that's meant as a compliment,' Dad joked.

'Of course,' Holly said, her voice still sullen. 'You're always looking out for me. And all I've ever been is a dick.'

'Language,' Mum scolded.

'Sorry.' Holly swallowed, the threat of tears finally past. 'It's true, though.'

'We beg to differ, but then we might be a little biased. Considering we made you and all,' Mum replied.

Dad moved his hand to her shoulder and gave it a squeeze. 'Now, how can we help? If you've murdered someone, your mum's a dab hand with a shovel.'

Holly let out a stuttered laugh. 'No shovels needed. Not yet, anyway.'

'That's good news,' Dad said, dropping his hand to his side. 'I've not had time to clean the shed this summer and I don't know if we can actually reach the shovel.'

'It's in the greenhouse, Harry. I was using it for the azaleas last week.'

Dad nodded, clearly relieved to know it was at least accounted for.

Holly swooped on the chance to change the subject. 'Is that the new one by the pond? It's lovely, Mum.' She wandered off, following the path again.

'It is. I have another to plant this week, if you fancy helping?' Mum replied, keeping pace at her side.

'I'd love that.'

'We could chat then, if you're still feeling sad?'

Holly sighed, closing her eyes as she shook her head. She didn't want to worry her parents. She'd put them through enough in the last few months. 'It's just heart stuff.'

'Heart stuff?' Dad repeated.

'Yeah, as in I like someone and they don't like me back.'

'Ah,' her parents chorused.

They walked in silence for a few steps before Dad piped up: 'So, who's that then?'

'Jen.'

Mum and Dad exchanged looks. Mum spoke first. 'Jen from next door?'

'So, she likes you and you don't like her back?' Dad added, seeking clarity.

Holly shook her head. Was he not listening? 'No, other way round.'

More looks.

'What's all the glancing about?' Holly asked with a confused laugh.

'It's just,' Dad said, looking increasingly bewildered. 'We've seen how she looks at you. The way the two of you are together. We'd just assumed the whole fake-dating thing had progressed. We're not blind,' he chuckled.

'Well, clearly you need to visit your other neighbours and get your eyes tested, because she's made it perfectly clear she only sees me as a friend.'

'Hmm.' Dad wasn't convinced.

Holly let a wavering sigh escape. It was one thing to battle her own doubt, but she didn't need her parents throwing further suspicion into the ring. All it was did was torture her, her mind running the same circles again and again and again. It was time to face the facts and accept the truth.

'She tells me nearly every time we meet that she doesn't want a relationship and that what we have is purely friendship.'

'In those many words?' Dad asked.

'Yep.'

Silence descended once more as a lady and dog passed in the opposite direction. Thankfully there were no sticks to jump.

'You know,' Mum said, looking to Dad as if for approval. 'I don't think we've ever told you the full story of how we met.'

'At the bank's Christmas party. You've told me plenty of times.'

Mum screwed her face up. 'Not quite. That's the ending, yes, but there's a little bit before that.'

'Really?' Holly's brow arched.

'So,' Dad began, taking the reins. 'As you know, we were

both mortgage advisers at the same bank, before I became manager.'

'Yes.' Where is this going?

'Well, it wasn't exactly love at first sight. For your mum, at least.'

'Harry,' Mum chided. 'You're making me out to be the villain, one sentence in.'

'Sorry,' he conceded with a chuckle. 'It was my fault. You see, when your mum started at the bank, I was engaged to someone else.'

'No, you were not!' Holly blurted, so loud the surrounding trees emptied of birds.

'It's true,' Mum said, sounding wistful.

'I'm not overly proud of it, but the heart wants what it wants. I knew as soon as I saw your mum that I couldn't marry Helen, so I broke it off.'

'Six months later he admitted that he liked me, but I'd never seen him that way. We weren't even really friends, to be honest. I'd not long started and we weren't in the same social circles.'

'So what did you do?' Holly asked Dad.

'Nothing, really.'

'So glad you told me: all my problems are solved,' Holly teased.

'Now, now,' Dad replied with a hoarse little laugh. 'The moral of the story is that it pays to be honest. If I hadn't told your mum how I felt she never would have even considered me.'

'What changed your mind, then?' Holly asked, peering around Dad to see her mother's face.

'It was the Christmas party and I'd had a few Babychams. I figured, why not? If we don't click it will be a fun one-night stand.'

'Mum!' Holly exclaimed. She'd never heard her mum speak like that.

'Well, it's the truth.'

'I can see why you've never told me the full story now.' Holly's cheeks burned.

'But you see my point now?' Dad asked, looking embarrassed too.

'Kind of.'

'You need to be honest with her. What did we always tell you?'

'I have no idea. I'm still processing the whole Babycham thing.'

Mum giggled before turning serious, wagging her finger in time with her words to emphasise her point. 'Liars always get caught.'

'Meaning?' Holly asked, confused.

'You can't tell Jen you just want to be friends when really you don't.'

'I wasn't going to tell her anything.'

'Holly, we didn't tell you this just for you to miss the point entirely,' Dad jibed.

'Honesty is the best policy. Got it.' Holly's eyes widened, a question bobbing to the surface of her mind. 'What about poor Helen?'

'She's happily married with four children,' Dad stated, pleased to prove she had a good ending.

'So it worked out for her too,' Mum added.

'Guess I need to be honest, then,' Holly said with a huff.

22

'Yeah, she's totally ghosting you,' Ryan said, and received a punch in the arm from Chloe for his honesty. 'Ow, what? I'm just telling the truth.'

'I know, but sometimes the truth needs a little padding,' Chloe said, giving his arm a stroke where she'd hit it. It was only light; he would live.

Jen tilted her head back and stared at the ceiling. She'd managed a five-mile run before conceding she couldn't literally run from her problems and needed to head home. Being alone felt like a bad choice, so she was currently sprawled over Chloe's armchair, third-wheeling the couple's movie night. 'It's true, but,' she said, thrusting a finger in the air. 'Do you think it's because she knows that I like her?'

The sound of the TV filled the room as neither dared to answer.

Jen shifted, her attention fixed on Chloe. 'Clo, come on, be honest.'

Chloe shook her head, her eyes pleading for reprieve. With a sigh she caved. 'Okay, yes. Going by what you told us, I think you've fucked it.'

'Urgh,' Jen groaned, slamming her head back against the chair's arm.

'I dunno,' Ryan said, giving his stubble a scratch. 'I mean, I can't see why else she would be ghosting you, but I don't think you were that bad. I think you should message her again, outright ask if you've done something to annoy her.'

Chloe looked at him with disgust. 'She can't double text again. Are you mad?'

'She needs to know!' he exclaimed, gesturing his empty palms towards Jen.

'But she made it obvious. Why else do you think she would be ignoring her?'

'I don't think it was obvious,' Ryan mumbled as he downed a good glug of his drink.

'How can it be more obvious than "It would take a special person for me to date again" to be followed with "and you're pretty special"?' Chloe asked, incredulous.

Jen pulled a face. 'The way you say it makes me sound like a total smooth talker. I might have paraphrased a little there.'

'What? How?' Chloe's face dropped.

'I don't remember the specifics, but it wasn't run-on sentences like that. Stuff happened in-between. But it felt obvious at the time.'

'It felt obvious,' Chloe repeated as if in a dream, taking the change of events in. 'So. Let me get this straight. You said, "I don't want to date anyone" and then five hours later you followed it up with the last part?'

'Right. Not that bad, but yeah, there was a sizeable gap.'

'Jen!' Chloe wailed, swatting the air like she might have been able to reach her bestie's leg. Lucky for Jen she was too far. 'And then you carry on like that yesterday? The poor girl probably has whiplash.'

'See, Jen needs to text again. Get a straight answer.' Ryan looked pleased with himself.

'He's right. I can't feel like this forever.'

Chloe considered it as she walked to the kitchen to get a refill. 'It's a risk, pal. You sure you don't want wine?'

'No, I feel sick.'

'Lordy. I've never seen you like this,' Chloe said, plonking herself back onto the sofa.

'It's like,' Jen whined, hands gripping her stomach. 'Everything hurts. I feel sick. I'm full of energy and I want to be pacing, but equally I just want to be in my bed with the covers over my head. I hate it.'

Chloe looked at Jen like someone might study a rare animal at the zoo. 'It's so weird seeing you like this. You're properly in love, aren't you?'

'Less of the L-word, please. Ryan already thinks I'm a psycho.'

'I never said nothing,' he countered with a smile.

Chloe set her glass on the coffee table before venturing over to Jen's side. 'What can I do to make you feel better?' she asked, crouching level with Jen.

'Invent a time machine and let me do over yesterday. Or better still, stop me going to the stupid Lovefest thing altogether.'

Chloe stroked the top of her best friend's head. 'I would If I could, Jen Jen.' She planted a peck on Jen's forehead. 'But alas, that's just outside my skill set.' She headed back to Ryan.

'So, we definitely not doing the second text?' he asked, putting an arm around Chloe as she got comfy again.

'We?' Jen queried.

'Yeah, this a group mission now.'

Jen liked Ryan. She'd seen Chloe smitten before, but it felt different this time. He was a genuinely nice bloke, unlike the arseholes Chloe usually went for. Jen hoped she kept him.

'Hypothetically speaking,' Jen ventured, pointing to thin air again. 'If I did, what would I say?'

'Personally, I would just ask if I did something wrong,' said Ryan.

'Really?' Chloe asked, looking shocked. 'Do you not think that's a little forward?'

'Nah. Why play games?'

Chloe pursed her lips, giving her head a little wiggle as if to agree.

'So just: did I do something wrong? That's it? Nothing else?'

'Not needed,' Ryan replied, slicing the air with a level hand as if it was the most logical solution in the world and there was no reason to question it.

Could she, though? What if Holly wasn't ghosting her? She'd look desperate as fuck. Double-texting was one thing, but being so forthright was another.

Jen looked at her phone again. Holly had read the message when she'd sent it this afternoon. Five hours later and there was still nada back.

She hated feeling this needy. It was a new emotion, and one she didn't want to get used to.

'Right. Ryan, I'm going to do it.'

Chloe bolted upright. 'Jen, I'm being serious, I don't think you should.'

'No, Ryan's right. Why play games? I need to know what's going on.'

Chloe let out a frustrated sigh. 'And what if she says she doesn't like you back?'

'I'm not going that far. I just want to know why she's giving me the silent treatment.'

'Okay. Worst case scenario: she says it's because you have feelings and she doesn't. What will you say to that?'

'I'll say. . .' Jen paused, weighing up her options. 'I'll say, okay. Cool.'

'Pffft.' Chloe leaned back into the sofa cushions, her arms crossed.

'I need to know. We have our date in a few days – I can't go on that without knowing what's going on.'

'Will it not be a bit bloody awkward either way?'

Jen shrugged. 'Well then, what's the harm?'

'This is going to end in disaster,' Chloe said, her voice sing-songy.

'If it was me and you, I'd want to know what I'd done wrong,' Ryan admitted.

'Yeah, but that's different. We're dating.'

'Right, I've sent it.' Jen said, stuffing her phone under the nearest cushion.

'No, you did not.' Chloe bolted upright once more, fear streaking her features.

'Yep, done and dusted, no taking it back.' Jen's heart hammered. She'd felt sick before, but now it was like she was on a choppy boat.

Chloe huffed as she slammed back into the cushions. 'Well, shit in my pocket and call me Derek. I need more wine.' She guzzled half the glass before speaking again. 'Did you really send it?'

'Yes,' Jen groaned. 'Oh crap, my phone just vibrated.'

Chloe and Ryan leaned forward in unison, their mouths hanging open.

She couldn't look. She'd expected Holly to take ages, a little more time to prepare herself. This was too quick.

'Well?' Chloe urged.

'Tell us what she's said,' Ryan pleaded.

Jen took a deep breath. 'I don't want to look.'

'If you don't, I will,' Chloe said, getting to her feet.

'Steady on. Right,' she grabbed her phone with a shaking hand as she puffed her cheeks out, her breath snagging. 'Okay. Fuck.' Jen's heart skipped a beat on reading the message. The bottom fell out of her world.

Chloe's face dropped, weighted with concern. 'What did she say?'

'Shit, not good, eh?' Ryan said, sounding super guilty.

Jen coughed, hoping she could keep her voice level. She was never much of a crier, but it was a real possibility right now. She tilted her eyes to the roof, warding tears off. 'It says: *You've done nothing wrong. Lines have gotten blurred and we're not on the same page any more. Just trying to get my head around it. Can we still be friends?*'

'Fuck,' Ryan said, the word lasting a few syllables longer than usual.

'Told you it was a bad idea,' Chloe said to Ryan.

'Well, at least I know now.' Jen was grateful to know, but it didn't stop her body going numb. The world was in slow motion, everything taking an age to process. She barely knew this woman, and yet it felt like her heart had just been ripped in two.

'Sorry,' Ryan muttered.

'I need to reply now or it's going to be in my head all night. What should I say?'

'I think I've done enough damage. I'm off to get a refill,' Ryan replied, and disappeared to the kitchen with his empty wine glass.

Chloe patted the empty space on the sofa. 'Come here.'

Jen didn't need to be asked twice. She scampered over and cuddled into Chloe's shoulder, her best friend hugging her close.

'It's going to be okay,' Chloe mumbled into the top of Jen's head.

'I know. But it still hurts.'

'Let's get really, really drunk when Ryan and I come to the cocktail night.'

'Sounds good.' The truth was, she didn't think she could stomach alcohol right now. Or ever again. Her belly felt like it was on a spin cycle.

Ryan rejoined them on the sofa, squeezing in beside Jen.

'Want me to get you ice cream or something?'

'Ice cream?' Chloe asked, her tone dripping with disgust.

'Aye, that's what girls are always eating in the movies when they get sad.'

'That's like pillow fights, is it not? Not an actual real-life thing. At least not for me. Do you want ice cream, Jen?'

'Nah,' was all she could muster.

This was exactly what she'd worked so hard to avoid for the last three years. Maybe she wasn't as in control as she thought; maybe her heart called the shots. She couldn't have dodged this bullet even if she'd tried. All this time she'd thought she was the one building the walls, but all along her heart was the one playing doorman.

Well, it knew now. Play shitty games, win shitty prizes.

23

Holly trudged up the stairs, each one harder to climb than the last.

Deliveries were nearly done for the day, but when she'd seen the name ping up as her next destination she'd had to fight the urge to dump the remaining orders and do a runner.

Chloe.

Jen's reply last night was the final straw and she wasn't embarrassed to admit she'd had a good cry in her room. The tears had helped ease the pain, but like all good band-aids, the feeling was only temporary.

It simply said: *Yeah, sure. Take all the space you need.*

Whatever reply she'd been expecting, it wasn't that. So calm and casual, like she'd known Holly's little secret for a while and already come to terms with it. She and Chloe had probably had a good chuckle over it.

Today wasn't so bad. She'd woken braced for change. Still, it was strange not waking up to Jen's usual messages. Holly had kidded herself it was just one of Jen's days off: she always texted closer to eleven on those. *See, you could never work. She's not a morning person.*

It had got harder to pretend as the day went on, and for the first time since she'd returned, Holly found herself noticing how little action her phone actually got. No one from London had been in touch since she left. Phones work both ways, but she was the one who'd been a mess. You soon find out who your real friends are when you hit rock bottom.

She'd spent the morning lazing around the house, a piece of toast hanging out of her mouth as she culled London people on social media. It was natural they'd prioritise their friendships with Shona when Holly was this far north, but she hadn't expected to be forgotten so quickly. Maybe she wasn't on their minds in the first place.

Old Holly would have let it sink a bad mood deeper, but today it was invigorating. *Bye! Sayonara!* No further ties to the old Holly.

She'd surprised herself with some of her answers to the sharing platter questions. Being around Jen made her relaxed, and instead of overthinking every little thing, walking on eggshells so as not to upset her partner, she found herself just answering. The audacity! Yes, she wanted kids. Yes, she had imagined her perfect wedding. No, she hadn't been to her dream holiday destination yet. Were omelettes a stupid last meal? Not to Holly. Yes, Jen might have joked about some of her answers, but in a way that made Holly feel listened to, not ridiculed. And she'd teased back, only for Jen to gratefully receive. Holly had dreams. Holly had opinions. And they damn well mattered, too.

Mid-afternoon, she was ready to channel this new energy into something productive, so she entertained herself with business research, scribbling ideas down like a madwoman and poring over the books she'd been gifted. She'd never even dared to write her designs down before, never mind the dreams beyond that, for fear of Shona seeing and mocking her. Now though, she had a five-year plan. Well, the start of one. It was all just a matter of putting the first steps into action.

She was a live wire today, a growing fire in her belly. Yes, it was mainly fuelled by a need to distract herself, but there was also a feeling of balance. She was capable, she was worthy: she just needed to damn well get on with things.

She understood Dad's intentions, but she was sick of having someone else call the shots. Now would be on her terms, not on someone else's plan – waiting until the moment was right for anyone but her. She'd done enough of that in the last decade. This was her time, and she was ready to seize control.

If Jen eventually liked her, fair game. But she wasn't going to delay her own dreams.

Holly paused on the stairs to Chloe's flat, letting her legs rest a little and hoping her heart was only going a mile a minute because of the climb, not the potential of who was upstairs.

She remained on the step. *What if Jen's there?*

Or worse, what if she wasn't? Should she go say hello? No. She'd just told her she had feelings and then she's going to show up at her door? *That doesn't look weird.*

Holly was dreading the date this week. She'd made it super awkward. Why couldn't she have waited until after Lovefest? Too late now.

An intimate evening of whisky and chocolate tasting. *Really? You couldn't have waited a week, Hols?* Something told her Jen would be civil. If anyone was going to make it awkward it would be Holly. What worried her the most was

how she would feel when she saw Jen. It was fine when
there was distance, but in the flesh? How could she be
friends who someone who drove her so wild? She'd all but
made up her mind the friendship would be over with
Lovefest.

Holly tensed her jaw and set off. *Let's make this quick.*

Far too fast for her liking, Holly was at Chloe's door.
Today's stuffy weather had her hot and bothered. She
probably looked crap. She pulled at her long-sleeved top
and adjusted her shorts.

A final breath and three hard knocks. Showtime.

Holly looked at Jen's door. *Please don't see me.*

After what felt like an age, the door creaked open to
reveal Chloe's beaming smile.

'Hey, Chloe. Hamper for you,' Holly said, already
turning to leave as she handed it over.

'Hey, wait.' The redhead leaned on the door frame,
resting the hamper on her hip.

Holly turned with the speed of a depressed sloth. 'Yep?'

'Can we, like, chat quickly? I promise, one minute. I
know you're busy.'

Holly faltered, hands in her shorts pockets. 'I have a lot
to do, Chloe.'

'Honest, one min. We could be done by now.'

No point in delaying the inevitable. Holly stole a final
look at Jen's door, just to be sure this wasn't some weird
ambush. 'Yeah, okay.'

Chloe pushed off the door frame. 'Great – not out here,
though. In you come.'

Chloe's flat was the mirror image of Jen's, but looked like
it probably hadn't been redecorated in a while. The kitchen
looked old and worn, despite seeming well-cared-for. A
picture pinned to the fridge caught her eye. Jen and Chloe at

a festival, cheeks smeared with face paint. Seeing Jen's smile made her stomach ache.

Holly lightly knocked her knuckles against Chloe's breakfast bar to expel a little of the nervous energy that was threatening to make her knees shake.

'Jen showed me your text,' Chloe said, her back to Holly as she placed the hamper on the counter.

Great. How fucking embarrassing.

Chloe continued, slowly walking to face Holly on the other side of the bar. 'I just want Jen to be happy—'

'So do I.'

'—and I've never seen her like this before. She's like a different person with you.'

'Okay?' Holly replied, confused about where this was going.

'She would kill me if she knew I was talking to you about this,' Chloe said with a wobbling laugh, as if she was as nervous as Holly. 'I just want to know: is there no chance, like, even the smallest one, you'll ever see her as more than a friend?'

'Me?' Holly asked, positive she'd heard Chloe wrong.

'Yeah, do you think, maybe with time, there might be a chance?'

'A chance that I'll like Jen? As more than a friend?' Holly repeated, really needing some clarity. Her heart stuttered. Was this a real conversation, or had she finally lost it?

'Yeah,' Chloe replied, her voice soaked in uncertainty. She ran a hand over her hair, buying time. 'I know you don't see her the way she does you. I just want to know if that could ever change,' She shook her hands in the air like she could dismiss what she'd just said and vanish the conversation from existence. 'You know what? I'm meddling. Sorry. I shouldn't have asked.'

Chloe's eyes met Holly's for a split second before she busied herself with grabbing two wine glasses from the cupboard, placing them by the hamper.

Holly couldn't move. Her brain had turned to mush. Everything tumbled into one. There was no sense in the world anymore. Did she even understand English?

'Jen likes me?' The words spilled out of her mouth, losing their spaces.

It was Chloe's turn to freeze. 'Isn't that what your message was about?'

'Erm, no. She's made it perfectly clear she isn't looking for a relationship.'

'I'm so confused,' Chloe said, joining Holly back at the breakfast bar.

'So am I. Jen likes *me*?' she asked, pointing to herself in case Chloe was getting her confused with the fridge or the kettle. 'That doesn't make any sense.'

'How?' Chloe's eyes said she was still catching up too.

'She told me only two days ago she wasn't looking for anything.'

'I think there's been a misunderstanding,' she replied, her features hinting that she was starting to put the puzzle together.

Holly shook her head, waving a hand in the space between them. 'She said, more than once, "I'm not looking for a relationship." How could I misunderstand that?'

Chloe sighed. 'Jen's a master at protecting herself. She hasn't let anyone in since Alison; she always has her guard up, so things don't come out like they should.' She paused, adding her final point with a chuckle. 'She's also a fucking idiot.'

Holly didn't find it funny. 'I'm not buying it. No one goes

three years thinking one way and then changes their entire perspective after three weeks.'

'Yeah, well, she didn't know you until three weeks ago.' Chloe's eyes said she meant it.

This wasn't how this delivery was meant to go.

Holly felt sick, her stomach twisted with excitement, her heart racing. This was a lot to take it. She needed air, and lots of it.

'I need to go. I still have loads of deliveries to do,' she stated, not giving Chloe the chance to protest.

She followed her into the hall, calling after Holly as she unlocked the door. 'Can you just go speak to her?'

Holly shook her head. It was all she could manage for fear of throwing up.

24

Jen studied the frozen pizzas, indecision rife. In the grand scheme of things, the choice meant nothing. But right now, it was all she had to focus on – the other option being a full-scale freakout.

A little over an hour ago, the highlight of her evening would be finishing the bottle of Sauvignon Blanc she'd just started. That was, until Chloe chapped at her door.

The rest was a blur.

Before Jen knew it she was taking a walk to the shop, attempting to mentally prepare herself and calm her nerves.

Her body buzzed.

Was this really happening?

Holly had messaged not long ago, asking if she'd spoken to Chloe. Then came the nondescript reply about popping round for a chat.

Jen looked at the pizzas for the thousandth time. She couldn't go own brand, she knew that much, but settling on a base type was impossible. Personally, she liked deep-dish, but what if Holly liked a skinny Italian?

Her heart skipped.

Holly liked her. It felt like she'd won the lottery.

Jen flicked her phone out of her pocket, realising she should probably text her, just in case deliveries were nearly done.

Just at the shop – you want anything? Getting you a pizza. Guess you'll not have eaten?

It all felt so casual. Surely there should be trumpets, a fanfare, some sort of grandiose soundtrack to all this?

Her phone buzzed. Jen furrowed her brow at Holly's reply:

I'm also at the shop. What shop?

Jen fired back:

Morrisons. You?

She picked up a deep-dish pizza and tucked it under her arm as Holly's reply came through:

What aisle?

Looking both ways confirmed she was alone. Was Holly here?

Pizza. You?

Wine. Meet me in the middle?

Jen slid her phone into her pocket, her gaze unmoving from the fogged-up freezer, inches from her nose. They were really going to do this. See each other for the first time, the first time truthfully as themselves, in the middle of the bloody supermarket.

Her heart hammered.

She flinched as her phone vibrated: a call incoming. Holly.

'Hey,' Jen said, her voice breathy.

'Hey.'

Silence.

'What's up?' Jen ventured, certain she should be moving already, but her legs had forgotten how to work.

'I can't see you. Are we in the same one?'

'I'm still at the pizza. One min.'

A few short steps and she was in the middle aisle. Ahead, in the centre of the empty aisle, was Holly, facing the other way as she looked for Jen. Wine tucked under one arm, a bouquet of flowers in her hand. At the sight of her, Jen's breath caught in her throat.

'Turn around.'

'Huh?'

'Turn around,' Jen repeated, biting on her bottom lip in an attempt to keep emotion under wraps.

Holly turned, her face lighting up. 'Hey.'

'Hey yourself.'

Without breaking eye contact Jen slipped her phone away, Holly mirroring the move.

It felt like forever until they were finally together, only inches apart.

'Hey,' Holly repeated, quiet like they were having to sneak about.

'Hey.'

'You got everything you need?'

'I thought you'd be hungry after your deliveries,' Jen replied, gesturing with the pizza box.

Holly nodded and Jen watched the rise and fall of her chest.

She wanted nothing more than to kiss her, but now wasn't the place or the time.

'Home?' Jen asked, sticking to the low volume rule.

Another nod.

Just like that, they were off, heading for the self-checkouts. Holly found her voice on the way, their pace gathering speed the closer they got to the exit. 'I thought your reply was weird.'

'Huh?'

'I spilled my guts out and you just replied about taking space.'

'It was hardly gut-spilling,' Jen teased, scanning the items through at record speed. The beacon above the till flashed red, needing approval for the booze.

'Eh, excuse me. It was near enough.' Holly tugged at the hem of Jen's jacket. There was a pause before she searched the periphery for staff. 'Why's no one coming?'

Jen went on tiptoe, scanning the shop floor. The lady at the checkout was too busy serving to even make eye contact.

They'd been here years.

'I thought you didn't like me,' Jen said, still looking for staff. Where the hell was everyone?

'You were the one saying you didn't want a relationship.'

Jen paused her search for help, shifting her focus back to Holly's brown eyes. 'I can see why that might have been confusing.'

'Ya think?' Holly replied, pulling a face. 'Surely there can't just be one person working in the whole fucking shop?'

The universe was definitely having a good laugh at their expense. Jen did a quick sweep of Holly, taking in her gorgeous legs and the way her baggy top accentuated all the right places. 'I've got booze at home. I can order us a pizza. Let's just go.' She grabbed her hand, Holly's fingers instinctively lacing with hers.

She didn't budge when Jen moved away. 'But your flowers.'

'It's the thought that counts.'

Jen gave another gentle tug and Holly followed. It wasn't long before they were in the main foyer and passing security. There was no denying the urgency to their step or the giddy look on their faces.

At least, that was, until they went through the first set of automatic doors.

The muggy heat hit, then the mist from the rain.

'Fuck,' Jen groaned, stopping in her tracks. The heavens had opened and torrential rain battered the flagstones outside.

Holly gripped Jen's hand tighter. 'It'll pass.'

'I can't wait.'

An old man lingered by the open door, his shopping bags discarded by his feet. He snagged Holly's gaze as she assessed the weather. 'Hope you brought your brolly, lass.'

Jen watched as Holly smiled, noticing the shift in the brunette's eyes as she switched gears from carnal Holly to small-talk Holly. 'No such luck tonight. Looks like I'll be getting soaked.'

Thunder rumbled overhead and the old man shuddered. 'Won't last long,' he said, looking to the sky.

Jen didn't want to wait; she'd done enough of that already. 'Where you parked?'

Holly nodded to the right. 'Just up by the trolley park. You?'

'I walked.'

Holly smirked. 'Looks like you're the one getting soaked then.'

Jen walked them towards the door. 'Will we go for it?'

Holly's chest wavered as she took a deep breath, her eyes wanton again as they dragged the length of Jen's body. 'Yeah. Ready?'

'You lead, I'll follow.'

Jen braced herself, ready for the deluge. A few short strides and it was like stepping into a shower. Fuck, it was cold. Two seconds and she was soaked to the bone, her hair clinging to her scalp as they ran.

Lightning flashed and they jumped into the car, the doors slamming as they collapsed into the seats.

Holly's eyes locked with Jen's.

Time to finish what they started two days ago.

Holly's lips crashed into Jen's, hungry and unapologetic. The initial frenzy sated, they relaxed, finding a rhythm as Jen brought a hand to Holly's jaw, pulling her closer.

For a second Jen forgot breathing was a necessity, preferring to focus on the way Holly's lips felt pressed to hers.

A moan echoed and Jen didn't know if it was from herself, Holly, or both, as their tongues intertwined. If it was her, it was from frustration; she wanted to be closer, but the damn confines of the car wouldn't allow it. To be fair, though, she could be right on top of Holly and it still wouldn't feel close enough right now.

She scooted nearer, her knees jarring on the gearstick, and pushed Holly back.

Holly responded with a smile, their lips still pressed together as she spoke. 'This is so much more fun when I'm not overthinking things.'

'You're telling me.'

The rain battered the car, and the world of Holly and Jen was once more illuminated by lightning. Jen didn't even flinch when thunder clapped right above them.

Holly did, though. 'Holy shit, that's close.'

Jen comforted her the only way she knew how: by sliding a hand under Holly's top, resting it at the bottom of her ribcage, not sure if she could go further and trust herself to stop. Her mouth explored Holly's neck, marking its journey to her collarbone with slow kisses.

Holly's hand gripped Jen's joggers, pulling her in.

The handbrake jammed into her knee. 'Ow, fuck,' Jen groaned, trying to reposition herself and failing.

'Let's get back to yours,' Holly said, her voice lower than Jen had ever heard.

She'd expected a slow night with Holly, maybe a movie after they'd had a chat. Not seriously contemplating if she could get away with touching her in the car park of Morrisons.

Jen stilled, her hand unmoving on Holly's ribcage, unwilling to lose the ground she'd gained but knowing it was for the greater good.

'Let's make it quick,' she said, rising level with Holly.

Holly's mouth grew into a grin, her brown eyes darker than usual. One last lingering kiss, then Jen stole herself away, clicking in her seat belt to prevent further temptation.

She ran a hand over her sodden hair, sweeping it back. 'Fuck, I'm so wet.'

Holly shot her a devilish smile as she reversed the car. 'Home in five, don't you worry.'

Jen nibbled her bottom lip, fighting the urge to expand on the joke. She was already fit to pop; talking about it wouldn't help.

The windscreen wipers worked overtime, doing little to clear the glass as they sat at the lights. The storm didn't show any sign of letting up soon.

'Imagine if we'd waited,' Jen said, eyes fixed on the traffic lights.

'That guy would have got a show.' Holly paused for a beat before talking again. 'Doesn't feel real, does it?'

'Not one bit.'

Holly's leg jiggled with nervous energy. 'Is it just me or has this been red forever?'

'Definitely taking longer today.' Jen traced two fingers

along the outside of Holly's thigh, her skin still slick from the rain, the blonde's digits gliding lazily to the edge of Holly's shorts. 'You have no idea how much I wanted you on Sunday.'

Holly turned to face Jen, her leg settling. 'Not half as much as I wanted you.' She ducked for a kiss, only to be stopped by Jen's voice.

'Green light.'

She laughed under her breath. 'Probably for the best. I don't think I'll be able to stop again.'

'Why didn't we do this sooner?'

Holly scoffed, pulling a face as she leaned over and batted the passenger sun visor down. 'You need a mirror? There's one there.'

'Hey,' Jen whined back, playfully grabbing at Holly's leg. 'I deserve that, though. I thought I was being obvious.'

'Obvious?' Holly barked between laughter. 'Jen, baby. Oh no, no, no. This has been a mess.'

'Really? Cause to me it felt super obvious.'

Holly stole a look before returning her eyes to the road. 'Are you sure you've not mixed the word up with something French that means the complete opposite?'

Jen crossed her arms, her jacket squelching, and pretended to be huffy. 'My flirting might need some work.'

'You can practice on me all you like now.' They turned onto Skirving Street, Jen's flat just around the corner. 'Right, shout if you see a space.'

'Here? We're miles away.'

'I know, but parking is crap at yours. I don't have the patience to drive about.'

'Me neither.'

They reached the bottom of Skirving Street, still spaceless. 'Do you want to go in? Save you getting soaked if I have to park way down here,' Holly said, indicating up Tantallon Road.

This felt so normal, so nonchalant, like they both weren't focused on the moment after they crossed the threshold of Jen's flat and tore each other's clothes off. Jen's core tightened, getting wetter.

'I'm not going anywhere without you.'

JEN WAS happy to be the one with the keys. She didn't know how Holly was being so calm. If it was the other way round she would be pawing away, not standing hugging herself, one eye on Chloe's door, like Holly was.

A puddle of water surrounded them on the landing, having taken a fresh soaking when they legged it from the car. It was going to feel great to get these clothes off, regardless of how it happened.

After what felt like a lifetime, the key turned in the lock, the door of Jen's flat tumbling open. She stepped aside, letting Holly go first.

Jen shimmed her jacket off as the flat door trundled shut with a click. She let the clothing fall to the floor, unwilling to waste another second.

In a heartbeat she closed the gap and pinned Holly to the wall, finally losing the distance that had kept them apart all this time.

Holly's breathing filled her ears, her own chest keeping pace.

'Fuck,' Jen moaned, her hands back under Holly's top. She ran her hand the length of Holly's torso, her muscles stiffening under Jen's touch as she followed the curve of her hips and waist, until she reached the wire of her bra. Jen's thumbs ran over her breasts. Holly's nipples were hard nubs, dying to be sucked.

You didn't need to ask Jen twice. She grabbed the hem of Holly's top and pulled it overhead, revealing Holly's aubergine-coloured bra.

'You now,' Holly panted.

Jen sucked on the nape of Holly's neck before taking a quick breather. 'I had planned on wearing something a little sexier for you.'

'Huh?'

Words were useless. Jen crossed her arms and lifted her T-shirt over her head, revealing her sports bra. She'd thought she was going to the shop; she'd meant to come home and change into something more suitable after. Never in a million years did she see this happening.

Flames burned in Holly's eyes. 'We're going to have to chat about what's sexy, because I think you're pretty fucking perfect right now.' With that, she pushed Jen against the wall, the feeling of Holly's appraisal stoking the lust that balled in the pit of her belly. She'd forgotten how much of a turn on it was to see the hunger in a woman's eyes as she took you in for the first time. Could you come from just a look? It certainly felt like Holly had the power.

Jen shuddered at Holly's touch, her muscles tensing as Holly's mouth bit and sucked under her ear, only breaking contact as her hands made light work of Jen's bra, soon to be chucked to the floor. Holly's bra followed.

It had been a lifetime since she'd felt skin against her own like this. She'd been worried she wouldn't remember how to do this, but muscle memory was a wonderful thing. Jen ran her hands up Holly's back, feeling every curve and valley, before resting them on her shoulder blades, pulling her closer. Holly's stiff nipples pressed into Jen's and a fresh flush of desire spread over her. Despite the goosebumps formed by wet clothing and cool air, Jen's skin couldn't be warmer.

Holly's hands found the waistband of Jen's joggers, slipping the soaking wet clothing to the ground. Jen stepped out of them, kicking them away.

Her new favourite thing in the world was feeling Holly's smile as they kissed. The sensation of her lips pulling, like she was fighting it, only to break out into a stupid grin two seconds later.

It was an unmatchable high.

'Can we go to your bedroom?' Holly purred.

'Of course.'

A few fumbling steps, neither wanting to break their kiss, and they were there. Holly pushed Jen onto the bed.

'These need to come off,' she said, pulling at the waistband of Jen's pants.

Jen nodded as Holly guided them off, dropping them to the floor, her eyes fixed on Jen's centre as she bit her bottom lip. There was that look again. Jen fought the urge to groan; she was so aroused that Holly might as well be touching her.

Holly edged forward, but Jen stopped her, a hand gently on her shoulder. 'Not until I can see all of you, too.'

Without losing her gaze, Holly shimmied her shorts and pants off. Jen's eyes drifted south. *Fuck.*

Holly was perfect.

'Is that better?' Holly asked, her thigh pushing hard against Jen's core.

The noise that escaped Jen's throat was indecipherable.

Jen didn't know where to touch first. Holly's boobs were incredible. But then there was her waist, her hips, her bum. Jen wanted all of her, all at once. She'd waited so long for this moment; she deserved to be greedy.

She settled on her bum, gripping a cheek in either hand as Holly's mouth found hers.

'I want to show you what I was thinking about when I touched myself on Sunday,' Holly said, pulling away, just enough so their lips were still touching.

'Yeah?'

Holly sat back, taking a final moment to recline and see Jen as one complete picture, the brunette's face the epitome of content. With a final lick of her lips, she began her journey south.

'I was thinking,' she said between kisses, her breath making Jen's skin tingle, 'what could have happened after Bar Orama, if I'd been a little braver.'

Jen felt so close, Holly's kisses only having reached her navel. It had been three years, but surely she couldn't be on edge already? No. She wanted to savour every second, not come with one touch.

She scrunched her eyes shut, one hand gripping the headboard, the other a pillowcase, and tried to focus on keeping herself together.

Holly stopped just below Jen's belly button. 'I've been wanting to taste you ever since.'

Holly's breath reached her core, heat flitting over her.

'I can already tell this will be better than I ever imagined,' Holly said, her voice sending vibrations through Jen's hard clit.

Jen bit her lip. *I can't come now.*

To Jen's relief, Holly moved lower, her mouth planting slow kisses on her inner thigh, slowly travelling north.

Jen's skin sparked with every kiss. She was close to bursting.

At the top of Jen's thigh, her face so close she could feel

the heat of every breath, Holly stopped. She kissed the crease between Jen's thigh and core.

'Do you want me to touch you now?' Jen didn't need to look to know she was smiling.

'Yes.' The word was a breathless whimper. Three years of repressed desire rushed in her veins, dying to be satisfied.

Holly's tongue ran the length of her core as a hand traced her thigh, the other cupping her bum, bringing her closer.

At Jen's clit she stopped, teasing before running her tongue flat against it.

Jen's back arched; she was dangerously close.

Holly worked, varying her pace, tending to Jen with careful precision. Jen's thighs ached as she fought to regain composure. Her lust was so tightly balled inside, so close to the edge, that half of her was begging for release, the other willing it to last forever.

She aimed for the latter, gripping the pillow tighter with every stroke of Holly's tongue.

'You're amazing,' Holly groaned. Jen couldn't answer, instead her response was lifting her hips, urging Holly deeper.

She was holding it together. Just.

Everything was going to plan until Holly ran her thumb down Jen's wet centre, tracing her lines before sliding two fingers inside her.

FUCK.

Holly matched her tongue's pace with her digits, curling them, finding Jen's G-spot with ease.

Jen pushed her hips hard into the mattress, pleasure building with every thrust.

Why had she avoided this for so long?

Why had she worked so hard to keep other people out?

Because there was no one on earth who could do this but Holly.

As Jen tumbled over the edge, her inner walls clenching around Holly's perfect fingers, she knew there was nowhere else she could be. Every single moment had led to right now. She'd never been so exposed, and yet she'd never felt so strong.

Her back arched, her thighs tightening as a second shockwave tore through her.

For the first time in a long time, Jen was alive.

'FUCK, THIS IS GOOD PIZZA,' Jen said, her mouth full.

'Pizza and sex. I might never leave,' Holly replied, unable to chew for the smile taking over her face.

'Maybe that's the plan.'

They ate in silence for a few minutes, Jen finishing off her slice before speaking. 'Just a shame I never got my flowers.'

Holly leaned over the pizza box on the sofa, wobbling on one hand as she kissed Jen. 'Tomorrow, promise.'

'I was just kidding, don't worry.'

'I wasn't.'

Holly chucked a half-nibbled crust into the box before moving it out the way, onto the floor. She gave Jen's knee a tap. 'Come on, stretch these out, please.'

Jen did as she was told, a quizzical look on her face. It switched to a smile when Holly scooted closer, lacing her own legs over Jen's.

Face to face, there was no way this smile was going anywhere.

Jen's heart rippled as she watched Holly get comfy. She

looked perfect in one of Jen's T-shirts and her pyjama shorts. She could never wear either again; it wouldn't be fair to do them such an injustice after experiencing Holly's flawless form.

She cupped Holly's calf with her hand, stroking her skin with her thumb. 'You really had no clue I liked you?'

Holly shook her head, her hands settling on Jen's hips.

'I thought I'd blown it on Sunday,' Jen replied. Was it possible to live on a sofa? She never wanted to leave this little bubble.

'How come?'

'Playing you that Wallis Bird song, being too touchy-feely, asking questions I probably shouldn't have.' Jen felt heat flush her cheeks.

Holly shifted closer, her hands not moving from Jen. Her face scrunched as she thought. 'The song was a thing? I didn't realise. It was track one on the album,' she said with a shrug. 'Touching – I just thought you were playful. And yeah, the question was a bit much, but I just thought you were weird.' Holly chuckled, giving Jen's sides a squeeze. 'What about me? You really didn't know?'

Jen's turn to shake her head. 'Not a clue.'

'I thought my Lovefest playlist would give it away.'

'Are they about me? I just thought they were love songs. To be fair, though, I wasn't really listening to the lyrics. I was just looking at you.'

'And thinking about omelettes.'

'Mainly the omelettes, yes.'

Holly inched forward, closing the distance between their lips. 'I think it's time I gave you another memory on this sofa.'

25

Holly watched Shawlands fly by from the back of an Uber. The place was hoaching. Last night's storm had breathed new life into the suburb, the sticky hot air now bearable again, and people were back out, soaking up Lovefest activities.

She should be too, but Holly was ten minutes late for her date.

It was her own fault: she didn't have a decent excuse. She'd been fannying about, taking her time getting ready, and before she knew it the minutes had slipped away. She wanted to look good tonight – it felt like her and Jen's first proper date. She'd even stopped by the florists earlier and picked up a bouquet. Yellow and white roses – they'd look nice in Jen's living room, complimenting her colour scheme.

At Jen's request, she'd gone with the same outfit from the improv night. She'd messaged earlier, jesting about today's plans, and hit out with:

Did you know you can see your whole leg when you sit down in that skirt?

To which Holly had simply replied:

Why do you think I wore it?

Holly read the messages Jen had sent after that, feeling slightly on edge at how un-PG they were. Not something to have within eyeshot of a stranger. She couldn't help but grin, so she bit her bottom lip and stared out the window, hoping she didn't look too weird.

Their date was meant to be tomorrow, but Annie had messaged this morning to say their whisky guy was ill and they'd be joining Chloe and Ryan instead. She'd been a bit sad at first, with their final date not being just the two of them, never mind the fact that Jen was hosting it. Until it was pointed out that it meant they could wrap it up as soon as Annie left and go out and do something proper.

That was way more appealing than being stuck for an hour in the company of a man she'd never met.

'You okay in here, love?' the driver asked, pulling in across the road from Jen's.

'That's perfect, thanks.' Holly's stomach twisted with anticipation. Only hours had passed but it had been hellish dragging herself out of bed. She could tell by Jen's face that she was seriously considering the financial ramifications of staying closed today. They had all the time in the world now; there was no point in acting like love-struck teenagers and shirking responsibilities. Plus, after four orgasms in twelve hours, her body could probably go a rest. Talk about one extreme to the other.

Holly knocked on Jen's door; Annie bounded over to unlock it.

'Sorry I'm late,' Holly said, giving a little wave to everyone in the room.

Holly's eyes were set firmly on Jen, who was making no

effort to hide the fact she was checking her out, the blonde's face like a kid in a candy shop. Annie guided her to the side of the counter, and retook her position next to Isaac and his camera.

She handed the flowers to Jen, whose smile was unabashed, but Holly felt a little strange having an audience. Jen kissed her on the cheek, dissolving any discomfort. 'Thank you.'

Annie flashed them a happy but questioning look before speaking. 'Holly, we've just finished Chloe and Ryan's video, so we'll do yours next and let you guys crack on with cocktails.'

'Video?' Holly asked. Was she meant to have prepared something?

Jen shot her a quick look. 'Annie forgot to tell us we were doing a couples' quiz.'

'We did the hamper – we've got this,' Holly said, taking her bag off and putting it under the counter. It was only then she clocked Jen's trousers. The sexy resort shirt had been exciting enough, but team it with black waxed denim and Holly was having palpitations. 'Nice trousers,' she said to Jen as she leaned on the counter beside her. Having an audience really was the worst. All she wanted to do was snog her.

'Thank you,' Jen replied, giving her bum a little wiggle. 'I knew you were bringing your A-game, so I thought I'd better make an effort.'

'Appreciated.'

'Do I sense a change in circumstances?' Annie asked, her focus remaining on the screen as Isaac set up the shot.

'Hmm?' Jen asked, her hands fiddling with the edge of the counter.

Annie pursed her lips, a smile pulling at their edges. 'Hmm, yourself.'

Jen beamed bright red. Holly chose to divert her attention to Chloe. It was more fun to keep people guessing than answer Annie outright. 'So, did you guys enjoy your hamper last night?'

'Oh my God,' Chloe gushed, 'that Brie is amaaazing.'

'And the chilli crackers were ace too,' Ryan added, gesturing with his finger and thumb like a chef.

'Your dad will be relieved to hear that,' Jen said to Holly with a playful grin.

In return she got a quick squeeze in the side. 'Don't mock Crackergate.'

'Right. We ready, ladies?'

'As ever,' Holly replied, making sure her skirt was positioned right and her top was nice and straight.

'It's just quick,' Annie said, sliding a whiteboard and pen from Chloe's side to in front of Jen. 'You write on that. Holly, you say your answers out loud.'

'Got it,' Holly said, ready for action.

Jen twisted to the side, holding the whiteboard close to her chest, out of Holly's sight. 'No cheating, Miss Taylor.'

'As if I would.'

Isaac pointed, signalling action.

'Okay, Holly and Jen, welcome to Lovefest's Couple's Quiz,' Annie said, off-screen. 'Question number one. Holly, what size feet does Jen have?'

Holly's cheeks burst with a snort before pulling a face, revealing she didn't have a clue. 'Crikey.' She looked to her own black boots then to Jen's trainers. She was a five; Jen's looked slightly bigger. Her hands were bigger than Holly's. Just.

'Going to have to rush you for an answer,' Annie said.

'Fii. . . siiii—' Holly started, her eyes narrowed as she tried in vain to read Jen's face.

'Hey, no cheating,' Chloe shouted with a laugh.

'Seven. I'm going with seven.'

'Final answer?' Annie asked.

Holly considered it. 'Yeah, as good a shot as any.'

'Okay. Jen, please reveal your answer.'

Jen sucked on her bottom lip, looking at the camera as she turned her board around, whipping it to face Holly. 'Sorry, Hols.'

'Seven, yass,' Holly exclaimed with a fist pump.

'And I thought that was the easy one,' Annie said with a chuckle. 'Nicely played, Holly. Right, question number two: What was Holly's first impression of you, Jen?'

Holly grinned, hiding a grimace and made a show of biting on her thumbnail. 'Am I to be honest?'

'Depends how you think Jen will answer.'

Chloe pulled a face, her eyebrows wiggling as she read Jen's answer over her shoulder. 'Seems about right.'

Holly thought. *How honest is too honest? How would Jen word this?* 'Okay,' she said, still thinking. 'Jen, the first time we met, and I mean this in the nicest way possible,' she continued, a hand over her heart as she exaggerated a cringing face. 'I thought you were a rude moany cow.'

Chloe snorted, having to put a hand over her mouth to control further giggles.

'Pfft, don't hold back, babes,' Jen replied, fighting her own laughter.

'I'm interested to see this one. Jen, reveal your board,' Annie requested.

Jen turned it, to reveal the word *Rude.*

'I'm so sorry,' Holly said, cringing again as she put a hand on Jen's waist. 'Like, you really were, though.'

Jen spoke over her shoulder to Chloe, 'Who said romance was dead?'

'Probably you,' Chloe shot back with another grunt.

'Hey!' Jen turned back to Holly, putting on her best puppy-dog face. 'It was true, though. Forgive me?'

'I'll consider it.' Without thinking, Holly gave Jen a quick peck on the lips. God, her lip balm tasted good. She couldn't go a whole evening without taking things further.

'Oi, oi,' Chloe goaded.

Holly's cheeks matched Jen's. A few days ago she would have second-guessed kissing Jen, but now it was the most natural thing in the world. Well, in this little room, with people they knew. She wasn't about to snog Jen on the number six bus or whatever. This was Glasgow, after all.

'What's our final question, then?' Jen asked, regaining composure and holding the whiteboard away from Holly.

'Okay, final question. Who do you think will say I love you first? If you've not said it already, of course.' Annie asked with a wink, despite still being off camera.

'Wow. Don't hold back, Annie. Em,' Holly turned the question over. She preferred the shoe one – this was much harder to guess.

Jen's narrowed eyes hinted she was debating, too.

'Were your questions just as hard?' Holly asked Chloe.

'We got *how many kids are you having?*' Ryan replied, his arms draped over his girlfriend's shoulders.

That would have been much easier. Less pressure.

Holly blew out, stalling.

'Ladies, time for an answer,' Annie pressed.

Jen shrugged. 'Fifty-fifty chance.' She scribbled on her whiteboard.

It was far too soon for this carry-on. Did she love her, though? She definitely could over time. Of course. But not less than twenty-four hours after they technically had started dating.

'So, who's going to say *I love you* first?' Holly repeated, still stalling.

'Uh-huh,' Annie confirmed.

Holly tilted her head, looking for an answer in Jen's eyes. It didn't matter.

Not really.

But she didn't want to look like a lovesick twat, or worse, that she didn't care at all.

'Me,' Holly settled on. 'Because Jen is rubbish at saying how she feels.'

Jen lifted her chin, the smile quirking her lips saying she wasn't surprised by that answer. *Phew. Bullet dodged.*

'Right,' Jen said, turning her board round. 'I also put you.'

Holly smiled: was that a good or bad thing? Was it expected of her now? Crikey, this was spiralling. She pushed the thought to the back of her mind.

'Three for three, ladies. Impressive,' Annie beamed.

'Touch and go with the shoes, but I got there in the end,' Holly replied, happy with herself.

'So, what do we get?' Jen asked, leaning over the counter. God, her arse looked good.

Isaac snapped the viewfinder closed. 'Nothing per se, but it's about getting the public vote.'

'The four videos will go online tomorrow and the voting form shortly after, so get sharing if you can.'

'Four?' Holly asked, wondering if she'd missed something else by being late.

'Debbie and Nick have dropped out, but you didn't hear that from me,' Annie replied, putting a finger to her lips.

'Debbie and Nick?' Jen gasped. 'Why?'

Annie shrugged. 'Debbie said she didn't feel a spark and wanted to leave the competition. I felt so sorry for Nick.'

'That sucks,' Chloe said, looking sullen. She gave Ryan a hug.

'I had my money on them to win,' Holly said.

'Hope you didn't bet much,' Jen teased.

'Just goes to show, you can't believe what you see online,' Holly offered.

They'd looked so happy from the start. In Holly's mind, they had been the ones to beat: suddenly the money felt closer than ever.

'So, cocktails then?' Annie asked, clearly trying to move the conversation on before she was asked to spill any more secrets.

'Aye, got some complicated concoctions for Chloe and Ryan to try their hands at,' Jen said, wiggling her eyebrows.

'I can't wait to see this,' Chloe gibed at Ryan.

'Hey, now. Just because you think I make tea the wrong way.'

'How do you make tea?' Jen asked, genuinely curious.

Ryan looked sheepish. 'Milk first, obviously.'

'Milk first? Are you a sociopath?' Holly blurted.

'That ain't right,' Jen said, looking disgusted.

'Told you, babe. Something wrong with you.'

Ryan huffed. 'Heathens, the lot of you.'

'I'm glad we didn't ask that for the quiz, Ryan. I might have had to disqualify you,' Annie joked as she put a notebook in her bag. 'I think that's us. Isaac and I will edit these tonight.'

'Thanks, Annie,' Jen said, moving to the door to unlock it.

'My pleasure.' Annie let Isaac go first, before pausing in the doorway, a mooshy look plastered on her face. 'I'm so glad this worked out for you. Lovefest is a success either way.'

Holly didn't know what to say to that. *Thank you? Any time?*

'You've killed it as usual, Annie,' Jen said, leaning on the edge of the open door.

'I don't know about that. Feels good to have made a difference, though.' With that, Annie was off.

Jen closed the door, checked it was locked, and spun round. 'Let's get this paaartay staaarted!'

Chloe slammed a lime on the counter. 'Ryan, see if I find out you go lime, tequila, salt? We're over,' she joked.

'What? Is that not right?' he replied, pretending to be baffled.

≈

'YOU GO AHEAD – I just need to talk to Holly about something,' Jen said, taking the final crate of miscellaneous cocktail paraphernalia through to the stockroom. She'd kitted out the counter with lots of props, but in reality all they needed were four shot glasses and a cutting board.

Chloe was unconvinced. 'Talk, my arse,' she said with a wink.

Holly's muscles tensed. Had she done something wrong?

Box stashed, Jen locked the front door as she laughed to herself.

Holly didn't move from her spot by the counter. 'Is this because I was late? Sorry.'

'What? No. Of course not.'

What else was there? The moody cow comment?

Jen leaned against the counter, the grin falling from her

face as she looked at Holly. 'You okay? You look like you've seen a ghost.'

'I'm fine,' she lied, her stomach twisting, and not just from tequila. 'What do you want to talk about?'

Jen took her hand in hers, giving it a wee squeeze. 'I was hoping for a snog, but something's up.'

Ah.

She really wasn't used to having a girlfriend who wasn't set on messing with her head.

Holly felt heat rise up her neck. 'I thought you were mad. I've totally gone and killed the buzz now. Sorry.'

Jen watched over Holly's shoulder for a beat, studying the street through the shutters. 'C'mon, let's get away from prying eyes.'

Holly followed Jen to the stockroom. She leaned against the table in the middle, feeling like a prize idiot. Jen straddled her legs, putting her hands on Holly's hips.

She had her serious eyes on again, the ones that could spark fires.

'I bet I can guess who's in your head,' Jen said, kissing Holly's brow. 'And I have a message for her.' She ducked to Holly's ear, her voice a whisper. 'Fuck off.'

Holly's chest heaved with laughter. 'If only it was that easy.' She fixed her focus on the corner of the room, unable to match Jen's gaze. 'Sorry again.'

Suddenly she was back in London, being called out for not trying hard enough with Shona's friends. Or if she did let go and be herself, showing Shona up, saying something that was apparently idiotic or embarrassing. She could never do anything right. Too quiet. Too loud. Too Holly.

'You don't need to say sorry.' Jen wrapped her arms around her, pulling Holly into a tight hug as she kissed her head. 'Did you really think I was mad?'

Holly nodded into Jen's shoulder.

She sighed, and Holly could feel the tenderness in her embrace. She was annoyed at Shona, not Holly. Sometimes it was like Jen was in her head, knowing exactly what she needed, even when Holly was clueless herself.

Holly tensed her jaw, preparing to speak. Her throat was dry but she forced a gulp. 'Old habits die hard, I guess. I know you're not like her.'

Jen's hold didn't waver as she spoke into the top of Holly's head. 'Good. We're team Jen and Holly now. I'm here to build you up, support you. I'm the one cheering you on, not tearing you down. And if life doesn't go to plan and the pieces fall apart, I'm here to hold you until they click back together.' She burrowed her nose further into Holly's hair. 'And you do it for me. Or not. You call the shots, Hols. There's no pressure.'

Emotion welled, as did the tears.

She couldn't cry; the night would be ruined. Instead, she leaned into the embrace, focusing on Jen's shallow breathing. Eventually, it felt safe to talk. 'Why are you so nice to me?'

Jen smiled. 'Because I like you. A lot.'

'A lot, eh?' Holly couldn't help but grin.

'Nearly as much as I like that skirt.'

Holly rose from the safety of Jen's shoulder, meeting her tender gaze. Those eyes could calm a stormy sea with one look, no doubt about it.

'You like this skirt? You haven't mentioned that before,' Holly teased. Tears still lingered but the sight of Jen's cheerful face pushed them back.

'Oh, have I not? Well, let me talk you through it.' Jen stepped back, giving Holly room to widen her stance. She dropped to a squat, pushing the split of the skirt open before running the back of her finger up Holly's bare leg. She spoke as she rose. 'My favourite part is the impressive split, but,' she said, pausing her finger as it reached Holly's inner thigh, 'I guess that's because my actual favourite thing is what's in the skirt. If you get what I mean?'

Holly shuffled her legs wider. 'I think I can take a guess.' She was happy for the distraction; tears were but a memory now.

Jen moved closer, her lips finding Holly's as her finger trailed further north. When she reached Holly's pants, she traced her hand over Holly's thigh and round to her bum, before pulling her closer.

'Can these come off?' Jen asked between kisses, her fingers poised over Holly's underwear. The taste of tequila and lime ghosted Holly's tongue as Jen nipped at her bottom lip.

'Of course.' She'd all but forgotten they were in Jen's stockroom. They could be anywhere right now, safe in their own cocoon. No one else mattered but them.

In a heartbeat Holly's pants were on the floor, pushed aside with her boot as Jen cupped her centre.

She was purposely stalling, driving Holly wild. One minute Holly thought she was going to fall apart and then Jen had her unravelling in a completely different way. That's what Jen did, though. Deflect and protect.

What had she done to deserve this masterpiece of a woman?

'I can already feel how wet you are,' Jen groaned.

'That's what you do to me.'

With that, Jen gently slid two fingers inside Holly.

'Fuck,' Holly moaned, leaning against the table to give Jen a better angle. It squeaked under the unusual pressure, more used to boxes of stock than being a prop for sex.

She'd never had sex in a shop before. The thought of the public being mere feet away made her clit throb, the danger intoxifying. Thank God for the privacy of the stockroom, though. Holly was no exhibitionist.

Jen sucked below Holly's ear as her fingers worked their magic. Holly was already so close; this was going to be quick, but she didn't care. There would be plenty of time for slow and sensual later tonight.

'You feel so good,' Jen mumbled into her neck.

Holly gripped the edge of the table, certain her legs were going to turn to jelly at any moment.

'Jen,' she said between heavy breaths, not bothering to complete the train of thought. It felt so good, the warmth of Jen's soothing words still hot on her skin, stoking the orgasm as it built.

Jen used her thigh for leverage, pushing behind her hand as she drove into Holly, her thumb now massaging Holly's clit.

Two strokes was all Holly could take before she became completely undone.

'Oh fuck,' Holly cried, her voice shattering as a second wave came.

She gently grasped Jen's wrist as she went for a third, panting into her shoulder as she fought to get her breath back. The world shone around them.

'You're going to kill me,' Holly laughed, smiling into Jen's lips as she kissed her.

'I can think of worse ways to go.'

∽

'You sure about this?' Jen asked Chloe as she placed a glass of white wine in front of the redhead. Cal's was jumping tonight; they'd been lucky to get a booth just off the dance floor.

'For sure,' she replied, finishing a pint of water. 'Fun can be sensible.'

'Sensible is four glasses of wine and a tequila?' Holly said with a chuckle. 'I'd love to see you letting your hair down.'

Chloe was on a late shift tomorrow,which meant getting up at nine instead of five. Apparently that would make all the difference. Holly shuddered at the thought. She wasn't downing the wine as much as Chloe and still savoured the luxury of staying in Jen's bed until late afternoon if she really wanted. Just a shame it would be Jen-less.

'It's not much different – you just take out the water breaks. And add a few more shots.' Chloe lifted her wine glass with gusto. 'Right, here's to Lovefest!'

Jen turned to Holly and they chorused a quiet 'Quack, quack.'

Chloe raised an eyebrow as she drank her wine, either really not wanting to know what that was about or too drunk to care.

Jen placed a hand on Holly's knee and gave it a squeeze. 'Isn't it crazy to think we all met here? It seems like a different place.'

Holly looked at the patrons filling the dance floor: a decidedly different crew to the Lovefest attendees. There were no inhibitions tonight, a lot less awkward chat, and a heck of a lot more grinding.

Who would have thought that night would lead to this? She'd been so nervous about coming home, feeling like a massive failure, like this was the beginning of the end. Little did she know it was actually the beginning. Now she was having an amazing night out with two new friends and her girlfriend. If she'd known Glasgow was this good she never would have left in the first place.

Had that night made such a monumental difference for anyone else?

'I wonder if Natalie met anyone?' Holly asked, remembering their lovely chat.

'Aw, did you talk to Natalie too?' Jen asked looking wistful.

'She was great, wasn't she?' Chloe chipped in.

'Well, now I feel left out,' Ryan said with a pout.

'Don't think you were her type,' Jen consoled.

'Holly, I need the loo. Will you come with me?' Chloe asked, shaking her hand in Holly's direction.

'Yeah, sure.' This felt full of agenda.

Shut up, head.

Chloe linked her hand in Holly's and weaved them through the dance floor. To Holly's surprise, Chloe shunned the stairs up to the toilets and took a sharp left to the outside seating instead.

Maybe my head isn't always wrong.

The cold air stole Holly's breath, a stark contrast to the sweaty atmosphere inside Cal's.

Being late in the night, outside wasn't too busy, and Chloe made short work of finding them a seat among the smokers.

'You having a good night?' she asked Holly as she scooted her seat closer.

'Yeah, are you?'

'Amazing.' The air was loaded. Holly's heart picked up pace. 'So.'

'Is this the good intentions chat?' Holly asked, a coy smile pulling at her lips.

'Good intentions chat?'

'Yeah, when you tell me if I hurt Jen you'll kill me.' Holly swooped her skirt over her leg, the chilly night air nipping at her bare skin.

'Ah,' Chloe said, realisation dawning. 'Not quite. I don't think you need it.' There was silence for a second, like Chloe forgot she'd been the one to drag Holly out here. Something clicked. 'No, I just wanted to say thank you.'

'Thank you?'

'Yeah.' She gave Holly's leg a jiggle. The street lights reflected off the hint of tears welling in Chloe's eyes. She focused on the church across the street, avoiding Holly's confused stare. 'You've given me my best friend back.'

It was the booze talking, but her words were anything but false. 'How so?' Holly asked, trying and failing to make eye contact.

Chloe let out a breathy sigh. 'Alison, fuck, Alison. If I ever see her again I will kill her. I will actually kill her.' It was Holly's turn to squeeze Chloe's leg. She continued, 'She fucked Jen up. Like, you can't even imagine. I kind of thought that was it: I've got used to the new Jen, but then you came along and it was like, *ping*,' She mimicked someone flicking a switch. 'The light came back on. Only it wasn't just a light, it was fucking Blackpool illuminations. She's Jen times ten.'

Finally, Chloe turned to Holly, the redhead's tears only just staying put.

Holly gave a half-smile. 'I've not done anything special.'

'It's not about doing anything. You just need to be you.'

Holly exhaled slowly. What do you say to that? 'We've got you to thank for all this.'

Chloe chuckled, the threat of tears lessening. 'It just felt wrong. No one kisses someone like that and doesn't have feelings.'

'I just never thought she'd like me back.'

'Don't worry, I'll be ribbing her forever more about her bloody mixed signals.'

Holly swallowed, feeling like there was still something not being said. This conversation was lovely and she didn't doubt Chloe's sincerity for a heartbeat, but still, you could light a match with the air around her.

'You really needing the loo or do you want to go back inside?' Holly asked, eager to wind things up.

Silence. Chloe chewed her bottom lip. Holly braced herself.

'Holly, we're both looking out for Jen, yeah?'

'Of course. I'm not going to hurt her.'

The church stole Chloe's attention again. She sighed, her breath fractured. 'It's not you I worry about.'

'No?'

'If I tell you something, do you promise not to freak out?'

Too bloody late for that, but okay. 'Of course. What's wrong?'

Chloe rummaged in her bag, finally producing a phone. 'Ryan's phone,' she offered with a half-smile. A few clicks and Facebook popped up. She breathed in, breathed out. Holly's heart picked up pace with every second. 'I'm showing you this because I don't want you seeing it, freaking out, and telling Jen. Okay?'

Holly shook her head. 'Depends what it is.'

'Fair.' Chloe found what she needed and passed the phone to Holly. She pointed at a comment. 'There.'

Holly read it aloud. 'Ae Rae: *Looking good, Jen. But then you always do.*'

Chloe sucked on her top lip. 'She's commented on all your Lovefest pics. She's blocked me and Jen blocked her, so she's not seen it.'

'Is that Alison?'

'Yep.'

Words escaped Holly. She passed the phone back to Chloe, feeling like a deflating balloon. 'Why did you show me that?'

'Because, like I said. I didn't want you seeing that and putting two and two together, telling Jen, worrying something was going on.'

'Should I be worried?'

Chloe's eyes widened. 'No. Course not. She's not been back in three years. Or at least not seen Jen in that time. I just didn't want you thinking Jen has anything to do with her.'

'You're sure about that?' It wasn't that she didn't trust Jen; it was just that Shona had proved that even if you knew someone for nearly half your life, they're still full of surprises. Three and a bit weeks was hardly enough to stake a claim on.

'One hundred and fifty per cent. My main concern is you mentioning her comments to Jen.'

'Why?'

Chloe huffed. 'This is just because she's suddenly seen photos of Jen online. There's been nothing in three years. If Jen finds out Alison's been saying stuff, she will freak out. Has she told you about the debt?'

'A little.'

'Yeah, well. They bought the flat together too. It's fine, she went to a solicitor,' Chloe said, fanning the air between them. 'Alison doesn't contribute, so Jen has a bigger share of the equity, but this shit is hanging over her, you know? I just see her so happy right now, more than she's ever been. Like, a totally different person to the person I met with Alison all those years ago, and I don't want to burst that bubble, yeah? Promise you won't tell her?'

Holly tensed her jaw. This wasn't how she'd expected her night to end. Tonight hadn't just been an emotional roller coaster: it was the whole freaking theme park.

'Yeah, sure.'

26

The next few days were a bit of a blur, in the best possible way. They'd enjoyed Saturday together in Jen's shop, Holly offering to work a full shift even though Jen couldn't pay her. It was a good thing, too, because the shop had been exceptionally busy. Holly was brilliant on the upsell and Jen's eyes had bugged at the day's total.

She'd caught herself slipping into a daydream as she watched Holly with the customers. She was just so natural: there was no pushy sales pitch, no falseness. Just Holly, being Holly. Jen's heart could have burst.

Sunday, they'd somehow managed to be apart during opening hours, with Holly only coming round for tea. Jen had even cooked between their extracurricular activities, much to Holly's amusement. 'Just because my fridge is empty, doesn't mean I don't know my way around the kitchen!' Vegetarian wasn't her forte but Holly was pleased with her attempt at spinach and ricotta cannelloni, and that was all that mattered.

Monday followed with a day in bed, both at terms with

Holly spending the evening with her parents. She'd barely seen them all week.

That was, until Catherine had declared there was more than enough roast dinner for Jen to join them too. And who was she to argue with that?

'This is so weird,' Holly said, adjusting the pillows behind her.

'What is?' Jen asked, propping herself up on one elbow. So this was Holly Taylor's bedroom. When she'd imagined Holly's abode she couldn't have been more wrong. The Taylors lived in a beautiful period property just on the edge of Langside, not far from Shawlands. It was graced with high ceilings, original features, more fireplaces you could shake a stick at, and as the pièce de résistance, Harry had even installed his own bar downstairs.

It was obvious Holly hadn't been back for long; it lacked any real personal presence. But little items remained, proving it had once been her childhood bedroom: pin holes in walls from posters, the sun-faded lilac curtains, and the 80s-chic fitted wardrobe, complete with a vanity unit decorated with old photos, being just a few.

'I dunno. It's just weird, having you in my bed.'

'You've been in my bed all week,' Jen retorted, stealing a quick kiss.

'I know, but,' Holly sighed, placing her hands on her belly and looking at the ceiling. 'I've never had anyone here.'

'No one? What about Shona?'

Holly shook her head. 'Nope. Not even once.'

Jen pulled a face. 'She did meet your parents, right?'

'A few times.'

'In eight years?'

'When we were up north she usually visited her parents.'

'Still.' She could sense Holly's uneasiness, so changed the conversation. 'Funny to think I knew your parents before I knew you. Your dad even had me out for a beer.'

'No he did not!'

'Hand on heart,' Jen replied, placing a palm over her chest. 'I helped him set up the deli's POS system, so he took me for a beer.'

Holly grinned. 'I vaguely remember him saying a lovely neighbour helped them with the till. He forgot to mention how hot they were, though,' she said, turning onto her side to mirror Jen.

'Might have been a bit awkward if he's said that, no?' Jen joked.

Holly wrinkled her nose. 'Yeah, come to think of it. Possibly. They really never mentioned me?'

'If they did it was nothing major. Sorry.'

Holly huffed. 'My fault. Main thing is, I'm here now.'

'That you are,' Jen said, leaning in for another kiss. She didn't make it quick this time.

Just as Jen's hand had found its way to Holly's right breast there was a knock at the door. They froze, as if staying still would render them invisible.

'Yeah?' Holly called, her lips still touching Jen's.

'Dinner's ready,' Harry chimed, thankfully not trying the door.

Only when she heard his footsteps retreat did Jen's muscles relax.

Holly bit her bottom lip before speaking. 'Back to yours tomorrow?'

27

'What's up?' Jen asked, her eyes narrowing as she looked at Holly.

'Huh?' she replied, shifting in the bath, suddenly aware she'd been in her own wee world.

'You had that faraway look on your face again.'

'Did I? Sorry. Just tired, I guess.'

Jen cocked her head, her hand finding Holly's leg under the bubbles and giving her calf a squeeze. 'See, usually I would buy that, but you've been odd since your dad and I made those Rusty Nails after dinner. Did I do something wrong?'

Rumbled. Holly thought she'd hidden it well. After her little chat with Chloe she'd made a point of keeping tabs on Alison by following her Instagram. In Holly's experience there was never smoke without fire, and if this woman was as bad as everyone made out she was one to watch. While Jen and Dad had made cocktails yesterday, Alison had updated her stories: a video of a suitcase being packed, ready for a week at home. Glasgow. Alison was coming to Glasgow.

Holly had sat on the knowledge all evening. Feeling duty-bound to tell Jen, warn her at least, but with Chloe's words ringing in her ears, she'd held off. Truth be told, she didn't want to pop their little bubble either. The last few days had been magical.

She'd tied her brain in knots, and so, needing a second opinion, this afternoon she'd messaged Chloe, but had no reply. A few aloof questions and Jen had let slip she was in a staff meeting and probably wouldn't be finished until well after eight.

So, here she was, supposedly enjoying a bath with her gorgeous girlfriend, all the while contemplating if she should tell Jen her ex was en route.

And that was all without worrying what Alison had planned once she was actually here. Holly kept reminding herself that Jen wasn't Shona. Still, it wasn't a scenario she'd wanted to ever repeat, never mind so fresh into a new relationship.

'You've done nothing wrong,' Holly finally replied, her eyes on Jen's shampoo bottle. 'Just me getting in my own head again.'

Jen's face pulled into a sympathetic smile. 'Anything you want to talk about? How can I make it better?'

She wanted to scoop Jen up and take her away from Glasgow. Surely Alison wouldn't be staying long? But with the closing of Lovefest in just a few days, that would be impossible.

Holly found Jen's gaze and held steady. 'I don't think it can get better than this,' she replied with a chuckle before turning wistful. 'I can't remember the last time I was this happy.'

Jen's features softened. 'Me neither.'

They held each other's stares for a beat, before Jen

lunged forward, looking for a kiss. She had only got half way when there was a hard knock at the door. She froze, the water sloshing about the tub.

'Can't be Chloe; her meeting won't finish for ages,' Jen said, listening.

Holly's heart hammered. Alison wouldn't have the balls to come straight here. Would she?

They listened in silence for a few seconds. Both jumped when the second knock came.

Holly rose out of the bath, grabbing her towel off the radiator.

'Where're you going?' Jen hissed.

'This doesn't feel right.' Holly said, pulling on her clothes even though she wasn't fully dry.

If this was Alison, she was going to put a stop to it.

A quick check in the mirror to look for panda eyes and she was good to go.

'Holly, wait,' Jen called, half-out of the bath.

'Jen, I can hear you,' came a voice through the letterbox.

It definitely wasn't Chloe.

'Holly,' Jen wailed, still scrabbling with her towel. It was too late; Holly was in the hall now.

With a final deep breath she flung the door open.

Please don't shake, legs. She gripped the door for support.

Alison had obviously made an effort before popping round. She was wearing a cute floral dress, a denim jacket, and black boots. Jen certainly had a type. On anyone else, Holly would have admired the outfit. She suddenly felt underdressed in her joggers and sweatshirt, like she should be spruced up too, level the playing field.

'Alison.'

She looked confused, like she was considering if she had

the wrong flat. Realisation kicked in, and her features hardened.

'And you are?'

'Holly.'

She could feel Jen lingering behind her.

Silence filled the space between them. Hard. Heavy. Harsh.

Alison looked past Holly, leaning in the door to make eye contact with Jen. 'Aren't you going to invite me in?'

Not a word from Jen.

'What do you want?' Holly asked curtly.

Alison pulled a face that Holly could have gladly slapped. She didn't, though. Her hand stayed on the door, ready to slam it if need be. It also helped keep her steady, as every part of her threatened to shake.

She ignored Holly and continued addressing Jen. 'Kev said you were seeing someone new.'

'You've spoken to Kev?' Jen's voice was distant, like she was in the next room. Holly could feel her at her shoulder, though, and she wasn't going to move. Jen needed her as a shield.

'Yeah, I'm doing a gig there tomorrow. I'm home for the week, so I figured, why not get in touch?' she said with a shrug. 'I'd really like to come in now, if your guard dog will let me.'

Holly looked at Jen, scared to linger too long, as if Alison would take the break in eye contact as an invitation and run in, like a sneaky animal.

'I don't think that would be wise,' Jen said, her voice still weak.

Holly contemplated slamming the door right then, but something told her Alison wouldn't take an abrupt end well.

She was here for a reason, and she wouldn't leave until Jen complied.

Alison pursed her lips, thinking.

Holly helped her along. 'Tell us what you want first.'

'I don't think it's any of your business.' A moment later, she reconsidered her stance on Holly's involvement. Her eyes didn't blink as she talked to Holly. 'Just wanting to catch up with Jenevieve.' A smile pulled at her lips. 'Sorry for the spoiler. Took me a good year to find her full name out, and then it was only because I finally met her mum.'

The anger radiating off Jen was palpable.

'A year?' Holly asked, keeping cool.

'Yeah, Jen's more guarded than the Tower of London. You'll soon find that out.'

Holly smirked. 'Sorry, it just seemed a long time. I spoke to Léonie on Facetime last week.' She hadn't. But she had learned the name of Jen's parents via the hamper. The slight twitch in Alison's mouth made the lie worth it.

She returned to ignoring Holly. 'I'd love to catch up, without company. Just a coffee or something? I'm here a week.'

Jen's silence spoke volumes.

Alison wasn't for backing down. 'Look, now obviously isn't the right time,' she said, glaring at Holly. 'See you around, Jen.'

As Alison turned on her heel to leave, Holly slammed the door. Maybe a little too hard for a communal space, but the neighbour's dog would stop barking. Eventually.

Without uttering a word, Jen stormed to the kitchen, grabbed a glass, and slammed the tap on full blast, downing water before gripping the edge of the counter, her breathing ragged.

Holly lingered in the living room doorway, unsure what she was meant to be doing or saying.

Eventually, Jen spoke. 'Why didn't you seem as surprised as me to see her?'

Holly opened her mouth to speak, but had second thoughts and snapped it shut.

Jen turned to face her, betrayal clear in her eyes. 'Holly.'

Holly gulped, suddenly finding the window the most interesting thing in the world as she fought to keep her tears at bay. 'I saw on her Instagram that she was coming home.'

'Is that why you were being weird?' Jen's tone was low, like she was just holding herself together.

Holly nodded.

Jen tensed her jaw. Her eyes focused on Holly as she nodded slowly. 'I think I need a moment alone, if that's okay.'

'Yeah, sure.'

'As in, I want you to go home.'

Shit. 'Sure. I'll get my stuff.' Holly lingered before turning back to Jen. 'I thought I was doing the right thing.'

Silence.

28

The next day, Jen was still mad at Chloe and Holly, although she could see the logic in their actions. But this wasn't the time for being huffy: she needed all the allies she could get.

A sinking feeling in her gut told her Alison's visit wasn't purely social. Her chest tightened. There was no way Jen could afford to buy her share of the flat: with the shop's cash flow how it was, no sane bank would help her. Which only left selling the flat, leaving her without a home. Jen rubbed at her temples; no point spiralling until Alison made her intentions clear.

She'd made a pact with Holly to let her know if Alison appeared again. Honesty had to come first – her and Holly's relationship was the number one priority, as much as she'd prefer not to be texting her about her ex. Or talking about her. Or thinking about her.

Holly was being surprisingly cool about it all, but Jen suspected the front was put up for her, and Holly was likely freaking out internally. Calm and jovial uptop, a mess underneath. Just like good ducks are.

The day was whizzing past, but every time the door opened Jen's heart skipped a beat, certain Alison would be walking through it.

She finally got her heart's desire just shy of three.

'Place looks good,' Alison said, breezing in without a care in the world.

Jen's heart stuttered before rising to a sickening pace.

'Thanks,' she managed.

Why wasn't it busy? It had been busy all day. Where were the customers now she needed them?

Alison leaned on the counter, a grin taking over her face. 'So, tell me what you've been up to?'

Jen tensed her jaw, wondering what the right response was. Adrenaline surged through her veins like a rip tide. 'Not much. How's London?'

'Amazing,' Alison replied, shifting her stance, obviously not happy with the welcome she was receiving. 'You would love it.'

'Yeah, well. I guess we'll never know.'

'You free tonight?'

Jen shook her head.

Alison didn't take the hint. 'I'm playing in Bar Orama. I'd love for you to come.'

Jen laughed under her breath. 'I'd sooner pull my own teeth out.'

'You know, you're starting to come off as rude,' Alison said, standing straight.

'What do you expect?'

No reply. Instead, Alison turned, her attention going to the cocktail pouches. Jen took her chance to text Holly one word: *Alison*. Hopefully that would be enough.

Alison picked up a pouch and turned it over as if reading

the label, but her mind was clearly elsewhere. After a deep breath, she spoke. 'I know I fucked up.'

'Good – I'm glad you've finally grown a conscience.' Jen stuffed some paperwork away to keep her hands busy and hide how badly they were shaking.

Pouch returned, to the wrong place, Jen noted. Alison circled back to the counter. 'Jen, just come for a coffee or something. Please.'

'I don't know what you think we need to discuss.'

Alison extended a hand to take Jen's, but she swiped it away. The brunette's eyes fell to the counter. 'If you're worried about Holly, just say you're meeting someone else or whatever. I won't tell.'

Jen couldn't help but chuckle. 'Your morals haven't changed, then.'

'What's that s—'

She was cut off by Holly entering with two takeaway coffees from the deli. At the sight of her Alison groaned, her eyes rolling to the ceiling.

Holly joined Jen behind the counter, placing a coffee by the till. 'Thought you might need a caffeine boost.' Her eyes never strayed from Alison.

Tension hung in the air like a guillotine.

Two seconds later, a customer swanned in. A quick side-eye told Jen he felt he'd walked into something; he just hadn't put his finger on the fact he was now the innocent pawn in a gunless showdown.

Even with Jen's quiet music playing you could have heard a pin drop.

Holly took a sip of her coffee. Alison's stare didn't waver.

The guy placed two pouches on the counter and Jen did her best to be normal. It was tough with the unmistakable crackle of conflict in the air. It was so buzzed that Jen swore if she reached out a finger it would spark, lighting the room like a plasma lamp.

Finally, he left, never knowing how close he was to witnessing a death.

Holly broke the silence after another sip of coffee. 'Need a hand with anything, Alison? Or you good?'

Alison's eyes flashed; Jen knew that look. Holly had about two more nudges before she detonated this bomb. 'I came here to speak to Jen, so if you could leave us in peace, thanks.' She pulled a face, her clipped tone saying she was trying to be polite for Jen's sake. Under any other circumstances, Holly would be headless by now.

Holly nodded, her face serious but light. 'Yeah, sure, no probs. I just want to finish having coffee with my girlfriend, then I'll be off.'

Ooft. Holly was being a badass. Was it weird that Jen was a little turned on just now? She'd never had anyone fight over her before.

The problem was, as good as Holly was, Alison was better. She was the queen of cool and getting what she wanted.

'Don't let me stop you, although you could have brought one for me too, since you obviously knew I was here.' She leaned on the counter, not going anywhere.

Tension descended further over the shop, like a smothering avalanche.

Jen couldn't bear the back and forth any longer. 'Bar Orama tonight, did you say?'

Alison perked up. 'Yeah, the gig starts at 7.30.'

'Early.'

'I know, right? And I don't have my band. But I want to test some new material, so I promised Kev a two-hour acoustic set.'

Jen nodded. 'Nice of you.' She swallowed hard, her body fighting what she planned on saying next. 'Right, I'll see if I can swing by, if I'm not too busy here.'

She could feel the shift in mood from Holly. She'd explain later. Alison was the one to convince just now.

Alison's face broke into a grin. 'Brilliant – I'll see you there.' She turned to Holly. 'Leave the bodyguard at home.'

With that, she was off.

Jen broke into a ramble as soon as the door clicked shut. 'I'm not really going, I just wanted to get rid of her. Promise. I'm not.'

Holly was white as a sheet. She groaned. 'Urgh, I feel a bit sick.'

Jen couldn't help but kiss her.

∼

'SHE'LL BE ROUND ANY MINUTE,' Holly said, sprawled on the sofa.

As a thank you for being so amazing about the whole situation, Jen was cooking Holly dinner. Veggie chilli, to be exact.

'Well then, she can just fuck off any minute, too,' Jen called from the kitchen, stifling a chuckle.

She emptied the water from a tin of kidney beans into the sink before tipping its contents into her simmering pot.

Today had been surreal.

It felt like her muscles were fizzing with nervous energy, anxiety fuelling her every move. Her mouth was dry, her head in a daze.

Jen thought she was used to living in a constant haze of stress, but this was something else.

If she hadn't been cooking for Holly the only thing

passing her lips tonight would be a glass of Sauvignon, then it would be straight to bed. The sooner the day was over the better.

Instead, she was busying herself with cooking and focusing on sex tonight. Sex with her lovely, caring, gorgeous girlfriend.

They'd been like teenagers all week and Jen was ready to ride this wave for as long as possible. She might not have the stamina she did back then, but by God, when you had Holly to worship, you soon found the strength.

Jen stirred in the kidney beans, having a quick taste of the mixture off the end of her wooden spoon. It was okay. This vegetarian lark was going to be a breeze.

Holly's arms wrapped around Jen, her head resting on her back. 'How's tea coming on?'

'Not quite Michelin star, but decent.'

'High praise indeed.'

There was a pause. A pause Jen didn't like one bit. She chose not to fill it, and see where Holly was planning on going.

The feeling of Holly taking a deep breath didn't help squash her nerves. Jen stirred the pot, even though what it really needed was a lid and the oven. She turned the gas off and braced herself.

'So,' Holly began, only to be cut off by Jen tilting her head back with a groan. 'Please, just listen.'

Jen bit her top lip. This was going to be about Alison. She was sick to death of talking about her ex.

Holly switched positions, leaning on the counter to face Jen, keeping the connection with Jen's hip pressed against her stomach. 'I need to show you something, and I won't lie, it's got me spiralling a little, like, I trust you and everything, but the last twenty-four hours have just been a bit much, an—'

Jen cut her off with a sympathetic look, taking her by the waist when she saw the sadness in Holly's eyes. 'Hey, wait, what's going on? We were joking a minute ago.'

Another deep breath. 'Yeah, but.' She tapped the corner of her phone on the counter, hesitation clear.

Jen closed her eyes, steadying herself before meeting Holly's gaze. ' I have no plans to talk to that woman. When she calls again, I'm going to tell her everything needs to go through my solicitor. You don't need to be worrying about me and bleeding Alison Rae.'

Jen held her stare, hoping the message would get through to Holly.

Her features remained unchanged, although Jen was sure Holly's eyes glazed as they slipped further down the rabbit hole of anguish.

Holly looked at the pot of chilli. 'Smells good; need me to do anything?'

'Tell me why you came over here,' Jen replied with a thin-lipped smile.

'You're right, I'm stalling.' With a gargantuan sigh she leaned her back against the counter, searching for something on her phone. 'She's not after your flat.'

'Huh?'

Holly held her thumb on Bar Orama's stories, pausing the video from playing as she turned it to Jen. 'Listen to the song she's covering.' She released her finger and the opening bars of Wallis Bird's 'The Circle' played. Alison strummed her guitar, bopping to the song as she leaned into the mic, her eyes closed, clearly feeling the lyrics.

She'd pulled a good crowd. Kev would be happy. Jen

couldn't blame him for wanting to make money, encourage new patrons.

'Right, so? It's a good song. We both liked the album.'

Holly chewed on her cheek, giving her head a wobble as she breathed out slowly. 'Yes, but given the context.'

Jen cocked her head. 'Hols.'

'Right, okay, whatever. But, then, the next thing is this post.' She stabbed at the screen, skipping through the stories before resting her finger, pausing once again. 'Actually, you know what? I just listened to it; I can't do it again. I'm off to the loo.'

She released her finger and kissed Jen's cheek. For a fleeting moment Jen wondered if she meant the toilet in the flat or somewhere else entirely, because something felt very final.

The sound of a cheery crowd erupted from Holly's phone. Alison was on stage, lights glaring off her. She'd barely changed. The same hairstyle, same make-up. Jen was fairly certain she was wearing the oversized denim shirt she'd bought her one Christmas, the one she loved to wear around the flat with little else on. Tonight, its sleeves were rolled to her elbows. Jen assumed she was wearing it with jeans, at least, or Kev's establishment had become a different one altogether.

Alison put a hand to her brow, searching the crowd as she spoke. 'I was hoping someone very special would be here tonight.' She narrowed her eyes, still scanning the sea of faces as she hit the pedals at her feet, getting ready for the next song. 'But I'm not seeing her. Jen, are you here?'

Jen's stomach dropped.

Off camera, in the distance, Travis's voice boomed: 'She's not here.'

Jen was sure she saw a hint of dejection in Alison's face,

but she styled it out. 'When you hear the song, you'll probably guess why that is,' she said with a wry smile. A ripple of laughter sailed through the crowd.

She strummed her guitar, adjusting the capo, before leaning into the microphone. 'This is brand new. It's called "Is It Really Over?"'

Jen's heart joined her stomach. She swallowed. Even though her mouth was drier than it had ever been. *Fuck.*

Half way through the first verse Jen realised she'd forgotten to breathe. She flitted her eyes to the living room, willing Holly to come round the corner. Help her make sense of what she was hearing.

Alison's song was full of remorse, atonement, and worst of all, longing. She wanted her back. Badly.

Jen felt sick.

Three years too late. She'd moved on, long ago. Maybe not into the place she was now, but definitely to a space where Alison no longer fitted. The thought of getting back together repulsed her.

Her future was Holly-shaped now.

No matter how many songs were written about her.

Jen closed the app, quite content with never seeing Alison ever again, and strode to the bathroom. Empty. She doubled back and found Holly on her bed, lying flat on her back, eyes closed, deep in thought.

She slid into position beside her, scooping her close as she kissed her nose, her brow, and finally her mouth.

'I have nothing to do with that,' she said, lying flat against Holly and slotting her head into the space between her girlfriend's neck and shoulder.

'It's about you, though,' Holly said, her voice unsteady.

Jen lifted her head, just to check she wasn't crying. Clear for now, she settled back into Holly's shoulder.

'I can't help how she feels. I didn't encourage it. We've not spoken in three years.'

She studied the rise and fall of Holly's chest. There was no telling what was going through her mind.

After what felt like a few lifetimes, she spoke. 'I know you didn't ask for any of this, but I can't do this again, Jen. If there's a hint, even the slightest little "what if" at the back of your mind, you need to tell me now.'

'What do you mean?' Jen asked, rising to rest on her elbow.

Finally Holly opened her eyes. 'If there's just one tiny skin cell on you that wants to see where things could go with Alison, I need you to say now. There's no shame in that; you were together a long time. I just need to know the truth.'

Jen shifted position again, trying to find ground that wasn't there; they were already as close as was humanly possible, and yet it didn't feel enough. She shook her head a tiny fraction, scared to move too much, emotion prickling at her eyes. 'Not even for a nano-second.'

Holly didn't look convinced.

Jen couldn't blame her. She'd just watched a video of her arsehole ex declaring her love. After everything she'd been through with Shona, she didn't deserve this. She wanted to bring her close and shower her with kisses, forever remaining in the bubble of Jen and Holly, safe and protected from the outside world. Jen was Holly's armour: it was her job to defend, not add further damage.

'You believe me, yeah?' Jen asked a still-unmoving Holly.

'Of course.'

'But?'

'Everything is still so raw from Shona. I'm trying to figure out if I'm an easy target or just a gullible mug.'

That stung, but it wasn't Holly's fault.

Jen brought a hand to Holly's face, cupping her jaw. 'You've never been gullible – you've been trusting. There's a huge difference.'

'I want us to work—'

'Me too.'

'—this is just a lot, especially at the start of a relationship, when I've just come out of one so toxic.'

Jen let the words linger for a moment, then said the only thing she knew could fix it, something she'd been thinking about all week. 'I know. But I love you.'

Holly's eyes changed, emotion flashing over her.

Jen filled the silence. 'You don't need to say it back, it's okay.'

It had only been a little over three weeks, and under any other circumstances she would have sat on the words a little longer, picked a better moment to say it, but she was done with being coy and guarded. Now was the time for saying how she felt, no matter what.

When Holly didn't say anything, Jen's stomach tensed. She wasn't expecting a gushing declaration in return, but something would have been nice. Had she even heard what she said?

'Please say something.'

'Sorry, I'm just—'

Jen cut her off. 'Honestly, I don't expect you to say it back. I just want some acknowledgement that you heard me. And you believe me.'

Why did she feel like crying?

Moments like this were meant to feel special, not like they were on the edge of despair.

Holly nodded slowly. Finally, her mouth attempted what Jen assumed was the start of a smile. 'Guess we got the couples' quiz wrong.'

29

The air in Shawlands was charged, everyone excited for Lovefest's closing party this evening.

However, Holly wasn't feeling it.

She checked her hair in the deli's basement mirror for the thousandth time. She'd considered braiding it, but had gone with a messy bun instead. She just didn't have the heart.

She tapped on her cheeks, willing this mood to leave her.

Jen was excited. They'd be meeting soon; hopefully her good mood would rub off on her.

She should be buzzed. In a few hours she could be a couple of grand richer, and the woman she'd fallen for had told her she loved her last night.

But Jen's words had felt like a chokehold on her heart. She couldn't afford to fall deeper with Alison still here. No matter what Jen said, Holly knew it wasn't over. Not on Alison's side, anyway.

Footsteps on the stairs caught her attention.

Memories of her first day flooded back. Little did she know what the month was going to hold.

However, it wasn't her mother this time.

'You good?' Chloe asked, her eyes finding Holly's in the mirror.

Holly sucked on her lips. 'Not really.'

'Good job I brought this then.' She held up a bottle of wine and two plastic cups.

'You're a mind reader.'

Chloe looked stunning. She'd styled her long red hair in an elegant updo, perfectly offsetting the cut of her dress, accentuating her perfect figure. Holly wished she'd found the energy to do her hair properly. Too late now.

'Come, sit,' Chloe said, patting the tatty sofa in the corner of the basement.

Holly did as commanded, holding the cups for Chloe as she poured. 'Can we just cut to the chase. What's your prognosis?'

Chloe sighed, managing a half-smile. 'It's a tough one.' She took a sip of her wine. 'I hated Alison when they were together, and even more when they broke up. We never got on.' Another sip of wine. 'The problem is, she's all sweetness and light in the public eye, but really she's a slimy, sneaky snake. She'll be up to something.'

It was good to talk to someone who got it. Someone who's first comment wasn't about how Holly was probably overreacting. She needed a straight opinion, and nothing else.

'So how do you get rid of a snake?'

'Cut off its head?' Chloe stifled a laugh. 'Sorry, sorry, not helpful.'

Holly downed a glug of wine, letting the heat of the alcohol settle in her bones. 'I trust Jen, you know that, yeah?'

'Of course.'

'I just can't help feeling something bad is going to happen.'

Chloe nodded. 'I know. And seeing Alison's video must have been heart-wrenching, but Jen loves you. Just focus on that.'

Holly went to chew on her thumbnail, but remembered she'd just painted them, so lightly tapped her lip with it instead. 'I'll just be so much happier when she goes back to London.'

'A few more days and you'll be rid of her. Then you and Jen can get back to your little love bubble.'

Holly's breath wavered. It felt like it had already burst. Their honeymoon period was over, the brakes pulled by a sharp shock of reality.

Chloe gave her knee a squeeze, picking up the reluctance. 'Does Jen know you're feeling like this?'

She shook her head. 'I couldn't. Not after she said that she loves me. I know how big that must have been for her and I didn't want to ruin everything.'

'But you need to be honest. Remember how well that worked last time?' Chloe replied with a sympathetic smile.

'I don't think there's anything Jen could say to stop me worrying, so there's no point bringing it up.'

Chloe didn't look convinced. 'Why don't we go find Jen? You'll feel better when you see her.'

LOVEFEST'S FINALE was hosted in a massive marquee that Annie had erected outside Langside Hall. It certainly had more of an impact than the bouncy castle did the other week. The tent was a hive of activity, and thankfully the weather gods had blessed the suburb with glorious sunshine as the party spilled over the square. A sea of happy, chatting, drink-clutching people surrounded the tent. Holly's stomach did a little twist with nerves; she hadn't expected to be on stage in front of so many people.

The upbeat pop music from the tent grew louder as they drew closer. Chloe gripped her hand, weaving them through the partygoers.

'I told Jen I'd meet her at the park railings – she's by the bowling club,' she shouted back to Holly.

'How come you didn't get ready together?'

'We did, but she had something to sort for Ben's deliveries. She left me here, but I thought I would take the chance to see you, instead of just replying to your text.'

Following the wrought iron railings surrounding Queen's Park, it didn't take long to find Jen. She looked stunning in black cigarette trousers and a black top. A ripple of desire flushed up Holly's body. Jen really was the jackpot.

Her smile was brighter than the summer sun when she spied Holly. 'You look great,' she said, giving her a quick kiss.

'All sorted with Ben?' Holly asked, taking Jen's hand as they strolled along the edge of the crowd.

'Yeah, just a bunch of last minute orders. I usually wouldn't, but it was a lot of money.' She turned to Chloe, shielding her eyes from the sun with her free hand. 'Where's Ryan?'

'At the food trucks. That boy never stops eating,' she replied with a smile.

They weaved through the straggling crowd, making their way towards the dozen or so food trucks and stalls peppering the edge of the square. Fairy lights hung between poles overhead. Once the light faded, this place was going to look magical.

Holly's mind wandered to their night on the rooftop. She wished it could just be the two of them again. A relationship under public watch just wasn't for her.

'There he is,' Chloe said, speeding up as she clocked her boyfriend. He was stuffing his face with a cheeseburger and looked like the happiest man on earth. Even more so when he saw Chloe.

Jen gave Holly's hand a squeeze, leading them to a quieter spot in the shade of a tree. 'You feeling good about tonight?'

Holly stepped closer, putting her hands on Jen's hips as she leaned against the tree's trunk. 'Yeah, I am, actually. I think we've got as good a chance as any. We've done all the sharing on socials that we can.'

'How about another snap, just to seal the deal?' Jen asked, whipping her phone out.

Just like that, Holly ducked into position in front of Jen, her girlfriend's arm pulling her closer. It really did get easier with practice.

'Quack,' Jen said, flashing a killer smile.

'Quack,' Holly chorused. Maybe everything was going to be okay.

∾

'SWEETHEART, YOU LOOK STUNNING,' Dad said, kissing Holly on the cheek.

Deliveries had taken a little longer than she'd expected and Holly was starting to worry her parents would miss their big moment on stage. But then, Dad didn't have the system perfected like she did. She'd have to go with him sometime, show him how to streamline the process.

'Thanks, Dad,' she replied, giving his side a wee squeeze.

'Let me get you some drinks,' Jen said, leaping up from her seat. They'd somehow managed to bag a table at the edge of the dance floor, everyone else more intent on dancing as they mingled. Neither Holly nor Jen wanted to risk getting hot and sweaty before the reveal. The notion wasn't deterring Chloe, who was cutting shapes with Ryan like nobody's business.

'Only if you're sure,' Dad said, taking a seat. 'I'm gasping for a beer after all those steps. Catherine, wine okay for you?'

Mum gave a decisive nod.

'Right, on it,' Jen said with a little clap before bounding off. The bar queues were massive; she was a good egg offering her services.

'You excited?' Mum shouted over the music. She scooted her chair closer to Holly's, making talking easier.

'A bit, yeah. Would be pretty surreal if we won.'

'Well, either way, we're proud of you,' Dad said, clasping her hand and giving it a jiggle.

'I didn't do much. You asked me to be part of the competition, so I just got on with it.'

Mum's eyes turned solemn. 'Not just this. We're proud of everything you've achieved.'

'Achieved maybe isn't the right word,' Holly said, keeping her tone as light as she could.

Mum shook her head. 'You've been through a lot in the last few years. Look how strong you are now. It's been a dream come true, having you back.'

Dad looked to Mum, snagging her gaze. 'In all senses of the word.'

'What does that mean?' Holly asked, perplexed.

Her parents were quiet for a moment, as if both were waiting for the other to answer. Dad watched the dancing crowd, anchoring himself. It was strange seeing him so emotional and transparent, especially in public. He took a deep breath before speaking. 'We know you give yourself a hard time, and yes, you've had some of your less-than-finer moments in recent years, but your mum and I,' he paused, getting his thoughts in order. 'We don't believe that was the real you. Shona had a lot to do with that. What matters now is looking forward, getting back on track. This is a fresh start for us all.'

'We just want you to be happy, love,' her mum said with a slight wobble of her lip. 'And I'd like to think you are now, yes?'

Holly took a long draw of breath. She couldn't cry. Why had they chosen this precise moment to be so candid? Lovefest really did make people act in peculiar ways.

She looked to Chloe and Ryan again, using them as a distraction while the threat of tears lessened.

This festival had felt like a total farce when she'd been flung into it, hot and stuffy from the train, in a bad mood from Jen's watery assault and feeling like the biggest failure to grace the earth.

But now, sitting here, it felt like everything had happened at the just right time. Lovefest wasn't just about getting a date: it was about loving family, friends, herself. She cringed. Thank God no one could read her mind. It was true, though. It might have the most ridiculous, embarrassing, godawful name, but Lovefest was the real deal. A force to be reckoned with.

Tears not going anywhere soon, Holly nodded gently, forcing a half-smile. Mum and Dad knew what she was trying to convey; words weren't needed just now. She gave their hands a squeeze and mustered another nod.

With incomparable timing, Jen appeared from the crowd, drinks in hand, a showstopping smile breaking across her face as she locked eyes with her girlfriend. For the first time in forever, Holly felt like the luckiest girl in the world.

30

_____

As their time to take the stage edged closer, the ball of nerves in Jen's stomach grew. Sitting wasn't helping the matter: she needed more than conversation to divert her mind.

'Will we have a dance?' she asked Holly.

'Sure, but we're agreed; nothing too strenuous, yeah?' Holly replied with a smirk.

Jen led the way, finding them a quiet corner away from the booze-fuelled revellers in the centre of the dance floor.

She'd never been a huge fan of dancing while sober, but it was better than fighting the urge to jiggle her knee every two seconds.

'I can't remember the last time I danced in public,' Jen shout-whispered.

'Me neither.'

The duo lingered, neither really knowing what do to. It only took the hint of a smile to play on Jen's lips for them both to erupt with the giggles.

Someone above was watching out for them and a slow song came on the speakers.

Jen caught Holly's gaze and closed the gap between them, placing her hands on Holly's hips as she rested her head on Jen's shoulder. Just like that, everything was natural again.

They swayed in time with the music, captured in the moment.

She'd half-expected Holly to leave last night but she'd stayed. Yes, the chilli was aptly named, and the atmosphere in the room had been like ice as they ate. But she'd stayed and the evening had defrosted to become relatively normal. If Jen ignored the wedge between them, anyway.

How dare Alison come back and demand anything of her?

It had to be now, didn't it? Right when Jen was finally slotting her life back together. Couldn't have been last August, or never at all?

She kissed Holly's cheek, desperately wanting to tell Holly that she loved her again. She couldn't say it without Holly reciprocating first. She gulped the words down. Much like double-texting, there was an etiquette to follow, lest she look loopy.

Still, it was freeing to have put herself out there and not get what her brain had been programmed to expect. Maybe she could get used to this whole sharing-how-you-feel carry on. There was no pressure with Holly. Everything would come in time; there was no rush.

Holly pulled back, locking eyes with Jen. For a brief moment she worried she could read her mind again. Although on this occasion it wouldn't be bad thing.

She kissed Jen on the lips, Holly's arms now draped over her shoulders.

'Do you think we'd be here if Annie hadn't set us up?' Holly asked, her eyes in a dream.

Jen considered it. 'I'd hope so. You work next door so we'd have to meet at some point.'

'I met you after being in the shop about ten minutes. Although I don't think I'd be dying for an introduction if it wasn't for the Lovefest event.' Holly bit her lip, suppressing a smile.

'I dunno, I think I could have brought you round with my devilish charm.'

'Oh, really?' Holly replied, pulling a face of playful indignation.

'Maybe you'd need a little intense till training, and I could offer my services.'

Holly cocked her head to the side. 'I could see that happening.'

Jen raised her chin, fighting the grin that was pulling at her lips. What she really wanted to do was snog Holly like her life depended on it, but she was very aware her parents were likely watching.

The sooner this evening was over the better.

The song switched to another upbeat tune and her dance moves failed Jen once more. 'Will we get some fresh air before our big moment?'

'Sounds perfect,' Holly replied, planting another kiss on Jen's cheek.

WITH TWILIGHT DESCENDING, the fairy lights were coming into their own; the route to the food trucks were looking more like a wonderland as the evening wore on.

Jen gave Holly's grip a little pump as they held hands. 'You nervous?'

'A bit.'

'Me too. Don't worry – if we have to do a speech, I'll handle it. You know how good I am with words,' she joked.

'Want to run it by me first?'

'Yeah, sure,' Jen replied, clearing her throat. 'Thank you.'

Holly waited, her breath bated. When nothing further came she snorted with laughter. 'Short, sweet, to the point.'

'As always.'

Jen was so lost in Holly's smile that she almost didn't clock who was glaring at them from the taco truck.

Alison.

Her heart skipped a beat.

Of course she was here. Where else would she be?

'Let's find somewhere quiet to sit,' Jen said, pulling Holly in the opposite direction, hoping she wasn't being too obvious.

'It's like you're a mind reader.'

With a final look to her ex and what she prayed was her best *stay-the-fuck-away* eyes, Jen led Holly back to towards the tree line.

What stunt was she planning on tonight? Was Jen's absence in Bar Orama not enough of a hint to her? She'd brought her friend Nikki along. Last time Jen had seen her she was picking up the last of Alison's boxes from the flat. She'd been a mess handing the stuff over and could have quite happily never seen Nikki again in her life. Her presence just about gave Jen a full house on the 'how fucked up can it be?' bingo card.

If she could avoid Alison for the rest of the night and stop Holly from spotting her, all would be well. Jen's gut said to tell Holly, but everything was already so twisted, and after the turmoil of last night her head was screaming that ignorance was bliss. They'd be on stage in forty minutes: surely she could pull this off?

'We finally meet,' boomed a deep, friendly voice, pulling Jen from her thoughts.

She turned to find the gay couple from tonight's competition, James and Scott, or the Daddy Bears as Holly playfully called them, heading their way.

The nickname was even more spot on in the flesh. They were big, hulky men who towered over them – James with a grey beard, Scott with a face of ginger fuzz – and were both in their late forties. They were anything but grizzly, though. James's eyes lit up with kindness as he stopped just short of their hiding spot.

'Can't believe it's taken us this long,' he said, flashing a smile.

'Me neither,' Jen replied, happy to now have a literal shield from Alison's prying eyes. 'How do you fancy your chances tonight?'

'We're in the running, that's for sure,' Scott replied, his deep voice a calming rumble. 'We're not in it for the money though.'

James snared his eyes and Jen noted the sparkle. 'What about you?' he asked, breaking away from Scott's gaze.

'Deffo just here for the money,' Holly joked, unable to keep a straight face.

Jen quickly grabbed her side, giving her a playful tickle without breaking eye contact with the lads.

'I meant, do you think you'll win?' James asked with a hearty chuckle.

Holly let out a low whistle. 'No idea, really. I thought Debbie and Nick had it in the bag.'

'I know,' Scott said, his eyebrows shooting skyward. 'Who saw that one coming?'

'Not Nick, that's for sure,' Jen said, still feeling sorry for the guy. Matters of the heart could be so unfair sometimes. 'What was your favourite date?' she followed with, trying to keep the conversation cheery.

The guys exchanged glances and scrunched faces as they thought. 'Tough one,' Scott replied, clicking his tongue against the roof of his mouth.

James' eyes lit up. 'Probably the spa day. It's not something I would have ever booked otherwise, but I loved it.'

'Golf for me,' Scott chipped in.

'Aye, you would say that.' James gave his boyfriend an elbow to the ribs.

Jen got the impression these guys would be fun to hang out with. It was a shame they'd never got to meet the other couples until now. She'd mention it to Annie – maybe next year the contestants could do a group activity too.

That was, assuming it would now be an annual event. Judging by the turnout tonight the Business Group would be silly not to.

'What about you guys? Did you have a favourite?' Scott asked.

They thought for a second, Holly answering first. 'Cycling in Queens Park.'

'Really?' Jen said, taken aback. 'My legs hurt for days after.'

'Yeah, because you thought you saw a squirrel.'

The guys exchanged looks.

'Long story,' the women chorused.

'I think cycling would have killed me,' James said, gripping his belly and giving it a shake.

'It nearly did me,' Jen laughed. 'Nah, I think cocktails were my favourite.'

'You can't say that,' Holly scoffed. 'You hosted it!'

'That's why I loved it.'

'Have to say it looked better than our gin tour. My head was banging after,' Scott informed.

'So much to do in Shawlands, isn't there?' Jen said, suddenly very proud of her wee suburb.

'And this is only the tip of the iceberg,' Scott boomed.

A comfortable break in the conversation settled between the couples.

'Right, I think we're going to grab another beer before we take centre stage,' James said, flinging his thumb towards the bar.

Scott did a little wave. 'Was lovely meeting you both.'

Holly and Jen chorused their goodbyes.

'They were so nice,' Holly said, looking loved up.

'They were, huh? Stiff competition, Hols.' Satisfied there were no parents in sight, Jen closed the gap between them, kissing Holly lightly at first before diving deeper.

Holly bit her bottom lip when she came up for air. 'What was that for?'

'Just so happy to be here, with you.' She couldn't rest on her laurels, though. All Jen wanted to do was grab Holly's hand and make a run for it. Instead she was trying her hardest to maintain eye contact while really watching her peripheral. *Oh, to be a lizard.*

Holly's face split into a grin as she played with Jen's hand. 'I'm happy too.'

'I know we have plans for our halves of the money, but do you want to go away somewhere, just the two of us, for a night or two? Won't cost much.' Since opening the shop, Jen had only ever been to France twice a year to see her parents. Time away with Holly would be a dream come true.

'I'd love that.' Holly's eyes flickered, the creases around

them deepening as she smiled. She was thinking something, and Jen wished to God she could mind read. 'And I—'

There was no time to hear the rest. Alison's face loomed from the crowd. 'I'm really thirsty; can we go to the bar as well?'

Holly looked confused and even a little hurt, but followed as Jen tugged on her hand, already a few steps ahead. 'Yeah, sure.'

Jen felt like she couldn't get her breath. This night was a racetrack – there was too much going on and all she wanted was to hit the pause button, rest her hands on her thighs, and pant.

No such luck.

The queue to the bar was a few people deep and Jen bounced on her heels as they waited. She felt like a sitting duck standing here. At least if they were in the crowd they would be a moving target. Time to ditch the bar distraction.

'Hey, bestie,' Chloe said, enveloping Jen in a hug from behind. She kissed her cheek. 'We're going to get a final beer, you in?'

Jen scanned the crowd. No sign. 'Sure, why not.'

Holly's eyes fixed on Jen, her stare hot on her skin. She couldn't make eye contact, not now. She was already picking up on her weird vibe, if Jen looked her in the eye she would look straight through her, reading her very thoughts and knowing exactly what was wrong tonight. She couldn't risk it.

'You go, Clo. You always get served quicker,' Jen said, her smile feeling faker by the second.

Chloe didn't need asked twice and took on her mission with gusto.

Jen inhaled a long, wavering breath. The night was

unravelling around her, control slipping further away with every heartbeat.

Holly put a hand on her waist and pulled her close as she whispered in Jen's ear. 'You okay? You seem, kinda. . . edgy.'

Jen found the confidence to make eye contact. 'Yeah, yeah. Just getting nervous about being on stage.'

Holly nodded, her face dripping with scepticism.

A realisation hit Jen like a thunderbolt. She flinched. What if Chloe saw Alison? Fuck. This was like herding cats. Jen pulled at her T-shirt's collar, feeling like she was at sea. In boat made of lava.

'Babe, seriously, you okay?' Holly asked, gripping her waist tighter.

Jen's voice was a near gasp. 'Yeah, just, I think I need some air.'

'Sure, yeah.' Holly patted Ryan on the back, stealing his attention from the queue. 'Ryan, we're just going to be over there, yeah?'

Ryan's brow creased with concern. 'Everything okay?'

'Just too hot,' Jen lied.

Holly led them through the crowd. 'You don't look good.'

'Thanks.'

'No, really. You've gone all pale.'

'I'll be good.' Jen's eyes were still firmly on the crowd. She'd lost her again. For now.

Chloe bounded into view, followed by Ryan, both clutching two beers in plastic cups.

'You having a whitey?' Chloe asked as she passed Jen her drink. She was only half-joking.

Holly scowled. 'Told you.'

Jen shook her head. 'Guys. Seriously. I'm good.' She

gritted her teeth and took a grounding breath before raising her cup. 'To Lovefest.'

'To Jen not spewing,' Chloe countered.

Jen's mouth was a straight line. 'Hey! But, yeah, let's drink to that too.' She couldn't help but laugh. Maybe a little too nervously. She gulped her beer, seeing half the cup away with ease. The alcohol pulled her heart from a sprint to a comfortable cross-country run.

Chloe and Holly eyed her. Ryan was oblivious.

Jen's heart thrummed in her chest, only made worse by the look Chloe was now giving her. It was bad enough feeling like Holly could read her. Chloe, on the other hand? She may as well start blabbing now.

'I'm good,' she said, preempting a question.

That only made Chloe's eyes narrow further.

'You want to chat?' her best friend asked.

Jen shook her head, taking another sip of beer. 'Just nerves. I'm good.' Chloe would be out for blood if she knew the truth. They'd be on stage soon.

Although, perhaps her time was up.

Over Chloe's shoulder Jen could see Nikki.

Straight past Holly stood Alison.

Jen hooked her pinky with Holly's, anchoring herself, ready to accept the inevitable.

Holly's smile filled Jen's chest. She focused on her eyes, choosing to ignore the figures that were surely getting closer. In the hazy light her eyes looked browner than usual, a deep mahogany Jen could easily get lost in.

Anger flushed over Jen.

Tonight should be all about Holly, but instead Alison was here to steal the fucking show. Jen's blood boiled. Alison had broken her heart once before – she wasn't going to ruin things with Holly too. Plus, something told her that if she thought breaking up with Alison was bad, losing Holly would be a thousand times worse.

She opened her mouth to speak, to tell Holly the truth and storm the ramparts, confronting Alison head on, see why the fuck she'd thought it was appropriate for her to come her and stalk her like a bloodhound all night – only to have Annie swoop in.

'Hey, guys. How's it going? Excited?' Annie's smile was on full beam, clearly happy with how well the evening was going. Today was testament to the success of Lovefest. She'd smashed it.

The group muttered agreement and quiet elation. 'When do you need us at the stage?' Chloe asked.

'Ten mins, if that's okay?'

More nodding and approval. 'Ten mins, got it,' Jen said, willing her nerves to hold steady.

Annie gave her shoulders a little wiggle. 'Right, I'd best be off. Need to have a quick chat with Isaac.'

When Annie left, Alison and Nikki were nowhere to be seen.

Was this a game? Were they purposely messing with her head as revenge for not going last night?

Jen tuned back into the conversation happening around her. '—if you fancy it. Jen?' Chloe said.

'Yeah?'

'You keen?'

'Huh?'

The furrow in Chloe's brow deepened. Any more of this and she was going to be left with a mark. 'Drinks at mine after?'

Jen nodded in earnest. 'Sounds good.' She watched as the muscles in her bestie's jaw tensed: once, twice, three times.

'Can we have a chat?' Chloe asked, her tone flat and serious.

'Sure,' Jen said with a gulp.

'Won't be long,' Chloe said, flashing a smile at Holly and Ryan.

Jen dropped Holly's hand and instantly missed the connection. But if she didn't appease Chloe now, the night would be a bust; better to give in sooner rather than later.

She sucked on her top lip, waiting for Chloe to speak as they negotiated the crowd.

Finally, at a good distance, she pulled Jen aside. 'The fuck is going on?'

'What do you mean?' Jen replied, trying to sound casual but managing the opposite.

'You're distracted, weird to say the least, and jumpy. Really fucking jumpy. This isn't just nerves.'

Jen sighed, her shoulders slumping. She took a deep breath. 'Alison and Nikki are here.'

Chloe's jaw hung slack for a beat before she pursed her lips, her eyes clouded with disappointment. 'Why didn't you just say?'

'I didn't want Holly to worry.'

'And this is better, how?' she asked, crossing her arms.

Embarrassment prickled Jen's skin in a wave. 'I'm being that obvious, huh?'

'Just tell her – she'll understand.'

'I want to go home,' Jen said, the words getting caught in her throat.

Chloe's face creased as she gathered Jen in a hug. She squeezed tight, kissing the side of her head. 'Aw, pal. It'll be fine. Promise.'

Jen held on, swallowing her doubts. Everything felt too much. Usually Chloe was the one to ground her, trick her into actually believing things would work out, but even her words of reassurance were falling flat. She needed Holly, too, and the only way that was going to happen was by being honest. Holly was strong, and if she trusted Jen she would take this in her stride. Still, Holly's reaction to Alison's video hung in the air. The hurt in Holly's eyes had seared a mark onto Jen's heart, one she didn't want to repeat.

Jen pulled away from Chloe's embrace, her throat still tight with hesitation. 'You're right,' she said, her voice getting lost in the crowd around them. She gave herself a shake. 'You're totally right, I'll be honest with Holly.'

Chloe smiled. 'Good lass. Now, let's get back to our dates and focus on winning that five grand.'

An excited chill tickled its way up Jen's spine. She'd barely had time to think about the money. Her new fridge was within touching distance; she could feel it. 'You go, I'm going to pee. I'll see you at the back of the stage.'

Chloe thought for a second before her smile grew, cementing her faith in Jen. 'Yeah, sure. Just don't be long. Wouldn't want you to miss me winning.'

Jen shot her a look. 'You mean miss *me* winning.'

Chloe rolled her eyes. 'Whatevs. Just don't be an age.'

She disappeared into the throng and Jen trudged towards the queue for the toilets, hands stuffed in her pockets. She didn't really need to go – she just wanted a moment alone, a second to get her thoughts in order.

A hand on her elbow made her jump.

Her breath came out as a growl when she saw who it was.

'Thought I'd never get you alone,' Alison said, her eyes playful as she bit the corner of her bottom lip.

'What do you want?'

'Is that just how you greet people now?'

'Alison.'

Finally, she took the hint. Nodding her head like a glum pigeon. 'Can we chat? Quickly. Then I'll leave. Promise.'

'Go on then.'

'Not here – somewhere quiet.'

'Where's Jen?' Holly asked as Chloe retrieved her near-finished beer from Ryan.

She took a sip before answering. 'Just nipped to the loo.'

'Is it just me, or is she being weird?'

Chloe pulled a face Holly couldn't quite decipher. 'She was. But we've had a chat. Everything's fine.'

'Anything I should know about?'

'She'll explain when she gets back.'

Well, that did nothing to stop the uncertainty coursing through Holly's veins. It ramped up a notch, her blood now sharp like acid. Distrust formed a ball in her throat, solid as beer washed over it.

She'd been close to telling Jen she loved her, just after they'd chatted to the Daddy Bears. The moment had felt right, the emotions of Lovefest getting the better of her, and the words had been half-out of her mouth before Jen yanked her away.

Now the moment was gone and her insides felt muddled. Something was up. Very up.

She gulped again, trying to rid herself of the lump in her

gullet.

Chloe sipped her beer and Ryan's eyes flitted between the pair. 'Am I missing something?' he asked, his voice unsure.

'Jen's just nervous,' Chloe offered.

He nodded slowly, not buying it but aware his time was better spent being a buffer. 'Will we make our way to the stage? Better early than late.'

'Good idea,' Chloe said, taking his hand.

Holly downed the rest of her beer. 'You go. I'm going to look for Jen.'

Chloe stopped mid-step. 'She'll be back soon – she's getting us at the stage.'

'I know,' Holly said with a decisive nod. 'I just want to have a quick chat with her before we go on. I can do it while we walk back.'

Silence hung for a beat, the gaudy laugh of a nearby stranger filling the gap.

'Right, okay,' Chloe answered with a small smile.

Holly moved through the crowd, making a beeline for the toilets.

She'd done this dance enough times to know the score. The distracted conversations, the quick glances. Lies that tripped off the tongue without a second thought. She'd believed Jen last night when she said Alison wasn't on her radar, but tonight was washing that trust out to sea. Just because you're paranoid doesn't mean they're not out to get you.

Jen's behaviour reeked of Alison.

There was no sign of Jen in the queue for the toilets, so Holly loitered, watching it move slowly.

There couldn't be many loos inside. If she marked the person fifth in the queue it would be a safe bet there'd been a full rotation when they came out. Unless Jen was having a full-scale panic attack.

Guilt crawled over Holly's skin. She hugged herself, arms crossed over her chest. Maybe Jen was just feeling nervous.

No. There had been more. Something in the way she was looking everywhere but directly at Holly.

She'd been spoiled with Jen's affection in the last few weeks. She'd gotten so used to being her sole focus that now the spell was broken, it was glaringly obvious.

The queue moved forward.

Holly continued to hold herself, wishing and hoping Jen that would be the next person to leave the toilets. She'd look up, flash Holly that killer smile, then take her hand in hers, lacing their fingers together.

Holly's breath stilled, a thousand *what-ifs* crashing through her mind.

She wanted to be delusional, chastise herself for letting Shona get in her head. She wouldn't tell Jen what she'd suspected. She probably already thought she was needy and untrusting.

'You okay?' The queue was blocked out by Daddy Bear James.

'Yeah, just waiting on Jen,' Holly replied, forcing a smile as she dropped her hands to her side.

'Aw, I just saw her – she was heading that way,' he said, pointing towards the back of Langside Hall.

'There?' Holly couldn't hide the surprise in her voice.

There was nothing there. Barely even a light, never mind a reason for Jen to be wandering about in the brush.

'Yeah, definitely her. She was with some brown-haired woman.'

Fuck.

32

'So?' Jen said, unable to hide the annoyance in her tone or posture.

'So?'

'Why do you want to chat?'

It was eerily quiet round the back of the hall, the building doing a good job as a sound barrier to the event happening on its other side. Its shadow spilled into thick, dark night, enveloping the unlit car park and grassland beyond the wrought iron fence.

Jen huddled herself against the stonework hemming the ledge above. This needed to be over, quick.

Even in the dark Alison's nerves were clear. She'd never seen her persona crack like this, even on stage. The change in dynamics threw Jen in a loop.

Alison played with the ring on her thumb, chewing on her lip as she thought. 'I didn't expect you to be like this.'

'What did you expect?' Jen nipped.

A hint of tears rimmed Alison's eyes and guilt clenched Jen's stomach. It shouldn't have, not after what Alison had put her though, but it was there, a heavy hand around her belly.

Alison let out a quiet laugh. 'I guess I've played this out so many times in my head, I thought you'd be happy to see me.'

'Happy? To see you?' Jen couldn't help but laugh.

'I deserve that.' Alison shuffled her feet. 'Did you really never miss me?'

How honest should she be? Was she actually considering being nice? Since when did preserving Alison's feelings factor into anything?

'Perhaps once or twice,' Jen eventually replied. The flicker of happiness in Alison's eyes made her feel like a bad person. 'I heard your song.'

If she felt bad before, the feeling was a tsunami of wickedness now. Alison broke out in a grin, her eyebrows arching into a hopeful frown. 'You did?' She played with the strap of her shoulder bag. 'What did you think?'

'Good beat.'

Alison's brows fell. 'And the words?' She stepped forward with a slight stagger.

'Are you drunk?'

She pulled a face. 'A little. Dutch courage after you didn't show last night.'

'Did you really think I would?'

Alison held her gaze and Jen was transported back to happier times together. She'd really thought they were the real deal. Now she couldn't imagine being with anyone but Holly. It was funny how something could feel so right one minute and so disastrously wrong the next. When they were good, they were good: when they were bad, they were bad. Alison wasn't who she wanted any more. She'd missed her chance and would have to get over it, just like Jen had done three long years ago.

'I think about you all the time,' Alison said, worrying her bottom lip with her teeth.

Jen didn't quite know what to say to that. *Congratulations, here's a medal?* 'A successful out musician like you? Surely you have girls falling at your feet.'

'Doesn't mean I want them.'

Time to cut this off. 'Look, Alison. When you left you made it perfectly clear there was no room for me in your life.' She went to argue but Jen cut her off. 'No, let me finish. Why would you think after three years with no contact that you could just swan back into my life and pick up where we left off? Like, really? You think I've been waiting here, pining for you to come back? You broke my heart,' Jen barked, stabbing at her chest. She took a breath, lowering her voice back to normal level. 'I don't know what's changed, but I can't do this, I'm sorry. I'm with Holly now.'

Alison rolled her eyes. 'As if. You've been together three weeks, tops.'

'So?'

'You can't feel anything after three weeks.'

'I love her.' The words were like cinder blocks to the ground.

Alison closed her eyes, as if recovering from a punch. 'Do you know how crazy those photos made me?' She spun on her heel, slightly off balance as she leaned her back against the stonework. 'I was always going to be visiting Glasgow this week. But then I saw those photos and it was like someone ripping my heart out.'

Jen bit her tongue. She didn't need to drive the hurt deeper. She took a seat a few feet up from Alison and picked her words carefully. 'What's changed? Why now?'

Alison moved her jaw from side to side, playing with the hem on her shorts. 'I knew you'd hate London. I didn't want to feel like I was sucking the life from you when I was off following my dreams. It didn't seem fair.'

'I would have coped. You know that. It was my decision to make.'

'I know.' She ran a hand through her hair, nodding aggressively. 'I know that now.'

'We can't change what you did.'

'No, but.' She blew out a long wavering breath. 'I can change things now. I came back because I found this bar. It's in Dalston – you'll love it. I thought if I bought it, you could run it?'

Jen was flummoxed.

Alison took her silence as a challenge and ran with it, filling the void. 'You, me? It would be like old times. We're a good team.'

She reached a hand towards Jen's but found only stone. There was one thing being nice, but misleading her was another.

Words were lodged in Jen's throat as her brain struggled to keep up with changing events. She looked at the hands in her lap as she shook her head.

'I've never stopped thinking about you. Loving you,' Alison said, her final sentence a near whisper.

Jen stood. 'I think I should go.'

'No, wait,' Alison blurted, grabbing Jen's wrist and pulling her close.

33

H olly crossed the grass, heading for the back of the hall. The building sat at a forty-five degree angle to the square, obscuring its back corner from sight. Never mind the fact that darkness crashed over its rear, shrouding everything it touched.

Goosebumps flushed over Holly's skin despite the evening's pleasant temperature. She hugged herself, willing her heart to calm down.

There would be an innocent explanation to this. There had to be.

Maybe James was wrong – maybe it wasn't Jen at all.

It felt like the small bank of grass was a mile wide. As she neared its edge, the thinning crowd disappeared around her. Soon it was only her and a single smoker. She watched as he paced the edge of the hall, wandering back and forth as he sucked on his cigarette. Despite the lack of company the air was still charged with laughter, the chatter of the crowd carrying on the breeze.

The smoker gave her a weak smile as she passed.

She returned it, ignoring the sickness sitting heavy in her stomach.

Her nerves were already shot, the urge to cry sitting on her chest like a boulder. Maybe she should turn around and go find Mum and Dad? Or just go to the stage, meet Jen there as planned?

She inhaled a long breath, the smell of smoke catching in her lungs.

No. She had to know.

She rounded the corner, light on her feet.

At first, it looked like there was no one there, but then—

The slightest movement.

Right in the far corner.

Holly's blood froze, like she'd been walking on ice and it had finally cracked, plunging her into sub-zero water below.

She gasped, her voice strangled.

In shadows was the unmistakable silhouette of Jen, her lips pressed to who she could only assume was Alison.

It didn't matter. Could be anyone. It wasn't Holly.

She turned on her heel, unable to watch any longer.

Holly closed her eyes, squeezing them tight as she walked. This was Shona all over again.

She stopped in her tracks. Fists balled.

'No. Not this time.' She fixed her stare straight ahead, her vision misted from tears.

In one swift move she marched back and rounded the corner.

She wouldn't be the victim this time. She wouldn't take this on the chin, playing it down to keep the peace. Fuck Jen. Fuck her to hell and back.

But there were only shadows.

Holly stopped, her heavy breathing loud now she was sheltered from Lovefest.

Were they hiding?

She listened but couldn't hear anything above the blood pumping in her ears.

'Jen?' she said, her voice cracking.

Silence.

She carried on, looping round the far side until she was back in the crowd. No sign.

She rooted herself to the spot. Surveying the sea of partygoers.

Just breathe.

Holly closed her eyes, taking a few deep breaths. She was aware she probably looked like an absolute weirdo, but regaining composure was the most important thing right now.

When she opened them, Alison's smug face was coming her way.

Every muscle tensed, a wave of raw fury surging through Holly.

'Jen'll get you at the stage now,' she said with a wink as she passed.

Holly couldn't move.

Part of her wanted to grab Alison and rip her head off. Another part wanted to throw up. The biggest chunk wanted to bawl her eyes out.

She chose to ignore it all and willed her legs to move, thundering towards the stage.

She couldn't let Mum and Dad down. If she failed to show for the winner's reveal it would make them a laughing stock. Talk of the town for all the wrong reasons.

All too quickly she was near the stage. Holly choked back the tears and pulled herself together, hoping the thin thread that held her pieces in place didn't snap before she could get this part of the evening over.

Her breathing was ragged, her mind a mess. But she had to do this.

A switch flicked in her brain and she mustered her best smile as she passed through the door of the marque. Jen stood with Chloe, looking slightly flustered, but what was new?

'Hols, there you are.' Jen's face twisted with concern. 'You okay?'

She went to take Holly's hand and she snatched it back, her jaw set. 'I'm grand.'

Jen's next question was cut off by Annie's arrival. Her eyes never wavered from Holly's, though. Confusion rippled over her features, followed by hurt, then what Holly could only assume was guilt.

'Right, we all ready?' Annie asked with a clap as she addressed the four couples. 'If we can all line up on stage, two on either side of me, that would be brilliant.' Nods of approval all round. 'Right, on with the show.'

Annie disappeared up the two small steps and behind the speakers. Whoops and cheers erupted from the crowd.

'What's wrong?' Jen shout-whispered into Holly's ear.

She ignored her. If she spoke, the tears would tumble out.

'Holly.'

She held Jen's stare and watched as her green eyes misted. Holly clenched her jaw. This would be over soon, and then she could go home.

Jen looked to the stage, then to Holly. But there was no time to linger, Annie was calling them up.

Holly took a final deep breath and prayed her mask stayed put.

Chloe looked over her shoulder, her smile a mile wide,

only for it to fall when she saw the tension between Jen and Holly. 'You okay?' she mouthed to Holly.

Holly shook her head.

Jen shrugged.

There wasn't anything that could be done. They had to go on stage.

This relationship had started out as acting and it would end as acting.

Holly sniffed, teetering on the edge. Not long now.

The two steps to the stage felt like a mountain. Jen and Holly took their places next to Chloe and Ryan as the crowd went crazy with clapping, shouting, and cheering. The place was packed. Holly's legs did a little wobble. Jen looked like a deer in headlights, but Holly guessed it wasn't to do with the crowd: her eyes had barely left her, searching for a connection, like Holly might magically gain the ability of telepathy.

She reached a hand out, her knuckles skirting Holly's. She allowed Jen to lace their fingers together but she didn't squeeze back. Instead her hand lay limp. Jen gulped.

'Let's hear it again for the couples,' Annie cheered. The crowd raised the roof once more.

Holly tuned Annie's speech out once more as she watched Jen. How could you say you love someone one evening and kiss someone else the next? The sourness in Holly's bones was more than anger. It was embarrassment. Thick, rotten, embarrassment. She'd been taken for a mug again.

She heard her name and flicked back to reality, putting on her best smile for the crowd.

'And now, the moment you've all been waiting for,' Annie said, pausing for effect. She held a large white envelope in her hands and made a show of opening it very slowly, pulling the top of the inner paper out a slither. 'The winning couple is—' She slid the paper out further, pulling a face that was either surprise or agreement, maybe a little of both.

Jen pumped Holly's hand again. She chose to focus on the crowd instead of meeting her gaze.

People stomped their feet, banged on the tables; anything to make a noise, the rumble resembling a drumroll.

'Chloe and Ryan,' Annie shouted, twisting towards the couple.

'Oh, shit,' Chloe squealed as Ryan picked her up, spinning as he kissed her. They nearly lost their footing on the tiny stage, but he settled her down just in time. Then it was Jen's turn to hug her best friend. Holly kept back, clapping with gusto.

It was well-deserved. She was over the moon for them, but she just couldn't summon the level of energy needed for excitement.

Tears streaked down Chloe's face as she and Ryan headed to the microphone. Ryan had barely blinked, his eyes permanently wide, his mouth fixed in a grin.

He laughed down the mic, a throaty chuckle as words failed him. 'I can't believe it,' he said, one hand running the length of his face, the other scooping Chloe at the waist.

'Thank you,' Chloe yelped. 'Like, thank you! That's all I can manage.' She laughed, happy tears getting the better of her.

The crowd *aww*-ed and laughed.

Jen gave Holly's side a squeeze, pulling her nearer as they lingered at the edge of the stage. She allowed it. Now wasn't the time to be creating distance, not when so many eyes were on them.

Holly searched the crowd for her parents, but the spotlights were too bright. She could barely see the edge of the dance floor, never mind the seating behind it. As soon as this was over she wanted to dash home.

Another crescendoing round of applause and Chloe and Ryan's speech was over. Holly felt dazed, winded, deflated.

She didn't even care that they hadn't won the money.

Of course they didn't.

Finally, it was time to leave the stage. Holly didn't break her stride as she reached the bottom step and was out of the marquee in a heartbeat. The night air stole her breath, the momentary lapse in composure all her mind needed to collapse, and the tears followed.

Jen was hot on her heels, skirting around her in an attempt to slow her down.

'Holly, wait.'

This was bad enough as it was. She didn't want to create a scene in the still-thick crowd. Holly aimed for the fencing on the edge of the park.

Jen didn't let up.

'Hols! Please!'

She stopped, only for a moment, enough to speak before she took off again. 'Fuck you, Jen.'

34

'Holly, come on, tell me what's going on?' Jen asked, out of breath from keeping pace.

Holly shook her head, getting faster.

Jen's calves burned as she fought to overtake. With a final burst of energy she pulled Holly into the park, away from the bustle on the pavement.

'Holly. Speak to me.'

Had she seen? It was the only explanation.

Jen felt sick. She swallowed the feeling, trying to focus on Holly's face, find answers. Tears welled in her eyes at the sight of Holly's sodden face.

'I'm not doing this again, Jen.'

'Doing what?'

Holly's face creased with exasperation. 'I saw you and Alison.'

The sentence hung in the air and every part of Jen froze before her heart sped up to a dizzying thunder.

'I—.'

Holly's chest rose and fell, the tears heavier than ever.

She sucked on her top lip, her eyes fixed on the treetops above.

Fuck, where were the words? Jen's breathing was ragged, her vision closing in.

'I pushed her away,' she finally managed.

Holly scoffed. 'Didn't look that way when I saw you.'

Jen shook her head. This couldn't be reality. This was a cruel joke. Had she hit her head? Dizziness muddled her brain.

'She kissed me,' she pleaded, a tear escaping.

A couple passed, arms linked as they took up the whole path. Jen and Holly moved aside.

'Holly,' Jen said, her voice verging on pathetic. She reached for Holly's hand only for it to be snatched away.

Holly's eyes were now fixed over Jen's shoulder as she wiped her cheeks. Jen turned, wondering what she was looking at, but only found the crowd. The party showed no sign of letting up. She should be with Chloe celebrating. That wasn't going to happen now.

'Come back to mine, let's chat,' Jen said, attempting to make a connection with Holly's hand again.

Holly shook her head, tucking her hands under her arms. 'No. I've seen enough. If this is how you act at the start of a relationship, how am I meant to trust you later on?'

Jen's heart shattered. A rug hadn't just been pulled out from under her feet; it felt like the entire world had.

'Holly.' Her name was all Jen could manage right now. Every other word was either lodged in her throat or deemed not good enough.

'I thought you were different,' Holly said, her bottom lip wobbling. 'And you were. You were worse.'

Jen's brow creased, not knowing what that meant.

Holly continued. 'I fell so fast for you. I felt like we had this connection, you made me feel so good about myself, and —' She paused, her shoulders slumping as she sucked on her top lip again. She raised a trembling hand to her mouth, resting her fingers there. 'None of it was real. I see that now.'

'Holly,' Jen said, her voice firm. But still nothing more would come. *Jesus fuck.* If she didn't find words fast she was a goner.

Blood roared in Jen's ears as she watched a group of young lads walk into the park. They were drunk and carrying on, having a good time. She made awkward eye contact with one before focusing back on Holly.

With another gulp, sentences finally broke through the dam in her throat. 'She wanted to chat. I told her I loved you. Then she kissed me.'

Holly was silent and Jen hoped that was because she was thinking it over and seeing sense. She wouldn't cheat on her. She'd never felt this way about anyone, why would she throw it all away for a crappy kiss with her ex?

Their lips had barely touched for a second before Jen had pushed her away and stormed off.

Holly nodded and Jen's heart swelled. It was going to be okay.

'Right. She kissed you. Got it,' Holly said, walking away.

Wait. This didn't feel right.

'You believe me, yeah?' Jen asked, tumbling after her.

'I can't do this, Jen. I can't do this.'

'Can't do what? Talk here? Please, just come back to mine.'

Holly shook her head, her pace increasing as she exited the park.

'We're done.'

Jen paused for a moment, the words like a shotgun to

her chest. In an instant she was back in motion. 'No, Holly, no.' She took Holly's shoulder and turned her back.

'Jen, we're done. Okay? We're done.' Tears were a torrent on her cheeks but her voice was firm. The harshness of her stare told Jen she meant it.

She watched as Holly walked away. Was it just her, or was the light fading? Jen gripped the tip of the wrought iron fence.

'Holly!' she screamed.

CHLOE FOUND her sitting on the bench by the bowling club. She'd wanted to go home; it was just across the road after all, but Jen found she had no life left in her. All she could muster was the few short steps to the bench, where she pulled her knees to her chest and bawled her eyes out.

Thankfully, everyone that had passed ignored her. Sometimes living in a city had its benefits.

'Pal, what's going on?' Chloe asked, sliding into place beside her and placing a hand on Jen's back. 'I've been looking everywhere for you.'

'Holly's gone.'

'Gone home?'

'She's left me.'

'Hold up. You're going to need to back this up a little. Is this to do with Alison?'

Jen sniffed, pawing at her eyes to gain some composure. 'She said she wanted to chat. Then she kissed me.' She didn't have the heart to go into detail.

'Alison?'

'Yep.'

'And you told Holly?'

'She saw.'

Chloe let out a sound somewhere between a whistle and balloon deflating. 'Fuck.' She rubbed Jen's back. 'So, what're you going to do?'

'I honestly don't know.'

'You can't just let her go.'

'I know, but she was mad. Really mad. I've never seen her like that.'

Chloe nodded silently, a hand still on Jen's back. 'You texted her?'

'Yep.'

'Phoned her?'

'Yep.'

'Any reply?'

'Nope.'

'Okay, give her time to cool off. Go to her house in the morning.'

'You don't think I should go round tonight?'

'If she's that mad she'll need a breather to see sense. This is all just a silly misunderstanding. Give her a night to sleep on it and she'll see it wasn't your fault.'

That didn't seem like a crazy idea, but Jen's head was screaming for her to go after Holly now. Chloe was right, though: if she went tonight their conversation would go round and round in circles again. A little time and space and they could be rational. Holly would hear her out.

'Come on, let's go home,' Chloe said, getting to her feet and extending a hand to Jen.

'You should stay, celebrate.'

Chloe shook her head. 'Nah, the only people I want to celebrate with are you and Ryan. We can do that back at the flat.'

Reluctantly, Jen got to her feet. She didn't have the

stamina to argue with Chloe. It would be a losing battle anyway.

Chloe linked her arm with Jen's. 'Can you believe we won?'

'I know. Rigged, for sure.'

Chloe poked at her side. 'You still going to say that when I give you money for your fridge?'

Jen stopped in her tracks. 'No. That's too much.' For a brief moment her troubles with Holly faded.

'A loan, obviously. I would quite like a holiday. But I chatted to Ryan and we're happy to wait until after Christmas. Your cash flow should be better then.'

Jen was lost for words. 'You're sure?'

'Course I'm sure. You're the closest thing I have to family.' She kissed Jen's cheek. 'Now, let's get home and have a glass of bubbly. I'll text Ryan.'

They'd only made it to the zebra crossing when Alison's voice boomed Jen's name.

Chloe turned faster than a spinning wheel and Jen had the common sense to grab her by the arm. Chloe's eyes burned with anger.

'Don't you fucking dare come any closer,' she growled.

A few passersby made faces at the outburst, but Alison paid her no heed and sauntered closer without a care in the world. Nikki wasn't far behind.

'I just want to say bye to Jen.'

'I think you've done enough.'

Alison diverted her attention to Jen, who was holding Chloe back as much as she was using her as a human shield. 'The offer still stands, for Dalston. Just call me. Or Instagram. Whatever works best for you.'

Jen had no time to reply as a voice in the passing crowd blurted, 'Oh my God, is that Alison Rae?' A young woman stopped in her tracks, her friends following suit. 'Oh my God, it is. Can I get a photo?'

A flicker of annoyance tripped over Alison's features, but her professional face won out, the mask falling into place in a heartbeat. 'Hey, hi. Yeah, of course.'

As Alison got into position, the woman's camera phone angled towards her best game face, Jen took her chance.

'I've got this,' Jen said to Chloe as she stepped out from the safety of her best friend. 'I'll save you any confusion, Alison. There is no hope in hell that I'll open a bar with you. Or get back together with you. Or want to breathe the same air as you, ever again.'

Alison's face went blank. She was either wounded beyond response, searching for a good comeback, or wondering how to play this in front of a fan. Probably a bit of all three.

Whatever it was, the moment was perfectly captured on camera.

Her fan didn't know what to do with herself. Jen felt a bit guilty at centring her in the crosshairs of their argument but she couldn't let the opportunity pass.

Alison mumbled her apologies with a smile.

But Jen wasn't done.

'Don't worry, I'm her ex,' she offered as explanation to the poor woman. 'You're a mess, Alison. These people think you've got it all together, but you're nothing special. Don't ever talk to me again.'

Alison's mouth hung open, torn between Jen and her fan. Once again, work was taking precedence. Nothing had changed.

When she still hadn't spoken, Jen turned on her heel, linking arms with Chloe.

'Fuck you, Alison,' Jen shouted, flipping her the bird over her shoulder.

Safely across the road, she pulled out her phone and called Holly again. Straight to voicemail.

Tomorrow. Everything would be sorted tomorrow.

35

'Holly,' Dad called through the door. 'Jen's here. Do you want me to let her in?'

'No,' Holly replied, her voice muffled from the duvet over her head. She pawed at her phone, retrieving it from her bedside table. 7 a.m.. Who the heck calls at someone's house this early?

'Can I come in?' Dad asked, rapping his knuckles gently on the doorframe.

'If you must.'

The door creaked open and in popped Dad, still in his pyjamas, the little hair he had sticking up at odd angles and his face shadowed in white stubble.

He slowly sat on the bed, his muscles still waking up. Holly didn't budge from her position, buried under her covers.

'Very early for a visitor.'

'I didn't know she was coming,' Holly snapped. Her eyes were puffy and her chest still tight from the tears she had shed the night before.

'I wasn't having a go at you,' Dad assured, placing his

hand on the lump in the covers that was her leg. 'I'm just saying, she must really want to talk to you if she's here so early.'

It was a fair point but one Holly wasn't for awarding. 'I still don't want to see her.'

Dad was quiet. She pulled the duvet down a fraction and watched him sleepily rub at his eyes. He'd have to get ready for work soon. 'Do you not think it would be good to hear her out?'

'I don't know what else there is to hear.'

Jen's texts and voicemails basically said the same thing: Alison kissed her and she was sorry.

Sorry she got caught.

Would she have been honest if Holly hadn't caught them? Something told her yes. Which made the decision harder, but it had to be done. She'd been too soft and forgiving before. Never again.

Dad stood, his knees popping like candy. 'Right, I'd better go tell her you're not up for visitors.' He stopped short of the door. 'Any messages you want me to pass on?'

The words she wanted to use weren't Dad-appropriate. 'Tell her I need space.'

'Space. Right. Got it.'

He closed the door and a fresh wave of tears spilled. She'd moved past anger and grief. Now, pure embarrassment washed over her.

Not just caused by Jen. Alison, too. She'd looked at Holly and thought she would be easy to get rid of, that it was no big deal to completely fuck her over.

Holly growled with frustration.

Moving back to Glasgow was meant to be about starting again, not repeating mistakes. Maybe she was stuck in an endless cycle of being second best. She could be happy single. Plenty of people were. Anything would be better than feeling like this.

The tears stopped as quickly as they started, her eyes likely fed up with producing the damn things.

She wiped her face on her pillow before propping it against the headboard and sitting up.

Time to brave her phone.

She was in the middle of reading a message from Chloe when it buzzed to life, a call incoming from Jen.

Holly stabbed at the red *end call* button.

Now wasn't the time for pleading phone conversations.

There was nothing Jen could say to make Holly see her face to face.

Jen didn't take the hint, though, and her phone buzzed again.

Holly cleared her throat before answering. 'What do you want?' Her tone couldn't be more monotonous if she tried.

'Holly,' Jen sounded surprised she'd answered. 'Please don't hang up.'

Holly was silent. There was nothing worth saying.

'You there?'

'Of course.'

'I'm still outside your house. I know your Dad said you wanted space but please, just let me come up. Let's sort this.'

Jen's desperation was clear and her raw emotion brought a fresh tear down Holly's cheek.

She took a stilted breath before answering. 'I need time to think, Jen.'

'Hols, what's there to think about? I didn't do anything wrong.' She almost kept it together but the final sentence was too much. Her voice shattered.

This was a mess. A huge, colossal, fucked-up mess.

'I'll call you when I'm ready to chat.'

Holly punched the *end call* button with her finger and flung the phone onto the bed.

She was braced for more tears, but none came.

She settled for lying on her back and staring at the ceiling instead.

Shona wasn't like this.

When the truth finally came out it was because she wanted to be in a proper relationship with Keira. Holly was nothing but a hurdle. An inconvenience to overcome. There was no begging or pleading for her to stay.

But was Jen's remorse enough reason to give her a second chance?

For once, Holly was going to put herself first.

36

'Still nothing?' Chloe asked.

Three days and the radio silence continued. If Jen thought not hearing from Holly for a day was bad, this was off the scale. It was like someone was holding Jen's head under water; she wanted to scream and shout, gasp for breath, but her lungs burned instead, the weight on her chest getting heavier by the day.

'Not a word.' Jen twisted her glass, making the ice in her old -fashioned twirl and clink. In a bid to distract from her spiralling misery, Chloe had called round tonight, armed with the ingredients for a multitude of cocktails. Three drinks in, and it was working. Slightly. Jen was slowly becoming one with her couch, regardless. The longer this went on, the more her energy was drained.

'What did Harry say?' Chloe asked, lightly jabbing Jen's thigh with her foot.

Jen took in a long breath, followed by a pitiful huff. She'd called into Taylor's Deli today, hopeful to see Holly. No chance. She'd had a long conversation with Harry instead. At least he didn't have any ill feelings.

'He's on Holly's side, of course. But he implied if I gave her some breathing space she'd come around.'

'Well, that's a positive, surely?'

Jen felt her bottom lip wobble. She steadied herself. 'I guess. But why's she not been in touch?'

'You're reading into the *I love you* thing again, aren't you?'

'She would have said it back if she felt the same way.'

'You're being far too hard on yourself. You said what you feel. But it's super early in your relationship. Just because Holly doesn't feel it now, doesn't mean she never will.'

Jen downed the rest of her drink and the heat of the alcohol settled in her throat, numbing the lump that had been lodged since the Lovefest event.

'I should have stayed single.'

'You won't be saying that when she comes running back.'

'I feel like she was looking for an out. I came on too strong.'

'Now you're definitely being stupid.'

Chloe was right. She was stupid. She'd given Harry a little wooden duck to pass onto Holly. It felt like the worst move in the world now. It was a silly little thing, a child's toy, something she'd found in the boutique along from her shop. The chunky wooden toy was no bigger than an inch-and-a-bit tall, with a mallard duck painted on either side. It felt innocent, cute; a token of how much Holly meant to her, when she'd handed it to Harry. Now it screamed desperation.

'I'm making another drink,' Jen said, getting to her feet.

'What's up next?'

She shrugged. 'I'll make you anything you want. I'm just having whisky.'

'Good thing you're off tomorrow.'

'Don't.'

'What?'

'Remind me that I'm off.'

'Is it not a good thing?'

Jen shook her head as she poured the whisky into her glass with a satisfying glug. 'At least if I'm at work I have something else to think about.'

'You never know,' Chloe said, joining Jen in the kitchen. 'Holly might come round here. She knows your schedule.'

There was a flicker of hope in Jen's chest. 'Has she said something to you?'

Chloe's face turned serious. 'No. Sorry. Just wishful thinking.'

'She's returning your texts, though?' Jen took a swig of her whisky and bared her teeth at the taste.

'Yeah, but we've not spoken in a while. I said what I needed to and left her to it.'

'Which is what you think I should do?'

'You just go with your gut. You can only do what feels right to you.'

Jen drank another gulp of whisky. 'Maybe I should take Alison up on her offer, move to London. Would keep me busy.'

Chloe whacked Jen on the arm. 'Good to see your sense of humour's still intact.'

'Can you imagine?'

'Let's pray things never get that bad.' Chloe topped the dregs of her old-fashioned with whisky. 'Look, give Holly time. She'll come round.'

'And if she doesn't, I'll always have you and Ryan to live vicariously through.'

'Speaking of which, I'm also feeling the little pitter-patters of the L-word.'

Jen's eyes grew wide. 'Shut up.'

'Early days,' Chloe replied, holding a hand in the air. 'I won't be saying it for a long time yet, but there's deffo potential.'

'Big news, Clo.'

'Tell me about it.'

Jen was happy for her best friend, but couldn't help the swell of longing that erupted in her heart. She missed Holly, and nothing would feel right until she won her back.

37

A week since the event and Holly felt no better. She'd made the right decision, but the gap Jen had left was all encompassing.

Phone calls and texts were easily ignored.

But the tugging in her chest wasn't.

Holly flopped onto the sofa, not entirely sure what she intended to do. TV felt wrong – nothing grabbed her attention. Books weren't easy to focus on. Her mind kept wandering. She'd drawn for a bit this morning but now she felt all fizzy inside, like a wind-up toy being held in place. Maybe a walk. Fresh air would do her good.

In a bit. She'd go for a walk in a bit.

Holly let out a long, breathy sigh, and rubbed at her eyes.

How could someone get under your skin after such a short amount of time? Heck, they'd only properly dated for a week.

This wasn't right.

She grabbed her phone from the coffee table, her finger

hovering over Jen's name. But she'd betrayed her trust in the worst possible way. There was no going back on that.

Fuck. She'd been going in circles for seven days.

Holly chucked her phone to the armchair and it bounced off, landing with a thud on the rug.

'Urgh!' she groaned. Her thoughts were nothing but mindless spirals, forever in a loop: she wanted to crack her head open and empty it.

Maybe Mum and Dad would let her get a dog. Company would be good right now.

She would be in the shop if it wasn't for the fear of seeing Jen. The less time she spent there the better. Plus, it lowered the odds of Holly cracking and going next door herself. God, she missed her. Everything felt wrong, like her hands were never in quite the right position, her breathing was out of sync, and her heartbeat was going at a new rhythm. Restless didn't cover it.

Holly hugged herself as she stared at the ceiling. *Who does this after a month?* It was ridiculous.

A knock at the door made her freeze.

She raised herself up on her forearm and listened.

Was Dad expecting a package? She couldn't remember him saying anything. Although, she wasn't the most attentive listener right now.

A second knock, harder this time.

She looked to the living room window, well aware she was in full view. What kind of delivery driver looks in a window? What if it was someone trying to sell gutter cleaning services? They might look in. If they were weird.

If it was a package they could leave a note, plus she was in no mood to talk to strangers. Especially about guttering.

She grabbed the closest pillow and hugged it to her

chest. Days were getting longer, no doubt about it. Five o'clock got further away every morning.

She listened for the sound of a missed delivery slip being put through the letter box but nothing came. She'd made the right call. Bloody cold-callers. Who parted with their money on their doorstep anyway? Idiots.

The weather didn't seem too bad. She could go see the Highland cows in Pollok Park if she went for a walk.

Holly sighed for the thousandth time, before placing the cushion back and sitting up at a speed that surprised herself. Her vision closed in, she scrunched her eyes shut, a hand to her temple until the feeling passed. *Yuck.*

No point moping about like some sad sack. Time to see the cows.

She looked a mess, but who cared? There was no one to run into. Trainers crammed on, she redid her messy bun in the hall mirror before shoving her denim jacket over her hoodie. She gave herself an assertive nod. *Looking like a break-up personified. Nailing it, Hols.*

Keys grabbed, she was halfway out the door before she clocked the car in the drive.

Jen.

She hadn't seen Holly, though. She was focused on what Holly assumed was her phone.

Could she sneak past without her noticing? Was it worth a shot? What was the etiquette when the person you've been avoiding all week camps out in your driveway?

Holly closed the door slowly, as if keeping her movement to a minimum might make her invisible.

When she turned, Jen was still on her phone.

She looked as bad as Holly. Worse, even.

Even from a distance Holly could see her sparkle was

missing. Her posture was slumped, her hair scraped back in a knot. Not the cool, calm Jen that was spinning circles in Holly's head.

Holly's heart thumped against her ribs, taken aback by Jen's arrival. What to do?

She'd lingered too long and Jen's eyes met hers.

The person in the driving seat of Jen's car was a husk of the woman she'd grown to love. Her smile was unsure, her eyes sullen.

Holly's heart stuttered.

Jen was halfway out of the car before Holly had even moved.

'Holly, please. Can we talk?'

A dimension didn't exist where Holly had the willpower to say no.

Just seeing Jen made Holly want to lean into her and be hugged until there were no more tears to cry. Which was stupid, because she was the one causing the heartache.

Holly nodded, sucking on her bottom lip as she got her thoughts in order. She opened the passenger door of Jen's car.

'You not going to invite me in?'

'I'm heading out.'

Jen slumped back into the car and waited for Holly to join her.

The car's interior became ten times smaller when Holly closed the door. The air disappeared, the mounting pressure like a submarine sinking to unknown depths.

Up close, Jen's eyes were red, her skin blotchy. Had she been at work?

'It's the middle of the afternoon. Why are you here? Saturday's your busiest day.'

Jen fiddled with her jacket, repositioning it unnecessarily. 'I couldn't stand being there any more. Talking to you is more important than money.' She shifted in her seat, turning to face Holly. 'I feel like I'm going out of my head. Tell me what I need to do and I'll do it – just tell me, Hols. I need you to forgive me.'

'Unless you've got a time machine you're kind of sunk.'

Jen chewed on her cheek as she looked out the windscreen. 'You got my texts?'

'And your voicemails.'

'And the duck?'

Holly nodded. The duck had almost cracked her. She'd had to shove it in a drawer. Every time she looked at it she wanted to cry.

'You still don't believe me?'

Holly considered her response. She wanted to reach over and kiss Jen, tell her everything was fine, but the logical part of her brain told her she'd been here once before. *You really want to be the third wheel again?*

'I believe that Alison kissed you, but it's not changed how I feel.'

Jen's eyes pleaded with Holly's. She reached over and took her hand: this time Holly didn't pull away. Her heart fluttered at the contact.

'How can that not change anything? That's like someone kissing me while I'm in Sainsbury's milk aisle. I had no control over it.'

'Not exactly, but. . .' Holly replied, her attention fixed on Jen's hand. 'You really think I want to spend my life worried Alison is going to come back and pull another stunt?'

'She's not coming back. I made it clear I was with you.'

Holly couldn't help the smile that flashed across her face. Chloe had filled her in on what happened after she left the Lovefest event. It was good to know Alison got a little taste of her own medicine.

Jen took advantage of the change in mood and stoked her thumb across the back of Holly's hand. A shiver travelled up her arm, straight to her chest.

'You know what I went through with Shona. I can't do that again.' Despite Chloe's efforts, the thought of Alison coming between them would always linger, a shadow following them at every turn.

Jen shuffled closer, her hand gripping Holly's tighter. Holly couldn't bear to look her in the eye. 'I'm not your ex. This was a mistake out of my control.'

'You could have told me she was there. You could have told me why you were being weird.'

'I know. I thought I was protecting you.'

Holly sucked on her lips. They could go in circles forever. Holly wiggled her toes in her trainers, trying to expel the jittery energy rising within. Her head was in a tug of war with her heart, and right now she had no idea who would win. Much more of this inner back and forth and Holly would snap. 'So, what do you want? Why are you here?'

'Holly, please.' Jen pulled her hand back, slamming her head against the headrest in frustration.

'I can't take the chance, Jen. I wasted my twenties on a relationship that was doomed from the start. Why is this any different?' As the words tumbled from her mouth, Holly's heart ached. She'd never felt for Shona what she did for Jen. Even at the start of their relationship. But Shona's cuts were so deep, the bruises still so fresh, that no matter how softly Jen tread Holly would always be on the defence. Perhaps Holly had gone into this too soon. But she hadn't set out to fall for Jen – this was never part of the plan. The realisation hit like a slap in the face: Jen wasn't the problem, she was.

Jen looked like Holly had ripped her heart out and stomped on it. The tears rimming her eyes were instant. 'You don't feel the same way as me. I get it.'

'And how would that be?' Holly sniffed, she couldn't see Jen cry without mirroring her emotion. She missed Jen's hand and desperately wanted her to reach over again. She couldn't be the one to do it though; too many mixed signals, to Jen and herself. God, why couldn't she just settle on one emotion? Did she want her or not?

'I love you,' Jen blurted, punctuating the outburst with a quiet laugh as if it was the most absurd sentence to ever fall from her lips. 'I understand that you don't feel it back but I do, I love you. I've never felt like this before. I've barely known you a month and now when I think of the future you're all I see. I can't walk away from this.' She shook her head as her fists clenched. 'This is too special to give up on. Tell me you don't feel something? Anything?'

The words danced on Holly's tongue but they still felt foreign, premature. The feeling that she'd had at Lovefest was dialled back, uncertainty dampening what she'd been sure of.

'Wow,' Jen huffed, misreading Holly's silence.

'It's not like that.'

'So what is it?'

Holly's mind buzzed. 'This is a lot. I thought I was going for a walk.'

Jen gave a quiet nod. 'So, what now? You get out of my car and it's back to silence?'

'No. I can't spend another week like this.'

A quiet laugh escaped Jen. 'So we agree about something.'

'I just—' Holly didn't even know where the sentence was going. She rubbed at her temple, willing her head to make the decision for her. 'I need time.'

'I'll wait.'

Holly didn't doubt it for a second, and that's what was killing her. Could she really trust Jen with her fragile heart, or was it better for them both to walk away now?

38

Jen hammered on Chloe's door again, finally hearing footsteps in her bestie's flat.

A bleary-eyed Chloe appeared in the gap as she slowly opened the door. 'Oh, it's you. The fuck, Jen?'

'She's texted,' Jen declared, swanning in, full force. 'Why you asleep at 6 p.m.?'

Chloe rubbed at her eyes, closing the door as she followed Jen to the kitchen. 'I was on an early. Why are you so – urgh – why are you so awake?'

'Because it's 6 p.m.. And Holly texted. She texted.'

Chloe snapped awake. 'She texted.'

Three days of radio silence. Three days of torturous radio silence and now a text. Jen felt like she could do cartwheels.

'What did she say?' Chloe asked, her words crashing into each other.

'She wants to meet tonight. On our rooftop.'

'The rooftop?' Chloe clasped her hands to her lips and let out an excited breath. 'Oh, wow.'

'This is good, yeah?' Excitement was replaced with a rush of nerves. 'Yeah?'

Chloe considered it. 'Rooftop is good. Romantic.'

'But?'

'What else did she say?'

Jen froze, looking around the room for the clue as to what the heck that question could allude to. 'That was it. Is that not enough?'

'I dunno, it's hard to judge tone by text.'

'So, you think this is could be bad?'

Chloe shrugged. 'I'm still waking up. Can you come back to me on that?'

'Chloe,' Jen whined.

'What? I'm only being honest.' She walked to the sink as she spoke and filled a glass with water.

'Yeah, well, I don't need honesty. I need hope.'

Chloe downed a few gulps of water. 'How did it go with the fridge guy?'

Jen leaned her forearms on the breakfast bar and arched her back out, relieving some of the tension from the last week-and-a-bit. 'Good. All fixed. Just need to fill it now.' She couldn't help but grin: Chloe always had her back, no matter what.

'Shaping up to be quite the day for you,' she joked, placing the now-empty glass in the sink.

'Thanks again. I don't know what I'd do without you.'

Chloe smirked. 'You'd find a way; you always do. So, what time you meeting Holly?'

'Eight thirty.'

'Yikes. Not long. What you wearing? Or are you sticking with what you've got on?' she joked.

Jen jiggled on the spot with nervous energy, looking at

her old T-shirt and running shorts. 'Well, obviously not this, but I don't know. Does it matter?'

'Of course it flipping matters! Now, let me put a bra on and we'll head over to yours. Forgive me if I fall asleep in your bed while I'm waiting for you to choose an outfit, though. You know I've been up since 4 a.m.? Knocking on people's doors when they're trying to sleep, honestly. . .' Chloe said, her head sinking into her crossed arms on the counter.

'Awright, calm the ham.'

Chloe's head sprung up. 'Wait, you've texted her back, yeah? I'm not going through this again.'

Jen laughed as she landed a playful punch on her best friend's arm. 'Come on, I'll pour us a wine.'

JEN HAD GOT HERE EARLY, not wanting to risk being late, but it was now ten to nine. Holly obviously hadn't had the same idea.

She'd been surprised to find both the close door and the roof door open and had expected to find Holly as she rounded the chimneys, her heart racing a thousand beats a minute. It had all but stopped, her shoulders drooping, her face falling flat, when she discovered she was alone. A few trips round the stacks to double check, but nope. No Holly.

Nothing left to do but wait.

She felt a little bad, being up here, and had no idea how Holly had managed to have the door open, but she took it as a good sign. Surely? There was forward planning here. She might not be here now, but she would be. Soon.

The sky wasn't as psychedelic as the last time. This evening, the sunset played out in more reserved dusky greys, fading to a cool ink-blue. But Jen could still feel magic in the air. This was their spot. Her skin tingled at the memory of kissing Holly here.

She'd paired a simple T-shirt with her wet-look jeans. Holly hadn't held back on expressing how much she liked them. Hopefully they would earn her extra points tonight.

Jen checked her phone before leaning her forearms on the railing.

She let out a wavering sigh.

Her stomach twisted. Was Holly going to ghost her? Or maybe if this was a break-up meeting she just wasn't in a rush to get here.

But it was here: their place. Why not a coffee shop or somewhere neutral?

Sickness settled in Jen's stomach.

All week she'd been imagining this moment. Holly turning up at her flat; Holly at her work. Bumping into Holly in the street. Any scenario when they could be close. Rekindle what they had.

She understood Holly's hesitation, but what happened with Alison was out of her control. It was unfair to end things on someone else's faults.

The door to the roof banged shut and Jen stood to attention. Where to put her hands? Oh God, how was she meant to stand? Her heart fluttered in her chest.

Should she hug Holly? Was this going to be awkward?

Jen pawed at her hair, her palms suddenly sweaty.

The sound of two guys chatting on the other side of the stacks brought her mood crashing to the ground.

Not Holly.

She found a bench among the greenery and plant pots and took a seat.

How long should she wait?

Fuck it. She sent Holly a text.

From her spot on the bench she could just make out the buildings resting against the sky, and the occasional blocks of yellow and white where top-storey lights were on. Jen's eyes traced the outline, for want of something better to do.

What was the game plan if Holly didn't turn up?

Her chest twinged at the thought. At some point she had to admit it was over.

Jen drummed her fingers on the bench. Nearly nine o'clock.

If Holly didn't reply, she'd leave at nine. Half an hour was long enough. After all, Holly had set the time.

She leaned back, hands in pockets, and blew out slowly, her right leg as jittery as if it was connected to a jackhammer.

It felt like there was no air. If she was inside she'd be going out for a breather.

This is torture.

The door slammed again, but Jen didn't bother to look up. Probably more smokers or the last guys leaving.

Eight fifty-eight. Holly had two minutes.

Then what? Jen's mouth went dry, her throat closing tight.

A sound like a broken whistle made her peek round the potted plants and chimney stack.

Despite the odd angle she recognised Holly's perfect silhouette straight away.

There, in the glow of the fairy lights, stood Holly, hunched over, hands on thighs as she struggled to catch her breath.

Jen stood, surprised to find her legs were able to hold her even though they felt like jelly.

'Holly?'

She looked up, her messy bun flopping to one side like it was falling apart, and a smile split her face in two. 'One minute,' she huffed, words a struggle as she held up a hand.

Jen took a few tentative steps closer, unsure what was going on. 'You okay?'

Holly gripped her chest, pulling at the collar of her top. Jen noted her hoodie and shorts; she'd not gone to the effort Jen had. A sour feeling twisted in Jen's stomach.

Finally, after a huge ragged breath, Holly spoke. Even in the failing light Jen could see the sweat pouring off her. 'Sorry I'm late.' Another deep breath. 'I didn't know there was football on at Hampden.' More panting. 'I ended up ditching the car and running here.'

Holly rose to her full height, hands on hips, and stomped her feet a bit. She let out a breathy, 'Fuck.'

What to do? Could Jen touch her? She hovered a hand near Holly's arm. 'You okay? You're not going to pass out or anything?'

Holly pulled a face. 'Jury's out on that one.'

'Come, let's sit.'

There was only the sound of Holly's breathing for a while. Jen was painfully aware of the physical gap between them. Jen fixed her eyes on the skyline, even though all she wanted to do was look at Holly, take her in. She was really here. It almost didn't feel real.

'Oh my God,' Holly said, her voice nearly back to normal. She wiped the sweat off her top lip. 'I am not a runner.'

'Did you really run all the way from Hampden?' It was maybe just over a mile, but no mean feat if you weren't used to running. The steep hill in Battlefield was a killer to even the accomplished runner.

Holly nodded, still looking like she might pass out a little.

'Why didn't you text?' Jen asked. 'I would have waited.'

'I'd already gone a fair bit when I realised I'd left my phone in the car.' She cracked another smile, laughing quietly as she undid her wrecked bun, bobby pins held between her lips, and twisted it back to how it should be. 'This was not how I'd planned my entrance.'

'I can imagine,' Jen said with a chuckle. She felt light-headed herself, her heart hammering like she'd been the one doing the running. People didn't smile and make jokes when they were on track to break someone's heart, right? 'How did you manage to get access to the roof?'

'I went to the library where Gabriel works. He spoke to Bazza for me.'

Jen's heart pinged with optimism. That was a lot of effort. 'Romantic.' The word felt taboo, but she needed to get a feel for where this was heading.

'Trying to be, I guess.'

Fireworks exploded in Jen's chest. 'So, you're not here to break up with me?'

Holly snorted. 'Break up? Why would I bring you here? That's what texts are for.' A sly smile pulled at her mouth. She hid it by biting on her bottom lip.

Jen clicked her tongue to the roof of her mouth. 'Miss Taylor, please tell me you do not break up with people via text.'

Energy fizzed through Jen like firecrackers. This was feeling like the old them.

'A girl never tells her secrets.' Her face fell serious and Jen's heart did a little flip. 'I'm sorry for the silence the last few days. I just had to get my mind round things.'

'Like what? Can I help?'

Holly played with the hem of her shorts. 'It's just, I didn't expect to have these big feelings for someone so soon after breaking up with Shona. On the one hand I feel like I still have a lot of healing to do, but on the other, I like you too much to be without you.'

Okay. A lot to unpack there. Jen's hands ramped up the clam-factor. She turned the words over in her head once more, making sure she'd understood what Holly was saying. 'That's okay – we can go slow.'

Holly twisted to face her. 'But that's the problem: I can't go slow when it comes to you.'

'So?'

Holly shrugged.

The fireworks puttered out, fizzling to nothing. 'I don't understand.' Whatever Holly wanted she could get. Anything. It didn't matter.

'I'm saying this is an all-or-nothing situation. And I think it would have been hard enough without Alison getting involved.' Jen went to speak, but Holly cut her off with a wave of her hand. 'Let's never mention her again. Anyway, I just, what I'm trying to say is, if you can accept me as I am, a little bruised and broken, then I think I love you too.'

There were no words to describe how Jen felt. Euphoric didn't even touch the edges. She leaned in and kissed Holly: the feeling of her smiling against Jen's lips made her whole body flush. God, she'd missed that.

Jen could have happily kept the connection forever, but now was the time for words, not action. She had to be sure they were completely on the same page. Communication was key and there was no more room for fucking up.

She pulled back and was surprised to see Holly's eyebrows raise with disappointment.

'You okay?' she asked, wiping at her top lip. 'Sorry I'm so sweaty.'

Jen scooted closer, losing the gap on the bench, and taking Holly's hand in hers. 'I just don't want you to feel you're rushing into this. If you need time, I'll wait, honest.'

'But then what? I mope around, missing you while I wait for the magic moment when everything clicks back into place?' Holly shook her head. 'Do you remember what you said to me in your stockroom, the day we did the couples' quiz?'

Jen's brow knitted. Nothing specific sprang to mind. She stroked her thumb over Holly's palm as she thought, relishing the feeling as her skin tingled, every brush igniting miniature sparks.

'Something about your skirt?'

Holly chuckled. 'Yes. That's exactly what I'm talking about.'

'I was hoping you'd wear it tonight.'

'I bet you were. I didn't have time to change. There was an accident near Hillhead and I had to change plans. I should have known to just text you then.' Her eyes wandered to Jen's lips before darting back to her gaze. A playful smile pulled at her lips and eyes. 'No. Not the skirt. You said, "when life doesn't go to plan, I'm here to hold you until the pieces click back together". Or something like that.'

'I remember that. I just didn't know I said it then.' Thinking about how Shona had treated Holly made her blood boil. She couldn't undo the damage, but it was her job to make sure Holly never felt that again. 'I meant it.'

'I know you did. That's why I trust you.'

Jen felt Holly's words like a flaming arrow to her heart. It stuttered a little as heat swelled in her chest, warmed by the sheer weight of them. She leaned closer and kissed Holly. A kiss to end all kisses. But it wasn't frenzied, like their first proper kiss in the supermarket car park. Neither was adverse to taking their time, rediscovering the ebb and flow of how their bodies moved together. Jen placed her hand on Holly's neck, pulling her closer.

In a dizzyingly swift move Holly straddled Jen. No interfering gear sticks here. Jen's cored pulsed: this had gone from nought to one hundred, quick.

A burst of laughter from the other side of the chimneys paused Holly's movement.

She leaned close to Jen's ear, Holly's panting breath hot on her skin. 'Will we go somewhere a little more private?'

'I thought you'd never ask.'

39

Holly rounded the corner to Jen's bedroom, feeling fresh from a super quick shower, and was pleased to find Jen had followed her direction to a tee. Not that 'you better be waiting naked in bed for me' was hard to mess up.

She dropped her towel and slid under the sheets.

Jen groaned as their skin touched; every possible part that could connect was now merged into one. Holly pulled her hips closer, pinning Jen with a hand on her lower back.

She'd missed this. Not just the physicality of Jen's touch, but the feeling she ignited in her –with Jen she felt solid, sound. All vulnerability vanished.

Jen's hand explored her waist, her back, her lower ribs, as if rediscovering forgotten territory. When Jen's fingers found her breast and her fingers played with her hardened nipple, Holly couldn't help but arch her back, the manoeuvre stealing her breath. Jen grinned, taking it as an invite and dropping her lips to Holly's collarbone.

She'd toyed with the notion of giving herself time, but there was no hope in hell she could resist this. Her heart needed patience and a little TLC, which Jen could no doubt deliver, but her body needed this – Jen's touch, Jen's unequivocal love. They could never just be friends, and going cold turkey wasn't an option. Once you knew what you were missing there was no going back.

Jen rolled onto her back, pivoting Holly's hip with her hand so that her thigh naturally slipped between her own. 'I want to taste you,' Jen said in a low purr.

'What's stopping you, then?'

Jen tipped her head upwards. 'I want you on top of me.'

'Oh, yeah?'

Jen nodded, adding a lingering kiss for good measure. She tapped the base of her neck. 'Come on, up here.'

Who was Holly to argue?

She swung her leg over Jen, who let out a low moan as Holly's wet core ground into her stomach.

Her hands gripped Holly's bum, urging her up, but she was in no rush. Especially not with Jen's boobs looking so damn good. She lowered her head, taking Jen's nipple into her mouth and circling her tongue a few times before sucking.

Jen groaned once more. 'That feels so good.'

With a delicate nibble, Holly released the taut bud. 'Yeah? You want me to keep going?'

'No, come up here. Let me have my fun now.'

Holly shimmied up, Jen's hands on her bum cheeks guiding her into position. A second of Jen's hot breath on Holly's core then no further time was wasted.

Jen's tongue swept the length of her as Holly grabbed the headboard for stability. 'You taste so good,' Jen hummed, her voice rumbling through Holly's centre.

Holly closed her eyes, unable to focus on anything but the way Jen's tongue felt. *Fucking hell.* Everything was different with Jen, right from the start. Every sensation, every feeling, every emotion was turned up to eleven. It was no wonder Holly had fallen for her so quickly. But she'd fallen into safe and secure arms, and that made all the difference.

Still, she'd had doubts when so much went wrong this evening, like the universe was sending her warning signals, screaming she'd made the wrong choice. Now though, now, as she pressed harder against Jen's tongue, there wasn't a single ounce of hesitation left.

Jen's arm snaked around Holly's back, holding her in place, her other hand finding Holly's core. She slipped two fingers inside.

Holly's stomach flipped, desire building with incredible force. She ground her hips into Jen's shoulders, matching the rhythm she'd created with her digits. Jen's tongue ran circuits, surprising Holly with every turn. She fought to focus on her breathing for fear of coming too soon. She wanted this to last.

But it was impossible to fight it. Jen was too good.

'Fuck,' she growled, her internal walls clenching around Jen's fingers. Her tongue wasn't to be stopped, though. She dipped and swooped, twisted and turned, pulling Holly to the edge again. She opened her eyes and watched Jen's face as she came. Even with Holly's limited vision, she could see she was smiling, enjoying every second. She closed her eyes and let Jen bring her to climax once more.

Holly pulled back and Jen gave her hip a squeeze. 'Wow,' Jen said, out of breath.

Holly couldn't speak: the orgasm still thrummed in her chest, choking any words. Instead, she smiled and tipped her head back, letting out a long satisfied sigh.

With Jen's guidance, she flopped into the mattress. She felt delirious, drunk on desire, and completely done in.

Jen turned to her and planted a slow kiss on her lips. 'I think that about makes up for the lost week.'

'And then some,' Holly replied, her voice still breathy. She lazily traced a finger down Jen's side. She could do this forever more and never feel she'd got enough of Jen. When she reached her hip, Holly used a finger to tip Jen onto her back.

She flipped the covers back, revealing Jen in all her glory, and drank her in.

'You're just something else, you know that?'

Jen shook her head, lost in Holly's eyes. 'The only thing that matters is that you think that.'

'I think I might be the luckiest woman alive,' Holly said, taking one of Jen's nipples between her lips as her hand slid between Jen's legs. Wet didn't cover it.

Holly felt Jen's breath go ragged as she slid two fingers inside her. Jen's thrusting hips said she'd found the right rhythm, so she copied it with her tongue, flicking the hard nub with careful precision.

As she felt Jen tighten, Holly switched position, moving between her legs so she could achieve a better angle.

'Fuck,' Jen groaned as Holly used the thumb of her other hand to circle her clit.

Jen wasn't going to last long either. A week-and-a-bit of pent up frustration had them both tightly wound.

She slowed her pace, hoping to relish the moment for as long as possible.

When Jen gripped the sides of her pillow with both hands, she knew it wouldn't be long.

A few more thrusts and Jen was over the edge, falling hard, groaning so loudly it made Holly's centre twinge with excitement and pride.

The orgasm rippled through her, the muscles in Jen's thighs clenched tight as Holly continued to run circles.

'Fuck,' Jen cried, the word shattering into a million pieces as she came.

She grasped Holly's wrist, stilling her, a satisfied chuckle escaping. She opened her mouth but couldn't find the words, so let out another quiet laugh as she pushed her head into the pillow. 'I, er—'

Holly slid her fingers out, enjoying making Jen shiver once more as she ran them up her core and over her clit.

She draped herself over Jen, kissing her shoulder as she got comfy.

'Wow,' Jen finally managed.

'Let's never break up again.'

'Deal.' Jen kissed the top of Holly's head.

ONE YEAR LATER

'Where's Ryan?' Jen asked Chloe as they queued for the bar.

'Where'd you think?' she replied with a smirk.

'Food truck again?'

'Boy loves his chips.'

Arms around Jen's waist made her jump. Her muscles relaxed when a familiar voice shout-whispered in her ear. 'You still not been served?' Holly joked. 'Chloe's losing her touch.'

'It's a lot busier than last time,' Jen offered, in her defence. And it was. Lovefest's closing event was crammed with easily double that attended last year. Annie had outdone herself.

Holly moved to fill the gap between her girlfriend and Chloe. 'Who do you think will win this year?'

'My money's on the lezzers,' Chloe said without hesitation.

'Lesbians never win,' Jen countered.

'On what basis? That we lost?' Holly laughed.

'Exactly. If we can't win, no one can.' Jen bit her bottom lip, suppressing a cheesy grin.

'Who do you think then?' Holly asked.

'Kirsty and Ross. They seem legit.'

Holly pulled a face. 'Faux-mance for sure.'

'Nah.'

'Telling you. It's obvious when there's no real intimacy.'

'You should have offered them some tips. Little Miss I Think We Should Kiss.'

'If it works, it works.' She leaned in and kissed Jen, getting slightly more lost in the moment than intended. Annie's earlier gift of a bottle of champagne had gone to her head.

'Sorry to break up the snogfest, but the queue's moving. You stay here and I'll get this round,' Chloe said, a hand on Holly's shoulder.

'We'll get you outside,' Jen called to her bestie.

It was a relief to exit the tent, the crisp August air a welcome change from the oppressive heat.

Jen found them a quiet spot near the park's railings and pulled Holly in for another kiss. Someone wolf whistled. *Hey, if you can't kiss at Lovefest when can you?*

'You good?' Jen asked, meeting Holly's gaze. 'You seem a little distracted today.'

'Me? I'm golden. Although. . .'

'What?' If Alison was here again, Jen was going to hit the roof.

'You know, it's work stuff, it doesn't matter.'

Relief flooded over Jen. Work stuff she could handle. She gave Holly's hips a squeeze. 'Still debating card sizes?'

Holly pulled a face, telling Jen she was pleasantly surprised. 'How can you always read me like a book?'

'It's a skill. I told you: just offer both.' Holly's business was nearly ready to launch – she just had the small problem of making a final decision on what size cards to get printed. It was cute how worked up she got over the small details.

'I told you,' Holly replied in a playful whine. 'You can't just offer both. A6 just seems so small.'

'And 5 x 7 an odd size.'

Holly pulled another face.

'I might have heard this debate a few times.' She pulled Holly in for another kiss. A year since they met, and Jen felt like her feelings for Holly were only just getting started. She found a new thing to love nearly every day. 'Whatever you decide, it will be the right choice.'

'How can you be sure?'

'Because if you're making it, then that's the only option.'

'So wise, Miss Berkley.'

'Beer for three, ladies,' Chloe cheered, finally emerging out the tent.

'Offt, that hits the spot,' Jen said, taking a sip. If last year was hot, today was like being next to the sun itself. No thunder to break up the heat this August.

Chloe chugged her beer in record time. 'Right, I'm going home to pee quickly.'

'Home?' Jen asked, a little confused.

'Yeah, it's just across the road and the portaloos here stink.'

'Makes sense. I might come with you.'

Chloe's eyes grew wide. 'No, no. I need to be super quick – we've got to pass the crowns over soon. Actually, can you do me a massive favour and find Ryan?'

Jen was sure Chloe shot Holly a conspiring glance. Something was going on. Holly had been looking at her phone a lot this evening, conversation falling quiet when Jen entered the room, and there was a moment when they were drinking at Chloe's earlier than Ryan said something Jen didn't quite catch, his girlfriend's elbow between his ribs shutting him up pronto, only for an excuse about flights to be made. Flights?! That had nothing to do with anything.

She wasn't sure if she should be excited or nervous.

'We can find Ryan, no bother,' Holly agreed, taking Jen's hand as if to emphasise she had no option but to comply.

'And what if I pee myself?' Jen joked.

'It's a chance we'll need to take.'

Holly weaved them through the crowd, heading for the food trucks. No sign of Ryan.

'You two are up to something.'

'Who?'

'You and Chloe.'

'What? Cause she needs to pee?' Holly laughed. Perhaps a little too nervously.

Jen narrowed her eyes, watching Holly as she looked for Ryan. Something was off, but she couldn't put her finger on it.

'WELL, THANKS FOR A GOOD NIGHT,' Chloe said, leaning on the banister outside their flats.

'You want to come in for a drink?' Jen asked, key already in the lock.

'Nah, I don't want to be hungover tomorrow. We're going on a walk.'

Well, that confirmed it. Chloe had never refused alcohol when off the next day. Although, Ryan had got her hooked on bagging Munros.

'Fair enough, see you tomorrow.' Jen watched as Holly

gave Chloe a hug, and Ryan even joined in with a wee squeeze of her shoulder. Nerves jangled in her chest.

'You okay?' Holly asked as Jen opened the door. 'You look worried.'

'I'm fine. It's j—' Jen's words caught in her throat.

Fairy lights hung in drapes from the top of every wall in the flat, circling every room, the orange glow washing over them as Jen ventured into the hall.

Holly held back, watching Jen explore as she clicked the front door closed.

'What the?' Jen asked, awestruck.

Holly beamed. 'I wanted to talk to you about something and I was torn between finding a way on to our rooftop again and speaking to you in private, so. . .' She held her hands out, showing off the compromise.

'It's amazing,' Jen said, enveloping Holly in a hug. 'But what do you need to talk to me about?'

Holly took her by the hand and led her to the living room. 'Come, sit,' she said, patting the space beside her on the sofa.

Jen's jaw hung slack: the place looked amazing. It was like being a in fairy tale. 'How did you manage this? You've been with me the whole night.'

'Ryan did the hard graft, with a little help from Chloe.'

Suddenly it all made sense. 'I've always liked him,' Jen said with a smile. But her heart was picking up pace, knocking against her ribs.

The only consolation was that Holly looked more nervous than her. 'So.'

'So.'

Holly wrapped her hands around Jen's as she let an apprehensive laugh escape. 'I had a whole speech planned, but it feels like my mind's gone blank.'

'That's okay,' Jen replied.

She cleared her throat. 'The problem is, there's no words, really. I can't find the right ones to say how much I love you.'

A smile pulled at Jen's lips.

Holly continued, 'You've changed my life in so many ways. I don't know what I would do without you.'

'Same goes for you.' Jen's teeth pulled at her bottom lip. Was this going where she thought it was?

'When I met you, I thought I was past repair. I wasn't in a good space, but after just a few weeks you turned everything around. I didn't expect to fall for someone when I came back to Glasgow –heck, I didn't even know you could fall for someone so quickly.'

Jen smiled, fighting the urge to interject and tell Holly how much she loved her.

'But I did, and now we're here.' Holly's smile wavered again, her eyes dropping to their hands. 'And I know it's only been a year, but in the same way I knew I couldn't be without you after just a few weeks, I know I can't be without you for the rest of my life.'

Jen snagged Holly's gaze and they held steady for a few heartbeats, before Holly fished down the side of the couch to retrieve a ring box.

'How long have you had that stashed down there?' Jen asked, surprised to find her voice cracking as happy tears welled.

'Not long; just a year or so,' Holly joked. Jen watched the orange glow of the fairy lights reflect off the tears rimming Holly's eyes.

She took a deep breath before standing from the sofa and dropping to one knee, opening the box to reveal a silver ring with a diamond set flush in the band. 'Jen

Berkley, will you marry me?' Holly punctuated the sentence with a quick, nervous laugh, and Jen's heart burst with love.

Jen sucked on her lip, trying to find some composure. It was no good: she let the tears fall as she answered. 'Yes, yes, of course, yes.'

A smile split Holly's face in two as she jumped up, knocking Jen back on the sofa as she wrapped her in an almighty hug and smothered her in kisses.

Jen held her tight as Holly sat back, straddling her knee. 'Guess I'd better put this on before I lose it.' She slipped the ring onto Jen's finger. *Perfect fit.*

One more kiss and Jen found her voice, emotion still choking her words. 'You wait here – I need to get something.'

'Huh?' Holly said, moving to let Jen up.

'Just wait here.'

Jen padded through to her bedroom, wiping at her eyes as she went, ridding her cheeks of tears. This wasn't how she'd seen the evening going.

She did a wee excited dance before straightening her shirt, aiming to look slightly presentable.

It didn't take long to find what she'd come for; she'd had it hidden for a good month at the back of the top drawer in her bedside table. She gripped the ring box in one hand, hiding it behind her back as she returned to the living room.

'Right, close your eyes,' she said to Holly, unable to hide the cheesy grin spreading across her face.

Holly looked sceptical but did as she was told.

Jen copied the position Holly had taken minutes before, getting down on one knee, open ring box held out with a shaking hand.

'Right, open your eyes now.'

Holly's face was a picture. It flitted from pure confusion to elation in seconds. 'What the? How did? Huh?'

'I've had it a while, but I was worried you'd think it was too soon.'

Holly shook her head, dumbstruck.

'So, is that a yes?' Jen joked. 'Going to be awkward if you say no when I've said yes.'

'You've not asked me anything.'

Jen thought back. *Idiot.* 'Aw shit, yeah.' She cleared her throat. 'Holly Charlotte Taylor, will you do me the honour of marrying me?'

Holly pretended to think for a moment before extending her hand, ready to take the ring. 'Of course.'

Jen was quite proud of her ring choice. She'd taken bloody ages choosing it with Chloe. *Actually, there's a thought.* Of course bloody Chloe knew they were both going to propose. Typical.

'Good choice,' Holly said, admiring the sapphire stone.

With a hand on her neck, Jen gently pulled Holly in for another kiss, both unable to hide a slew of tears.

'Chloe helped me pick it,' Jen said, pawing the fresh tears away.

'You're kidding?' Holly replied with a snort of laughter. 'No guesses why she's got three bottles of champagne on ice tonight then.'

'She'll be dying to know what's going on.' Jen brought her lips closer to Holly's as she pushed her back on the sofa, slotting quickly between her legs. 'But I'm sure she can wait half an hour.'

Will you leave me a review?

I hope you enjoyed Love Charade. If you have a moment I would really appreciate an honest review on Amazon and / or Goodreads. Reviews help me grow as an author and help new readers know what to expect. The more people that take a chance on my books, the more books I can write. It doesn't need to be anything fancy, a few words will do. Thank you.

∼

Allie McDermid is a lesbian romance author. Her debut novel, Love Charade, was published in July 2022.

Born and raised in Perth, Allie now lives in Glasgow with her ever-growing gang of cats. She is partial to a good scone.

ALSO BY ALLIE MCDERMID

Want to know what happens at next year's Lovefest? Buy Love Detour, today.

LOVE DETOUR

Kirsty Hamilton would do anything for family, but when her mother insists she enters a dating contest to publicise her cafe, her commitment is put to the test.

Rhona Devi dreams of travelling the world. When she takes on a photography job to earn some cash, she never expects it to lead to her biggest adventure yet.

Rhona thinks she deserves a chance. Kirsty doesn't see the point. Will they be able to meet somewhere in the middle?

Book two in the Lovefest series features a love on a time limit romance oozing with sexual chemistry and flirtatious banter.
Buy Love Detour today and see if love truly can defy the odds.

ALSO BY ALLIE MCDERMID

Need to know more? Enjoy year three of Lovefest, today!

LOVE MAGNET

Gemma Anderson is new to lesbian dating. Recently divorced and looking for love, the annual dating festival is a last resort after a string of failed matches.

Steph Campbell has long come to terms with being perpetually single, so working in her bar during the most loved-up season of the year, she hardly expects to encounter a match.

Gemma is letting her head rule her heart. Steph is content to just be friends. Will they find a way to put their differences aside?

Book three in the Lovefest series is filled with slow-burn romance, lashings of spice, and a sassy granny who kills it with one-liners. Buy Love Magnet today and discover if opposites really do attract.

Lightning Source UK Ltd.
Milton Keynes UK
UKHW010624070922
408462UK00003B/367

9 798839 887633